Sweet on You

A BRADFORD SISTERS ROMANCE

Sweet on You

BECKY WADE

BETHANYHOUSE
a division of Baker Publishing Group
Minneapolis, Minnesota

© 2019 by Rebecca C. Wade

Published by Bethany House Publishers
11400 Hampshire Avenue South
Bloomington, Minnesota 55438
www.bethanyhouse.com

Bethany House Publishers is a division of
Baker Publishing Group, Grand Rapids, Michigan

Printed in the United States of America

Library of Congress Cataloging-in-Publication Data
Names: Wade, Becky, author.
Title: Sweet on you / Becky Wade.
Description: Bloomington, Minnesota : Bethany House Publishers, a division of
    Baker Publishing Group, [2019] | Series: A Bradford sisters romance
Identifiers: LCCN 2018048942| ISBN 9780764219382 (trade paper) |
ISBN 9780764234057 (cloth) | ISBN 9781493418763 (ebook)
Subjects: | GSAFD: Love stories.
Classification: LCC PS3623.A33 S94 2019 | DDC 813/.6—dc23
LC record available at https://lccn.loc.gov/2018048942

Cover design by Jennifer Parker
Cover photography by Mike Habermann Photography, LLC

Author is represented by Linda Kruger.

19 20 21 22 23 24 25   7 6 5 4 3 2 1

To the best writer friends a girl could ask for—
Katie Ganshert, Courtney Walsh, and Dani Pettrey.

Thank you from the bottom of my heart.

This one's for you.

CHAPTER

One

Five hundred and eleven days had passed since he'd seen her last. Five hundred and eleven days that had been hollower and duller and at times brutally lonely for him because Britt Bradford hadn't been physically present in any of them.

Five hundred and eleven days constituted a streak that, within minutes, would finally come to an end. Because he, Zander Kingston Ford, had returned home.

He sank his hands into the pockets of his sweat shirt and walked beneath the cherry trees arching over the entrance to Merryweather Historical Village. On this morning in early April, pale pink blossoms covered the branches.

He catalogued the details of the village the way a landowner might, with proprietary intensity. He knew this village, this town, and this corner of Washington state very, very well. This place, more than anywhere else on earth, had become his home.

The landscaping around the base of the village's buildings looked fuller than it had before he'd gone, and a fresh load of gravel had been laid on the walking paths. Everything else was exactly as Zander remembered. The deep green of the lawn that all thirteen historical structures faced. The white trunks of the aspens between the buildings. The pale gray of the clouds rolling in from the Pacific. The wooden sign hanging outside Britt's chocolate shop that spelled *Sweet Art* in black letters.

None of the stores that occupied the buildings would open for another hour. However, he knew that Britt would have arrived in her kitchen at six this morning.

In his lifetime, Zander had acquired knowledge about many things: technology, writing, adventure sports, travel, history. But he was a true expert at only one subject. The subject of Britt.

As soon as he'd awakened this morning, anticipation and apprehension had gone to war inside of him. Anticipation, because he was shamefully desperate to see her again. Apprehension, because he'd left Merryweather for several reasons a year and a half ago. But the greatest of those reasons had been her.

He was halfway across the village on his way to Sweet Art when the shop's door swung open and two women walked out. One of them was Britt. He would have recognized the natural confidence of her posture even if he'd been twice as far away. She was neither tall nor short. Simultaneously slim and strong. Perfectly proportioned.

Zander's progress cut to a halt. His breath stilled in his throat.

Britt and the other woman paused on Sweet Art's porch to talk. Britt wore her white chef's coat with exercise pants. She'd collected her dark brown hair into a knot on the top of her head just like she almost always did when making chocolate.

The women parted, and Britt turned his direction, back toward her shop. Her attention swept past him, then stopped. Lifting a hand to shield her eyes, she zeroed in on him.

His heart froze for an instant, then restarted with hard, drumming beats.

With a whoop of sound, Britt pounded down Sweet Art's steps and sprinted in his direction. The village seemed to be sound asleep, but even if it had been packed with people, she'd have run to him exactly the same way. She wasn't shy.

Joy—deep, simple joy—pulled his mouth into a grin. He opened his arms and caught her with an *oomph*. Then he spun her around in the air twice. Carefully, he set her back on her feet, steadying her the way he always had emotionally. She hugged him tight, pressing the side of her face against his chest for several long moments.

She was in his arms. Britt was in his arms. Her silky hair whispered against the underside of his jaw. Her crisp perfume—the one she'd adopted during the two years she'd spent in France after graduating from culinary school—filled his senses with the smell of flowers, blackberry, orange, and sunshine. Greedy to catalogue every sensation, he worked to file them all away—

She broke contact and lifted her face to smile at him.

And just like that, standing in the middle of Merryweather Historical Village and looking into her face without continents separating them, the biggest part of his soul—the part that had been missing for a year and a half—locked back into place.

He loved her.

Instantly, the pleasure of that truth was cut in half by pain. Loving her was his greatest blessing. But it was also his greatest curse, because she didn't love him the way that he loved her. Zander was no stranger to loving people who didn't love him back. He ought to have adjusted to it by now, but where Britt was concerned, he never had. They were friends. Britt had always thought of him as her very good friend.

She set her palms on his shoulders. "You came back."

"I promised you I would."

She had the features of a warrior princess. Her eyebrows communicated determination. Her almond-shaped brown eyes revealed fierce creativity. Her chin broadcast independence. Her lips were full. Her nose straight and slender.

"You got taller," she accused.

"Nope. I'm still five eleven."

"Then I must have gotten shorter."

"You're exactly the same."

She appeared gratified by his statement. "You look tired."

"That's because I am. You look well rested."

"That's because I am. Your hair's longer than usual."

"I know. It's bugging me."

Britt tilted her head, peering at him closely. "I'd sort of forgotten about the pinpricks of light blue in your eyes."

"I'd sort of forgotten that you have a few tiny freckles on your cheekbones."

"You forgot about my freckles?"

"I admit that I did."

"I'm scandalized," she said. "Have you lost weight?"

"Maybe a couple of pounds."

"Did I gain weight?"

"Definitely not."

"That's what you'd say even if I *had* gained weight."

"Yes," he acknowledged. "Because I'm no dummy."

Her pale pink lips ticked upward at one edge. "You've been gone a really long time, Zander."

"I know."

"And you were very far away."

He gave a nod.

"I missed you."

"I missed you, too." The words felt stupidly small. Like calling Mount Rainier a hill. Until he'd left her behind, he'd had no idea he could be as desolate as he'd been without her.

She stepped back and set her hands on her hips. "It's . . . sort of . . . scrambling my brain to see you again."

"Yeah." After such a long time, it was surreal to be here. With her. The last eighteen months had changed him, but he selfishly hoped that they'd changed nothing about her. While he'd been gone, she'd been going about her small-town routine, the same small-town routine she'd been going about for years. Which is why he'd been able to convince himself that he wasn't missing anything in her life that he couldn't bear to miss.

"I was expecting you to sleep until noon today," she told him.

"I should have." He'd only been able to string together four hours of sleep after reaching the Inn at Bradfordwood, the bed-and-breakfast Britt's mom owned, in the middle of last night.

"What happened? Couldn't stay asleep?"

"Nope." *Because I couldn't wait to see you.* "Jet lag bites."

"How long did it end up taking you to get here from Tokyo?"

"The trip from Tokyo to Honolulu and from Honolulu to Vancouver took twenty-eight hours. Then I rented a car and drove the rest of the way."

"Brutal." Britt linked her arm through his, and they walked in the direction of Sweet Art. "I'm glad you're home, but I'm sorry that it's for such a sad reason."

"I am, too." Three days ago, his aunt Carolyn had called him in Japan to tell him that her husband, Frank, had died suddenly. The news had gut punched him. Uncle Frank had been like a father to him for well over a decade.

Even as Zander had hunted for available flights to Washington, the ruling thought in his head had been, *This can't be right. Frank can't be dead.* His subconscious was determined to pick a fight with reality.

The reality: Uncle Frank had been hardworking, reliable, humorous, and devoted to his wife, twin daughters, and two nephews. Uncle Frank had also been found dead in the driver's seat of his truck this past Saturday, apparently killed by a heart attack.

"How's Carolyn doing?" Britt asked.

"As well as can be expected."

"And you?"

"Okay."

"Really?"

"Yes," he said. "How've you been?"

"Fine."

"You haven't gotten yourself into trouble lately?"

"Not lately."

"You've been behaving?" A note of disbelief marked his question.

"I didn't say I'd been behaving." She shot him a wry glance. "I simply said I hadn't gotten myself into trouble *lately.*"

"Ah. Dating anyone?" *Please, God, let the answer be no.*

"Not at the moment."

They'd kept in regular contact with each other through texts and FaceTime calls, but he'd purposely avoided asking about her boyfriends, because he hadn't wanted to know.

"I was dating this guy named Anthony, but we broke up three months ago."

"You've been single for three whole months?" The average interval between Britt's boyfriends: 2.5 seconds.

"I know! I'm proud of myself."

"What happened with Anthony?"

"He was an interrupter. I could never finish my sentence."

He held Sweet Art's back door open so she could pass first, then entered the kitchen that occupied the rear of her shop's square footage. Here, the rich scents of chocolate and coffee hung in the air. Walls of white subway tile gave way to counters of stainless steel. Open shelves held ingredients as well as turquoise, gray, and white mixing bowls.

Britt waved him toward one of the stools that framed her large central island. "Sit."

"I can help—"

"You're jet-lagged and sleep-deprived. Sit."

Zander did so while she moved around the room, cleaning her work space and updating him on her family. Her older sister Nora was busy planning her wedding, which would take place in six weeks. Her oldest sister, Willow, had married last summer and was living with her husband in nearby Shore Pine. Her parents were finishing a two-year stint in Africa as missionaries.

Kitchen clean, Britt washed her hands, then grabbed a small plate off a shelf. "Hang on a sec." She vanished through the swinging door into her shop and returned carrying four chocolates on the plate. She stood at the kitchen's side counter for a moment, studying the white Easter-egg-shaped chocolates assembled there, no doubt debating whether to add one to his plate.

Even when still and quiet, Britt *radiated* energy. He could feel the life in her, the suppressed movement.

She added an Easter egg to the assortment and set the plate before him.

He studied the chocolates. "What do we have here?"

"You tell me."

He shouldered out of his sweat shirt like a boxer shrugging out of his robe before a fight.

Britt laughed. "It's so nice to feed someone who has a sophisticated palate for chocolate. Finally!"

"No one around here cultivated a sophisticated palate while I was away?"

"No. They're all still novices. You're the only one who's ever taken advantage of my excellent coaching."

He picked up a hand-dipped dark chocolate. He'd taken advantage of her coaching, but not only that. He'd also read numerous books on the subject of chocolate.

"I knew you'd choose that one first," she said smugly.

Dark chocolate with nuts had long been his favorite combination. He let the chocolate soften in his mouth, then chewed slowly. He'd thought he'd stored the taste of her chocolate successfully in his brain. Now that he was tasting it again, he realized that . . . no. His memory hadn't done it justice.

Crossing her arms, she leaned her hip against the island and waited for him to make a guess.

For her dark chocolates, he knew that she used either seventy-two percent extra-bittersweet, sixty-four percent bittersweet, or fifty-five percent semisweet. For her lighter, sweeter chocolates she used thirty-eight percent milk chocolate or twenty-nine percent white chocolate. "Sixty-four percent bittersweet chocolate with macadamia nuts and Grand Marnier," he said.

"It's rum, not Grand Marnier."

"You're not going to give me credit?"

Britt shook her head. "I would have given you credit if you'd stopped after macadamia nuts. You were trying to show off when you said Grand Marnier. Pride was your downfall." Her eyes sparkled with amusement.

"I can do better."

"Prove it." She handed him a napkin and a glass of ice water.

He sipped the water, as she'd taught him to do between chocolates, then ate a truffle. "Seventy-two percent extra-bittersweet chocolate dipped in white chocolate and rolled in pumpkin pie spice."

"Yes!"

He lifted his eyebrows to gloat. "I nailed that one."

"You did," she agreed. "Even though you couldn't resist showing off again by noting the pumpkin pie spice."

"Yeah, but this time I was certain. I've been gone a long time, but I'm still a chocolate savant."

"You may still be a chocolate *sous* savant—"

"Not all of us can be master chocolatiers."

"—*if* you can nail at least two of the remaining three chocolates."

"I thrive under pressure."

"And I thrive at humbling those whose taste buds have deteriorated during their international travels."

"You're about to eat those words." He'd sought out chocolate in every country he'd visited. He'd sampled it, sent Britt pictures of it, and mailed the best of it back to Washington for her to try. If he screwed this up, it wouldn't be because he didn't know chocolate. It would be because he was too distracted by Britt, who was wearing purple tennis shoes, who'd painted her short fingernails gray, whose name was stitched onto her chef's coat in cursive.

He ate a dome-shaped molded chocolate.

For years, he'd been praying that Britt would fall in love with him or that he'd fall out of love with her. God hadn't answered either prayer. So when he'd left on his trip, he'd hoped the passage of time might change his heart. However, Zander's love for her had proven stronger than his own willpower.

Than distance.

Than time.

He wanted to be far more to Britt than her friend. But if he told her that, she'd react with pity and probably misery on his behalf. The admission would crack the rare dynamic they shared, and then they'd be forced to pretend the crack didn't exist.

He wasn't willing to do or say anything that might put their friendship at risk. Because even though their friendship was torture for him at times, it was also the best thing in his life.

Britt couldn't get over her tugging, tingling sense of awe. *Zander was in her kitchen*. Zander!

Her Zander.

To have him here felt both strange and familiar. Very familiar. Very strange.

"Thirty-eight percent milk chocolate with hazelnuts and cinnamon," he said.

"Right again."

She'd met him just days after they'd both started their freshman year at Merryweather High School. Back then, Zander had been as thin and defiant and mistrusting as a wounded animal.

His early life with his parents in a rough St. Louis neighborhood had never been a cakewalk. But things had begun to unravel beyond repair the year Zander was twelve, when his dad had gone to prison. Zander and his older brother, Daniel, had spent the next two years with their drug-addicted mom until the day their home and their "normal" had literally gone up in flames. It had taken Britt ages to pry the story of that day out of Zander.

Before the smoke had cleared, CPS had removed the boys from their mom's care. Their custody had gone to their mom's sister, Carolyn Pierce, and her husband, Frank. Zander had been carted to Washington, world-weary and withdrawn.

He'd made Britt work hard to earn his friendship, but almost nothing else she'd done had proven as worthwhile.

She watched him eat the puffed rice chocolate.

The fourteen-year-old boy she'd once known was long gone. He'd been replaced with this worldly, adult Zander, who was a roaring success and had nothing left to prove.

15

Earlier, when she'd been standing on Sweet Art's porch, a clang had gone through her when she'd recognized the lean lines of his body, his dark hair, his introspective loner aura.

To her relief, Zander looked very much the same. His pale skin struck a distinct contrast with his hair, which verged on black. His jaw, cheekbones, and nose were all sharply defined. Straight eyebrows. Thick eyelashes. Zander had a romantic, slightly heartbreaking, usually serious face. He could pass as either a nineteenth-century poet or one of those harshly handsome vampires from *Twilight*.

He was wearing clothes she remembered him wearing before he'd left—a gray T-shirt that said *Atari* across the front and his favorite pair of jeans. He hadn't added to the sleeves of tattoos running down his arms.

Her intuition told her that something within him *had* altered, though. He'd traveled the globe alone for a year and a half. Anyone who'd experienced something like that would return home changed. Matured. More self-reliant. She shouldn't be surprised and she shouldn't mourn because he wasn't precisely as he had been when he'd left.

Nor should she worry about the caution she could see in his ocean blue eyes. Given time, she'd be able to coax him to lower his shields.

For today, it was enough that *he* believed *her* to be exactly the same. That's what he'd said when they'd been standing on the green. *"You're exactly the same,"* he'd told her, even though she wasn't. Since he'd seen her last, she'd been scarred in ways he knew nothing about. Thank the Lord he hadn't been able to tell.

"Thirty-eight percent milk chocolate," he said, "with puffed rice, pecans, pistachios, and candied orange peel."

"Nope. Puffed rice, *almonds*, pistachios, and candied orange peel."

"Shoot. Now I have to get this Easter egg right, because I'm determined to retain the level of chocolate sous savant." He popped it into his mouth. His eyes narrowed on her as he swallowed.

"Twenty-nine percent white chocolate shell with a salted caramel ganache center."

"The Easter egg was too easy."

"It was nice of you to tee that one up for me."

"It truly was. I'm surprised by my own generosity."

"Every one of those chocolates was delicious, Britt."

"Thank you." She set his plate in the sink. "Coffee?"

"Please."

"Still drinking café au lait?"

"Yep." He followed her into Sweet Art's retail space. "Still drinking cappuccino?"

"Yep." She went to the espresso machine. "This is the first time you've been back in the States since your book released. Did you see it in the airport in Vancouver?"

"I did, actually."

"It's everywhere. Wal-Mart, Target, the grocery store. Every time I spot it, I want to grab it off the shelf and shove it at all the strangers in the store. I'm ridiculously proud of it, even though I didn't have anything to do with it."

"You did have something to do with it." He hooked his thumbs around his belt loops, a habit he'd long had. "When I told you I was thinking about writing a book, you're the one who convinced me I could. When I was working on the rough draft, you talked me out of quitting at least five times."

"Because you're my friend, but also because I knew the book was going to be a success. I was right."

A lone dimple sunk into his cheek. "Do you know of any stocks destined for success?"

"You're not going to need to invest in stocks. You're going to earn plenty of money and then some through your writing career."

Three years earlier, Zander had begun writing a thriller aptly titled *Geniuses*, about a genius enlisted by the FBI to outsmart and catch an evil genius. It was dark, smart, and filled with twists. A handful of publishers had entered a bidding war over the manuscript, which had then been heavily backed by the winning publisher. The advance Zander received had enabled him to quit the tech job he'd had here in Merryweather, pack his laptop into his carry-on, and write while traveling abroad.

Geniuses had released nine months ago and raced to the top of the *New York Times* bestseller list, where it still sat.

Britt plucked two mugs from the cupboard. When he leaned over and closed the cupboard for her, she swallowed a rush of affection because his compulsion to close doors and drawers was another of his old habits.

They sat at the bar that ran the length of one wall, contentment warming her like a sunrise. She liked feeding chocolate and coffee to strangers. But she *loved* feeding chocolate and coffee to Zander. Especially now, when he needed comfort in the wake of his uncle's death.

She blew on her cappuccino. She had a large family and a wide network of friends. Zander had only his brother, Frank, Carolyn, and herself. When Frank had died, Zander had lost one of his inner four, and she'd do just about anything she could to help him. "Nikki heard that Frank left work Friday afternoon and wasn't seen again until he was discovered in his truck the next morning."

"Right. Carolyn thinks he must have had the heart attack on his way home from work on Friday."

"Why wasn't he found until the next day?"

Zander hefted one shoulder. "He parked his truck perfectly on the side of the road. It wasn't until the next day that someone got suspicious and called it in."

"He was found on Shadow Mountain Road?"

"He was."

"Which isn't on his way home."

"No, it isn't. Carolyn's best guess is that he was running an errand when he had the heart attack."

"Poor Frank," Britt said. "Poor Carolyn."

"The suddenness of Frank's death is bad enough, but the fact that Carolyn wasn't with him at the end makes it even worse."

"Friday night must have been terrible for her."

"It was. She was up all night panicking, trying to reach him on his cell phone."

"That's awful."

"I'm going to the police station with her in the morning. They'll give us the preliminary autopsy report then."

Zander's journal entry, four years ago:

> Britt's the closest person to me, yet we're not close enough. "Not close enough" is starting to feel like a chain. It's keeping me inside a room when I know there are mountains and oceans outside the room. I can't get to them, though.
>
> I'm chained up.
>
> I know Britt, but I don't know what it's like to kiss her. I don't know what it's like to honestly tell her how I feel.
>
> I'm chained up.

CHAPTER

Two

The following day a tall, broad-shouldered man let himself into the police station meeting room where Zander and Carolyn waited. "Good morning. I'm Detective Kurt Shaw."

Zander and Carolyn rose to greet the officer with handshakes. "Carolyn Pierce."

"Thank you for stopping by the station, ma'am."

"You're welcome. I'd like to introduce you to my nephew, Zander Ford."

"I think we went to high school together," the detective said to Zander. "I graduated with your brother."

Recognition clicked. Kurt and Daniel hadn't been close friends, but they'd gotten along well with each other. As far as Zander could recall, Kurt had gotten along with everyone. He'd been a scholar athlete who'd seemed older than his years—steadier and more responsible than his classmates.

"I remember," Zander said. "You and Daniel both played baseball."

"We did. Nice to see you again."

"Likewise."

Kurt must have started losing his hair at an early age because he was probably only thirty, yet had already shaved his head. His recessed eyes were set into a kind, forthright face. He wore navy pants and a maroon-and-blue checked shirt. Both looked like they'd been pulled out of a dry cleaning bag this morning.

Kurt set the file he'd been carrying onto the table as they took their seats. The white-walled room contained one rectangular window and no decoration, save for a framed print of the American flag and a bulletin board with the round insignia of the Merryweather police force tacked to it.

"Zander, are you up to speed on what happened to your uncle?" Kurt asked.

"Carolyn's filled me in, but I'd like to hear it from your perspective, if you don't mind."

"Not at all." Kurt adjusted the position of his large black sports watch, placing the face directly on top of his wrist. "This past Saturday morning at approximately nine o'clock, our office received a call about your uncle's truck. It was parked on the shoulder of Shadow Mountain Road in a no parking zone. One of our officers was in the area, so he swung by to investigate. He reached the truck at 9:10 and found your uncle slumped over in the front seat. He checked Frank's vitals. When he could find none, he called the police chief, who contacted me. We arrived shortly after to process the scene. In time, Frank's body was released to the medical examiner, who has forwarded me his preliminary findings." Kurt opened the file. "Just so you're both aware, the formal autopsy report won't be available for approximately six weeks."

"At this point," Carolyn said, "my family and I would be grateful for any information at all. We just . . . we can't believe what's happened."

"I understand." Kurt regarded Carolyn with compassion, then glanced over the report. "The medical examiner has determined Frank's cause of death to be acute myocardial infarction. A blockage of blood flow to the heart."

This can't be right. Frank can't be dead, Zander's brain insisted yet again. "A heart attack."

"Yes." Kurt turned his attention to Carolyn. "Did your husband have heart issues, Mrs. Pierce?"

"He did, yes. He had some blockages in the past that they treated with stents. His doctors prescribed medicine and encouraged him to eat well and exercise and avoid stress. I thought we had it under control," she finished weakly.

"Was he good about taking his medicine?"

"He was."

Carolyn sat with her legs crossed, hands mounded on her upper knee, unnaturally still. Her face was a little too oval and her nose a little too long to be considered conventionally beautiful. Yet at the age of sixty, Carolyn's features still held their own unique brand of attractiveness.

She'd parted her long, wavy, blond-gray hair down the middle. As usual, she'd dressed in a loose top, belt, skirt, sandals. Even her artistic turquoise earrings were familiar to Zander. Yet she wasn't herself today.

She worked in a gift shop on Merryweather's Main Street, and her customers all adored her for her peaceful, friendly, optimistic personality. The shock of Frank's death had stripped those qualities from her. Zander could see and feel her tension. She reminded him of a rubber band stretched too far then held immobile to keep from snapping.

Zander's parents' relationship had been rocky. But Carolyn's relationship with Frank had been smooth. Frank had told everyone who'd listen how lucky he was to be married to Carolyn, how much he loved and valued her.

Every morning Frank had made her tea. Every evening when he'd arrived home from work, he hugged her. He'd joke about her affection for incense sticks until he could make her laugh.

"What's that smell?" he'd ask.

"Ylang-ylang," Carolyn would answer.

"I'm trying to watch basketball here. Ylang-ylang and basketball don't go together."

"They do in this house, Frank Pierce."

Zander could only imagine how devastating it must be for Carolyn to sit here beside him, listening to a detective half her age tell her that her husband had died of a heart attack. Of all people, Frank's death would affect her the most.

"Does it say in the report what time he died?" Carolyn asked Kurt.

"The medical examiner estimated Frank's time of death to be around five a.m."

"Wait." Carolyn's features sharpened. "Five p.m. or five a.m?"

"Five a.m. on Saturday morning," Kurt said.

"Then . . . where was he?" she asked. "From the time he left work on Friday afternoon until the time of his death?"

Foreboding twisted Zander's stomach.

"I wanted to ask you about that, actually," Kurt said. "To see if you had any idea where Frank might have gone."

Pain and confusion drifted in Carolyn's eyes like fog. "No, I don't have any idea at all. I'm sorry, I'm baffled. Frank and I—" Her voice broke. "We'd talked on Friday about having shrimp scampi and salad for dinner that night. I expected him home at the regular time. When he didn't come home, I started calling him on his cell phone."

"What time did you start calling?" Kurt asked.

"Around six forty-five. At midnight, I called 9-1-1."

"Was Frank in the habit of staying out late from time to time?"

"No."

"Had he ever stayed out all night before?"

"Never."

"Does he typically answer his cell phone when you call?"

"He does, yes."

"As you know, Shadow Mountain Road connects Merryweather to Shore Pine," Kurt said. "His truck was pointing toward Shore Pine when we found it. Can you think why he would've been driving in that direction?"

Carolyn's forehead wrinkled. "There's a plumbing supply store there that Frank likes. Zander, can you think of anything?"

23

"Jim, his coworker and friend, lives in Shore Pine."

"Yes, and our church is there." She gave an anguished shrug. "I really don't know. I can't fathom why he would have been driving there at that time in the morning."

Kurt leaned back in his chair. "Jim Davis called me. Is that the same one you mentioned?"

Zander and Carolyn nodded. Frank had worked construction at Chapman and Associates ever since he and Carolyn had moved to this part of Washington as newlyweds thirty-three years ago. Jim had joined the company shortly after Frank, and the two men were good friends.

"Jim said that Frank received a call on the jobsite around four thirty on Friday afternoon. After answering it, he walked away to continue the conversation. Jim couldn't hear what was said, but he could see that Frank was upset. Shortly after, Frank left for the day. Do you know who might've called him?"

"No," Carolyn answered.

"Was Frank involved in an argument with anyone? Was he in trouble financially?"

"No. Are . . ." Carolyn inhaled raggedly. "Are you thinking that someone might have . . . had a hand in Frank's death?"

"No. Frank's death was caused by a heart attack. I'm simply trying to get a sense of his whereabouts during the hours that are unaccounted for."

"Did you check Frank's phone?" Zander asked. "To see who called him at work?" Based on what Carolyn had told him, he knew the police had taken Frank's cell phone and several other items as evidence.

"Yes, but I hit a dead end. The call was placed by a burner phone." Carolyn looked puzzled.

"A burner phone is a pre-paid, disposable phone," Zander said to her.

"Which means we can't access records on the person who purchased it." Kurt hunched forward and once again scanned the report. "The medical examiner noted that Frank had a bullet wound

24

in his left outer thigh. Do you know when and how Frank received that injury?"

Carolyn regarded Kurt as if he'd spoken his question in a foreign language. "The scar on Frank's leg isn't from a bullet wound. It's from a metal stake that fell and hit Frank while he was working at a construction site back in 1985. I remember because I met him shortly after, when we were both living in Seattle."

A long silence answered. Kurt met Zander's eyes before returning his focus to Carolyn. "Ma'am, the medical examiner is certain that the injury was caused by a bullet."

Zander scowled. Frank had told Zander the story about the metal stake whenever his old injury acted up.

"How can the medical examiner be certain?" Carolyn asked.

"Because he was able to recover the bullet, Mrs. Pierce."

Quiet descended, thick and cold.

Frank had lied. He'd lied to both Carolyn and Zander about the injury.

A knock sounded, and a deputy stuck his head into the room. "Sorry to interrupt, but there's a call for you, Kurt."

Kurt excused himself, shutting the door softly behind him.

Carolyn's skin had paled, and two wrinkles shaped like brackets dented the skin on either side of her lips. She extended her trembling hand to him, and Zander immediately took firm hold of it. He pulled the file toward them. "Would you like to look over the report yourself?"

"No, thank you. I can't bear to."

Zander picked up the papers and read them carefully, using his photographic memory to take mental snapshots of them.

"Zander," Carolyn said after a time, her voice low.

He set the sheets aside and faced her fully.

She stared sightlessly out the window. "I need to know what happened to Frank. I definitely . . . I just *need* to know. For myself. For Courtney and Sarah."

Frank and Carolyn's daughters were in their early thirties, both married. Courtney was five months pregnant with her first child.

"It's just that I don't think I can handle any more . . . surprises about Frank at the moment," Carolyn continued. "It's all . . . it's really all I can do to put one foot in front of the other."

"If you want me to, I'll find out what happened to Frank for you."

Weary hope sprang to her face. "You'd do that?"

"Of course." Once, he'd been an orphan convinced that he didn't need saving. But then Carolyn and Frank had proved him wrong when they'd gone ahead and saved him anyway. If he could save her—even from the heartache of the questions surrounding Frank's death—he would.

"I don't know if it's fair of me to ask that of you," she said. "It probably isn't. I'm putting too much responsibility on you, aren't I?"

"No. You're not." He had a manuscript due to his publisher at the end of the summer, but he'd been working on it consistently while he'd been overseas. He could continue his writing pace here, spend the bulk of his time doing what Carolyn needed done, and still get his manuscript in on time. "It'll be a relief to have something tangible to do. Tracking down answers is tangible."

Tears gathered on her eyelashes. "Thank you." She tried to smile. "I love you."

"I love you, too, Aunt Carolyn."

Britt had taught Zander to cook and, frankly, she'd done an outstanding job.

Dating men was entertaining. Dancing with men—enjoyable. Kissing men—pleasurable. Competing with men—exciting. But cooking with Zander was a dream.

He stood beside her in her cottage's kitchen, seasoning a tray of Broccolini while she chopped a shallot for the citrus vinaigrette she'd pair with her arugula and pear salad.

Zander wasn't in Norway or Spain or Singapore.

He was right next to her, and they were cooking together in perfect synchronicity.

He slid the Broccolini into the oven. "What'll it take? About fourteen minutes?" he asked her.

"Thirteen," she teased, knowing he was physically incapable of setting a timer or alarm to an odd number.

He winked. "Fourteen it is." After adjusting her kitchen timer, he set the ingredients she'd need for the vinaigrette near her cutting board. Champagne vinegar, olive oil, an orange, a lemon, pepper grinder, salt shaker.

The salmon filets Britt had purchased earlier waited, prepped. She planned to pan fry those last, right before she, Zander, and her sisters sat down to dinner.

As soon as Willow and Nora had learned of Zander's return, they'd contacted Britt, demanding to know when they could see him. Tonight's dinner was Britt's answer, and so far, her sisters were making good use of their time. They were currently setting the table and pelting Zander with questions about his Grand Tour.

Britt listened to their conversation with one ear while pouring a golden stream of olive oil into her bowl. Phillip Phillips' gravelly voice eased from the speakers. A breeze stirred the white curtains that accented the dining room windows. Whenever the temperature hovered above fifty and below eighty, Britt kept at least a few of her windows cracked. She craved fresh air and the extended daylight of the spring and summer months.

Tonight, dusk was hesitating extra long, as if unsure of its welcome. The peachy pink sky suited the satisfied state of Britt's heart.

There'd been a time when a gathering that included herself, Zander, and her sisters had been commonplace. But this particular grouping had become very rare. Mostly because of Zander's long absence. But also because the Bradford family was changing and expanding.

Britt's oldest sister, Willow, had married Corbin Stewart last summer. Nora would be marrying John Lawson in a month and a half. Britt was acquiring brothers-in-law faster than shipments of cacao beans, and her sisters' schedules were busier than ever. Not that she held that fact against Corbin and John or her sisters. Her brothers-in-law were great guys, handsome guys, accomplished guys. If Britt were to marry, which was a big if, she'd always known it wouldn't happen until after her sisters were married. Everything was progressing exactly as it should.

Even so, she occasionally missed the old days when she'd been—let's face it—the crux of Zander's and Willow's and Nora's social lives.

She gave the salt shaker a hearty twist and watched the flakes dot the top of her vinaigrette.

"We've finished setting the table," Willow told her.

"Can we lend a hand with the cooking?" Nora asked.

"Thanks, but we've got it under control." Her sisters were well-meaning, but Britt had no interest in talking amateurs through the creation of this dinner. Sharing cooking duties was, in her opinion, sort of like sharing the creation of a piece of artwork. Better left in the hands of the people who had a clue. "Your main job tonight is to inflate Zander's ego by giving him lots of undeserved—"

"Well deserved," he corrected.

"Attention," Britt finished.

Zander shot her a small smile. She smiled back, glanced down at her work space, then glanced back at him and found that he was still watching her.

"What did you think of New Zealand, Zander?" Nora asked. "I've been dying to go there ever since I learned that's where they shot *Lord of the Rings*."

He was tugged back into Willow and Nora's inquisition as he closed two drawers, then began rinsing the dishes and utensils Britt had used.

One side of her kitchen ran along the rear wall of her house. Acacia wood topped the half wall that formed the other side, which emptied to her living room. On top of the acacia wood, she'd placed seasoned nuts, grapes, brie, and crackers.

She lived at Hackberry Lane Cottages, Merryweather's only community of small homes. The floor plans of the cottages varied, but none of the houses were larger than hers, which rang in at fifteen hundred square feet. The exterior of every home in the miniature neighborhood looked similar: taupe-painted siding with white trim, a roomy front porch, two stories tall, shimmering windows, steeply pitched roof. The structures were aligned in two rows that faced each other across a garden zigzagged by stone pathways and bursting with spring flowers. A petite wooden fence framed the garden, and a sidewalk framed the fence. A row of trees hid their parking lot from view at one end of the complex. The other end of the complex flowed into protected woodland.

The moment Britt had heard about the Hackberry Lane development, she'd visited the sales office. And the moment they'd shown her their plans, she'd plunked down her money.

Not all of the spontaneous decisions she'd made in her life had turned out well. One spontaneous decision in particular had almost cost her her life. But, fortunately, she'd never once regretted her spur-of-the-moment decision to buy her home. She'd embraced the entire concept—the small environmental footprint, the sustainable ethic, and the fostering of connection with neighbors.

The majority of the residents had decorated their cottages in cottage style. Not Britt. While charming was fine for the outside of her house, she'd kept the interior modern, crisp, and simple. White walls. Sleek leather furniture. A thin Kilim rug patterned in shades of blue and white.

". . . the detective told us that Frank had a bullet wound in his leg," Zander was saying.

"*Wait.*" Britt ceased her movement. "Wait wait wait. My mind must have wandered. What are you saying?"

"I was saying that yesterday Kurt Shaw, the detective—"

"I know Kurt," Nora said.

"So do I," Willow said. "He grew up here in Merryweather."

"His mom," Nora told Willow, "is Racquel Shaw—"

"But what did he say when you met with him about Frank?" Britt asked Zander.

"That Frank died of a heart attack, just like we thought. He also said that the injury Frank had on his leg was caused by a bullet.

Which means the story he told my aunt and everyone else about the scar on his leg was false."

"Intriguing," Nora said.

"Why would he have lied?" Britt asked.

"He might have been ashamed or embarrassed," Willow suggested.

"Could be," Zander said. "It seems strange to me, though, that he wouldn't have told Carolyn the truth. Why wouldn't he have told her?"

The sisters shrugged in response. Britt popped a red grape into her mouth and chewed thoughtfully. She broke another from the stem and pitched it to Zander so accurately that he caught it in his mouth.

Tonight, he'd combined his jeans with a muted orange T-shirt that made his eyes look especially blue in contrast. His inky hair stuck up in casual disorder. Five o'clock shadow darkened his cheeks.

"I'd like to find out more about Frank's old injury, if I can," Zander said. "Nora?"

Nora perked up. She loved to be helpful.

"What would be the best way to look up information on that?"

"Do you know Frank's full name, his birth date, and the location of his birth?"

"Yes."

"Then I'd recommend you start by plugging that information into one of the genealogy websites and running a search for records."

Britt hurried toward the staircase. "I'll grab my computer."

"We don't have to do this right now." Amusement tinged Zander's words. "Think of the Broccolini."

"I've never stopped thinking of the Broccolini." Britt climbed the stairs two at a time. "And we absolutely *do* have to do this right now. My curiosity's piqued."

"There's no stopping her when her curiosity's piqued," Britt heard Willow say.

"No," Zander replied, "there's not."

"'Never lose a holy curiosity,'" Britt called down to them. "That's an Albert Einstein quote."

She grabbed her computer, descended the stairs, and handed it to Nora. Nora set it on the bar top near the brie and booted it up.

Red-haired Nora had dressed with trademark vintage flair tonight in a sleeveless turtleneck shirt and turquoise capris. A genealogist who ran the Library on the Green Museum that anchored Merryweather Historical Village, she'd never met a search for historical information she didn't like.

Willow stood next to Nora wearing a plum-colored sundress, absent-mindedly straightening a lock of blond hair between her thumb and pointer finger. She still looked as slim and sophisticated as she had when she'd been a model, even though she'd retired from modeling more than a year ago. Since then, she'd opened a clothing and housewares store in Shore Pine called Haven.

The three sisters shared a father, but had been born to different mothers. As a result, they didn't resemble one another strongly.

The click of the keyboard punctuated the air as they watched the computer screen.

Zander had spent so much time at Bradfordwood, the sisters' childhood home, that he'd become a de facto family member. He'd been included in countless family parties and functions. He'd accompanied them on several trips and, for a long time now, he'd treated Willow and Nora like sisters . . . . minus the fighting, disagreements, and rivalry.

"Okay," Nora said to Zander, hands poised above the keyboard. "I'm ready."

"His full name was Frank Joseph Pierce."

She entered the information.

Britt checked on the Broccolini—browning nicely—then resumed her position next to Zander.

"He was born on February second, 1955," Zander said, "in Enumclaw, Washington."

Nora hit return. "Here he is." She angled her head toward the topmost search result. "I'm just going to click on his name to bring up some additional information about him." A hitch of quiet. "Hmm." Seriousness weighted the single syllable.

"What is it?" Zander asked.

"Well." Nora drew Zander nearer the screen. "Frank Joseph Pierce was born on the day you supplied in the town you supplied. But look at this." She pointed to one of the dates provided. "Frank Joseph Pierce died in 1956."

Britt stared in confusion at the blocky black numerals.

Nora clicked on a link that brought up a death certificate. Britt's vision raced over the information. Frank had drowned in August of 1956, when he'd been just a year and a half old.

"This must be the wrong person," Zander said.

"It's possible." Nora spoke calmly. "However, it would be unusual for more than one Frank Joseph Pierce to have been born in a small town on the same day." She returned to the previous screen and scrolled down.

Britt had gotten to know Frank well, through Zander, when she'd been a teenager. In more recent years, she'd worked side by side with Frank on Merryweather Historical Village's annual O Holy Night Christmas Concert. From time to time, he and Carolyn invited her to dinner parties. She invited them to join her when a guest chef served a meal at the Village. She saw them at wedding showers and baby showers and fundraising events. Every few weeks, Frank stopped by the shop to drink coffee and visit with her.

Nora selected another listing for Frank Joseph Pierce. This time, the details about the Frank Britt knew, *their* Frank, populated the screen. His wedding certificate. A listing of the times he'd appeared in the census.

This was what Britt had expected to see when Nora had run her initial search. Yet all of this now felt as obsolete as a rotary phone in light of the death certificate they'd viewed first.

She peeked at Willow. Willow peeked at her. A pulse of *What in the world is going on?* passed between them.

"This documents my uncle's life," Zander said.

"Yes," Nora answered.

"But there's also documentation about the life of someone with the same name who died when he was a toddler."

"Yes."

The kitchen timer sounded. Zander used a dish towel to extract the Broccolini from the oven, then made his way back to them. "So even though it's unusual, two babies with the same name *were* born in the same place on the same day."

"That's the conclusion I'd reach if I could find separate birth certificates for each," Nora agreed. "But I can't." She checked and rechecked. "Here's the birth certificate belonging to the Frank who drowned." She enlarged a scanned image of a simple, old-school birth certificate printed on beige paper. It listed the date of birth and then the place of birth: Enumclaw, King County. Mother's maiden name: Gladys Mortensen. Father's name: William Pierce.

"And here," Nora said, "is the birth certificate belonging to your uncle."

The very same birth certificate appeared. Beige paper. Place of birth: Enumclaw, King County. Mother's maiden name: Gladys Mortensen. Father's name: William Pierce.

In the silence that followed, Britt's thoughts spun. They came to a stop on the nonsensical realization that her earlier goal of having the salmon ready at the same time as the Broccolini was shot.

"Two separate people are sharing the same birth certificate," Nora said.

"Maybe the birth certificate is right, and it's the death certificate that's wrong," Zander said. "Could the death certificate for the boy who died have been issued to Frank by mistake?"

"Excellent question." Nora centered young Frank Joseph Pierce's death certificate on the screen again. "Frank's death certificate includes information about his birth. And look, the details of his birth that are listed here all agree with what we know to be true. The day. The place. His parents' names."

Gladys Mortensen. William Pierce.

"The details line up," Nora said. "Which makes me think this death certificate was issued to the right person."

"What other explanation for this could there be?" Zander asked.

Nora faced them, leaving one hand on the bar top. Thoughtfully, she clicked a fingernail against the laptop's metal surface. "Before computers were as prevalent as they are now, people who were in the market for a new identity would occasionally search cemeteries for gravestones. They'd find someone of roughly the same gender and age as themselves."

"And?" Britt asked.

"They'd jot down the person's full name and birthday. Then they'd call the local hospital, impersonate the dead person, and ask to be sent their birth certificate."

Willow frowned. "But how?"

"Hi, this is Mary Smith," Nora said, "and I was born in your hospital on June seventeenth, 1942. I'm so very, very sorry, but I've just moved and searched through every single packing box, and I can't find my birth certificate anywhere. Is there any possible way for you to reissue me a new one? If so, you'll save my marriage, and I'll be forever grateful. Truly! So grateful."

"And just like that a person could get their hands on a birth certificate that didn't belong to them?" Willow asked.

"Back in the day, the answer was sometimes yes," Nora answered. "Once a person had possession of a birth certificate, they could visit the DMV and apply for a license. The DMV would take a photo and attach it to the name on the birth certificate. Once they were granted a driver's license, a world of possibilities opened to them."

Zander scratched the back of his neck. "You think Frank stole a dead child's identity."

"I think it's possible." Nora sighed. "I've been researching genealogy for years, and I've only seen evidence of a potential stolen identity one other time. It's rare. But I *have* seen it." She considered him, concern in her eyes. "I'm sorry, Zander. I know this isn't what you'd hoped to find."

After they finished dinner, after they ate vanilla toffee bar crunch for dessert, after Willow and Nora went home, Zander sat next to Britt on her living room sofa.

Britt had a way of cooking—choosing ingredients and blending flavors—that was unique to her. He'd missed her food. Tonight, finally, he'd had the chance to eat a meal of hers for the first time in what felt like a decade.

But the information Nora had uncovered about Frank before they'd sat down to dinner had caused his chest to tighten with anxiety. He regretted that he hadn't been able to taste the food like he'd wanted to.

Britt looped her arms around her bent knees, her socked feet flat on the sofa. She never wore shoes or slippers inside her house, only socks. He tried not to notice how well her jeans fit or the creamy V of skin at the base of her neck, revealed by her purple shirt. She'd braided her brown hair loosely and pulled the braid forward over one shoulder.

He sat against the sofa's back, his palm tucked behind his head, his feet crossed on one of the two shellacked wooden stumps that functioned as her coffee tables.

The intensity between them caused the air particles separating his position from hers to vibrate. From his perspective, anyway. She probably didn't feel what he felt. To Britt, the air between them was likely as flat as the surface of a windless lake.

Memories of the many, many other times they'd sat just like this moved through his mind. They'd talked, laughed, discussed decisions big and small, worked on some harebrained plan of his or hers—usually hers—and watched movies from this spot.

Sitting next to her tonight felt different, though. Because so much time had passed and because of the push-pull battle happening inside of him. Love pulling him to her. Futility pushing him away.

Before he'd gone abroad, he had years of practice at stuffing down his emotions toward Britt. It had never been easy. Even so, he'd become very good at it. He'd been able to manage himself inwardly and outwardly when they were together. The push-pull battle had been bearable. At least, it had been bearable right up until the night she'd thrown him a dinner party at Bradfordwood to celebrate his book contract.

She'd been dating a guy named Tristan at the time. When she'd told the guests about Tristan, her cheeks had been pink, and she'd looked excited and happy and infatuated and, all of a sudden, he'd known what he had to do with his advance.

He had to leave.

Until that dinner party, he hadn't had the means to leave. But on that night, he'd had the means, which had, in turn, allowed him the luxury of hitting his limit. He'd taken the getaway car his newfound money provided because he'd understood that he owed himself a chance to move on. He'd needed to prove his independence from her to himself.

The night of the dinner party, the push-pull battle had not been bearable.

Nor was it bearable now.

Either he'd outgrown his old coping mechanisms or they'd become so rusty they were of almost no use to him.

Good grief. He really needed his coping mechanisms. She was assessing him without a shred of self-consciousness, and he was almost afraid to meet her eyes, for fear of what she might see.

She was far more comfortable in her own skin than anyone else he knew. Certainly more so than he was. He'd only recently grown into himself on his trip. Britt hadn't needed travel to grow into herself. She'd always been exactly who she was.

"I'm trying to think of things that would explain why two separate people would have the same birth certificate," Britt said.

"Me too."

"I can't come up with anything, but I wish I could."

"So do I. I'm trying to process the fact that Frank may have taken a child's identity. . . . That he may not have been who he said he was."

"He was so genuine. He seemed to me like an open book. It's hard to imagine him needing to change his identity—let alone him actually doing it, then keeping it a secret."

Groaning, Zander bent forward. His feet thumped onto the floor as he pressed the heels of his hands against his forehead. "How am I going to tell this to Carolyn?"

"You'll find a way."

"She told me that she can't handle surprises right now."

"She also told you that she needed to know Frank's story, right?"

"Right."

"It sounds like this identity thing might be part of Frank's story. If so, then the truth is the truth. This surprise isn't your fault, and you can't change it."

He drew in a heavy inhale. "I told Carolyn I'd find answers for her. I'd hoped the answers would make things better. What if they make things worse? What if I uncover something disturbing or depressing?"

"That would stink, but again: The truth is the truth."

"What if I uncover something dangerous?"

"Then knowledge is power. If Carolyn's in danger, then it would be better to be informed than ignorant."

Taking his time, he sat up fully. "Happy, law-abiding people don't change their identities. Only people who are in trouble or who want to escape from something change their identities."

"You have a point."

Zander worked the situation in his mind. "Let's assume Nora's right, that my uncle isn't the real Frank Pierce. If so, then how can we find out who he really is—was?"

"I have no idea."

She looked gorgeous and eager to help him. *Do you want to help me, Britt? Then love me. Love me back.*

Here's the thing, though: He knew his predicament wasn't Britt's fault.

He'd have nothing to complain about if he could adjust his

feelings for her to the level of her feelings for him. He'd tried for years to care about her in the same way that she cared about him.

Zander wanted to fall in love and get married and have kids and maybe write books from an office with a view of the water. He wanted all that, but he couldn't have any of it until he could find a way to change the way he felt about her. He knew this.

The last time he'd seen his brother, Daniel had made Zander promise that he'd do everything he could to let Britt go.

Zander had promised.

Yet, sitting two feet from her, he was powerless to stop the longing from roaring through his bloodstream. If he kissed her, he could prove his longtime theory that kissing her would taste like chocolate.

"Let's brainstorm ways to confirm Frank's identity," she said.

"Fingerprints?" he suggested. "Do you think the medical examiner would have taken Frank's fingerprints during the autopsy?"

A spark illuminated her face. "If so, we can ask Detective Shaw to run his prints."

"Which might be in the system if Frank committed a crime in his younger years."

She resettled the end of her braid. "What about the bullet that was removed from Frank's leg? Could that lead us to some clues?"

"Possibly." He noticed she'd used the word *us*. She'd assumed this search was *their* search, and with good reason. They'd tackled their problems together in the past. "I'm wondering if the town of Enumclaw could be a clue."

"Right. Because why would Frank have been shopping in that particular cemetery for a new identity unless he had a connection to the town?"

He nodded. "On the other hand, he may not have had any connection to the town. He might've been driving through Enumclaw, spotted the cemetery, and decided to pull over to search the gravestones."

Her lips twitched with skepticism. "Would you put something that random into one of your books?"

"No, because random chance doesn't work in fiction. But in real life, people do inexplicable things all the time."

She reached for the bowl of chocolate-covered cashews on the side table and offered them to him.

"No thanks."

She adjusted into a cross-legged position, wincing a little as she did so, almost as if the motion had hurt her.

"You okay?"

"Fine." She set the bowl in front of her ankles and popped two cashews into her mouth. "What if the bullet wound is connected to Frank's decision to change his identity?"

"It probably wouldn't hurt to search for news stories about shootings that happened in the general area of Enumclaw shortly before Carolyn met Frank."

"Because Frank already had the bullet wound and the new identity when they met."

"Correct."

"What year was that?" she asked.

"1985."

"If I were a betting woman, which you know that I am—"

"Yep."

"—I'd bet on us. Working together, I think we have a shot at figuring this out."

"Thanks, but I'm planning to look into this by myself. In other words, *alone*." He tried and failed to keep his expression serious.

Her chestnut-colored eyes lit with fire. "I'd like to see you try to stop me from joining you."

"That's what I was afraid you'd say." Those were the words he spoke. However, the truest, hungriest, most selfish part of him was very glad that she was determined to join him in this. He wanted her as his ally. He wanted her near him.

Which was idiotic.

If they spent hours working side-by-side, he had no confidence in his ability to resist her. Nor did he trust that he'd be able to make himself return to Japan and finish his trip when the time came.

Once the funeral was over, he discovered what had happened to Frank, and Carolyn was on her feet again, he needed to leave Washington. He still had six months of travel plans left to complete.

Even so.

Regardless of all that.

He wanted her near him.

Phone call from Zander to Detective Kurt Shaw:

Zander: Some friends and I were checking online records last night and we came across two entries for Frank Joseph Pierce. One was for my uncle. The other was for a child who died in 1956. But here's the troubling thing: Both of them share the same birth certificate.

Kurt: What?

Zander: Nora Bradford was there. She's a genealogist, and she suggested that my uncle Frank might've assumed the identity of the deceased Frank Pierce. Would my uncle's fingerprints have been taken during the autopsy?

Kurt: Yes, they would have.

Zander: I'm wondering if they could confirm his identity. Either as Frank Pierce or as . . . someone else.

Kurt: I'll check to see if the prints have been run. If not, I'll make sure that they are. Then I'll get back to you with results.

CHAPTER

Three

Why in the world would I want to put dark chocolate and red pepper in my mouth at the same time?" Nikki Clarkson demanded the next afternoon. "If I want to eat a red pepper, Britt, I'll order chili at The Griddle. And you know how suspicious I am about dark chocolate on principle. I like my chocolate with plenty of milk and plenty of sugar, thank you very much."

"Don't you think it's good for the soul to try new things?" Britt asked. It was good for her soul, heaven knew. She'd wither away from boredom if she had to do the same thing and eat the same thing and look at the same things every day.

"What's good for my soul at this particular moment is a milk chocolate pecan turtle." Nikki pointed a long French-manicured fingernail at Sweet Art's display case. "I'll take that one there, third from the end, because it's the biggest."

Britt grumbled about unadventurous customers as she reached for the chosen turtle.

Nikki worked for Nora as the office manager of Merryweather Historical Village. She'd been widowed twice, dressed her curvaceous figure in clothes reminiscent of her '80s heyday, and was one of Britt's most regular customers.

Today she'd caught the sides of her dyed brown hair into a

barrette, sprayed her bangs, and let the permed strands corkscrew around her shoulders.

"Don't mind Britt's grumbling," Maddie said from her position at the cash register, where she'd recently finished ringing up a newlywed couple with a fondness for white chocolate macadamia popcorn. "Britt has always been too impatient with routine for her own good."

Maddie, Britt's high-school-friend-turned-employee, ran the business side of the shop. She waited on customers, managed the online store, handled accounting, ordered supplies, organized their weekend staff, and more.

"Nikki," Britt said sweetly, "do you want a job here at Sweet Art? Maddie's position is about to become available."

Nikki released a throaty guffaw. "You don't want me working here, believe you me. I'd become distracted every time a halfway decent-looking man walked in. Why do you think Nora keeps me shut away upstairs at the Library on the Green like I'm some kind of nun or a person with an infectious disease? Which I'm not!"

"The nun or the person with an infectious disease?"

"Neither!"

"Speaking of halfway decent-looking men . . . Have you seen Zander since he got back into town?" Maddie asked Nikki.

"Mercy, yes. I happened to be in the office the other day when Zander stopped by to say hello to Nora." Nikki hadn't paid yet, a truth that didn't stop her from extracting the turtle from its bag and taking a bite. She moaned while chewing. "Zander's always had a special place in my heart. He's so somber and watchful! He reminds me of a Dickens orphan. Tragic and brooding and gorgeous."

Britt couldn't wait to tell Zander that Nikki had likened him to a Dickens orphan.

"Those tattoos on his arms make me wonder about the tattoos I *can't see*," Nikki said.

Britt's eyebrows sailed upward.

Nikki grinned. "The tattoos on his *upper arms*, I mean!" She threw a balled napkin at Britt. "If I can't have Zander for myself—because, let's face it—he might be a little too young for me . . ."

If Nikki's "a little" meant thirty years, then she was right on the money.

". . . then I'd like for him to end up with you, Britt," Nikki finished. "When you bottle your sassiness, you're actually not half bad."

"Yes!" Maddie exclaimed. The gold highlights in her brunette curls caught the light. "Thank you."

"Are you thanking her for labeling me as not half bad?" Britt asked.

"I'm thanking her for agreeing with my belief that you and Zander should end up together."

Britt made a dismissive sound. Why couldn't people accept that a man and woman could be friends? *Just* friends? Over the years many, many people had suggested that she date Zander. Maddie had been advocating for it for eons, and Britt sensed that her sisters would jump on the bandwagon, too, if she gave them a chance.

It irked her, because they all seemed to think that dating a man was superior to friendship with a man, when Britt's experience had confirmed the opposite.

From the day she'd met Zander, with his reserved personality encased in hard-to-know armor, she'd wanted him as her friend.

Perhaps because boyfriends were so transient and so . . . fluffy. Ultimately, inconsequential.

Perhaps because, as fun as it was to feel sexually drawn to someone, she hadn't felt sexually drawn to Zander at the start. There had been some exceptions to that since. But why dwell on the exceptions when they only proved the rule? She and Zander were friends. That's how they thought of each other. That was their dynamic. And their dynamic had been in place, unchanged and unbreakable, for a long, long time.

She trusted him. She appreciated every facet of him. She both liked him and loved him. And all of that, all the things she *did* feel—trumped lust. Friendship wasn't a consolation prize. It wasn't less than. It wasn't second best!

"Is Zander hiding back there in the kitchen by chance?" Nikki asked. "I could use a little pick-me-up."

"Nope, he's not here." More's the pity. Time passed much more slowly when Zander wasn't around. "I'm not in the habit of stashing men in my kitchen, FYI."

"Maybe we *should* get in the habit of that," Maddie suggested. "I'll gladly volunteer Leo for the position."

For more than three months, Maddie had been dating handsome history professor Leo Donnelly.

The two were crazy about each other. Just like Willow and Corbin and Nora and John. Britt had been an early proponent of each of those romances. Now that they were all so disgustingly moony over each other, though, she sometimes had to indulge in hidden eye rolls. "I refuse to pay my employees to be sidetracked by their boyfriends," Britt said.

Maddie sighed and sailed toward the kitchen. "She's a brutal taskmaster," she told Nikki before vanishing from sight.

"You haven't met any handsome new bachelors in their fifties or sixties lately, have you?" Nikki asked Britt.

"No, I—"

Sweet Art's front door opened to admit a long-haired, six-foot-tall man.

"Clint!" Britt called happily.

"Hey there." He wore a leather vest sans undershirt, a cowboy hat decorated with a peacock feather, jeans, and boots. The getup was purely an expression of taste since he'd never lived in a cowboy state, only in a cowboy state of mind.

Nikki slid her the evil eye. "I just this minute asked you if you'd met any handsome new bachelors," she accused.

"Clint's not new to town. He works at . . ." Britt raised her voice to include Clint in their circle of conversation. "I was just going to say that you work for my parents at Bradfordwood as landscaper."

"Don't forget that I also work as the inn's maid."

"You mean to tell me," Nikki said, "that you've been keeping a man who knows how to garden and how to clean all to yourself?" She managed to look both outraged with Britt and appreciative of Clint simultaneously.

"I didn't know I was keeping him to myself," Britt shot back. "I assumed you two had met."

"Are you single?" Nikki asked Clint.

"I am."

Nikki whistled. "Today is my lucky day."

"I'm Clint Fletcher." He proffered his hand.

"I'm available. So nice to meet you." Nikki preened as if she'd said something terribly witty while they shook hands.

Despite the bravado that Clint's clothing and hair suggested, his personality could be described as tentative. He was sometimes unsure of himself and always eager to please. He appeared to be taking Nikki in with a combination of interest and naked fear.

"Clint," Britt said with a grand hand gesture, "it is my very great honor to present Nikki Clarkson to you. I thought you two might know each other because Nikki works for Nora at the library."

"Do you come to the Historical Village often, Clint?" Nikki asked.

"Not often at all. This is probably only my second or third time here." He slid a paper from his back pocket and handed it to Britt. "Casey would like to give chocolate to all of the inn's guests on Easter Sunday. I volunteered to stop by with his order form."

Casey worked as innkeeper at the Inn at Bradfordwood. "Awesome. Thanks."

Nikki rested her arm against the top of the display case and swept out an imposing hip. "How old are you, Clint?"

"Sixty."

Her heavily made-up eyes enlarged, and Britt almost laughed. Watching Nikki in action had long been the best entertainment in town. "I'm the same age!" Nikki exclaimed. "When's your birthday?"

They exchanged birthdays and realized that Nikki was just two months younger than Clint. "Well, that's perfection right there, that's what that is," Nikki said. "How do you stay in such good shape?"

"Well, I was once a professional performer—"

"What kind of performer?"

"An actor," he answered shyly. "But interpretive juggling paid the bills."

"Interpretive juggling," Nikki said, awed.

"I still act, in addition to the work I do for the Bradfords. Since I don't juggle anymore, I had to find another way to stay fit. So I took up Pilates."

"Fabulous," Nikki replied. "I gave up exercise in 1992, but I've recently been thinking that I'd be excellent at Pilates."

"Britt?" Maddie's voice drifted from the kitchen.

"I'll be there in a minute. The show I'm watching out here is too good to miss."

Britt's words brought Maddie out immediately. "What's too good to miss?"

Britt nodded at Clint and Nikki. "The interaction between these two."

"Some privacy would be welcome right about now," Nikki said.

"You're in my shop," Britt reminded her. She set her palms beneath her chin and blinked several times. "Don't mind me."

Maddie set her palms beneath her chin and blinked, too. "Don't mind me, either."

Nikki gave a huff and turned to Clint. "Is it any wonder that Britt doesn't have a boyfriend?"

"I've had lots of boyfriends," Britt said.

"But you haven't managed to keep a single one."

"I haven't *wanted* to keep a single one."

"Anyway." Nikki gave Clint a these-immature-people-are-so-tiring expression. "When is your next Pilates class? I'd love to join you."

For Zander, arriving at Frank and Carolyn's house when he was a teen had been like arriving at an island of calm after a long, stormy voyage at sea.

The small bedroom with the twin bed and navy-and-white striped bedspread had held peace. The acres thick with trees that surrounded the house had brought comfort. The food they'd served him—casseroles and stir-fries and tacos and chicken salads—had steadied him. So had Carolyn's reliability and Frank's sense of humor.

On the days when Daniel had baseball practice after school and couldn't drive Zander home, Carolyn had always been waiting for Zander in the carpool line in her Subaru Outlook. Not once had she forgotten.

Frank had insisted that Daniel and Zander watch funny movies with him on Sunday nights. He'd felt duty-bound to give them an education in films like *Blazing Saddles* and *Monty Python and the Holy Grail*.

Looking at Carolyn and Frank's house now through adult eyes, Zander could see its modesty. The house had been built more than twenty years ago without the use of imagination. The front was flat. Its sides, gray. Black shutters. Two utilitarian stories. Neither Frank nor Carolyn had a green thumb, so nothing more interesting than hedges accessorized the exterior.

Inside, however, the house overflowed with color. Carolyn collected stained-glass windows. All sizes and shapes of them covered every inch of wall space. Sitting inside the living room felt like sitting inside a greenhouse.

When Kurt Shaw had arrived and Carolyn had ushered him in, he'd chosen to sit in Frank's weathered TV-watching chair.

Courtney and Sarah, Frank and Carolyn's daughters, occupied the sofa. The identical twins looked just like their father would've if he'd been female and thirty-two years old. Both had Frank's dark hair, his hazel eyes, and his sharp-cornered smile that dug into the apples of their cheeks. Not that he'd seen a smile out of either of them over the past days.

They lived ten minutes apart from each other in Seattle, attended the same church, and spent a great deal of time together.

They'd been incredibly gracious about sharing their mother and father with Zander and Daniel. Especially because, having only spent time with Courtney and Sarah five times during their childhoods, Zander and Daniel had been near strangers when they'd moved into the girls' former bedrooms.

Carolyn sat across from Zander, looking as fragile as she had when they'd visited the police station. Was her neck strong enough to support the rope of peach-colored beads she'd coiled around it?

Zander had tried to soften the news the best way he knew how when he'd told Carolyn about Nora's suspicions concerning Frank's identity. Even so, it had still sent Carolyn, Courtney, and Sarah reeling. All three looked shell-shocked, as if unsure when they'd receive the next blow.

"Zander told you that he found information on a second Frank Pierce, correct?" Kurt asked Carolyn.

"Yes."

"Two people were using one birth certificate," Kurt said, "which meant the birth certificate had been paired with at least one of them incorrectly. I had your husband's fingerprints processed, and it turns out that he's not the one the birth certificate belongs to."

Zander's attention honed on Kurt like a camera focusing.

"Then . . ." Carolyn's voice trailed away to nothing. She cleared her throat. "My husband wasn't Frank Pierce?"

"No."

"Who was he?"

"James Richard Ross. Have you ever heard that name before?"

Bewilderment filled her eyes. "I've never heard that name before in my life. James Richard Ross, did you say?"

"Yes."

"Are you . . . are you completely sure about this, Detective Shaw? That my husband was this other person?"

"Yes, ma'am. Very sure." He extracted three pages from the file and spread them across the coffee table. "He was born in 1954 in

Chicago. His mother had five other children, some older, some younger, with a total of three different fathers."

Carolyn and her daughters stared at Kurt, faces glazed.

"Your husband dropped out of high school after his sophomore year," Kurt continued. "It wasn't that his grades were bad. In fact, from what I could tell, he was bright. I'm guessing that his desire to make money overrode his desire to get an education. He wasn't listed as part of his mother's household in the 1970 census, which means he'd left home by the age of sixteen." He leaned over and pointed to a mug shot of a teenager. The black-and-white picture showed an expressionless kid with a John Lennon haircut. "Is this your husband?" he asked Carolyn.

The paper shuddered slightly in her hand as she picked it up and studied it. Zander knew—no doubt everyone here knew—what her response would be. The teenager in the photo was undeniably Frank.

"Yes," Carolyn finally said. "This is my husband."

"He was arrested three times," Kurt said. "Once for underage consumption of alcohol when he was seventeen. Once on a drunk and disorderly charge when he was twenty-four. And once for robbing a gas station when he was twenty-six."

On the kitchen counter, an incense stick that smelled of cloves burned.

"What did he steal from the gas station?" Sarah asked.

"All the money out of the cash register and safe, as well as food and beer. He and a friend named Ricardo Serra committed the crime together. Does the name Ricardo Serra ring a bell?"

They shook their heads.

"James and Ricardo both served time for the crime," Kurt said. "Your husband was released from prison in November of 1983."

"I met him a year and a half later," Carolyn said.

"I found documents confirming that James Richard Ross was working in Seattle around that time. But after that, he vanishes from government records."

Courtney knotted her hands together on the upper ridge of her pregnant stomach. "You think that my dad turned his back on everything that had come before and started over?" she asked Kurt.

"Yes. How did he explain his lack of family to you?" Kurt asked Carolyn.

"He said that his father abandoned his mother when he was four. That his mother died when he was eleven, and that he was then raised in the foster care system."

So many lies. The revealing of them made Zander feel as though the foundation of this house might be torn in half at any second by an earthquake.

Today was Friday, and on Monday, he, Carolyn, Courtney, Sarah, Daniel, and many others would be attending Frank's funeral. The programs had already been printed and they clearly stated his birth year as 1955 and his name as Frank Joseph Pierce. What was Carolyn supposed to put on her husband's headstone now?

Would Carolyn still be able to trust, in retrospect, the relationship she'd had with Frank? Could Frank's girls still trust the relationship they'd had with their dad? Could *he* still trust the relationship he'd had with Frank? Or did Frank's lies force everything into question?

No.

He'd had so few good family relationships in his life. He needed to hang on to his belief in Frank's love for him.

"You mentioned when we met at the station that a bullet had been removed from Frank's leg," Zander said to Kurt. "Could testing the bullet potentially provide us with useful information?"

"Useful information concerning the circumstances surrounding the shooting?" Kurt asked.

"Exactly." If Zander could understand the shooting, which had happened around the time when Carolyn met Frank, perhaps he could understand Frank's change of identity.

"It's unlikely. Ballistics information will only provide us with details on the weapon the bullet was fired from. Also, I'd only have cause to analyze the bullet if I was investigating a crime." He addressed Carolyn directly. "Which I'm not, since we know that Frank's cause of death was a heart attack."

"I understand," she said.

The detective stood and said his good-byes.

"I'll walk you out." Zander fell in step with Kurt as they made their way down the front walkway. "Do you think Frank's change of identity could have had anything to do with his death?"

"Are you concerned that it might?"

Zander gave a grim nod. "I don't see anything in the paper work you brought that might have motivated a man to change his identity. What if he got involved in some kind of dangerous situation after his release from prison that caused him to take the extreme step of becoming someone different?"

"And?" They came to a stop near Kurt's GMC.

"And that situation came back to haunt him last Friday?"

Kurt spun his key ring around his index finger once. Twice. "After lying dormant for thirty-five years?"

"Maybe."

"I'd be willing to look into that possibility if I had evidence that pointed to murder. But I don't. Frank died of a heart attack."

"Possibly brought on by extreme stress?"

"But far more likely brought on the old-fashioned way, by a blood clot. While we were waiting for the autopsy results to come back, the chief and I went through Frank's truck from top to bottom. We dusted for prints and searched for fibers. We hunted through his phone, his phone records, his work and home computers, his browser history. We didn't find anything out of the ordinary."

In other words, Kurt had completed his responsibilities concerning Frank. He'd gone above and beyond, in fact, by researching James Richard Ross and bringing his findings to them. Kurt couldn't spend any more of the Merryweather Police Department's time digging around in Frank's distant past.

"What about the fact that Frank was missing for several hours before he died?" Zander asked. "Does that raise any suspicions in your mind?"

"It's strange, but no, it doesn't really raise suspicions. It's not extremely unusual for people to stay out all night or go off the grid for a day."

"It was extremely unusual for Frank, though."

"I hear you. However, Frank was a grown man, free to stay out all night if he wanted to."

Zander thanked the detective and returned to the now-empty living room. His aunt and cousins had moved to the kitchen. The subdued tones of their conversation drifted to him in snatches. The pages containing information about Frank stared up at him from what had once been a benign coffee table.

Zander memorized the sheets one by one, grief gathering in his chest. Grief because he'd never see Frank again, but also grief for the difficult childhood his uncle had faced.

What had happened to the teenager in the photo? What had his eyes seen once he'd become an adult? What could have occurred after his release from prison that might have motivated him to abandon his true identity as James Richard Ross?

Zander wasn't on the Merryweather Police Department's time. He couldn't run ballistics on a bullet, but he could contact Frank's relatives in Chicago and ask them for information on his uncle. He could search newspaper reports for shootings that occurred near Enumclaw in 1985.

He'd do his best to dig up Frank's secrets. Because Carolyn had asked it of him. Because his sense of unease concerning Frank's death wasn't shrinking, but growing. Because there was a chance that Frank's secrets might help him keep Carolyn, Courtney, and Sarah safe.

Text message from Britt to Zander:

Britt
I forgot to mention earlier that Nikki Clarkson came by the shop the other day and told me that you remind

her of a Dickens orphan. Isn't that hilarious? And also somewhat apropos?

Zander
A Dickens orphan?

Britt
Tragic and brooding and beautiful, she said.

Britt
I believe she said beautiful, anyway. It might have been gorgeous.

Britt
Maybe it was gorgeous.

Zander
I'll take gorgeous, because that's the honest truth.

Britt
It really is.

Zander
I'll also accept orphan and brooding.

Britt
But you take exception to tragic?

Zander
I do. It sounds needy. How about you let Nikki know that I'm a giant celebrity now?

Britt
Sure. Right after I finish doing every other possible thing I could do in the universe.

Zander
At the very least Nikki should upgrade me to wealthy Dickens orphan.

Britt

I like wealthy DickenSIAN orphan better.

Britt

I'm going with Dickensian. I like saying it. Dickensian.

Britt

Zander Ford, wealthy Dickensian orphan.

CHAPTER
Four

The day after Frank's funeral, Britt sat on her mountain bike, hands braced, one foot on the pebbled ground. Her breath came hard as she eyed Zander with both irritation and respect.

She wasn't interested in leisurely outings on mountain bikes or snowboards or rock-climbing mountains. In fact, she loved adventure sports precisely *because* she could make them into a competition.

Zander claimed he hadn't been on a bike since leaving for his Grand Tour. If not, whatever he'd been doing to exercise his muscles and cardiovascular system had been working. He was just as hard to beat as he'd ever been.

"Good effort, Britt." He needled her deliberately.

"It was better than good. I'd—"*pant pant*—"call my effort valiant."

"I wouldn't go that far." He shot her an affectionate smile that lifted her spirits and made her forgive him for beating her.

Yesterday at the funeral he'd looked bleak and lost. Seeing him like that had left her feeling equally lost and almost desperate to help him through the hard knock of Frank's sudden death. Zander had suffered too many hard knocks already.

Not today—and maybe not for a long time—but eventually,

Zander *would* return to his full self. She refused to have it any other way.

It was critically important to Britt that Zander Ford find happiness.

The woman at the front office of Forest Lawn Cemetery in Enumclaw had given them a map. She'd drawn lines in blue pen illustrating the route to the grave of Frank Joseph Pierce, which she'd marked with an X.

Zander came to a stop. "Here," he said.

Britt halted beside him in the heartbreaking portion of the cemetery named Baby Land. Kneeling, she cleared an infringing grass root from one corner of the small headstone.

FRANK JOSEPH PIERCE

BELOVED SON

2/2/1955–8/20/1956

Before this, they'd visited Enumclaw's library to hunt for information. They'd decided not to search for Frank Pierce, seeing as how Zander's uncle couldn't very well have remained in Enumclaw after pilfering the name of one of its residents. If their Frank was to be found in Enumclaw, he'd no doubt be found before he'd switched identities, under the name James Ross.

A friendly librarian had helped them search 1950s newspapers and city directories, but they'd come up empty. If James Ross had ever lived in this town, he'd left no discernible trace.

The sounds of nature wrapped around them as they paid their respects to a boy whose short life had ended abruptly in tragedy.

It was creepy here. But then, Britt had always found cemeteries creepy. She usually only visited the one outside Merryweather with her family on Memorial Day, to leave flowers on the grave of her Grandfather Bradford, who'd died before her birth.

Cemeteries reminded her—uncomfortably so—of her own mortality. Everywhere she looked, graves. Hundreds upon hundreds of graves. Corpses lying under the ground in different stages of decomposition.

Because of her faith, she knew she was supposed to look forward to heaven with anticipation. Or at the very least, have reached a truce with the idea of death. Instead, she'd drifted further and further from a truce since early last summer when she, like baby Frank here, had gained experience with drowning—

Don't think about it, Britt.

She hated thinking about it. In fact, she worked hard *not* to think about it whenever the memories came. But sometimes, like now, the memories overpowered her resolve, the same way the swollen river had overpowered her mastery of her kayak when it had swept her fast around the outside of a bend.

By the time she'd caught sight of the submerged tree, there'd been no avoiding it. The current rammed her kayak sideways against it. When she tried to yank herself free, she lost her balance and pitched into the rapids. The kayak flipped and surged against the embankment. The tremendous force of the water thrust her body beneath the river's surface and against the strainer, the tree's underwater branches.

She wasn't a novice. She'd acquired a great deal of experience with Class II+ rapids. She'd paddled that stretch of river numerous times. But recent rain combined with the newly fallen tree had conspired against her, and before she'd had a chance to process what was happening, she found herself trapped and looking death in its murky, cold, watery face.

The river pressed against her with crushing force. Panic and the need for air clawed her brain.

Blindly, she groped for her kayak. She could only feel its smooth body. Nothing to grab on to. Terrified, she reached out farther, then farther. Her fingers curved around the edge of the cockpit. Marshaling all her strength, she pulled as hard as she could, freeing the bow from the bank. The kayak swung out and began to tug downstream through a narrow opening in the branches.

She pushed off desperately against the branch beneath her feet and the kayak towed her into open water. She'd come up wheezing, injured badly—

And *really*. That was enough of that. Time to abort her charming little walk down memory lane.

She made a production out of retying both her shoelaces.

Zander didn't know what had happened to her that day because she'd opted not to tell him. She hadn't wanted to ruin even one of his days overseas. And she definitely hadn't wanted to risk the possibility—if one of her sisters had called him from her hospital room—that Zander might cut short his trip and return home. She'd wanted him home. But on his own terms. She refused to be the one responsible for forcing him to end his trip of a lifetime.

She hadn't remained silent about her accident for his sake alone, however. She'd also remained silent for her own sake.

Independence and adventurousness were two of the qualities she knew Zander appreciated most about her. She hadn't wanted him to think less of her. Nor had she wanted him, who'd always cautioned her to be more careful, to know just how careless she'd been and just how badly she'd screwed up. It was humiliating.

She'd been seriously injured the day of the accident. Even so, she hadn't been able to bear the pity and coddling her family and friends had tried to foist on her when she'd been recovering.

Yes, she'd been hurt. But she'd also been fine.

Fine.

Only Zander wouldn't be fine at all if he found out that she'd hidden her accident from him. He'd be wounded and angry and rightfully so.

She pressed to her feet.

Zander continued to peer at the grave, his face inscrutable.

"What're you thinking?" she asked.

"That Frank must have stood on this same spot decades ago and looked down at this very same thing."

"It's crazy to think he then decided to become Frank Joseph Pierce."

"Right. He arrived here James and left here Frank."

"In an odd way, it's almost as if he gave this child a chance to grow into a man. Because of your uncle, Frank Pierce lived an adult life." Britt clasped her hands behind her back. Had they been here long enough? It seemed like long enough.

"Why would he have come to this cemetery?" Zander murmured. "In this town?"

"We know Frank moved to Seattle around the time he changed his identity. Seattle's only an hour from here."

"It seems to me that a city kid from Chicago would have made his way straight from one big city to another big city," Zander said. "Chicago. Seattle. If so, then what was he doing in Enumclaw?"

"And why exactly did he need this boy's identity?"

Zander looked across his shoulder at her. The blue of his eyes tempted a person to think he might have the ability to see into souls. "I wish I knew," he said.

"You bet. Good-bye." Zander ended the call on his cell phone, then set the phone facedown on the desk inside his room at the Inn at Bradfordwood. He'd just finished talking to the last of Frank's relatives that he'd been able to find.

According to them, Frank had not been involved in their family's life since around the time he turned twenty. They were aware of his underage drinking arrest. And one sister had heard a rumor of his drunk and disorderly charge. But none were aware that he'd robbed a gas station or been sent to prison. None had a clue why he'd moved to the Pacific Northwest or, indeed, even that he *had* moved to the Pacific Northwest. And, unfortunately, none of them knew why he'd changed his name.

All of the siblings he'd spoken with had agreed that the Ross family's home life had been extremely difficult. Poverty, alcohol, and arguments had marked their mother's relationships. Frank's half sister had told Zander that Frank hadn't run away from home so much as he'd simply gotten a job at the age of sixteen and moved out.

Frank's brother told Zander that Frank had fallen in with a group of rough boys during his freshman year in high school. One of them had been Ricardo Serra, who later became Frank's partner in crime. *"Ricardo was very smart, but slick, you know?"* Frank's brother had said. *"He never struck me as somebody who could be trusted."*

Restlessness clawed at Zander as he settled his vision beyond the room's window toward the spring green forest.

Casey, the soft-spoken man who managed the inn, had served breakfast a few hours before. Zander had decided that he'd spend the time between breakfast and lunch each day working on his manuscript. However, his laptop lay beside him on the desk, shut and cold. Since arriving in Merryweather, he hadn't yet managed to focus his mind enough to write.

His lack of productivity wasn't the inn's fault. In fact, he'd be hard-pressed to think of any place more ideal for writing. The inn had been constructed of stone in the late 1800s in one corner of Bradford's two-hundred-acre plot. Dense woods hid the structure from the rest of the world. Its own entrance road linked it to the nearest street.

Zander remembered when Britt's mom, Kathleen, had decided to renovate what had once been the property's dower house and change it into an inn. He'd walked with Britt and her mom through these rooms back when they'd been covered in dust, as surely as the furniture had been covered in sheets. The bathrooms had been few and far between. The kitchen small, dark, and ancient.

Kathleen had kept the building's quality and character intact, but she'd added every possible comfort when she'd overhauled the place. The downstairs common room and dining room and the inn's five guest rooms and their adjoining bathrooms were now on par with what you'd find at a Four Seasons.

As soon as Britt had heard he was returning for Frank's funeral, she'd insisted he stay here. He hadn't needed convincing. He was comfortable here, in this inn owned by the family he knew so well. The Bradfords often housed friends and family here free of charge, and though he wasn't okay with staying here without paying anything—especially because he might be staying for weeks—he knew he'd be able to sweet-talk Kathleen into a payment arrangement later.

So, no. His irritability and wrecked concentration wasn't the inn's fault.

Pushing to his feet, he set his hands on his hips.

Maybe he needed a walk? A run? Maybe he should get in his rented Jeep Wrangler and go . . . where? He knew for sure he should pray. Too much time had passed since he'd spent a significant amount of time in prayer.

His guilt over that fact only increased his reluctance.

He'd go for a walk because he just—he needed *out*.

After exiting the inn's front door, he crossed a small bridge over the creek, then took the walking path that bent to the right. Moist wood and moss scented the air. The grumpy gray clouds matched his mood.

He'd never gone to church while growing up in St. Louis. The Bradford family, Aunt Carolyn, and Uncle Frank had first introduced him to church. As much as he appreciated their efforts, in the end, Britt had been the one who'd motivated him to cultivate a relationship of his own with God during their high school years. He'd wanted what he'd seen that she had. And when she'd explained how overwhelmingly God loved him, Zander had wanted that, too.

Years later, when he'd been in college and Britt had been in France apprenticing under master chocolatiers, he'd realized Britt's second-hand faith wasn't going to be enough to sustain him over the long haul. He'd been gut-wrenchingly lonely during that stage of his life. In need of God's presence. Eager to trust someone far bigger and more permanent than he was. He'd deepened his communication with God and reaped the benefits.

For the next several years, he'd felt close to God. His heart had been fiery and committed.

Over time, though, his enthusiasm had begun to dry.

He'd attended churches all over the world during the past eighteen months. He'd watched people in every language and culture praising the Creator of all things. He'd worshiped alongside them.

He'd hadn't worshiped from a place of gratitude, however. He'd worshiped from a place of duty.

His former closeness with God seemed distant to him now, like clothes that had belonged to him when he was much younger. Between then and now, life had changed him—

Was that right?

No, to say that *life* had changed him wasn't specific enough. Certainly, age and experience hadn't helped. Neither had the demands and pressures of his adult life. If he was honest with himself, though, the worst enemy of his faith had been his own disappointment.

He'd started praying that Britt would fall in love with him when he was a teenager. He'd continued praying that same prayer all the years since.

When you prayed for something every day and heard nothing but silence for more than a decade, it ground down your hope like corn into cornmeal. Zander had begun to wonder if God could still be good while denying him the one thing he'd prayed for most. Could he depend on a God who refused to give him what he'd waited years for?

The right answer was yes. God was still good. God was still dependable. However, disillusionment had driven a wedge into his relationship with God. What had once been simple was now complicated.

He watched an orange-chested robin glide into the air. The branch it had left trembled.

His walk hadn't helped cure his restlessness because his restlessness couldn't be fixed through a change in location or activity. He was restless because he didn't want to do the work he should be doing. His grief over his uncle weighed down both his body and his heart. And he missed Britt.

He didn't know how to exist in Merryweather, unless she was beside him.

Since his return, he'd either been with her and thinking about her, or apart from her and thinking about her. There was no other category. At the reception following the funeral, his awareness had tracked her instead of concentrating on the blur of faces offering him condolences. While making calls in his room just now, he'd wondered if Britt was tired today after staying up late with him the night before binge-watching *Star Wars* movies.

During his months overseas, she'd sometimes been more than seven thousand miles away. Now she was only five miles away. *Five miles.*

He could drive to Sweet Art in under ten minutes.

He should do that. He should go see her.

He turned toward the inn, then stopped. It was madness to get even more tangled up in her than he already was.

Missing her wasn't fatal.

He'd return to his room, and he'd try to write because he needed to protect himself from her as much as he possibly could.

Text message from Britt to Zander:

Britt
You haven't been searching the Internet for shootings that might have involved Frank without me, have you?

Zander
I wouldn't dare.

Britt
Thatta boy. Do you want to meet at my house tomorrow night to see what we can find? I'll have my laptop and you can bring yours.

Zander

I talked with Nora, and she told me that the odds are against us if we simply search the web for news stories about shootings that happened thirty-five years ago. She thinks we'll have better luck if we look through back issues of the Seattle Post-Intelligencer. They're stored on microfilm at the Central Library in Seattle.

Britt

I'm game for a trip to Seattle tomorrow if you are. I can leave work as early as 1:15.

Zander

You're going to be tired at 1:15 on a Friday. I don't want you to feel obligated to visit the Central Library with me.

Britt

Since when have you known me to feel either tired or obligated? I'm going with you and I'll be ready to leave at 1:15.

CHAPTER
Five

Seattle's Central Library had reveled in her three lives.

Her first incarnation, a Beaux-Arts design built with funds supplied by Andrew Carnegie, had opened in 1906.

Her second incarnation had come in1960, at a time when it had been en vogue to construct large civic buildings in the style of Ugly Utilitarian Monolith.

For her third incarnation in 2004, she'd made her debut wearing a dazzling garment of glass and steel that jutted upward and outward at shocking angles. Either her Dutch architect, Rem Koolhaas, had been drunk when he'd drafted her, or he'd been floating in a sea of creative brilliance. To Britt's way of thinking, he'd been floating in a sea of creative brilliance.

She loved the newest version of the library. For a woman who was as ceaselessly curious as she was, the library's more than three hundred thousand square feet offered countless wonders. Though she'd visited at least six times previously, this was the first time she'd attempted to comb through the library's microfilm collection.

An excellent male librarian, who was wearing a tie and cardigan sweater (as male librarians ought), had gathered film for them containing old issues of the *Seattle Post-Intelligencer*. He'd given her and Zander side-by-side projectors and a crash course on how to use them. Then they'd gotten to work.

They'd been at it for two hours already.

On the drive from Merryweather to Seattle in Zander's rental car, Britt had scrutinized the pages Kurt had given to Carolyn concerning Frank's early life. They'd talked through everything they knew about Frank's years as James Ross, including the little bit Zander had gleaned from the family members he'd spoken with on the phone.

Carolyn had told them that Frank had received the wound on his leg shortly before she'd met him in June of 1985, so Britt and Zander suspected Frank had been shot in April or May of 1985. After some debate, they'd decided to add a month before and after to give themselves a wide margin of error. Thus, they were searching for articles about shootings in issues of the Post-Intelligencer that ran between March and June of that year.

"I'm done going through mine," Zander said.

"I only have a few left." Britt adjusted the microscope on her projector as she skimmed an article about a wife who'd shot her husband.

"I think we should add one more month to both ends of our timeline, just in case," Zander said. "What do you think?"

"I sort of feel like we're trying to sip from a fire hose as it is. There's just *so much information.*"

"I know. But what if Frank got shot at the end of February, and we miss it because we don't look at February papers?"

"I hear you about February, but why look at July? Carolyn met Frank in June."

"So she says. Her memory isn't always the best, and she met him a long time ago. It's possible that they met in July or even August."

She straightened the legal pad they'd set between them. On it, they'd listed the shootings they'd found so far that might have involved Frank. Most of the articles about shootings mentioned the parties involved by name. All those had been excluded. So far, they'd compiled a record of only six incidents. Below each, they'd jotted the date, the location, and a few details about what had occurred.

"I'll look through the July papers," he said. "Are you game to look through February?"

"Anything for you, Zander." Man, the gun-toting wife in this article had really been mad at her husband, somewhat justifiably. He wasn't a good person. He also wasn't Frank. Britt moved on.

Zander vanished in search of their librarian and additional microfilm. When he returned, they threaded new reels into their projectors.

What they didn't know about Frank seemed as large to Britt as a tidal wave. What they did know seemed as small as a seashell.

They had no way of knowing whether the shooting had occurred near Seattle. It could've happened anywhere in the United States or even the world, for that matter. They didn't know if the shooting would factor into a big news story or no news story or a small news story about something as minor as a disagreement at a bar between two men backing opposing sports teams.

She skimmed another article, then went in search of the next. Nora deserved an extra dark chocolate cashew truffle the next time Britt saw her, because Britt couldn't understand how her sister did a job this detailed, slow, and painstaking on a daily basis.

Britt sort of wanted to poke her strained eyeballs out with forks.

Half an hour later, Britt's ears perked up at Zander's sharp intake of breath. "Did you find something?" she asked.

"Maybe," he replied slowly.

She swiveled toward him.

"I'm looking at a story about the art that was stolen from the Pascal Museum," he said.

"When was that?"

"July 5, 1985. Do you know anything about the heist?"

"It definitely rings a bell. Did a shooting happen in conjunction with it? If so, I don't remember that part at all."

"One sec." Tendons bunched and flexed at the hinge of Zander's jaw. She watched his profile intently as he read the article. He'd found something. She could tell by his posture.

Her heart began to pick up speed.

"At three a.m. on July fifth, three robbers broke into the Pascal." Zander's concentration remained on the screen. "They loosened bolts at the rear of the property and removed an entire window from its frame. They succeeded at disabling the security cameras but didn't disable the alarm because the alarm had a fail-safe they'd been unaware of. The three paintings they took were three of the most valuable the museum possessed. *Girl Before a Door* by Pablo Picasso, *The Pianist* by Marc Chagall, and *Young Woman at Rest* by Pierre-Auguste Renoir. Because they took three pieces of art, the heist is often referred to as the Triple Play."

"Go on."

"The alarm alerted the security guard on site, but the robbers were so fast that they'd exited the building by the time he was able to locate them. He saw them running down an alleyway behind the museum. He pulled his gun and was able to get off a few shots as they climbed into a dark gray Audi. The license plate on the rear fender of the Audi was covered. The security guard didn't know whether he'd succeeded in shooting anyone. Nor was he able to give good descriptions of the robbers because they were all dressed in black with ski masks over their faces."

"Okay, so I'm fascinated by the art heist angle," Britt said. "However, it's really unlikely that any of this relates to Frank because we don't even know whether or not anyone was shot."

Zander moved his focus to her. In the distance, she heard the gurgle of a quiet conversation, the distant *bing* of an elevator. "Aunt Carolyn used to work at the Pascal," he said. "That's where she and Frank met."

The tiny hairs along Britt's arms lifted. She peered at Zander while struggling inwardly to comprehend. "I don't think I ever knew how they met." The Pascal Museum was housed in a mansion that had once been the residence of the wealthy Pascal family. In the late seventies, when the matriarch and patriarch died, their children turned the house into a gallery filled with their parents' art collection and the pieces they themselves had acquired. The Pascal had received a mention in every "Ten Things Not to Miss in Seattle" article Britt had ever read.

"When Carolyn was in her early twenties, she gave tours of the Pascal and worked at their ticket counter and helped behind the scenes with events," Zander told her.

"What brought Frank to the Pascal?"

"He had a job doing construction in the city at the time." His forehead quirked. "At least, he *told* Carolyn he had a job doing construction. He came to the gallery because he loved the art."

"At least," Britt said, "he *told* Carolyn he loved the art. Did he display a lot of admiration for art when you knew him?"

"No, not that I can remember." He leaned back in his chair, crossing his arms. "Let's imagine for a minute that Frank didn't visit the Pascal because he loved the art. Let's imagine he visited because he was casing the museum in order to plan a heist."

Britt nodded. "A heist would have given him motivation to move from Chicago to Seattle. Once he moved here he would have needed to spend time, maybe months, planning the robbery."

"So he visits the Pascal often to study its collection, its security, the entry points, the layout."

"And in the process, he gets to know the woman who works at the ticket counter," Britt supplied. "It turns out that she's extraordinarily pretty and friendly."

"He and his accomplices proceed to rob the museum. They get away with three paintings, one for each of them. However, the security guard fires at them as they're getting away, and Frank is hit in the leg."

Britt rubbed her palms together slowly while she thought. "Where would Frank have gone for medical treatment? I mean, he couldn't very well show up wearing black at a local hospital with a gunshot wound in his leg. The police would have been all over him."

"I have no idea where he might have gotten treatment. Maybe from a small-town doctor? Not associated with any hospital?"

"Maybe."

"The police would also have been keeping an eye out for a dark gray Audi," Zander continued. "So the three men must've found a safe place where they could get Frank's leg sewn up and where they could switch out the car."

In record time, Britt had gone from wanting to poke out her eyeballs to suspecting she may have missed her calling as a detective. "I can't imagine how we'd be able to find either the doctor or the Audi now."

"Neither can I."

They sat without speaking, Britt's brain assessing the new information from every angle.

"After the heist," Zander said, "Frank continues to visit the Pascal. Eventually he asks Carolyn out. They date for several months, then get married in the summer of 1986. Shortly after that, they move to Merryweather."

"And the rest is history."

"So . . . help me think." Zander scratched the back of his neck. "Why would someone who'd stolen a painting from a museum return to that museum after the fact?"

"To set his sights on more art? If he was successful there once, he may have developed an appetite for more."

"Except that another heist never occurred."

"Could he have returned to the museum because of Carolyn?" As soon as Britt voiced the suggestion, it struck her as absurd. It was too far-fetched to think that a person in possession of a multimillion-dollar masterpiece would return to the scene of his crime for a girl. Doing so was altogether too dangerous. "On second thought, I can't imagine why any man would be willing to risk so much for a woman."

Zander's blue eyes met hers with intense steadiness. "I can."

In that moment, sitting inside a marvel of a library, Britt's stomach tightened with a sweet-hot tingle of physical longing.

For her very good friend Zander Ford.

His handsomeness had not, of course, escaped her notice for the

70

past thirteen years. His angular face was both aloof and observant. Young and hard. His body communicated a casual, effortless grace. Proficiency had been woven into the fabric of him.

Everywhere Britt went with Zander, women eyed him with proprietary interest.

His attractiveness wasn't up for debate.

That didn't mean, however, that she should allow hormones to hijack her body. Over the years, she'd experienced twinges of jealousy over him and flashes of silly infatuation. There had been times when she'd suspected him of experiencing twinges of jealousy and moments of silly infatuation over her, too.

Whenever a rogue romantic notion for Zander had overtaken her, she'd simply steamrolled it. Fortunately, he'd dealt with whatever rogue romantic notions he may have had for her in the same way. They'd never said anything to each other on the topic, thank God. A conversation about it would have been incredibly awkward, for one thing. It might have hurt their relationship, for another.

She'd handle this current pang the same way she'd handled those that had come before. She'd steamroll it.

"Frank may have returned to the museum after the robbery specifically so that suspicion *wouldn't* swing his way," Zander said.

Britt considered that. "If so, he must have waited a few weeks before returning. Otherwise, wouldn't he have been limping?"

Zander dipped his chin in agreement. "There are things about the heist that make me doubt that Frank could have been involved."

"But there are other things that point to his involvement."

"The main one is that we can put both Frank and Carolyn at the Pascal the summer of the robbery."

"And let's not forget that Frank had been convicted of robbery in the past." Still, it seemed like a stretch to imagine that Zander's uncle Frank, who'd sat across the table from Britt a month and a half ago at a guest chef night in the village, had once pulled off a world-class art heist.

A monotone voice flowed from the speakers. "The library will be closing in fifteen minutes."

"Ready for dinner?" he asked.

"Yep." They'd made a reservation at Place Pigalle, a Pike's Place Market restaurant within walking distance of the library.

Zander began taking photos of the art heist article. "Over dinner I want to research—"

"I already know what you're going to say."

His lips formed a wry smile. "I was going to say that I wanted to research . . ." He made a challenging, finish-my-sentence gesture.

"Whether or not the stolen paintings were ever found."

As Britt and Zander walked in companionable silence down city streets that slanted sharply toward Pike's Place, Britt's attention split between the sidewalk, the distant view of Puget Sound, and the ties that had knotted herself and Zander to food and to each other.

Britt's love of food had sprouted in elementary school. She could still recall the first time she'd made cookies with her mom. She'd stood on a chair near the counter, and her mom had handed her measuring cups and spoons pre-filled with ingredients. She'd dumped them into a bowl and stirred.

Fifteen minutes later, she'd been mesmerized when the thing they'd made—with ingredients in their pantry that were boring individually—had come out of the oven as warm and gooey chocolate chip cookies. She'd realized that cooking was like a craft project you could eat. From that point on, she'd turned the full force of her creativity in that one direction.

By the time she and Zander entered ninth grade, she was already an accomplished, experienced cook. Fourteen-year-old Zander had known nothing about cooking. He appreciated food as passionately as she did, however, because he was almost always ravenously hungry.

The first time he'd come to Bradfordwood to hang out, they'd baked a lemon cake with lemon glaze. He'd been clueless in the kitchen, but when it had come time to eat the cake, he'd exhibited his prowess by consuming twice as much as she'd been able to.

After that, he'd proven himself a quick study. He'd memorized every recipe they'd worked on together using his photographic memory. To this day, recipes didn't naturally stick in Britt's head. She had to make a recipe at least a dozen times before she could remember the exact quantities and ingredients. Not Zander. He looked at a recipe once, and there it was, accessible in his brain forever.

Every weekend through high school, they'd met either at Frank and Carolyn's house or at Bradfordwood to cook. Instead of a soundtrack, they had a food track from that season. It included thin crust pizza, fried chicken, cinnamon rolls, homemade ice cream, and peanut butter cookies.

After high school Zander accepted a full-ride academic scholarship to University of Washington–Tacoma and Britt had gone on to The Culinary Institute of America at Greystone. Each time she'd returned to Bradfordwood from California, Zander had made the trip to Merryweather, too. They'd cooked the sophisticated dishes she'd learned at school. The food track of that season: ricotta omelets, scallops with browned butter, pan-roasted pork chops, berry tarts.

She'd moved home from France the same summer that he'd moved home from Tacoma with his degree. They'd both, suddenly, been members of the work force. Her, as owner of Sweet Art (thanks to the hefty gift of capital her mom and dad had given her when she'd completed her apprenticeship). Him, as a computer engineer with a software design firm.

For the first time they'd had enough income to afford restaurant dinners. They'd explored all the small and large, casual and fancy eateries in the region around Merryweather. Even so, they'd never given up cooking together. The food track of that season: almond-crusted duck, red snapper, steak, soufflés.

Then one night, out of the blue, Zander had announced to a tableful of people that he'd decided to leave Washington and travel. He hadn't discussed his decision with her privately first, which had confounded her.

73

In the days leading up to his departure, the prospect of a long separation between them had weighed on Britt, but it hadn't seemed to weigh on Zander at all. Which had confounded her, too.

Then he'd gone. And she'd missed him. And missing him had stunk. She'd remained behind in their small hometown, watching photos of one glamorous destination after another appear on his private Instagram. He'd flourished without her while she'd struggled without him. If it had occurred to Zander that his absence might have left a black hole in her life, he'd never let on.

And she'd never said anything to undermine his happiness. She'd supported his Grand Tour the way a true friend should, because she'd always believed that he deserved a turn to see the world. There'd been no money for travel during his childhood with his parents or his teenage years with Frank and Carolyn. But even if that hadn't been the case, she herself had once enjoyed two years overseas. She could hardly begrudge him the same opportunity.

They reached Place Pigalle, a diminutive restaurant perched atop other structures like a hatbox atop a stepladder. Memories of the other times she and Zander had eaten together swirled through Britt's thoughts as the hostess led them to a linen-covered table positioned beside a window.

Britt paused to compare the merits of the available seats. She always took her time choosing and had been known, when she chose incorrectly, to leave a seat that had bad mojo.

The hostess waited with their menus. Zander, well aware of Britt's quirks and immune to bad chair mojo, stood patiently.

She lowered into a chair and . . . ? Excellent mojo.

Zander took the remaining seat, and they proceeded to discuss the menu options as if they were about to commit to a deed of sale on a house.

When her French onion soup and his butter leaf salad appeared, he gave her a contented nod. He spoke volumes through that one, wordless nod. It said that he felt nostalgic about this, too. That he remembered all the foods she remembered. That he hadn't outgrown his affection for eating. That he was just as pleased to be sitting here with her as she was to be sitting here with him.

The browned cheese on top of her soup clung to the bowl as she drew the spoon upward. "I'm really, really curious about the fate of the paintings that were stolen from the Pascal." She blew on her steaming bite.

"The other diners will think we're cretins if we hunch over a screen at a fancy restaurant." He was already reaching for his phone.

"Yep."

"Which has never stopped us before."

"Nope."

He scooted closer to her, set his phone between them on the table, and typed *Whatever happened to the paintings stolen from the Pascal?* into Google. The first article that arose was titled "Chagall Returned." They bent their heads over it and read as they ate.

A year and a half ago, the Chagall had come up at a private auction in Singapore. A British art dealer had immediately recognized the painting as the one stolen in the infamous Triple Play. He'd contacted the authorities and the painting was eventually returned to the Pascal's museum director, Annette Pascal Spencer.

"What about the Renoir? And the Picasso?" Britt asked.

After some searching, Zander found a story detailing the discovery of the Picasso. In 1996, a Colorado antique store owner attended an estate sale following the death of the property's wealthy owner. Among other things, the antique store owner purchased the painting that had been mounted on the wall above the multi-millionaire's bed.

He'd loaded the items into the back of his truck and transported them to his store. As soon as he put the painting on display, customers began marveling over just how much it resembled an authentic Picasso.

Upon closer examination, the man discovered a few horizontal cracks in the paint, which indicated that the piece may have been rolled. Warbles at the edges of the canvas suggested that it might have been cut from its frame at some point in its history. Thus, he began researching Picasso's works and stumbled upon a mention of the Picasso stolen during the Triple Play.

"I almost fell out of my chair," the antique store owner was quoted as saying, *"when I found an article about the heist and saw a picture of the missing Picasso. It looked exactly like the one I'd just purchased, so I called the police."*

As with the Chagall, the Pascal Museum brought in experts who'd verified the painting's provenance.

"When I think about how I piled that painting into the back of my truck, it sends a shiver down my spine," the antique store owner had stated.

"I'd love to know how the paintings ended up in Singapore and Colorado," Britt said.

"I'm guessing that the robbers sold them on the black market."

Britt slid her bowl toward Zander so he could taste her soup. He scooted his salad toward her.

"So if Frank was involved in the Triple Play, and he was the one who sold either the Picasso or the Chagall on the black market, we can assume that he would've made a tremendous amount of money on the deal," Britt said.

"I find it hard to believe that Frank could've had that kind of money stashed away."

"Did he ever show any evidence of a big nest egg? Take you guys on an expensive trip? Buy a boat? Purchase land somewhere?"

"No, never. I'd call him frugal. He was the one who did the grocery shopping for the family, and he always spent time on Sunday nights cutting out coupons. Imagine the kind of discipline it would have taken to spend your life cutting coupons, taking your kids to matinee movies only, and turning out lights to save on electricity if you had hundreds of thousands of dollars in a secret account."

"Awe-inspiring discipline," Britt said. "Was Frank a highly disciplined person?"

"About some things. He worked out three times a week. He

never missed a Trail Blazers game on TV. He never drank more than one drink. He paid his bills and his taxes on time."

Zander's salad tasted of lime and beets and crunchy roasted nuts.

"He was really undisciplined about donuts, though," Zander continued. "He never could drive past the Edge of the Woods Bakery without stopping and buying an old-fashioned."

Below their table's window, boats crisscrossed the water between the mainland and Bainbridge Island.

"What about the Renoir?" Britt asked. "What happened to it?"

Zander ran Internet search after Internet search. No luck.

"If the Renoir was found a year or two after the heist, before the Internet was a thing," Zander said, "then information about it might be hard to find online."

"Do you remember the title of the Renoir?"

"*Young Woman at Rest*," he answered without a pause. "Let me try that."

He typed it in and an article from 2015 appeared. "The Mystery of the Missing Renoir Still Unsolved," its title proclaimed.

"Oh, fiasco," Britt whispered. She'd adopted the term *fiasco* because she liked saying it. Fiasco. Its dance of syllables and vowels rolled off the tongue like antipasto or Tabasco.

"The Renoir's still missing," Zander said.

"Did your uncle ever show any evidence of having a world-famous masterpiece hidden in your attic?"

"No. If Frank stole the Renoir, he would have stolen it for money, right? So what motive could he have had for keeping something like that all this time?"

"Fear of getting caught selling it?"

Zander returned his focus to his phone's screen.

He'd pushed the sleeves of his black henley up his forearms, so she could see the sinuous lines of the tattoos that ended at his wrists.

Just like she remembered their shared food, she remembered when and why he'd gotten each of the tattoos that now ran down his arms in a complete tapestry. From the start, he'd known how he'd wanted them to interlock. But he'd gotten them slowly, one by one, over time, as he'd been able to afford them.

The slow pace at which he'd acquired them seemed almost quaint to her now that he'd earned so very much money for his book.

Her study of his forearms, wrists, and capable hands caused the magnetism that had overtaken her in the library to return. Hot and insistent.

She jerked her vision to his face. No help to be found there. A gust of air from the vent riffled his hair, and Britt had a disastrous urge to reach out and run her fingers through the strands.

For heaven's sake!

For the next minute straight, she stared fixedly at her food.

Seattle Magazine, July 2015:

Thirty years have passed since the "Triple Play," the most infamous art heist in Washington's history.

In the early morning hours of July 5, 1985, three masked thieves broke into the Pascal Museum in Seattle and cut three masterworks by Renoir, Picasso, and Chagall from their frames.

No arrests were made in conjunction with the case, and the identities of the thieves are still unknown.

In time, both the Picasso and the Chagall were recovered and restored to the venerated walls of the Pascal. However, the Renoir is still missing, despite the efforts of local law enforcement and the FBI.

French impressionist Pierre-Auguste Renoir (1841–1919) painted *Young Woman at Rest* in 1876 using oil on canvas. The piece depicts the upper body of a woman seated. Renoir captured his subject, Nina Lopez, a professional model, wearing a softly patterned pastel dress and sitting on a sofa. Her hands lay serenely in her lap. A pink flower adorns the light brown hair spilling down to her waist.

The piece is rendered in the gentle oranges, reds, greens, and blues typical of Renoir's work at the time.

The painting was purchased by Mr. and Mrs. Claude Pascal, owners of a chain of French department stores, in 1931. Later, when World War II erupted, the couple booked passage to America for themselves and their extended family, with the intention of returning to France as soon as it was safe to regain occupation of their properties and possession of their belongings. Before they departed, they stored their art in numerous locations. Several pieces, including *Young Woman at Rest*, were placed in the Parisian vault of a friend.

In 1941, the Nazis discovered the vault and took ownership of all the art within. Of the approximately 650,000 art objects appropriated by the Nazis during World War II, 100,000 remain missing.

By the time World War II drew to an end, the Pascals had opted to settle permanently in Seattle and had opened the department store Beau, which has become a local institution.

For years Claude Pascal, his wife, Aline, and their son, Lucien, tirelessly sought to locate *Young Woman at Rest*. In 1968, twenty-seven years after the painting was stolen, investigators pinpointed its whereabouts. A judge determined the Pascals to be the rightful owners of the masterpiece, and *Young Woman at Rest* was subsequently returned to them.

"Our entire family gathered to celebrate its homecoming," recounts current museum director Annette Pascal Spencer. "*Young Woman at Rest* was my grandmother's favorite painting. Because of its history with the Nazis and our long search for it, the piece was extraordinarily special to every one of us. We were ecstatic to have it back."

After the deaths of Claude and Aline, their son and granddaughter, Annette, chose to honor them by turning their mansion into a gallery. In 1979, the doors of the Pascal Museum opened to the public. And in 1985, via the Triple Play, *Young Woman at Rest* was stolen from the Pascal family for the second time.

"I was promoted to the role of museum director six months before the heist," said Annette, now eighty-three. "Because of that, I've always felt somewhat responsible for the painting's fate. I'll

never stop working and waiting and hoping for the painting's recovery. Never. I'll continue searching until the painting once again
hangs on the walls of the Pascal where it belongs."

The museum has long offered a reward for information leading
to the retrieval of *Young Woman at Rest*. If you have any knowledge
concerning the location of the painting, please contact the Seattle
Police Department.

CHAPTER
Six

"Well . . . yes. The robbery of those paintings did happen around the time that I met Frank," Carolyn said to Zander the following Tuesday. "But you can't think that Frank had anything to do with the Triple Play. Can you?"

"If you'd asked me a few weeks ago if I thought Frank could've had anything to do with an art theft, I'd have said no," Zander answered. "But I wouldn't have believed that he'd had a past life or a rap sheet, either."

Zander had arrived at The Giftery, the gift shop on Main Street where Carolyn worked, to take her to lunch. Since she was the only employee present at the moment, they'd leave once her co-worker returned from break.

His aunt slowly emptied a new roll of quarters into the drawer of her cash register. *Plink. Plink plink. Plink.*

Carolyn had decided of her own volition to return to her job today. Eight days had passed since Frank's funeral, and she'd told Zander last night that without Frank and without work, she didn't have anything to do but float in a sea of grief. She wanted her familiar routine and interaction with her coworkers and customers.

Long earrings swayed from her earlobes today. Her wavy hair looked shiny and clean. She'd ironed her blue shirt and black skirt.

However, dark circles smudged the skin beneath her eyes, and her wrinkles had etched deeper.

Aunt Carolyn's aura of peace had been punctured. She had daughters who loved her and a grandchild on the way and friends and siblings. However, none of those people could replace her husband.

Zander understood. If Britt died, his life wouldn't be worth a penny to him. He honestly didn't think he'd be able to go on—

A woman near Carolyn's age with short blond hair entered the shop.

"Sunny," Carolyn said, coming out from behind the counter.

"Carolyn." Sunny embraced Carolyn with sympathy and kindness. "How are you?"

The two talked quietly while candles, women's bath products, signs, coffee mugs, boxes of chocolate, locally made jellies, stationery, and many other feminine items crowded around Zander. The Giftery always made him feel the way he'd feel if he entered a women's restroom. Like testosterone wasn't allowed.

He carefully moved his elbow away from a display of Easter decorations. Tiny eggs, rabbits, ducks, and flower ornaments hung from a tree. An Easter tree? He'd never heard of such a thing.

"Sunny, this is my nephew, Zander Ford."

"Pleased to meet you," Sunny said.

"You too."

"Zander's going to take me to lunch," Carolyn explained.

"Excellent." Sunny hitched her large purse higher on her shoulder. "I stopped by to check on you, but I have several errands to run. I'll swing back by when I'm done, and we'll chat more then."

"Perfect."

"Nice to meet you," Sunny called as she sailed from the shop.

When he'd first moved to Merryweather from inner-city St. Louis, the fact that just about everyone here knew one another or knew *of* one another had made the town seem ridiculously small. He'd expected to feel bored at best and claustrophobic at worst. Instead, he'd grown to appreciate Merryweather's close-knit community.

Here, he hadn't been another nameless, faceless kid being herded through the public school system. Here, he and Carolyn belonged. Here, after eighteen months in foreign countries, he was known.

Carolyn assisted two women who were buying matching coffee mugs. When they'd gone, Zander pitched his voice low to mask it from the handful of people still browsing. "Just so I have the timeline right in my head . . . did you meet Frank before or after the Triple Play?"

She fidgeted with the ring on her finger that contained a green oval stone. "Before. He visited the Pascal summer long."

"How often?"

"Very often. He was a museum member, so he could come whenever he liked. We didn't say anything out of the ordinary to each other on his first few visits, but as the days went by, we talked a little bit more and flirted a little bit more each time." Sorrow darkened her gray eyes.

"Did he ever ask strange questions?" Zander asked. "About the museum's security, for example."

"Not that I can remember."

"Was the museum closed for a while after the robbery?"

Her forehead furrowed. "I believe that . . . yes, it was closed for a time. Maybe a week or ten days? So that the police could investigate and we could repair the window and have new security systems installed."

"And Frank returned to the museum as soon as it reopened?"

"I think so. If not right away, then very soon after."

"Was he limping?"

"No. At least four or five times he showed up when I was scheduled to give a tour so that he could join the tour group, even though he'd heard it all before. It was after one of those tours that he asked me out on a date."

"You said yes."

"And we had a great date. To Orcas Island." Her chin wobbled. "I can't believe he's gone, Zander. I keep waiting for it to sink in, and it still hasn't."

"I'm so sorry. We don't have to talk about this now."

"No, I asked you to discover what happened to Frank, and you're doing just that. The least I can do is answer your questions." She fidgeted with the ring again. "Where was I?"

"Your first date with Frank. To Orcas Island."

"That's right. After that, he started coming to the museum on his lunch break every day. We'd sit together in the courtyard garden and eat our packed lunches at one of the little tables."

"Did he dress like he'd come from a construction site?"

"He did."

Carolyn's redheaded coworker bustled into the store. "I'm here to relieve you so that you can take your lunch break! Ah, your handsome nephew's here." She grinned. "It's good to see you, Zander."

"Thanks. It's good to see you, too."

Carolyn retrieved her purse, then he and his aunt walked down Main in the direction of the restaurant she'd chosen for today's lunch, the Soup and Sandwich Company.

An enormous white cloud blocked the sun, giving the light a muted feel. Spring breeze scented with cut grass rippled American flags and awnings.

As soon as the Historical Village came into view, he instinctively sought out Sweet Art and strained for a glimpse of Britt. One glimpse.

But no. None of the people walking around the village or sitting on its benches was her.

After their visit to the library on Friday, Britt had spent Saturday with her sisters. He'd spent the day accomplishing tasks that the publicity department at his publishing house had arranged for him. Two interviews and a Q&A session followed by a book signing.

When he'd told his publisher about his return to US soil, they'd jumped at the chance to schedule media events. He was glad that his publisher was working hard to promote his book, glad that *Geniuses* surprising popularity made events like the interviews and book signing possible. It's just that parting from Britt in order to spend a day surrounded by strangers made him feel more lonely than he did when he was actually alone.

Sunday, he and Britt had gone hiking at Olympic National Park and last night, Monday, he'd brought a to-go order of chips and tacos to her house, and they'd eaten them while watching episodes of *Once Upon a Time*. Britt had tossed a chip at the TV every time a character had done or said something she didn't approve of.

"I'm trying to think back to the Triple Play robbery," Carolyn said. "I remember that the museum held all kinds of activities the day before because it was the Fourth of July. That night we hosted a catered dinner for our benefactors. I was exhausted by the time I got home. The next morning a friend of mine who worked at the museum called to tell me about the heist. I turned on the TV and watched a story on the morning news. I was stunned. The museum had cameras, a security guard or two on duty at all times, an alarm system. I couldn't imagine how anyone had been able to get away with those paintings. Plus, I felt terrible for Annette Pascal. She was and is wonderful. Did you know that she and I still keep in touch?" She looked across her shoulder at him as they walked.

Gently, he steered her around a puddle. "No, I didn't."

"I started looking for a job when I was twenty and had a hard time finding one. I only had an associate's degree, and I wasn't exactly in high demand on the job market. Annette interviewed me personally and we got along well. Do you know much about her?"

"Very little. Only what I've read in articles."

"She's stylish and intelligent and articulate. Very self-controlled. I wouldn't say that I'm any of those things." She huffed wryly. "Even so, she took me under her wing and gave me a job at the museum which, at the time, was like a dream come true for me." She laced her hand around his arm, and he crooked his elbow. Her shoulder rested against his as they made their way forward. "Annette and I stay in contact through cards and lunches when I'm in Seattle or when she comes this direction. There's no telling how much money she's personally spent trying to find the painting that's still missing."

"*Young Woman at Rest*."

"Yes. Of the three that were stolen, that's the one she always wanted back the most."

"Do you remember it from when it was hanging in the gallery?"

"I do. It was beautiful. So much so that it almost glowed from inside, as if a lantern was shining out from behind the canvas. It had a whole wall to itself because it was just that special."

They passed a bookshop and a bar.

"I can't stand to think that Frank might have been one of the men who took those paintings from Annette. He was good." She spoke in a way that made him think she was trying to convince herself, to shore up her cracked trust in her husband.

"Yes, he was."

"If Frank had been one of the robbers, he would've brought a lot of money to our marriage."

"Yes."

"I'm the one who handled our family's finances. I can assure you that Frank didn't bring any money to our marriage except what he made working construction. Remember his coupon clipping on Sunday nights?"

"I remember." Zander nodded at a passerby walking a dog. "If it's all right with you, I'd like to take a look at Frank's home computer, work computer, and cell phone."

"Certainly. You're welcome to."

"Kurt Shaw told me that he and the police chief already searched them and found nothing. But it can't hurt for me to double check."

"Until the morning we met with Detective Shaw to talk about Frank's autopsy," Carolyn said, "I was certain that I knew Frank through and through. So very certain."

"I also thought I knew him through and through."

"Every time I've been presented with information that's different from what he told me, my knee-jerk reaction is to push it away. It's painful to think that Frank lied to me, that I didn't know him like I thought I did," she said. "I still do want to know the truth, however. Even if it is painful. I think Courtney and Sarah and I are entitled to the truth."

"I agree."

"I have to remember that the one thing I know for certain about Frank is the one thing that matters most: I know that he loved me. No matter what, I can hang on to that." She gave her head a slight shake, as if to throw off the tears hovering beneath the surface. "He loved Courtney and Sarah and Daniel and you." She squeezed his arm. "He loved you. You believe that. Don't you?"

Heat constricted his throat. "Yes."

"Frank and I weren't given any sons of our own, so imagine our surprise—"

"—and horror." He knew where she was going with her sentence.

"Imagine our surprise and *delight* when we were given two boys to take care of. You and your brother made our lives complete. You were no trouble."

"Never?" he asked skeptically.

"Well, almost never."

"You're remembering us as angels now that we're grown."

"I'm remembering that it was a joy to have you under our roof. I'm so proud of you. And Frank was, too."

"I couldn't have asked for a better aunt and uncle. It blows me away, what you did for us."

"It was our pleasure." Ever since he'd come to live with her, she'd taken every opportunity to insist that it was their pleasure to provide for him and Daniel—even when he'd known doing so had sometimes been expensive and tiring and stressful.

"It's good to have you here, Zander. But it would be selfish of me to keep you in Merryweather if you're ready to leave and finish your trip."

His body braced against the idea of leaving. "I'm not planning on leaving until we know what happened with Frank." He had no sense of closure. Not about Frank. Not about Britt.

Apprehension continued to churn within him whenever he considered how Frank's change of identity coupled with his disappearance the night before his death might impact Carolyn's safety.

"When you decide that it's time for you to leave," she told him, "whether or not we've been able to discover what happened to Frank, then I want you to go ahead and leave. I would never want to hold you back."

"I'm not ready to leave yet, Aunt Carolyn."

"Just promise me that when you are, you'll go."

"I promise."

The next morning at Sweet Art, Britt poured all five of her senses into the great love of her life.

Chocolate.

At the moment, she was tempering the chocolate, the step in the chocolate-making process that gave beginners trouble. It wouldn't dare to give her trouble, however. After years of spending the largest share of her time, passion, and ability on chocolate, she'd become one with the medium.

She could taste the idea of a recipe before she made it. She'd traveled internationally to the birthplaces of chocolate to learn each culture's secrets and to sample the nuances of their cacao beans. She read about chocolate. She attended meetings with fellow chocolatiers during which they all talked gleefully about chocolate. She often dreamed about chocolate.

She flirted with breakfast dishes, lunch dishes, dinner entrées, and other types of desserts. But in truth, she was monogamously committed to chocolate and unswervingly determined to create the most delicious chocolate she possibly could.

Back when they'd started Sweet Art, she and Maddie had both worked six days a week. Three years ago, they'd been able to hire part-time employees who operated the store for them on Saturdays and Sundays. Two years ago, they'd added a virtual assistant who worked several hours a week on marketing. A year ago, Britt had begun bringing in her pastry chef friends to assist in making chocolate for large custom orders or busy holiday seasons.

She and Maddie had good heads for business and worked well

as a team. They'd grown Sweet Art the same way a gardener might cultivate a garden. They'd expanded their online business. They'd sold their chocolate into retail stores across Merryweather, Shore Pine, and Seattle. They'd courted mentions in food magazines, travel sites, and blog posts.

Soon they'd have the funds to hire even more help. In the coming year, Britt hoped to begin scaling her business so that she could sell her chocolate to stores in neighboring states. After that: world domination.

When she'd arrived today, she'd gone through her familiar routine—donning her chef's coat, catching her hair into a bun and adding a stretchy, shoelace-wide headband in case any strands dared to wander.

Deftly, she stirred the dark chocolate while turning and testing in her mind the idea she had for a brand-new truffle.

Since her chocolate inspirations were sometimes mercurial, she'd learned to jot them down as soon as they came to her. She kept track of them in little notebooks she had stashed in her car, her purse, her house.

Ordinarily, she pondered a new recipe until the urge to create jangled from her fingertips. Only then would she shut herself up in her kitchen—at any time of the week, the day, the night—and indulge in a fit of artistic productivity.

This morning, her fingertips had not been jangling. In fact, she was having to stretch to reach an inspiration that wasn't yet full-bodied because her motivation was less about art and more about chocolate as distraction.

She really needed to lose herself in chocolate because she really needed a reprieve from these ill-advised, uninvited, embarrassingly *moony* feelings she'd been having for Zander since their dinner in Seattle.

A memory of that dinner formed diamond sharp. Zander, who was wry and faithful and as constant as time, sitting near her, wearing that black Henley. His powerful concentration focused on her, just as it always did when he listened—

A pang of desire tightened within her.

This is *exactly* what had been happening!

And it was wildly annoying.

She seeded the chocolate by adding a handful of finely chopped cold chocolate to the warm, melted chocolate. More stirring. More chocolate fragments added. She tested it with a thermometer out of habit rather than necessity when she sensed that she'd brought it to temper. The thermometer confirmed her intuition. Eighty-six degrees. Now to reheat it slightly to finish the tempering.

The day that Nikki had met Clint at Sweet Art, she'd mentioned that Britt hadn't "managed to keep" a single boyfriend. "Managed to keep" made it sound as though Britt had tried hard to keep her boyfriends. Actually, she hadn't tried hard because she hadn't wanted to keep them.

She lined up cream, cocoa butter, salted butter, rum, vanilla, and crème de menthe and imagined how different quantities of each would affect the outcome. She wanted this new truffle to blend the flavors of dark chocolate, white chocolate, peppermint, caramel, and salt into a perfectly balanced melody.

She'd had more boyfriends than either Willow or Nora. More than Willow and Nora combined.

Britt liked men and she liked dating them.

According to scientists, falling in love generated a huge endorphin rush, and Britt believed it to be true. Dating someone you liked intensely *was* a huge endorphin rush. As it happened, she was a woman who liked endorphin rushes. Bungee jumping? White-water rafting? Skydiving? High-wire walking? She'd done them all. Few things, however, were quite as much fun as developing a crush on a new boyfriend.

It was the sustaining of said crush that she'd never successfully accomplished. One or three or five months into a relationship, her crush would wear off like sunblock she'd forgotten to reapply after swimming. She'd realize that her infatuation had led to indifference instead of love. Then, he or she—but almost always she—would end things.

She was fine with her pattern. It's not like she was in a hurry to find a man who had the super-power ability to convert a crush into love.

In just over a week, she'd be turning twenty-seven, which, to her, seemed on the young side for marriage. I mean, *marriage*. Marriage was a heavy, forever kind of commitment.

She cherished not having anyone to answer to.

On the other hand, there'd been no one to tell her he didn't want her kayaking on a flooded river because he was scared she'd hurt herself.

She cherished that she could decide she wanted to take a trip to Canada, then leave for Canada the very next morning.

On the other hand, she didn't have anyone to take a spur-of-the-moment trip to Canada with.

She cherished her freedom.

On the other hand, when she saw Willow with Corbin and Nora with John, she sometimes suspected that belonging to someone might be worth a few sacrifices.

An hour later she sampled her truffle.

Her lips tipped downward while she chewed. The artist had now become the critic. The peppermint was nice. The ratio of cream to salted butter, pleasant. But something was off. Something wasn't as deep and rich and unique as it should be. What?

She wasn't certain. She'd need to reflect on it then refine the recipe repeatedly across a period of days.

She wasn't content with this truffle, but, all in all, she was content with her life. She had Sweet Art, her family, friends, her cottage, a world to explore, and Zander—

Pang.

She squeezed her eyes shut, willing the pang away. Carefully, she opened her lids, as if scared that another wayward pang might jump out from behind the stove and ambush her. She popped the rest of the truffle into her mouth.

If she fell in love with a man one day who didn't bore her, who didn't try to change or control her, who made the sacrifice of her freedom worthwhile—then fine. Great.

But if she never met a man like that, then fine. Great.

Text message from Britt to Zander:

Britt
You're still planning to come to Willow and Corbin's on Sunday for Easter lunch, right? Pretty please?

Zander
I'll be there.

Britt
Whew. I won't have to force you there with a cattle prod. Did you finish going through Frank's computers and phone?

Zander
I did. Even if Frank had tried to cover his digital tracks, I have confidence that I would have found something if there was anything to find.

Britt
You didn't find anything?

Zander
Not a thing. My uncle's devices held exactly what you'd expect from a man who loved his family and worked hard and followed the letter of the law.

CHAPTER
Seven

Zander glanced in his rearview mirror, eyes narrowed.

He'd decided to write at the Merryweather Coffee House for the next few hours. A new black Expedition had been behind him most of the way from the inn to town. Not close to his bumper. Far back. But consistently there.

The Expedition's presence hadn't registered as noteworthy until it had taken the same turn off the road that Zander had. Then the next turn, too, toward Merryweather's downtown.

Zander took a left, drove a block, then pulled into a parking spot on the street. Two cars moved through the intersection behind him before the Expedition turned left, as he had, driving toward his position.

Zander scrambled to get the camera on his cell phone ready.

He caught a glimpse of the driver—a man wearing a baseball cap—as the Expedition rolled past. Zander snapped a photo of the rear license plate, then watched the SUV disappear into the underground parking structure favored by tourists.

He tapped his thumb against his steering wheel, waiting for the SUV to reappear. It didn't. Which probably meant that the man had parked and exited via the stairway that emerged on Main. Most likely it had been a coincidence that the Expedition's destination was located so near his own. Merryweather's Main Street served as a hub for the whole community.

Flicking up the hood of his rain jacket against the drizzle, he walked toward the coffee house. He kept an eye out for the man in the baseball cap. No sign of him.

The guy could be behind him.

If so, Zander didn't want him to know he was aware he'd been followed. So, after two blocks, Zander pretended to answer his phone. This was likely insane, but the pretense gave him a reason to stop. He set his shoulders against the exterior brick wall of the flower shop and turned his focus back in the direction he'd come, hoping that he gave off the impression of staring at nothing while listening hard to the nonexistent person on the other end of the line.

Plenty of people made their way up and down the street. Even so, Zander spotted the man in the black baseball cap almost at once.

The man stood approximately twenty yards away, studying a display window. He wore gray track pants and an exercise sweat shirt. Perhaps in his early thirties, he gave off the impression of fitness and toughness. Maybe a military vet? If not, he could pass for a UFC fighter.

Suspicion ran thick through Zander's veins.

If Frank had robbed the Pascal Museum, then anyone who knew what had happened that night could be following him in hopes that he'd lead them to the money they believed Frank had hidden away. Or they might want the Renoir. Or they might worry that Frank had left behind evidence that could incriminate them.

Alternatively, Frank could have gotten himself involved in something illegal in recent years. If that was the case, then military guy might be keeping an eye on him for any number of reasons.

What should he do?

He spoke nonsense into the phone as he swiveled to peer down the street toward the coffee house. A short distance beyond it hung The Griddle's sign.

Zander checked the time. 11:37. On a Thursday. He'd taken

his aunt out to lunch enough times over the years to know that Merryweather's police chief had a standing lunch date with his adult daughter at The Griddle on Thursdays. They ate early, and with any luck, would already be inside.

Zander finished his imaginary call and made his way to The Griddle. Sure enough, the police chief and his daughter sat at their usual table near the front window.

He hesitated, pushing the hood from his head. He might be overreacting. In fact, the chances of that were strong.

Zander wasn't concerned for his safety in an immediate sense. If military guy knew he was staying at the inn, then he could have jumped Zander in the woods when he'd gone running this morning.

This wasn't about his current well-being. This was about the ominous storm he'd sensed on the horizon ever since he'd learned that his uncle had taken Frank Pierce's identity. A growing number of unknowns continued to feed the storm, giving it power, making him worry about a threat he couldn't name. He had an opportunity to address one of those unknowns, and he'd rather be proactive than sorry. He'd rather make a fool of himself than do nothing.

He crossed to the chief's table. "I'm sorry to disturb you, sir."

The police chief's daughter startled slightly. The chief regarded him with friendly inquiry. He had a neatly trimmed white beard and dark, intelligent eyes.

"I'm Zander Ford, Frank and Carolyn Pierce's nephew."

"Yes, son," the chief replied, "I know who you are."

"Again, I apologize. But I think there's a man outside who's following me."

For a moment, no one spoke. Then the chief glanced fondly at his daughter. "Will you excuse me for a minute, honey?"

"Of course."

"Be right back." The older man followed Zander to the restaurant's foyer. He'd dressed in a black police uniform with stars embroidered into the collar, a badge over his heart, and his last name—Warner—written across a gold pin. Zander relayed all that he'd observed since leaving the inn.

"Let's go introduce ourselves to this person and see if we can't determine what's going on," Chief Warner said.

Military guy was now positioned three storefronts down from The Griddle in a protected spot under an awning. Since Zander had last seen him, he'd continued to move in the direction Zander had taken. He held his phone, his concentration fixed on it as he tapped its screen.

"Excuse me," Chief Warner said to him as they neared. Everyone in the area, including the man in the baseball cap, looked to him. "A word with you, sir, if you wouldn't mind."

Military guy responded to the chief's words with an expression of mild surprise, nothing more. "I don't mind."

"Silas Warner, police chief." The chief extended a hand.

"Nick Dunlap."

They shook. "This gentleman here thinks you've been following him," the chief said. "That true?"

Nick spared Zander a brief, annoyed glance then returned his focus to Chief Warner. "No, sir."

"You don't know him?" the chief pressed.

"I've never seen him before."

"It's just a coincidence that you both took the same route into town and ended up within a few feet of each other?"

"Yes, sir. Must be."

"Did you enter town on Valley View Highway?" The chief's manner was far more conversational than interrogative.

"I did."

"Coming from?"

"Portland, Oregon, this morning. I'm on a road trip and stopped here to stretch my legs and get food."

"Where you headed?" the chief asked.

"Today? Seattle."

"Are you under probation?"

"No, sir."

"Have you ever been arrested?"

"No."

"Do you have your driver's license on you?"

Nick inclined his head to the side a few degrees. "I do."

"May I see it?"

"For what purpose?"

The chief gave a relaxed shrug. "I just like to be thorough."

Nick paused. "Sure." In order to pull out his wallet, he set his phone on the ledge near Zander. The phone's upturned screen revealed a text message conversation. Zander made out the initials *TR* centered in a circle at the top above small print that read *Tom R.* He leaned in to read more, but the phone went dark.

Nick passed his license to the chief, who carried it down the nearby alley until he was beyond earshot. He spoke into his shoulder microphone.

Nick had full control over his irritation with Zander. Nevertheless, it was an almost palpable force. "Look, man. I'm not following you."

Zander sized Nick up, saying nothing, letting Nick register his own irritation level. One thing he knew: Merryweather's Main Street attracted locals or tourists who were either female or over the age of sixty. What it didn't tend to attract? Young male military vets traveling alone.

In under a minute, the chief returned. "Here you are, Mr. Dunlap." He handed back his license. "Enjoy your time in Merryweather."

"Thank you, sir."

Zander and the chief fell in step, leaving Nick behind. "His record's clean," the chief said.

"I mentioned earlier that I took a picture of his car's plate. Would it be possible to run that and see what comes up?"

"I'll have Kurt run it when I get back to the station. Like I told Mr. Dunlap, I like to be thorough." They stopped before the restaurant and he extracted his phone. "License plate number?"

Zander rattled it off and the chief recorded it in his phone. "Got it."

"I'm sorry if I wasted your time."

"It's all right." The grooves of the older man's face held compassion. "I'm sorry about what happened to your uncle, son."

Zander nodded. The chief clapped him on the upper arm and returned to his daughter.

Zander watched Nick enter the taco shop across the street.

If he'd wasted the chief's time, the way that it looked he had, he really was sorry. Sorry to have cut into the man's lunch hour. Sorry to have made himself look paranoid in the chief's eyes.

An overactive imagination was an occupational hazard for writers. He wrote about dark characters, after all. A serial killer in his first book. And in his current manuscript, an assassin. Had he been wrong about Nick?

Maybe.

Then again. Maybe not.

A clean record in the past didn't guarantee innocence in the present.

Zander was immediately welcomed inside Corbin and Willow's house by Corbin himself on Easter Sunday. Corbin was easy to talk to and had a great sense of humor. Even so, Zander could feel himself withdrawing more than usual whenever he was around the guy. For years, he'd watched Corbin play football on TV. Every time he and Corbin talked, *that's NFL quarterback Corbin Stewart* filled Zander's head until there wasn't room for much else.

He was going to have to get over himself. Corbin had joined the Bradford family when he'd married Willow, which meant Corbin would be part of Zander's life from now on.

More than a decade after leaving St. Louis, Zander still had trouble squaring the hardship of his early life to the life that had come after. The Bradfords' acceptance of him. A *New York Times* bestselling book. Now Easter lunch with Corbin Stewart.

He made a quick scan of the guests in the room. Willow, of course. Nora and her fiancé, John, were here, as were John's parents and John's sister's family. He spotted Britt's grandmother, Britt's uncle, and two Bradford cousins and their families.

Britt, he didn't see, which meant she was probably cooking.

After greeting everyone, he entered the kitchen.

"Oh good!" Britt smiled at him. "There you are. I'm putting the finishing touches on my potatoes gratin. Prepare to be dazzled."

"I always am."

She sprinkled the top of the potatoes with salt. "Everything else is ready. They're not as desperate for me to save them with my culinary skills as they sometimes are."

Zander hooked his thumbs through his belt loops and studied the impressive kitchen. "This house has changed since I was here last."

"That's because Willow's worked her magic on it. I've accused her more than once of falling in love with Corbin for his house." Turning, she slid her baking dish into the packed oven. "Every time I come here I feel like I'm inside a shoot for *Architectural Digest*." She came around the kitchen island and hugged him. "Happy Easter, Zander."

His gut clenched. "Happy Easter, Britt."

They parted. She scooped up some pistachios from a decorative dish. "Would you like some?"

"Sure."

She put half her handful on a napkin for him and the other half on a napkin for herself. They stood leaning against the island, facing each other, while she shelled pistachios.

She wore casual clothes most of the time, but on days like today when she dressed up, she appeared just as comfortable in her more formal wardrobe. A bright blue geometric pattern decorated her sleeveless white dress. The straps of her white high heels wrapped around her ankles. Her dark brown hair fell to the middle of her chest. She had on big silver earrings and three silver rings and she was ridiculously beautiful.

She caught him staring. With a flick of her fingers, she reminded him of his pistachios.

He ate two.

"Did you see any black Expeditions on the way here?" she asked.

"Not a one."

"Bummer."

"How can you consider the fact that I wasn't followed by a suspicious military vet in an Expedition a bummer?"

"Because the incident with Nick added just the right level of intrigue to the proceedings." When he'd told her about his run-in with Nick, Britt had responded with avid interest. "You have to remember how very sleepy things usually are around here."

"I don't think you're going to be able to depend on Nick to liven things up. The plate on his SUV belongs to a rental car, which fits the traveler story he gave the police chief. I'm starting to think he was telling the truth."

"But what if he wasn't?" She raised a pistachio and an eyebrow.

He opened his mouth, and she lobbed the nut to him. He made a clean catch.

"Did you look through the profiles I sent you of the Nick Dunlaps on Facebook and Twitter?" she asked.

He, Britt, and Nora had all spent time looking for Nick Dunlap online over the past few days. Britt had volunteered to comb through the social media sites. She'd compiled links to all the Nicks she'd found that might be their guy and emailed the list to Zander. He'd studied the pictures associated with each one. "None of them were him."

"Shoot. Are you sure?"

"Yes."

"I had big plans. If you'd been able to find him on Facebook, for example, then I was going to hunt for Facebook friends of Nick's named Tom R."

"Genius. And yet. None of them was him." They'd all drawn a blank with Nick, even Nora.

Britt chewed thoughtfully. "What do you think about asking Kurt Shaw to contact the rental car company that owns the Expedition? They'd have all kinds of information on Nick."

"I already asked Kurt about the rental car company's records. He's unable to request personal information without cause. Americans tend to dislike it when people trample on their privacy."

"*Bummer.*" She tossed another nut into the air. Again, he caught it in his mouth.

He watched her shuck a few more pistachios. She'd painted her square fingernails black since he'd last seen her.

"Where were you supposed to be traveling this week on your Grand Tour?" she asked.

"China."

"I hear China's overrated."

"Likely."

"Not very many people live there, and it's not very large, after all."

"And the history there doesn't date back very far."

"Not far at all."

"It's better for me to be here running into dead ends as I try to research my uncle's life."

Britt's small, white-haired grandmother, Margaret Burke, entered the kitchen clothed in an old-lady suit and a mink coat Britt and her sisters had nicknamed "Old Musty." She always wore pearl earrings and her hair in a bun. Her bone structure was perfect, her sense of optimism less so.

"Would you like some pistachios, Mrs. Burke?" he asked politely.

"Goodness, no. They get stuck between my teeth." She zeroed in on him. "Nora and John and I missed you at Easter services this morning."

"I went to church with Carolyn," Zander said. "She wanted to attend the early service before driving to Seattle to spend the day with her daughters."

"You went to the *Presbyterian* church?" Margaret asked, as shocked as if he'd just announced that he'd visited the Kremlin.

"Yes, ma'am."

"I went to a service at Victory Fellowship," Britt said, interceding on his behalf like a soldier bravely drawing enemy fire.

"Did they have a sermon?" Margaret asked. "Or just a great deal of loud music? Because if it was just a great deal of loud music, then it was a concert you attended. Not a service."

"They had a sermon," Britt said lightly.

"Did they offer an altar call?" Margaret asked.

"They have a reception room where you can meet with pastors after the service if you want to talk about salvation or need prayer or want to join the church."

Suspicion tightened Margaret's lips. "It sounds like Victory Fellowship is trying to make everyone too comfortable. Reception rooms," she scoffed. "Coffee and tea. Big TV screens. Seats with cushions."

"I'm not sure," Britt said, "that being comfortable in church is a bad thing—"

"Many years ago," Margaret interrupted, "our pastor would stand at the front at the end of the service. We'd sing 'Softly and Tenderly,' and between verses he'd spread out his arms and entreat people to make a decision. Guilt and discomfort are both motivating *and* convicting. Your generation is in need of more convicting. Much more convicting."

"Mmm-hmm. When was the last time you went forward during an altar call, Grandma?"

"1946." Margaret took her time eying her granddaughter and then him. "How old are you now, Zander?"

"Twenty-seven," he answered.

"When I was twenty-seven, I'd already been married for several years. I was the mother of one child, with another on the way."

"Yes," Britt said, "but that was—"

Zander cleared his throat to warn her because he knew she was about to say *forever ago*.

"Things have changed," Britt said. "A lot of people are getting married at an older age. Or not marrying at all."

Margaret blanched.

"I think you've just caught a little bit of marriage fever," Britt said to her grandmother, "now that Willow's married and Nora soon will be."

"My dearest dream, my *only* dream, is to see all three of my granddaughters married." Margaret tipped up her chin in a way that reminded Zander of a wrongly accused prisoner facing the gallows.

"Now who's using guilt and discomfort to motivate and convict?" Britt gave her grandma a kiss on the cheek, then went to check her potatoes.

"I still believe that the right man would be willing to marry a woman your age, Britt," Margaret said, "although time *is* of the essence." Margaret's attention swung to him. "You plan to marry, don't you, Zander?"

"Yes, I'd like to."

"Are you courting anyone at the moment?"

"No, I've been traveling for the past several months."

"Men have been known to fall in love with foreign women while traveling," Margaret said.

"Grandma, no!" Britt snapped straight, looking outraged. "He's definitely not allowed to fall in love with anyone from a foreign country. I can't have him living the rest of his life in a place like Fiji. No, no, no."

"He's allowed to do whatever he'd like," Margaret said to her granddaughter. "He's twenty-seven."

"He's not allowed to do *that*."

"I don't know, Britt," he said. "I'm going to Korea next, and I think I could really go for a Korean woman. They're gorgeous, and they seem really smart and calm."

"Not allowed! Plus, you just stereotyped Korean women."

"Is it a stereotype if the traits are positive?"

"When you're done traveling, you're going to come right back here to Washington," Britt said, "and you're going to fall in love with a local girl."

Done. He'd already fallen in love with a local girl.

"I . . ." She paused, looking flustered.

She very rarely got flustered. Had she read his mind? Or maybe the idea of him falling in love with a local girl had bothered her for some reason?

Let that be it. Hope multiplied inside of him.

Britt flipped a lock of hair over her shoulder. "In fact, while you're finishing your tour, I promise to keep an eye out so that I'll have some good dating prospects waiting for you when you return home."

Zander's spirits took a sharp, sharp turn south.

"Like I said, time is of the essence," Margaret stated. "I'd appreciate it if you'd keep an eye out for a husband for Britt, Zander."

Not going to happen.

If Britt married anyone other than him he'd have to move to Iceland and live in a hut without Wi-Fi. "Excuse me." He moved toward the kitchen's sliding door. "I want to see what Willow and Corbin have done with the yard."

He couldn't care less about the yard. He needed a minute to adjust to the uppercut punch of disappointment he'd just taken.

He walked beyond the view of the kitchen and kept going, inhaling the cool air.

"I'll have some good dating prospects waiting for you," she'd said.

As far as he was concerned, dating was a cuss word.

Britt delighted in discussing the subject. He hated it.

God knows he didn't want to hear about the guy she'd met at a party, or about their first date, or about her concerns over his neediness. Almost as bad? Their discussions about his dating life.

Britt had often tried to play the role of matchmaker for him. Truth be told, she wasn't terrible at it. She knew him, and she knew what type of woman would suit him. Most of the time, he'd sidestepped her attempts to set him up. But occasionally, he'd gone out with the women she'd recommended.

When his dating attempts failed, Britt would kindly suggest that he might be too picky.

He'd never argued. He *was* too picky.

Because he only wanted her. There wasn't enough real estate in his heart for anyone else.

Britt didn't want to own that particular piece of real estate, and a lot of the time, he didn't want her to own it, either. The situation he'd locked himself into was stupidly painful.

So he'd repeatedly forced himself to give dating a shot. A handful of times, he'd dated a woman for a month or more. In those instances, he'd told himself to give it time. Why was he demanding so much? Relationships shouldn't be rushed. He'd get to know the woman gradually, treat her as well as he possibly could, and maybe the feelings would come.

Once, he'd lectured himself into going out with Bailey Benton for three whole months. Bailey had been in law school. Her personality had been quick. Her laughter genuine. Her hair red.

But the feelings had never come.

They hadn't come because of one simple truth: He was in love with someone else.

When Bailey had looked at him with melting softness, he'd felt like a jerk for two reasons.

One, because he'd known he was stringing her along and wasting her time. Bailey had deserved to be with someone who wasn't constantly thinking to himself that dating her was a counterfeit version of what he really wanted.

Two, because he hadn't been able to shake the notion that he was cheating on Britt. Britt, who regularly had boyfriends of her own. He'd finally come to the conclusion that it wasn't Britt he was betraying, exactly. Each time he went out with someone else, it was his love for Britt he was betraying.

It had been a relief to take a break from dating while overseas. For eighteen months, he hadn't had to hear the woman who was perfect for him tell him she'd found someone perfect for him who wasn't her.

The Easter-themed tablescape Willow had created was, as Britt had expected it to be, a bona fide work of art.

Pink and white peonies flowed from squat vases onto varying sizes of moss-covered spheres. Nestled within the delta of flowers perched tiny terra-cotta pots sprouting real grass and silvery votive candles twinkling with light. Britt found her china plate by locating the pale pink egg stenciled with a *B* sitting atop a sea-foam green linen napkin.

She ate ham, green beans, a bread roll, a deviled egg, corn, and potatoes gratin. She avoided eating Grandma's offering: green Jell-O with fruit and nuts suspended inside it.

When lunch concluded, they moved outdoors for an egg hunt on the enormous grounds of Willow and Corbin's house.

She and Zander made their way to Winnie, the four-year-old daughter of Britt's cousin. Winnie squatted near her basket, both hands over her face, crying.

"Bad hair day?" Britt asked.

"I'm terr—terrible at finding eggs!" Winnie wailed.

That's true, Britt mouthed to Zander above Winnie's head. *She is terrible.* To Winnie she said, "Chin up, sister. If you join forces with Zander and me, I think we might be able to find more eggs than either of your brothers."

Her tear-stained face lifted.

"I graduated with a minor in egg hunting," Zander told the girl.

"And I was once crowned Miss Easter Egg." Britt smiled and gestured for Winnie to stand.

The girl rose.

When Britt bent to unbuckle her shoes, the kayaking injury in her side tweaked with pain. She stilled for a second, pressing her hand to the spot. The ache subsided and she kicked her shoes free.

"Uh-oh," Zander murmured. "Britt's getting serious."

"And you should, too," Britt told Winnie. She tugged off Winnie's Mary Janes and frilly socks while the little girl giggled.

When Zander picked up Winnie's pink basket, Britt arched a brow at him.

He returned her look. "Real men carry pink Easter baskets."

"Of course they do." She grabbed Winnie's hand. "Ready?"

"Nobody's holding his hand." Winnie pointed at Zander.

Britt took hold of Zander's free hand. She'd held his hand plenty in the past. When her family prayed before dinner. When she needed to tow him somewhere in a hurry. But this time, the masculine strength and texture of it sent a hot thrill all the way to the backs of her knees, where it gathered and sizzled. Every other sensation, except the exquisitely acute sensation of his hand holding hers, fled.

"Now I'm ready," Winnie announced.

"Hmm?" Britt tried to remember what Winnie was talking about.

"I'm ready to hunt for eggs," Winnie clarified.

"Right. Of course."

They hurried forward. As soon as they reached the first egg hunting spot, she let go of Winnie's and Zander's hands.

She made a show of looking for eggs even though she was approximately as coherent as a sleepwalker. Her hand, the one that Zander had held, felt entirely different than her other hand. More sensitive. As if the skin of that hand had been bathed in starlight.

Holding hands was sweet and snuggly and cozy. Respectful. Chaste. But it wasn't powerful.

Or at least it hadn't been before. The touch of Zander's fingers just now had seethed with power and intimacy—

Fiasco, Britt. Fi-as-co.

Holding hands with a man did not rattle her! Nor did telling Zander that he needed to come back to Washington and fall in love with a local girl. But right after she'd said that to him earlier, an unpleasant lump had come into her throat and she'd felt like she was choking on her statement. The prospect of Zander falling in love with a local girl had struck her as ghastly—the last thing in the world she wanted. To cover, she'd made an overcorrection and said something dumb about searching for prospects for him.

She'd never had a problem setting him up in the past!

Zander found hidden egg after hidden egg.

Britt couldn't spot a single one.

This new infatuation with him *must* end. She'd become, because of him, as terrible an egg huntress as Winnie.

Note passed between Britt and Zander in ninth grade:

BRITT: Would you go with Hannah to the mid-winter dance as friends? She doesn't have a date yet, and it would help me out if you'd go with her. Plus, it would be fun to have you as part of our group that night.

ZANDER: If it would help you out, then sure. No problem.

Note passed between Maddie and Britt in ninth grade:

MADDIE: Hannah is really excited about going to the mid-winter dance with Zander. She won't admit it, but I can totally tell that she's crushing on him.

BRITT: No, I don't think so.

MADDIE: Trust me! She is. Do you think he's into her?

BRITT: Not in that way. I mean, I really love Hannah. But I don't think her personality is quite right for Zander. They're not a fit.

Note written by Britt in ninth grade:

Mom, Zander's shoes are really worn out, and his jacket's too small. Will you take me shopping this weekend so we can buy him new stuff for his birthday?

CHAPTER

Eight

Two days later, Britt evaluated her most recent attempt at the peppermint truffle.

Better. Though still not quite right. Something was lacking. Its finish was bland. Not complex nor interesting enough. Yet.

How to fix it? How to fix it?

She sat cross-legged atop the chair at the desk located in Sweet Art's kitchen. Though she wasn't currently looking at Zander, she could feel his presence as if he were a heater and she a freezing person.

He'd taken up his usual position at the central island, empty at this point in the afternoon. She finished work at two o'clock each day, and the clock read 2:10. She'd already put her kitchen to bed.

She carefully arranged the papers Zander had brought with him when he'd arrived. Just in case they were wrong about Frank's involvement in the Triple Play, they'd divided up their list of Seattle-area shootings that had occurred in 1985. Then they'd each chased down as much information on those shootings as they could.

So far, none of the research they'd gathered was leaping out at her.

She looked toward Zander.

He motioned to the peppermint truffle she'd given him to sample. He'd eaten half. "Have you considered adding rosemary to this recipe?"

"Interesting suggestion. Sophisticated suggestion. But, no. That's not the direction I'm wanting to go with this one. I'm thinking butterscotch."

"In that case, almond extract, perhaps?"

"Excellent, Daniel-son. But expected."

He smiled at the *Karate Kid* reference, popped the rest of his truffle into his mouth, and regarded her solemnly as he chewed. He'd gotten his hair trimmed since she'd seen him yesterday. The edges of it were perfectly straight now but the top was still the way she liked it best—longer and in a mild state of disarray.

His soft brown long-sleeved shirt suited his austere looks. His worn-in jeans fit him as if they'd been tailor-made. When he'd entered Sweet Art a few minutes ago, he'd brought with him the luxurious scent of his cologne. The fragrance always made Britt think of leather and cognac and handmade suits and rich, exotic spices—

She fought to return her focus to the pages in front of her before her wayward thoughts cobbled together a mutiny. "I don't see anything promising here."

"I don't either."

"In that case, it's a good thing that we made an appointment with Nora. She's our best hope at finding information on Ricardo Serra."

She and Zander had talked at length about the potential avenues they could explore next with their investigation. They'd decided to research Ricardo, the friend of Frank's who'd helped him rob a Chicago gas station when they were both in their twenties.

"It's certainly possible that Ricardo and Frank committed other crimes together before and after robbing the gas station," Britt said. "Imagine that I'm Frank—"

"You look nothing like Frank—"

"—and that I'm released from prison around the same time as

my buddy Ricardo. It's not like employers will be lining up to hire either of us. We're only experienced at stealing stuff, and we're in need of money."

"It's also possible that Frank left prison, decided to clean up his act, and never stole so much as a pack of gum again. The way he lived the past thirty years supports that theory."

"Point taken. But maybe Frank and Ricardo cooked up one final scheme before they retired? One so big that they'd be able to live on the income for a very long time."

"Three robbers carried out the Triple Play."

"So somewhere between Chicago and Seattle, Frank and Ricardo recruited one more. Maybe another friend from high school?"

He tapped his fingers lightly against her work station. "Maybe."

Britt slipped out of her chef's coat and lobbed it into the shop's laundry hamper, then straightened the royal blue exercise top she'd been wearing underneath.

He held the back door open for her. She preferred to arrive and exit through Sweet Art's back door since she was likely to either a) see someone she knew inside Sweet Art's shop or b) see something that needed her urgent attention inside Sweet Art's shop. When she left at the end of her workday, it was usually best to dart out the back like a thirteen-year-old avoiding a middle school dance.

Her Nikes crunched gravel as they crossed the short distance to Nora's Library on the Green Museum. One of Britt's favorite job perks? The freedom to dress for work either in work-out gear or jeans paired with casual tops.

Once again, Zander held the door for her. Britt crossed the threshold into Nora's library. The two-story structure had begun life in 1892 as an apothecary and was the only one of Merryweather Historical Village's buildings that occupied its original site. The others, including Sweet Art, had all been carefully relocated to the village.

Britt was more of a let's-go-paragliding and less of a let's-go-to-a-museum person. Even so, she loved Nora's library, with its books and artifacts and towering old windows.

Nikki hurried over to ogle Zander. "Hello, handsome."

"Hi, Nikki."

"You look like you're on your way to play lead guitar for a band or pose for a romance novel cover," Nikki said.

"Nope. Just hanging out with Britt."

Nikki leaned in and sniffed near his shoulder. "Is that Polo cologne you're wearing?"

"No."

"Because even though I'm old enough to be your mother—what's age, after all? So arbitrary!—if it's Polo, then you're going to have to take me out dancing right here and now."

Zander laughed. "It's not Polo."

"How are things going with Clint?" Britt asked.

"I've been to two Pilates classes with him. You should see his single leg circles. Poetry, I tell you! Have you ever done Pilates?"

"Yes," Britt said. "It's great—"

"It's miserable," Nikki stated. "Pilates makes my inner thighs tremble. I haven't exerted myself that much since I competed in a three-legged race to win tickets to a Duran Duran concert, and so far, the Pilates isn't even paying off. Clint hasn't asked me out, and you know how I am about that. I talk big, but I'm old-fashioned in the sense that I expect the man to ask *me* out. I want to be pursued! If a man can't summon the courage to ask me out for chicken strips, mashed potatoes, and green beans, then what chance do we have as a couple?"

"He won't be asking you out for chicken strips," Britt said. "Clint eats Paleo."

Nikki's heavily eye-linered eyes rounded. "Land! What does that mean?"

"No grains, no sugar," Britt said.

"Just meat, vegetables, nuts, and fruit," Zander said.

"No pancakes?"

"Paleo pancakes only," Zander said.

"No Pillsbury crescent rolls?"

"No," Britt said.

"I pretty much live on carbs," Nikki told them. "How about a teensy little cracker? Would Clint eat that?"

"No."

"Well, I suppose I could go without carbs if Clint and I go out on a date. Have you noticed his biceps?" she asked Britt. "He has very good biceps."

"I'm well acquainted with Clint's biceps." She ought to be. Clint had been walking around Bradfordwood in leather vests for years.

"And I've always loved men with long hair," Nikki said. "Very mountainous, you know?"

"Oh yes," Britt said. "Clint's quite the mountainous Pilates man."

"Will you please give him a call and encourage him to ask me out?" Nikki asked Britt.

"Why not ask Nora to give him a call? You work with Nora, and she knows Clint as well as I do."

"She's already told me that she won't be party to this. I think she's tired of playing the role of my wing woman. But I'm going to need a wing woman with Clint. I sense that he needs a subtle push."

"Do you categorize my calling him and encouraging him to ask you out as subtle?" Britt asked.

"I do, so long as you don't mention that I told you to call. Just say that you noticed sparks between us that day at Sweet Art and wanted to make sure that he followed up by asking me out because I'm a very endearing person. And you think we'd make a great couple."

"Anything else you'd like me to say?" Britt asked dryly.

"You can mention my fabulous figure if it seems appropriate."

"I can't imagine a scenario in which that would seem appropriate."

"You can mention my delightful personality, then. And my good taste in chocolate."

"You eat milk chocolate pecan turtles."

"Because I know what I like." She winked as she moved off to check on a trio of patrons. "And I like Clint Fletcher."

God have mercy on Clint, Britt thought as she and Zander climbed the stairs. The library's second floor held a sitting area, Nikki's office, and Nora's office.

They found Nora behind her desk, a mug of steaming tea at her elbow. The pastel-striped rug, the jaunty tulips in a vase, and the carefully curated books filling Nora's bookshelves communicated just how much Britt's older sister adored her job.

All of the Bradford sisters had been lucky in that way. They'd each found their way to careers they loved. Nora had a passion for genealogy and history. Britt was crazy about chocolate . . . always and forever chocolate. And Willow was devoted to the housewares and clothing she offered at her new store, Haven.

Haven had been a roaring success ever since word had gotten out that renowned former model Willow Bradford was doling out fashion and decorating advice via her store. And luckily for Britt, Willow sold the gift boxes of Sweet Art chocolate she ordered for Haven almost as soon as she stocked them.

"Two of my favorite people." Nora stood to give them hugs. "I thought I heard your voices downstairs. Did Nikki scandalize you?"

"She did," Zander answered.

"Good to hear that the status quo has continued uninterrupted." Nora sat again behind her desk as Britt and Zander eased into the patterned chairs facing her. "Would either of you like tea?"

"We just had mediocre chocolate, so I'll pass on mediocre tea," Britt said.

Nora responded to Britt's jab exactly the way Britt had known she would, with a look of exaggerated offense. "My tea is the pinnacle of excellence, as you well know. Zander? Would you like to taste the pinnacle of excellence?"

"Thanks, but no. After this, Britt wants to go mountain climbing. If I have tea now, then Britt will blame the caffeine for giving me an unfair advantage when I beat her."

"I admire your foresight," Nora said to Zander. "No amount of caffeine could help me beat her. At anything. Ever."

"Except perhaps Trivial Pursuit," Britt said.

Smiling, Nora took a sip of tea. "So." She set her mug on a coaster that read, *If you walk a mile in my shoes, you'll end up at a bookstore.* "When you texted me earlier, you mentioned that you'd like to research Frank's old accomplice."

"Yes," Britt said. "How should we go about finding more information?"

"You dare insult my tea when in need of assistance?" Nora teased.

"Pretty much," Britt said brightly. "I know you well enough to know there's only one thing you like better than tea—"

"John."

"—assisting people with research," Britt finished.

"Speaking of John, your wedding is coming up soon now," Zander said.

"In less than a month," Nora answered. "I can't wait."

Nora had been engaged once before, years ago. Her fiancé had fallen in love with someone else a few months before their scheduled wedding, breaking both their engagement and Nora's heart.

In the end, though, Nora's ruined engagement had been revealed for what it truly was—a blessing in disguise. John Lawson was far more perfect for Nora than her first fiancé had been.

At this point, Nora's bridal showers, the bachelorette getaway weekend, and the wedding preparations were all complete. The only things left: their parents' return from Africa and the wedding itself.

"You deserve every happiness," Zander said to Nora.

Britt's sister beamed. "And for that, I'll take pity on you and lend you a hand with your research. Bring the chairs around."

Britt situated her chair next to Nora, and Zander claimed Britt's other side. The monitor remained centrally located, though Nora slid her wireless keyboard in front of herself.

"Do we have any idea how old Ricardo is?" Nora asked. "A birth date would really help."

"He and Frank were in the same grade at school, so they had to have been close in age," Zander said. "Frank was born in early 1954. So Ricardo was likely either born that year or in the fall of 1953."

"And we know that Ricardo was living in Chicago when?"

"Between around 1970 and 1983."

"And that the gas station robbery occurred there," Britt said.

Nora surfed to one of her genealogy sites and filled several fields with the information they'd provided. Her search returned numerous results. Three of the Ricardo Serras listed seemed like possible matches. They pored over the records, but there was no way to verify whether any of the profiles belonged to *their* Ricardo.

Nora scribbled the birth dates of the three men onto a notepad.

Ricardo James Serra, June 29, 1954
Ricardo Arthur Serra, February 1, 1954
Ricardo David Serra, October 14, 1953

"We might be able to find him in the Illinois Inmate Database," Nora said, "if we can match an inmate named Ricardo Serra with one of these birth dates."

Nora typed *Serra, Ricardo* into the Illinois Inmate Database.

In response, an error message appeared. *Inmate not found. The inmate's sentence may be discharged.*

"Drat," Nora said. "Their database doesn't include information about inmates who've completed their sentences. But there's a number listed here—" she squinted at the screen and scrolled down slightly—"for their Department of Corrections." She punched the string of numbers into her cell phone. "They might be able to provide information about someone who was formerly incarcerated over the phone."

While Nora conducted her conversation, Britt became increasingly attuned to Zander's physicality and nearness.

She sensed his body's warmth. Noticed the cadence of his breathing. Imagined the blood pumping through his fit, hard body.

His hands set atop Nora's desk, fingers loosely clasped. The tip of one thumb rested against the center of his other palm. His nails were short and clean. A delta of veins ran beneath the skin on the outside of his hands, leading to his knuckles.

She wanted to trail a fingertip along one of his veins, dip it into the hollow of his palm.

The thought caused a delicious sensation to draw at her middle. Her skin flushed with heat.

Great Scott! What was her problem?

It was so ill-advised to indulge in these flights of fancy over her friend. Her friend!

Nora disconnected the call and adjusted to face them. "Ricardo was released in November of 1983."

"Same as Frank," Zander said.

"According to the woman I just spoke with," Nora said, "Ricardo was only incarcerated in Illinois that one time. And this date here," she circled the birth date next to the name *Ricardo David Serra* on the notepad, "is his birth date."

"Can you check to see if he was ever incarcerated in Washington?" Britt asked. "In case he ended up here like Frank did?"

"Sure." A few swift clicks and Nora navigated to the inmate site for Washington. "This site, I'm more familiar with." Her fingernails clicked keys. "Ricardo's not currently in jail in Washington. Like the last website, this one won't give us information about former inmates. If we want that kind of data, we'll need to send them an email with a request."

"I'm for that," Zander said.

"It might take them a few days to get back to us." Nora filled out the form, then hit Submit. "There's one other inmate database we should check. The federal inmate database. It's slightly more comprehensive than these other two."

"It contains the names of prisoners convicted of federal crimes?" Britt asked.

"Exactly."

"Like?"

"Art theft, for one." The faintest upward curl lingered at the edge of Zander's mouth as he met Britt's eyes.

"Here we are," Nora said a moment later.

The words jolted Britt's focus back to her sister.

Had she stared at Zander a mite too long just then? She'd gotten lost in the ocean blue of his eyes.

Details about Ricardo were centered on Nora's screen.

Ricardo David Serra
Age: 65
Race: White
Sex: Male
Released: January 22

"January twenty-second of this year?" Britt asked.

"Right," Nora answered.

"This proves that Ricardo didn't give up his criminal pursuits back in 1983," Zander said.

"Not only that," Britt said. "The timing is suspicious. Ricardo was released from federal prison, and a few months later Frank receives an upsetting phone call while he's at work. He's found dead the next day. What if that phone call was from Ricardo?"

"Is there a way to find out what crime Ricardo committed that landed him in federal prison?" Zander asked.

"Yes," Nora answered, "but that may take me a little bit of time."

"How can we get ahold of a current address for Ricardo?" Britt asked.

"Why do you want his current address?"

"So we can contact him," she said matter-of-factly. "If he lives anywhere nearby, I want to talk with him. I've got about a million questions I'd like him to answer."

Zander stared at her like she'd suggested swimming with polar bears. "You're not going to talk with Ricardo Serra," he said.

"Not alone, I'm not. We'll talk to him together."

Zander's journal entry:

What if Frank actually was involved in the Triple Play? What if Frank's old life came back to haunt him in the form of Ricardo Serra? What if I was followed?

It's three a.m. I'm sure Britt is sleeping soundly, because she's too brave to be terrified.

I'm going to have to be sensible . . . and terrified . . . enough for the both of us.

CHAPTER
Nine

Zander was having a rotten time at Britt's birthday party.

She'd chosen to celebrate at 12 Lakeside, a new and modern restaurant with an industrial vibe and exposed ductwork. It was located at, yes, 12 Lakeside in Shore Pine and positioned so that the windows overlooked views of the lake at sunset.

For the past forty-five minutes, he and the other guests had been socializing and snacking on appetizers at the bar. Soon they'd move to tables for dinner.

Of Britt's two dozen party guests, Zander knew all but five. Three of those five were men. One of those three was named Reid. Reid looked to be around Zander's age, but unlike Zander, Reid obviously loved to party.

Zander had always been suspicious of people who loved to party. He himself only functioned well in small groups and at a decibel level that enabled him to hear himself think.

So far, he'd watched Reid throw back two afterburner shots. That, Zander could forgive. But Reid's unceasing flirting with Britt—not so forgivable. Britt's laughing amusement at Reid's flirting—even worse.

Zander tried to focus on his current conversation with Nora's fiancé, John, and Willow's husband, Corbin. They were discussing the recent Masters Tournament.

"Did you see the shot Jordan Spieth hit on sixteen?" Corbin asked.

"Unbelievable," John answered.

Zander didn't like golf and hadn't watched the Masters, but he nodded in a way he hoped communicated interest.

Zander had behaved like a saint in the face of all the beginnings, middles, and ends of Britt's relationships. Tonight, though, he was realizing that he no longer had the stomach for it. He flat-out couldn't stand to watch a new relationship develop between Britt and Reid.

You're acting like an idiot.

She'd been a better friend to him than anyone. She always had his back. She supported him and sacrificed for him and believed in him even when he struggled to believe in himself. She accepted his flaws and understood his idiosyncrasies. She told it to him straight when she thought he was wrong. And she insisted on helping him every chance she got.

In light of all that, he didn't exactly have the freedom to opt out of information on Britt's current and future boyfriends. He'd never told her he loved her, so it wasn't like she had any reason to think that a flirtation with Reid might hurt him. She was free to flirt with anyone she wanted. If he couldn't stand to watch her with Reid, then the best he could do for himself was look in a different direction.

That's what he told himself.

Unfortunately, logic didn't change a thing. The iron-sided self-control that had enabled him to stand silently to the side during her past romances had frayed. When he first returned to Merry-weather three weeks ago, his true emotions concerning Britt had been simmering under the surface. Now they were boiling.

Maybe the time had come to tell her how he felt. If he did, things might never be the same between them. He could lose her and his relationship with the rest of the Bradfords, too.

And for what?

Did he expect her to promise she'd never date anyone again once she found out that he loved her? Did he expect her to say, *"Thank goodness you mentioned that you love me, Zander. Now that you've said the words, it occurs to me that I love you, too."*

No. Most likely she'd react with compassion and questions. She'd try to make him feel better even as she'd be forced to tell him that she loved him, too . . . but in a platonic way.

Imagining that caused his chest to tighten defensively because he'd spent the bulk of his early life reconciling himself to his parents' inability to love him in the way he needed.

He could clearly picture his mom and dad in his mind's eye, even now. His mom's delicate blond beauty. His dad's dark hair and harsh, pointed face. He could hear kindness in her voice, disapproval in his.

His mom, Adele, had been both the sweetest person and the weakest person he'd ever known. Unsure of herself, funny, caring. A dreamer placed in a rough St. Louis neighborhood where dreams were liabilities. She'd been too soft for the world and for the man she'd married.

Intense and hard to please, Caleb Ford had always been convinced that he'd received less out of life than he'd deserved. It had never occurred to him that he'd received little out of life because he'd allowed laziness to cripple his smart brain.

His parents had raised him and Daniel on talk of the ways in which their ambitions would one day make the family rich. His mom had wanted to become a singer. His dad a poker pro. However, neither of them had been capable of the steady, day-in, day-out work that would've paid the bills, given them a shot at achieving their goals, and provided their sons with a sense of consistency.

Zander had been twelve when his dad had gone to jail for grand larceny, a circumstance that had left him and Daniel alone with the far less dependable of their two parents. Their mom.

The recreational drug habit she'd acquired in her early twenties had become, by her late twenties, a crutch she used to cope. By her mid-thirties, her addiction controlled her far more than she controlled it.

In addition to feeding themselves, clothing themselves, and getting themselves to and from school, Daniel and Zander became responsible for their mother's care.

When conscious, she spent her time looking for more drugs, apologizing, spouting empty promises, getting jobs, losing jobs, telling them how much she loved them, and pretending to be a normal mom by going on cleaning binges.

For two years he and Daniel tried to parent her. Then one summer day when Zander was fourteen, she left a candle burning too close to her bedroom curtains before passing out. By the time he and Daniel smelled smoke and ran to her room, flames had devoured the curtains. Daniel carried their mom into the hallway. Zander filled mixing bowls with water and ran repeatedly to her bedroom to toss water on the fire. Daniel beat the flame with a blanket.

No use. They had no fire extinguisher, and the water and blanket were no match for a fire that quickly leapt beyond their control.

They led their mom outside and collapsed beside her on the curb across the street from their burning apartment building.

"What's happening?" she'd asked dazedly. "Whose apartment is that? Why doesn't someone put out the fire? Daniel? Whose apartment is that? Zander? What's happening?"

Pity and love and hatred and sorrow for her had twisted inside him.

Sitting on that curb, Zander comprehended that life as he'd known it was finished. He and Daniel would be taken from her and part of him . . . part of him had been glad. The other part felt guilty because of his gladness.

He and Daniel left for Washington. His mom remained in St. Louis. His dad remained in jail.

Carolyn and Frank had given him a home. The Bradfords had drawn him into their circle. Over time, Daniel, Carolyn, Frank, and the Bradfords had become Zander's family.

Four years ago, his mom had succeeded at the one thing she'd put her mind to. An overdose. Since then, his dad had succeeded in getting released from prison, committing another crime, and getting thrown back in.

The pretty sound of Britt's laughter collided with his dark memories. Zander blinked, tugging his attention back to his surroundings.

Britt stood at the bar wearing a turquoise sundress that fell to the floor. There was a name for that type of dress, but he couldn't remember what it was. She'd knotted her hair at the base of her neck in a messy bun. The look was pure Britt. Casual, self-assured, stylish without trying.

"Can I get either of you another drink?" Zander asked Corbin and John.

"I'm fine," Corbin answered.

"Same here," John said.

Zander excused himself and made his way through the crowd toward Britt.

Since their meeting regarding Ricardo the day before yesterday, Nora had received a reply from the Washington State Department of Corrections informing them that Ricardo had never been an inmate in their system.

They'd also learned more about Ricardo's federal conviction. He'd served two years for stealing three porcelain Ming Dynasty figurines from the home of a wealthy elderly couple in California and then transporting them over state lines.

Nora had assured them that she'd continue to search for past convictions, past arrests, and his present-day address.

When Zander had taken Carolyn to lunch yesterday, he'd updated her on the information Nora had discovered. He'd also asked her if she'd be willing to go through Frank's things, in case Frank had hidden evidence of his past life inside their house.

"I've been meaning to go through his things," she'd told him. "Not because I'm ready to give anything away, but because his things are comforting. What should I look for?"

"Anything out of the ordinary," he'd said. "Keys, photos, a piece of paper with names and telephone numbers on it. Anything."

After he'd parted from Carolyn, he'd called Detective Shaw and brought him up to speed on the Triple Play heist and Ricardo's rap sheet. Shaw had been interested, but he'd also politely pointed out that no evidence tied either Frank or Ricardo to the Triple Play.

"Having fun?" Zander asked Britt as he took the position beside her at the bar.

"I am." Color tinted her cheeks. A strand of dark hair fell across her forehead and curved around the upper shell of her ear. "You?"

"Yes," he lied. "I've eaten four pot stickers. My life is complete."

"Have you met the people here you don't know?"

"Nah, but I'm fine. I know plenty of people here, and small talk with strangers makes me irritable."

"I saw you over there looking irritable a minute ago. Is that why?"

"I must have been thinking through a problem with my plot—"

Reid elbowed his way between them. "Excuse me, buddy. Just let me catch the bartender's eye real quick. An empty glass is a crime at a birthday party, eh?"

Zander was forced to take a hurried step back. His shoulder bumped the glass of wine the woman behind him was holding. He shot out a hand to steady her glass before any of it could spill. "I apologize."

"No problem."

Reid did not seem sorry. "Everyone have something to drink?" he asked loudly, looking to the right and left. He had dark blond hair and dressed like he'd been born rich and attended Princeton. "The birthday of a girl as beautiful as this one is a reason to celebrate, so speak up if you need another."

"I was standing there," Zander said to Reid in a flat voice.

"Huh?" Reid's face swung to Britt for confirmation.

"Yep," Britt said. "He was standing there. Reid, this is my friend Zander. Zander, Reid."

"Well, no problem, buddy. I'll move out of your space as soon as the bartender here pours me another shot. What can I order for you? You look like you could use a couple of beverages."

"I'm good," Zander said.

"No, really. I'm going to get you something. A beer at least."

"No."

The bartender poured another afterburner for Reid. "Your friend Zander seems kind of angry," Reid said to Britt.

"He's not usually angry, no," she said. "Serious is more his style."

"Nobody," Reid declared, "is allowed to be angry tonight because—"

"I'm allowed," Zander said with quiet menace, "to be whatever I want to be."

"—it's your birthday!" Reid raised his glass to Britt. She nodded in response. He turned away from the bar and stumbled, spilling a third of his drink on Zander's sleeve.

Instinctively, Zander thrust out his arms to set Reid away from Britt. It wasn't quite a shove. But close.

"Hey." For the first time, antagonism cracked through Reid's expression. "Do you have a problem with me?"

"More than one."

"Zander." Britt stepped into his line of sight and gave him the type of stare a teacher gives a student to keep him in line.

How was he in the wrong here?

Several of the guests turned curious eyes their direction.

Britt handed Zander napkins. "Everything's fine," she said lightly to Reid. "Apologize to Zander for spilling your drink on him."

"I didn't spill my drink—"

"You did," she insisted.

"If I did, I didn't mean to."

Zander ground his teeth.

"Everything's fine," Britt whispered to Zander. With those two words she communicated that she trusted him not to wreck her birthday party by causing a scene.

Problem was, Reid had been right about one thing. Zander *was* angry. Angry enough to want to punch Reid in his smug face.

"Sorry about that, man." Reid bobbed his chin and moved away.

Ferocity and the smell of rum filled Zander's senses. Frustration beat against his temples.

Britt opened her mouth to say something to him just as the hostess raised her voice and asked the group to follow her into the dining room.

When the guests separated to occupy two long tables, Zander deliberately allowed others who didn't often get to see Britt the chance to sit near her. He took a chair close to the end of her table, then wished he'd sat at the other table entirely because, from his position, he had a direct view of Reid. Reid sat three seats down from Britt, which didn't stop him from joking with her throughout the meal.

The harder Zander tried not to watch their interaction, the more a headache built within his skull. By the time everyone rose to watch Britt slice her birthday cake, a vise had tightened around Zander's head, and his mood had turned into a storm cloud.

Britt saw him approaching and met him halfway.

"I'm going to go," he said.

Her face fell. "What? No."

"I've got a bad headache."

"A headache cake and coffee can't cure?"

"Yeah. I'll catch up with you later."

She placed a hand on his forearm. The simple contact instantly stopped his progress.

"I'll swing by the inn," she said. "After this."

"No. Stay here and have a great time. You'll be exhausted after this."

"I don't think so."

"No, really. Go home and get some sleep. It's okay."

A groove formed between her brows.

As everyone began to sing "Happy Birthday," Zander slipped from the restaurant, desperate for quiet, solitude, and a reprieve from the pain in his head and in his heart.

Britt knocked on the door of Zander's room at the Inn at Bradfordwood at 11:07 p.m. Thanks to the fact that her parents owned the inn, she had keys to the inn's front and back doors on her key ring.

She heard rustling.

She knocked again, softly. "You're not asleep already, are you?"

"In bed" came Zander's response. His voice wasn't sleep-roughened.

"But not asleep. So open up."

Several seconds later he opened the door wearing drawstring pajama pants. Rumpled dark hair. Brooding eyes.

The smooth skin of his chest and abs made her mouth go instantly dry. They'd spent the better part of many summers in swimsuits. But something indefinable had shifted between them recently, and seeing him shirtless suddenly felt both intimate and dangerously thrilling.

"I disobeyed your order not to come by," she stated.

"I see that." The stony angles of his face informed her that he was still aggravated with her. She'd known when they'd been at the bar with Reid that Zander was aggravated. And she'd been able to tell, even though he'd been at one end of the table and she at the other during dinner, that he was aggravated. She didn't want him aggravated with her on her birthday.

"Following orders was always Willow's strong suit," she said. "Never mine."

"I feel for your parents."

"So do I," she said heartily.

He flicked on lights, then went to the room's chest of drawers. She shut the door behind her. With his back to her, she watched him shrug into a gray T-shirt. He did so in one fluid motion that caused his muscles to ripple.

"I brought you a slice of birthday cake and a bottle of Advil," she said. "It's vanilla with buttercream frosting and confetti sprinkles from Stacy's Bakery. Well, the cake is anyway. The Advil is regular brown-coating flavor."

Once his attention settled on her, she lifted the to-go box of cake in one hand and the bottle of Advil in the other. She tested a persuasive smile.

It wasn't terribly unusual for them to have disagreements. She was strong-willed. He was equally strong-willed, in his quieter way. They upset each other sometimes.

Because neither could bear to have the other mad at them for long, though, the offending party never failed to make things right with the offended party. Tonight, she was the offending party. Which, to be honest, rankled a little bit.

Yes, she'd given Zander a warning look when Reid had spilled his shot on Zander. The shot spilling hadn't been Zander's fault. However, the shot spilling hadn't been *her* fault, either. As far as she could tell, she was only technically guilty of having delivered a warning look.

"Would you like cake and Advil both?" she asked. "Just cake? Just Advil?"

"Just cake, please. I took Advil earlier."

"And did it succeed in knocking out your headache?"

"For the most part."

"Excellent."

He motioned to the armchair in the room's corner. She made herself comfortable and stashed the Advil in her purse.

Zander sat on the bed opposite her. *His* bed.

Their eyes locked. He said nothing as sexual tension stretched between them, charging every passing second with wattage.

Zander looked away, breaking the contact. Then he rose from the bed, clearly having thought better of sitting there. He angled out the desk chair, which was farther away from her, and sat. His bare feet rested against the room's rug.

To distract herself from her attraction to him, Britt popped the

129

wrapping around the prepackaged plastic utensils the restaurant had provided. She opened the to-go container and passed everything to him.

He took his time with his first bite of cake, chewing, swallowing. "It's delicious."

"I agree."

"But not as delicious as your vanilla cake with buttercream frosting."

"Which is why you're my friend and not Stacy's."

He extended the cake back to her, one of his eyebrows hitching up. He was asking her without words if she wanted some of the cake.

"Don't mind if I do."

She used the same fork he'd used to section off a bite. Stacy really had made an excellent effort with this cake. It was just a little too dense and a little too sweet. Otherwise, very admirable.

She handed the cake back to him. He handed it back to her. In that way, they polished off the slice the way they'd polished off so many dishes in the past.

His laptop rested on the desk positioned in front of the room's large window. The yellow legal pad he used for notes, research, brainstorming, and more lay beside his computer. One coffee mug and a pen sat on top of the pad. Three books formed a pillar on his bedside table. The rest of his belongings must have been put away, because no other evidence of him existed except for a delectable hint of his scent in the air.

"Reid moved to town a couple of months ago," Britt said. "He's friends with Hannah's boyfriend, Kyle. Hannah asked me if Reid could come tonight so that Kyle would have someone other than her to hang out with. Inviting Reid was my attempt to organize a playdate for grown men in order to make Hannah happy."

He regarded her steadily.

"I wouldn't have invited him, however, if I'd known it would make *you* unhappy. And I'm sorry about the surly look I gave you after Reid spilled his drink on you. You were an innocent bystander, but of the two of you, you were also the one I knew had the ability to keep his cool."

"I almost didn't. Keep my cool."

"But you're an honorable person, and so you did."

"I was on my way to becoming a dishonorable person back when I met you, Britt. Honor sometimes feels like a jacket that's too tight."

"No way. You were born with an honorable soul, Zander."

"I wasn't. If I'm honorable at all, it's because of you."

Her heart kicked, then drummed. "Well." She dashed a trailing piece of hair back into her bun. "Thank you for resisting the urge to brawl with Reid in the middle of the restaurant. Brawls tend to bring the atmosphere of a party way down."

"I can't stand that guy."

"I noticed." She tipped her head. "Was he really *that* bad, though?"

"Yes."

"I found him only slightly tiresome."

"I found him hugely tiresome."

"He was entertaining," she said cajolingly. "He seemed to get along well with most of the guests."

"Please, keep going," Zander said, deadpan. "I'd love to hear a long list of Reid's sterling qualities."

She laughed. "Zander! You're not making this easy for me."

"No." He gave her a begrudging smile undergirded with both sheepishness and a trace of ferocity.

She'd been imagining that she'd show up here and say she was sorry and that he'd immediately forgive her. Maybe even say he was sorry for his rudeness toward Reid.

He wasn't behaving as contritely as she'd hoped.

"How about you tell me what's bothering you?" She waited for a long moment.

"Frank's death."

"Yes. Something else is also bothering you. What is it?"

He scrubbed his hands through his hair, dropped them to his thighs. "I think that I'm . . ."

Silence.

"You think that you're what?" she asked with kind insistence.

"Lonely."

Her emotions constricted with sympathy, as well as a prick of hurt because, clearly, her friendship and the time they'd been spending together hadn't been enough to save him from loneliness.

"I've been traveling for months," he continued. "I was lonely then, but at least I had things to see and do to distract me. It seems worse now that I'm home. Now that Frank is gone."

"Is there anything I can do?"

"No. I don't even know why I'm struggling as much as I am. I have my writing, our research into Frank's past, and Carolyn to keep me busy."

"And me."

A brief pause. "And you."

"Do . . . Do you think it's time for you to leave and continue your Grand Tour?" It pained her to ask the question. Inside, her psyche was wailing, *Nooooo!* "As much as I'll miss you, I don't want you to be stuck here against your will."

"There's still a lot I need to figure out about Frank before I can leave."

"That's not technically true. Carolyn and Nora and I can keep looking for information after you go."

He scowled. "No."

"*Yes.* Of course we can. It's unlikely that any of us are going to find anything, anyway. Whether you're here or not." She gestured impatiently. "What if you postpone your trip for years and we never unearth even one more clue?"

He released an edgy breath. "I don't feel right about leaving yet."

"You sure?"

"Yes."

"Okay." And *thank God.* She was saying the noble things, but she absolutely did not want him to go. "Just know that when you do feel right about leaving, I'll support you. Fully. Because I'm very unselfish like that."

"Very."

"Anything else you want to tell me?" she asked.

"I think I've spilled my guts enough for one day."

"By your standards, perhaps even enough for one week."

"Probably enough for one year," he admitted. For the first time all evening, humor and affection settled into the lines around his eyes. He'd gotten over his aggravation.

Zander really was painfully good-looking. Mercilessly so. How was she supposed to regain their usual dynamic with him *looking* like that? All Dickensian and poet-like? What chance did she have? She'd been somewhat boyfriend-starved for the past few months.

"I brought something else." She extracted a medium-sized wrapped gift from her purse. His gift, to her. He'd deposited it onto the pile of presents at the restaurant. "You left before cake and before I had a chance to open my presents. Is it okay with you if I open it now?"

"Sure."

She ripped off the paper and exposed a gleaming silver antique chocolate mold in the shape of a teddy bear. "Oh," she breathed, pleasure suffusing her. The handwriting on the white tag tied to the clasp read *1930s. Anton Reiche Dresden. German.*

The history of chocolate making fascinated her so much that she'd framed black-and-white photos from America's chocolate-making past and hung them in the interior of her shop. She'd devoted one long shelf in her kitchen to her private collection of chocolate-making antiques.

Long ago, chocolatiers had used intricately crafted molds to fashion chocolate into charming designs. So far, she'd collected French molds in the shape of a rabbit and an Easter egg. One American mold in the shape of a rooster. And a German mold in the shape of St. Nicholas.

The silver bear peering up at her with a contemplative expression was not an inexpensive piece. Nor easy to find. She lifted her chin to beam at Zander. "I'll treasure this. I might even make some teddy bear chocolates from it." She rose to give him a hug.

He straightened and enclosed her in his arms.

The hug didn't feel the way their hugs usually felt. She was all too aware of his body and the fact that she was female and he was male and maybe there was some truth to the theory that men and women could never truly be *just* friends, after all—

She didn't want anything about their relationship to change. Letting it change meant risking his presence in her life. And that was too, too high a price.

"Thank you," she murmured.

"You're welcome."

Britt didn't like to think of herself as a coward, but she swept up her purse and moved to the door before she did or said anything that couldn't be undone or unsaid.

She paused on the threshold and raised the chocolate mold. "Because of this I forgive you for your rudeness to Reid and for walking out on my birthday party." She grinned.

"I didn't ask for your forgiveness," he countered, amused.

"Right, but you should have, so I forgive you." She turned to go.

"Britt."

She glanced back.

"Happy birthday," he said.

The sight of him in bare feet and pajama pants and a gray T-shirt was perhaps an even better gift than the teddy bear chocolate mold. "Thanks."

She strode to her car with the long, purposeful strides of a woman determined to resist a powerfully sweet temptation.

Phone call the following morning from Britt to Zander:

Britt: As if we needed more proof that my sister Nora is a genius—which we don't—she just called to tell me that she's located a current address for Ricardo. And listen to this. He lives here in Washington.

Zander: Where?

Britt: Maple Valley. Which proves that he and Frank both started out in Chicago and both ended up near Seattle. Which, in turn, makes me suspect that Ricardo was one of the thieves involved in the Triple Play.

Zander: We don't even know if *Frank* was involved in the Triple Play.

Britt: It's only an hour and a half drive to Maple Valley. Easy.

Zander: Not easy. Ricardo could be dangerous. He's been convicted of crimes twice.

Britt: Yes, but both times for theft. Not for assault or battery or anything that had to do with harming another person.

Zander: My uncle is dead, and it could be that Ricardo is somehow involved.

Britt: We'll take precautions.

Zander: Like?

Britt: We'll follow him to a public place and talk with him there. We won't give him our names.

Zander: We're going to use aliases? Like in a movie?

Britt: Or in a bestselling book by an author I know.

Zander: My characters do crazy things like hunt killers and use aliases for one reason.

Britt: Which is?

Zander: They're fictional.

CHAPTER
Ten

I want to drive to Maple Valley to talk with Ricardo," Britt told her sisters the next day over lunch at the Edge of the Woods Bakery and Tearoom. "But Zander doesn't think it's safe, and I'm having a hard time convincing him otherwise."

Britt and Willow had just accompanied Nora to her final wedding dress fitting, where they'd clucked appropriately over how fantastic Nora looked in her gown.

They were carving out time for a sisters lunch before all three returned to work. So far, Britt had selected a seat, decided that seat didn't suit her, and forced her sisters to play musical chairs until she'd found the right spot. They'd placed their orders and their iced tea had been delivered.

"Convincing Zander of stuff didn't used to be so hard," Britt said.

"Hmm," Willow said noncommittally.

"I noticed that he slipped out of your birthday party early." Nora sipped her tea. "What was that about?"

"He couldn't stand that guy Reid."

"The well-built blonde?" Willow asked.

"Right."

"He seemed gregarious," Nora said.

"If I knew what that meant, I might agree," Britt told her.

"Gregarious means affable. Convivial."

Britt smiled. "Way to define a big word with more big words, Nora."

"Gregarious means outgoing. Social. How's that?"

"Better," Britt replied. "And yes. Reid is outgoing and social for the most part. But he and Zander almost came to blows when Reid spilled his drink on Zander's shirt."

"Really?" Nora's brown eyes widened.

Another noncommittal "Hmm" from Willow.

Britt zeroed in on her oldest sister. "What are those *hmm*s a placeholder for? What are you not saying?"

Willow gave her an innocent look. "Nothing."

Suspicion needled Britt. "Nora?"

She, too, put on an innocent look. "Nothing."

Britt could guess the direction of their thoughts.

They were thinking that Zander hated Reid because Reid had been flirting with her. And Reid's flirting would only have caused Zander to hate Reid if Zander liked her as more than a friend.

Their server arrived and set their plates of food before them. Willow knew the woman personally and inquired about her children while Britt considered her bistro salad. Goat cheese, spiced pecans, dried cranberries, pulled chicken, and sliced apples dotted a base of spinach.

Over the years, each time Maddie had suggested to Britt that Zander liked her as more than a friend, Britt had done everything she could to blow the idea off as absurd. Her sisters knew this. Even though Britt sensed that they agreed with Maddie, Willow and Nora had been too tactful and too careful to confront Britt openly on the topic of Zander.

Which had suited Britt perfectly. In the past, whenever they'd reached a point in a conversation—like the one they'd reached now—where a discussion of Zander's feelings toward her had become an option, Britt had avoided talking about it. So had Willow and Nora.

No doubt her sisters had avoided discussing Zander's feelings because they'd known Britt wouldn't take it well. But now that she was thinking it through from their perspective, it seemed logical to assume that they'd avoided that discussion for Zander's sake, too.

Willow and Nora were two of Zander's biggest admirers. It could be . . . Great Scott. It could be that they'd remained quiet out of loyalty to *him*, not wanting to blab about a subject Zander himself had never broached.

For two weeks straight since her trip to the Central Library with Zander, Britt had been at war with herself over him. Praying over it hadn't helped. Waiting for her infatuation to fade hadn't helped. Scolding herself hadn't helped. Neither had her attempts to lose herself in her newest truffle recipe.

Until now, she hadn't wanted to hear Willow and Nora's thoughts on Zander. But now she did.

When their server left, Britt said, "I have a confession to make about Zander," before either of her sisters had time to reach for their forks. The statement had the desired effect. It immediately commanded Willow's and Nora's full attention.

Britt tended to view her sisters through a lens of deep familiarity. When she saw Willow, she saw gentleness and steadiness. When she saw Nora, she saw kindness and trustworthiness.

It took more scrutiny to notice that the pale pink of Willow's top complemented her pale pink lip gloss and blond hair. Her highly observant green eyes were set into startlingly perfect features.

Nora wore a navy cardigan, accented by a thin belt at her waist. Her side-parted cinnamon-colored hair framed a pale, heart-shaped face. A face so approachable that it invited confidences.

"After thirteen years of friendship," Britt told them, "I seem to be developing a . . . crush on Zander."

Both sisters' mouths hinged open. Then, simultaneously, both began to smile.

"I keep tying to ignore these ridiculous swoony feelings," Britt continued, "hoping that they'll go away. But so far that hasn't been working."

Their smiles grew.

"Neither of you is looking sympathetic," Britt noted.

"Oh! Sorry about that." Nora attempted an expression of contrition and failed.

"I guess," Willow said, "I'm happy because . . . maybe . . . this is a good thing?" She gave an elegant shrug.

"Yes! Have you stopped to consider that this might be a good thing?" Nora asked.

"No. I've had Zander in my life all this time and we're as close as we are because we're *friends*." A movie reel of images whipped through her brain. She and Zander sitting together at high school football games. She and Zander eating the chocolate soufflé they'd made. She and Zander kayaking. She and Zander painting the inside of her house before she moved in. She and Zander dancing at a club to brighten her spirits after her relationship with one of her boyfriends had disintegrated. He was the one she called when she needed help, when she received good news or bad, when she was discouraged or elated or uncertain. "Breakups don't usually happen between friends, but they happen all the time between boyfriends and girlfriends."

"I hear you," Willow said. "But not every romance ends in a breakup. Mom and Dad's hasn't."

"John's and mine hasn't," Nora said.

"Corbin's and mine hasn't," Willow said.

"You're suggesting that Zander and I might fall in love and live happily ever after?"

"Why not?" Willow asked.

"Who better to fall in love with than him?" Nora spoke in the reasonable tone she used when guiding her library patrons toward the next sensible step in their ancestry research. "You already know him very well, and you already like him tremendously."

"You share history," Willow added. "You have the same interests. He's wickedly smart."

"He's a Christian," Nora said. "You know his character."

"Plus," Willow added, "he's handsome."

"That dark hair!" Nora sighed. "Those blue eyes!"

Willow nodded. "He's got that whole fiery but introverted thing down."

If her sisters were trying to be impartial, they were doing a terrible job. "And in this happily-ever-after scenario of yours, you assume that Zander will want to date me and then love me forever. Even though he's never given me a reason to think that's the case."

Her sisters regarded her with hopeful patience.

"Do you think he wants to date me?" Even as Britt asked the question, the muscles at the back of her neck constricted. Some uneasy part of her didn't want to hear their answer. Why? Why was it hard to confront even the idea that Zander might want to date her?

"Are you sure you want to know what we think about Zander's feelings?" Willow's level gaze cautioned Britt not to plunge thoughtlessly into information that might end up changing things she didn't want changed.

Was she sure that she wanted to know? *Yes. No.* "I'm sure."

Their plates of food continued to sit before them, untouched. "You need to keep in mind that this is just my opinion," Willow said. "I'm not speaking for Zander."

"Me neither," Nora said. "I've never talked to him about this."

"Nor I," Willow said.

"Fine," Britt told them.

"And you won't hold what we say against Zander?" Nora asked.

"No."

"Or let it damage the relationship you have with him?"

"Oh, good grief," Britt said irritably. She already knew what they were going to say because they wouldn't have bothered with such a big lead up if they were simply going to say he didn't want to date her. They might be a few years older than she was, but there was no reason to treat her like she was twelve. "Just spit it out."

Willow's posture radiated calm. "My answer is yes. I think Zander wants to date you."

"So do I," Nora said.

She'd anticipated what they'd say. Even so, hearing it out loud rattled her old beliefs so fiercely that it stole her breath. "Let's eat." She speared a bite of salad.

Ordinarily, she found the tearoom soothing. All at once, the hum of conversation among the largely retirement-age diners, the whitewashed walls, and even their table's bouquet of daffodils and green berries grated on her nerves.

As Britt chewed, she watched a drip of condensation zigzag down the exterior of her glass.

Willow spoke first. "If Zander does want to date you, then that might explain why he doesn't want you anywhere near Ricardo, who might be dangerous. And why he couldn't stand Reid, who might become your next boyfriend."

Britt took another bite of salad and directed her vision beyond the tearoom's windows. Neat storefronts marched down the opposite side of the street, their cheerful signage and awnings contrasting with the day's drizzly weather.

Here's why it was hard to confront the idea that Zander might want to date her: Because she knew that Zander's love was a very serious thing. He wasn't someone who loved lightly or easily. He didn't slide into and out of relationships like she did. His love had gravity. Depth. His love held within it the potential of disaster for him. If he loved her, how was he going to come out of that intact?

She didn't want to injure him in any way. But if he loved her, then she may have been injuring him every time she'd fallen for a new boyfriend—a horrifying thought. If he loved her, how could she *not* injure him?

If he loved her, how could their friendship survive?

If he loved her, why hadn't he told her? Likely because he'd known she didn't feel the same way.

She'd been far too immature and headstrong at age fourteen and twenty and even at twenty-four to settle into a love-with-an-uppercase-L relationship with anyone. She'd been well aware that commitment would cost her a measure of her independence, and she hadn't wanted to give any of it up.

Why should she? She'd never longed for a serious boyfriend or a husband. She could support herself. Her work fulfilled her.

Those were all sentiments she'd expressed often to Zander. Had she hurt him when she'd said all that?

"She's not saying anything," Nora observed to Willow as if Britt wasn't within earshot.

"I think she's processing."

"Right. She looks like she's deep in thought."

Britt swung her chin to them, narrowing her eyes. "If you've never talked to Zander about this, then what evidence do you have to support your theory that he wants to date me?"

Nora swallowed a spoonful of soup and dabbed her lips. "The first time I met him, I could tell how he felt about you based on his body language and the way he looked at you."

"No!" Britt exclaimed. "Not the first time you met him."

"All right, then," Nora allowed. "The second time. It was very early on, little sister of mine."

"Remember when he gave you his concert ticket so that you could see Nickelback with your friends?" Willow asked. "You forgot to buy your ticket until it was too late, and when you tried, they were sold out."

"He gave me his Nickelback ticket because he got sick," Britt said.

Willow looked at Britt as if Britt were being purposely obtuse.

"Remember when he drove you thirteen hours to San Francisco so that you could go on that private tour of the Ghirardelli company?" Nora asked. "Nobody voluntarily drives someone thirteen hours for the fun of it."

"Remember how sad he was for the entire two years that Britt was in France?" Willow asked Nora.

"I do."

"I didn't know he was sad," Britt said.

"That's because he didn't want you to feel bad for him while you were having the time of your life," Willow said.

"Remember when he took a week off work to help you get Sweet Art ready and open for business?" Nora asked.

"Which reminds me." Willow rearranged her plate so that she could rest her forearms on the lip of the table. "He learned about chocolate because of you. How many books has he read on the subject?"

"I don't know. Several."

"He didn't read them because he has a passion for chocolate."

"But he does have a passion for chocolate," Britt argued.

"Why, though?" Willow asked. "Does chocolate seem like a common thing for a good-looking young guy to become passionate about?"

Britt felt duty-bound to play devil's advocate. "Zander's had girlfriends over the years!"

Both sisters' faces told her they thought the comment was beneath her.

"Those relationships were very halfhearted," Nora said. "Brief and few and far between."

Britt groaned. "If all of this is true, then why did he leave Merryweather?"

"Because he lost hope that things were ever going to work out for the two of you," Willow answered. "And he refused to watch you fall for any more men who weren't him."

"No," Britt said.

"Yes," her sisters replied in unison.

Willow and Nora glanced at each other. "Jinx!"

Britt had talked at length with Zander about his decision to travel. He'd told her that he wanted to expand his boundaries, see the world, make it on his own. Was it possible that *she* had been another of his motivating factors?

She needed time to mull over all of this and contemplate her history with him through this prism.

"Zander's wonderful," Nora said.

"Incredibly wonderful," Willow agreed. "I think I can say that I speak for Corbin, Nora, John, Mom, Dad, Maddie, Hannah,

Mia, and everyone else who loves you when I say that we'd *really* like for you to consider him as a boyfriend."

Quiet descended.

"Keep in mind that he hasn't asked to be my boyfriend," Britt said. "If he does make a move, I have no idea how I should respond because I want to be smart about this."

"It's not easy to make a move on a person who doesn't ever seem to need anyone," Willow pointed out. "'I'm fine' could be your mantra, Britt."

Britt rolled her eyes. "Move on to another topic, please. This one's giving me hives, and I'd like to enjoy my poor, neglected salad."

Humanely, Willow took it upon herself to ask Nora a question about her honeymoon plans.

Early in her life, Britt had learned that Willow's mom had left Willow behind when Willow was a baby and that Nora's mother had died young.

Unlike her sisters, no childhood tragedies had befallen Britt. Her mom and dad were married. They loved each other, and they loved her.

All three Bradford sisters called Kathleen, Britt's biological mother, Mom. And for all intents and purposes, she *was* mom to all of them. She'd married Garner Bradford when Willow was five and Nora three. However, she'd only given birth to Britt, a fact that never failed to stir guilt within Britt.

She'd always feared that Willow and Nora viewed her as the sister with all the advantages and all the luck. Privileged. Maybe even spoiled. Thus, for as long as she could remember, she'd understood that she—in all fairness—should never have troubles, never need anything, and never complain.

Once, when she was ten, she'd burned her inner wrist on the edge of a cake pan.

"That looks like it hurts," her mom had said, enclosing Britt in her arms.

Britt stood in her mom's warm embrace that smelled like home and felt like safety, for a good two or three seconds. Then tears rushed to her eyes and emotion cinched her throat. Appalled, she jerked away and went to the sink to run the burn under cold water.

"Honey," Mom said, "let me help you—"

"I can do it myself."

"All right, but let me take another look at that—"

"It's okay. I'm fine." She felt her chin trembling, so she ducked her head and stuffed down the tears.

The burn hurt. Really hurt.

But Britt said nothing more about it.

Instead, she'd continued baking the cake as if her arm wasn't smarting viciously. As if everything was as right as rain.

In the end, Zander agreed to visit Ricardo with Britt.

His agreement had little to do with his desire to pick Ricardo's brain regarding Frank's past and everything to do with his refusal to allow Britt to meet Ricardo alone.

"Left here," she instructed him. "The GPS says we're just five minutes away from Ricardo's house."

He steered his Jeep left.

"Then right there." She pointed. "Then your first left."

He cut a quick glance in her direction.

When he'd pulled up at the Hackberry Lane Cottages at eight a.m., an hour and a half ago, Britt had been waiting for him in the parking lot. A hiking backpack slumped at her feet. Her hair poured over one shoulder. She'd chosen a long ivory T-shirt, black jeans, and a short black jacket for today's road trip.

This was the first time they'd seen each other since she'd come to his room at the Inn at Bradfordwood after her birthday party on Thursday. He'd been spoiling for a fight that night, fixated on the fact that the two of them were shut inside a room dominated by a bed. He'd admitted to her that he was lonely. It was a miracle that he'd managed to stop there, that he hadn't said anything unforgivably stupid.

He'd filled Friday and Saturday with writing. Running. Time spent with Carolyn. He'd talked with his brother, and they'd decided that Zander would fly out in a couple of weeks to see him.

Daniel had encouraged Zander to set aside his expectations where Britt was concerned, accept that they had no future as a couple, and open his mind to new people.

Zander had heard everything Daniel had to say. More than that, he'd agreed with the principle. But now that he had Britt to himself for the next several hours, he didn't want to waste time setting aside expectations or accepting that they had no future or opening his mind to new people. He only wanted to enjoy every minute alone with her.

"This neighborhood is fancier than I expected for an ex-con," Britt said.

The homes testified to an earlier, more tasteful time. Each had been carefully restored and stood on a roomy parcel of land.

"If Ricardo was Frank's accomplice in the Triple Play," Zander said, "he's a rich man thanks to the painting he stole."

"You think he'd still be rich from that thirty-five years later?"

"If you sell a Picasso on the black market and invest the money well, you can live large for a very long time."

"If he was living large off Triple Play earnings then why did he steal Ming dynasty figurines?"

"Good question."

"Ricardo's house should be coming up on the right. Yep, that's it. Number fourteen fifty-six." White-painted brick and black shutters marked the structure's exterior.

Zander slowed, then parked two houses down. They'd decided to stake out Ricardo's home until they saw him leave. Then they'd follow him to his destination, which would, hopefully, be a populated place where they could speak with him safely.

Britt leaned nearer her window. "There's someone outside. Do you see that man kneeling in the flower bed?"

"I do."

"Is it Ricardo?"

"Hard to tell from this distance."

Britt shuffled through the sheets of paper on Ricardo that Nora had printed for them and found Ricardo's most recent mug shot. She squinted toward the figure gardening in the yard. "I think that might be him. This street seems perfectly normal, by the way. Maybe we should approach him in his yard. It's public enough."

"For now, let's stay in the car like we planned."

They sat, watching the man garden. Gentle sunlight sloped over them, then hid as bands of clouds passed by. Neighbors walked dogs. Others peddled down the road on bikes. Some pushed strollers along the sidewalks. Every resident of Maple Valley seemed eager to take advantage of the sixty-two degree weather.

The setting possessed no whiff of danger. In fact, the only people on the street receiving nervous glances were him and Britt. They looked conspicuous, sitting in a parked car, doing nothing.

As the clock ticked off the passage of time, Britt's nearness began to feel more threatening than did a conversation with Ricardo. Every time Zander inhaled, he drew the scent of blackberries into his lungs. He could perceive the energy lacing her muscles and tendons. Her hand relaxed on the center console. Just inches away, his own hand burned with the desire to interlace their fingers.

"If we wait," Britt said, "and Ricardo goes inside, it could be hours before he leaves the house again."

"True."

"I really don't think he's going to murder us on his front lawn or try to shove us inside his house so he can murder us there. At the moment, he mostly seems interested in pulling weeds and planting annuals."

"Let's go talk to him."

"Really?" She sent him an alert, expectant look.

He nodded. "Remember that we're going to use the names we decided on."

"Right. I'm Adele."

"And I'm Caleb and our last name is Kingston." He'd decided

to keep it simple by using his parents' first names and his middle name, Kingston. "We live in Seattle."

"Got it."

"We're not going to mention Carolyn or Courtney or Sarah or Merryweather or anything that might allow him to locate us. We're also not going to mention the Triple Play, because if he was involved, we don't want him knowing that we're hunting for clues."

"Deal." She exited the car in a flash.

Zander hurried to catch up with her. "Frank's my uncle, so I'm going to take the lead."

The breeze snapped a strand of her hair. "I'll do my best to practice restraint."

"You have the ability to be restrained, you know. You exercise it every time you flavor chocolate."

"I have to. Too much of anything will ruin the recipe."

"This meeting we're about to have with Ricardo is like that."

The sun highlighted pale glints of laughter in her brown eyes. "Are you suggesting that too much of me will ruin this meeting?"

He allowed himself a grin. "You said it. Not me."

They'd almost reached the walkway leading to Ricardo's front door. "I admire the fact that you're speaking to me in chocolate metaphors, by the way," she said.

"I can't create chocolate, but I can be trusted with chocolate metaphors."

"You probably *could* create chocolate. You know a lot about it."

"Not that much."

"More than any other non-chef I know. Why is it that you learned so much about it?"

Of all the times to ask him that question, why now? They were almost within earshot of Ricardo. "I learned about chocolate because you love it."

Ricardo caught sight of them. He sat back on his haunches and regarded them with a friendly expression.

"Hi," Zander said. "Are you Ricardo Serra, by chance?"

"I am." He removed a slim cigar from his mouth and clambered to his feet.

"I'm Caleb Kingston."

"Adele," Britt supplied.

"Nice to meet you." Ricardo shook hands with them both. "What can I do for you?"

Zander pushed his fingers into the front pockets of his jeans. "We knew James Ross." If by some chance Ricardo didn't know that James Ross had taken the identity of Frank Pierce, then Zander had no intention of telling him.

Surprise hitched Ricardo's brows upward. "That's a name I haven't heard in a long time."

"Unfortunately, James passed away recently," Zander said. "After his death, we discovered some things about him we hadn't known before. One of those is that the two of you were friends. We were hoping we could ask you a few questions."

"We're trying to fill in gaps so that we have a more complete picture of him," Britt added.

Gray streaked the dark hair that Ricardo wore long around his face. The lines marking his olive skin gave evidence of his sixty-five years. His body, however, was lean and fit. He'd dressed in a collared golf shirt, battered jeans, and flip-flops. "I'm sorry to hear that he died." Ricardo and James had once attended a down-on-its-luck high school in urban Chicago. Now Ricardo looked rich and well-traveled, like someone who'd feel right at home at a five-star resort in Bali. "What happened to him?"

"He had a heart attack," Zander answered.

"Ah." The syllable carried a somber note. Ricardo took a pull on his cigar. "How did you find out that James and I were friends?"

"I spoke with some of James' siblings," Zander answered. "One of them mentioned that the two of you met in high school and were friends for many years after that."

"And how did you find me?"

"Computer address search." Zander hoped his nonchalant tone

made it sound as if Ricardo's address had been easy to pinpoint. In fact, it had taken veteran researcher Nora days.

"We decided to drive over when we saw that you live nearby," Britt said. "We're in Seattle."

Ricardo took another drag on his cigar, assessing them with pleasant interest as he exhaled sweet smoke. "I'm happy to answer questions, but I don't think I'm going to be able to help you much. James and I were young when we knew each other."

"What was he like back then?" Britt asked.

"We were both a couple of punks." Ricardo's mouth curved with nostalgia. "We drank and smoked and got ourselves into fights as often as we could. We were trying to convince everyone how tough we were."

"We learned that James was convicted of robbery," Zander said, "and served time."

"That's right. James and I both."

"Shortly after he was released, James moved to Washington." As always, charm flowed from Britt. She was confident, which gave everyone else confidence in her. "Did you move here around that time, too?"

"Yes. James and I drove west together, actually, in my old Volkswagen van."

"When was that?" Zander asked.

"The spring of 1984."

"Why did the two of you choose Washington?"

"We were in need of work, and we'd heard that the job market here was good. Plus, my mother's sister lived here. We moved in with her until we got our feet under us."

"You both moved in with her?" Zander asked.

"Right. A month or so later, James moved out."

"Where did he go?"

"To an apartment complex in the Renton area."

"Do you remember what it was called?"

"I do." Ricardo released a soft chuckle. "It was called The Ridge. Even then it was old. It's long since been torn down."

"If James was able to get an apartment, then I'm guessing he found work pretty quickly," Zander said.

"We both did. James got a job in construction. I got a job at a restaurant washing dishes. I've been in the restaurant business ever since." His eyes crinkled. "Luckily for me, I don't wash dishes anymore."

"Did the two of you remain close?" Britt asked. Her features were arranged in easygoing lines, but Zander could sense the focus beneath the surface.

"For several months, yes. Then we each started to make friends at work. I moved to a suburb a ways from his. We saw each other less and less, and then we lost touch. I remember trying to contact him at some point . . . a year, a year and a half, maybe, after we'd come to Seattle. No luck. I couldn't reach him. I've never heard from him or about him again. Until today."

Zander scratched his jaw. "We know that James was shot in the leg after moving to Washington, but we never could get him to talk to us about it. Do you know anything about that?"

"He was shot in the leg?" Ricardo asked, puzzled.

"Right. He had a bullet wound in his thigh."

"I don't know anything about that."

"He never mentioned a leg injury?" Zander asked.

"No. Back when I knew him, his leg was fine." If Ricardo was lying, he was outstanding at it. Every word sounded like truth to Zander.

"Did you meet any of the friends James made working construction?" Britt asked.

"Yeah." He seemed to rake through his memory. "I met his buddies a couple of times, but I don't remember their names."

"Did James have a girlfriend?" Zander asked.

"Not that I knew of." The sun came out and Ricardo shielded his eyes with one hand. "Did James ever marry and have a family?"

"Yes," Zander told him. "He did both."

"Good for him." Ricardo gestured with his cigar to his impressive house. "My wife and I got married two months ago. She's the best thing that ever happened to me."

"Congratulations," Britt said.

"Would you like to come inside and meet her? Have a cup of coffee?"

"Thanks, but we can't today," Zander said. "We have an appointment."

Ricardo smiled understandingly. "Sure, sure. I'm glad you two stopped by. I only wish I could have been more help."

Note passed between Britt and Zander in tenth grade:

BRITT: Why did you quit the debate team?

ZANDER: I changed my mind about it. I'm going to be busy with soccer.

BRITT: I was the alternate, so now that you've quit, Mrs. Covington has invited me to take your spot. You definitely didn't quit just so that I could be on the team, did you?

ZANDER: Definitely not.

Note passed between Olivia and Britt in tenth grade:

OLIVIA: Mia told me that she thinks Zander's looking really cute lately. They'd make an awesome couple! Please tell me he's feeling the vibes between them, too.

BRITT: No, I don't think so.

OLIVIA: Oh no! Really? Maybe you should encourage him to consider Mia. She's such a doll.

BRITT: I know! I really love Mia. But I don't think her personality is quite right for Zander. They're not a fit.

Note from Britt to Carolyn in tenth grade:

Here's the check to cover the cost of Zander's soccer camp this summer. Thanks for agreeing to keep this between us. I don't want him to know that I'm paying for it. And I don't want my parents to know that I'm paying for it, either. They think I'm spending my allowance on practical things like clothes.

CHAPTER
Eleven

Now that she, Willow, and Nora had hauled the *Zander wants to date you* possibility out of the shadowy back closet of their sisterhood, Britt was finding it hard to concentrate on anything else while in Zander's presence.

They'd left Ricardo's, driven halfway home, then pulled off the freeway in Gig Harbor for lunch. They were now polishing off their meal from a picnic table at Sunrise Beach Park. A view of Puget Sound, Vashon Island, and majestic Mount Rainier preened before them.

Britt kept her focus affixed to the setting, because each time she'd looked at Zander today—while driving to Maple Valley, while talking with Ricardo—she'd wondered whether her sisters' theories could be true.

I mean, they *could* be true. But were they?

Willow and Nora had made an outstanding case, after all. They'd pointed to behavior of Zander's that supported their argument.

It's just that every time she began to think they might be right about Zander, she started to feel dizzy . . . as if nothing about her world was quite as she'd trusted it to be. As she'd wanted it to be. As she'd set it up to be.

If Willow and Nora were right about Zander, that meant she'd been wrong.

She knew Zander much, much better than her sisters did. Before he'd left on his Grand Tour, she'd hung out with him constantly. She'd texted with him endlessly. She'd shared her truest self—all of her hopes and frustrations and weaknesses—with him. She'd been on the receiving end of his words and body language a hundred times more often than Willow and Nora had.

She'd concluded that his feelings for her were the same as her feelings for him.

It was true that he'd sacrificed for her in a million ways. But she'd sacrificed for him, too. That's what friends did. Her motives hadn't been romantic, so why did his motives have to be romantic? Couldn't he have done what he'd done for her in the name of friendship?

Yes.

But *had* he?

It's possible—and this is what had been keeping her awake the last two nights—that she'd concluded that his feelings mirrored hers because that conclusion had been the most convenient for her.

The idea that Zander loved her: scary and thorny.

The idea that Zander felt friendship toward her: easy and safe.

She had the sinking sensation that she'd been willfully wrong about him. Because that's what had made her comfortable.

Inwardly, she groaned. She certainly wasn't comfortable anymore. She didn't know what to think about Zander. Nor did she know what to think about her new preoccupation with thoughts of kissing him.

She took another bite of the cold rice, chicken, and curry salad she'd made early this morning. Britt wasn't one for picnic lunches stored in decorative wicker baskets. She was one, however, for power lunches stored in her oft-utilized hiking backpack. In addition to the salad, she'd packed sliced fruit, a baguette and butter, and bottled waters for the two of them. For dessert, she'd included her latest attempt at the troublesome peppermint truffle recipe.

She chewed critically. The next time she made this chicken curry salad, she'd add a pinch more curry and extra green olives. And what was it about the flavors of baguette and butter that paired so deliciously? The taste of both were simple on their own. Bland bread—springy on the inside and crispy on the outside. Bland butter—creamy and salty. Together? Perfection.

"I believed Ricardo." Zander scooted his plastic dish and fork away from him, indicating he'd finished eating.

"So did I." Smoke wisped from the chimney of one of the homes on the far side of the water. "When we came up to him and explained that we were friends of James he reacted exactly the way I imagine someone who'd lost touch with an old friend would."

"I agree."

"And despite the fact that Ricardo was released from prison recently, I don't think he had anything to do with Frank's death."

"My gut's telling me the same thing," Zander said. "But in this case I don't want to trust my gut because thieves like Ricardo are probably good at playing a part, at putting themselves in the shoes of the person they want you to believe they are, then responding and speaking the way that person would."

She steeled herself to meet his eyes. Could he? *Her Zander?* Have loved her all these years? "When I was talking to Ricardo, I didn't feel as if I were talking to an experienced actor playing a part. I felt like I was having a normal conversation with a normal person."

"We never did see Ricardo's wife," Zander pointed out.

"You think he lied about having a wife?" Britt asked with surprise.

"I don't think he did. I'm just saying he could have."

"Why would he do that?"

"To make himself seem less threatening."

"To what end?"

"To get us inside his house?"

"Under the guise of having coffee with his wife?"

"Yep."

"So that, in actuality, he could slash us to pieces?" she asked.

He shrugged. "Slashing to pieces sounds a little extreme."

"Over the top," Britt said.

"He'd probably just shoot us."

"Naturally." Britt considered Zander's hypothesis. "I think his wife is real. He wouldn't lie about that because it's too easy for us to verify her existence, or lack thereof. I'll ask Nora to check into Ricardo's personal history just to be sure. She's already planning on doing more research into his criminal history." Britt opened the container bearing her truffles and extended it to Zander.

He took one. "Ricardo's rich enough to afford to pay someone like Nick to follow me."

"True."

"And he lives close enough to Merryweather to have met with Frank the day he left the jobsite and never returned."

"Also true. However, I'm not convinced that Ricardo would have wanted to meet with Frank, because I'm not convinced that Ricardo was one of the Triple Play robbers. If he was, then wouldn't it make sense that both he and Frank would have changed their identities? Or both he and Frank would have kept their original identities?"

"That would make sense, yes."

"Instead, Frank changed his identity and Ricardo kept his the same." Britt gestured from Zander's truffle to Zander. "Eat." They both bit into their chocolate.

The recipe had so much promise. It offered layers of flavor—complicated, innovative flavor. She could taste in this truffle the thing that made her heart beat faster, the promise of greatness.

It wasn't great yet, though. The consistency wasn't quite right, and this batch possessed too much rum and not enough of . . . something elusive that she hadn't figured out yet. "I'd like to hear your feedback, chocolate sous savant."

The rich green backdrop of pine trees sharply outlined his masculine profile. "Perhaps a little too much rum."

"Yes." Earlier today, he'd told her he'd educated himself on chocolate because she loved it. That was something a person might do for a friend. Right? "I may try adding a hint of ginger to the white chocolate."

"Will that be bright enough to contrast with the peppermint?"

She knit her forehead. "I'm not sure." She'd created enough recipes over the years to have reason to believe that she'd uncover this particular truffle's secrets eventually. Even so, the uncertainty of the current creative phase didn't sit well with her. At the moment, this truffle was eighty percent chocolate and twenty percent doubt. Doubt—about Zander, about chocolate—had never coexisted well with her.

Her attention flowed to the touch football game beginning to take shape on the stretch of beach below them. She motioned her chin toward the players. It looked like a large group of college-aged friends. Guys and girls both. "Want to join them?"

Zander considered her with a small, uneven smile.

Something other than chocolate greatness had the ability to make her heart beat faster. *He did.* There was power in that particular smile on the face of her friend—the quiet, brilliant man.

"Yes," he said. "But only if we're on opposing teams."

"I wouldn't have it any other way."

They talked smack to each other while stashing the backpack in the car and making their way to the beach.

The players were glad to welcome two more. Zander gave their names.

"Wait," said a beautiful blonde dressed head to toe in Lululemon. "Are you Zander Ford, the author?"

"Yes!" Britt answered before Zander had a chance to. This person recognized Zander! Pride sunburst within her more strongly than it would have if she'd been the one recognized. "Have you read *Geniuses*?"

"I have," the blonde chirped. "Oh my gosh, it was amazing."

"It really was," Britt said.

"Thanks." Zander appeared both pleased and sheepish.

"I couldn't put it down." The girl eyed Zander, as if deciding whether he'd fit into the tuxedo she had picked out for her future groom.

This female stranger had fallen prey to Zander's unattainable vibe and fantastic book, which wasn't at all uncommon. The unattainable vibe had attracted women even before the release of the book.

What was uncommon? The emotion that overtook Britt in response to the girl's interest.

Possessiveness.

A few seconds ago, she'd liked the girl. Now she wanted to step in front of Zander and tell her in no uncertain terms not to get her hopes up.

Britt was losing her marbles. Honestly, it was almost frightening. These newfound feelings for Zander were just too . . . fraught. Too unsettling.

The girl asked Zander questions about his writing process, which he fielded good-naturedly.

"Shall we start?" Britt asked the group at large, interrupting the girl halfway through a question.

"Sure," one of the guys answered, and the two teams coalesced.

Just empty your head, Britt. Simply enjoy a Sunday afternoon game of touch football.

For the next hour, they played. The teams progressed up and down a "field" they'd marked off with pieces of driftwood. Cool breeze coursed through Britt's hair. She ran. She caught passes and dodged to stop the opposing team's plays.

A hazy blue sky watched over them, the water of the Sound glimmered, sun kissed Britt's cheeks, and she and Zander bantered. They behaved as they always had when competing—ribbing each other, making predictions of grandeur, and laying down outrageous boasts.

In the end, Britt's team won.

She approached Zander, flushed with victory. "Everything's right with the world when the worthiest team wins."

"Funny. I was just going to say that everything's wrong with the world when the worthiest team loses." Exertion and sea air had dampened his sable hair.

"Thank goodness that's not what occurred here today." She scooped up an aqua piece of sea glass and brandished it. "I'm going to take this home as a trophy to remind me of today's game. Every time I see it, I'll have an excellent reason to gloat."

He attempted to jab upward on the bottom of the glass so that it would spring from her grip.

She jerked it out of range just in time and, laughing, turned and ran.

He chased her. "Hand the sea glass over, and no one will get hurt."

"Never!" She raced along the beach away from civilization. Her tired legs responded to the test, obediently drawing from her stores of stamina. It was hard to sprint on sand, but she was doing it, a fact that filled her with a heady sense of strength.

She could hear Zander close behind her. She wanted to believe she was faster. It was probably closer to the truth to assume he was humoring her. She followed the shore's long curve, then slanted up the beach, away from the water.

She glanced over her shoulder, tendrils of hair streaming in front of her eyes. He was gaining. She shrieked and tried to increase her speed just as one of her feet sank into a wet patch of sand. Her balance pitched forward, and in the next instant she landed with a giggling *oomph*. One of her feet tangled between Zander's legs and he fell, too. She rolled partway onto her back and found him above her. He'd braced the weight of his upper body on one of his arms.

"I warned you," he said with a huff of amusement.

She grinned. "I'm the winner of today's very important touch football game, and I'm dead set on keeping my trophy at any cost." Pleasantly cool sand supported her overheated limbs.

"At any cost?" he asked.

"Any."

They were both breathing hard.

His face was near and their position . . . oh. Their position was very intimate.

Adrenaline shot down her body to her toes.

Her sense of caution reared awake and began issuing warnings. She waited for Zander to move away.

He didn't. By slow degrees, seriousness overtook his features. Then raw need flared in his dark blue irises, followed immediately by conflict. His focus flicked to her nose, her lips, then down toward her knees.

What should she do? Her thoughts split apart like a firecracker. Her body clamored to kiss him. Her emotions were drawing her to him—

"What's this?" he asked in a tight voice.

"Hmm?"

He was looking at her waist. With effort, she recovered enough from her daze to lift her head. She saw that her shirt had flipped up at the hem when she'd landed, exposing a few inches of her abdomen above her jeans. A portion of the raised pink scar she'd received during her kayaking accident was fully visible.

Her heart seemed to spiral into the cold, dark depths of a well.

Fiasco. He'd seen the scar, and it was too late to hide it from him. Shoot, shoot, shoot.

"It's just a scar," she said. "No big deal."

"No big deal?"

She levered her elbows underneath her and edged backward. "It looks worse than it is."

"It looks worse than it is." His gaze seared hers.

She sat, then rolled forward onto her feet and straightened tall because she couldn't bear to talk to him about this from a position of weakness.

He, too, rose to standing. Color stained his cheeks. He'd shed his sweat shirt early in their football game and was wearing a black T-shirt that revealed his tattooed arms. His hands hung at his sides, but they didn't look relaxed. Tension arced along every tendon. "When did you get that scar?" he asked.

She pressed her back teeth together and resisted the urge to cross her arms defensively. She double-checked to make sure her shirt had fallen back into place. It had. "I got it early last summer—"

"When exactly?"

"The end of June."

"How?"

She pressed two fingertips against her temple.

"Britt." He gestured angrily. "Don't make me drag it out of you. I need—I need to know what happened, so tell me. Please. Everything."

She dropped her hand. "I was paddling the gorge—"

"Alone?"

"Yes. As you know, I sometimes go out alone when my paddling friends aren't available."

"Water conditions?"

"High," she admitted, chin lifted. "There'd been a good deal of rain."

"*Britt*," he growled, infusing her name with censure.

"That section of the river is only class two."

"Class two plus," he corrected, "when it hasn't rained. The run-off makes the gorge unpredictable—"

"—and dangerous," she snapped. "Yes. I'm aware." She'd already received this sermon from her doctors, parents, sisters, friends. She'd even heard it from Mike, the guy that sold adventure sports equipment to her. Their sermons had been unnecessary because she'd *lived* the lesson. The river and her painful recovery had been excellent teachers.

Thick clouds swept in front of the sun. "What happened?" he asked.

"I went wide around the bend at the basalt wall."

He acknowledged that he knew the place with a nod.

"That area has always been clear before. But this time, a tree had fallen into the water. It was mostly submerged, and by the time I saw it, I couldn't avoid it."

His mouth tightened.

"My efforts to free myself only made it worse, and before I knew it, the current had pushed me underwater and against the branches."

"A strainer."

"Yes. I managed to grab hold of my kayak. I yanked it hard, and it swung out. The river pulled it down river and dragged me out."

"And?"

"I hung on until the water slowed, then kicked over to that spit of land in the center of the river." She didn't mention that crawling onto the island had been agonizing. "I had my life vest on and my phone was in its waterproof case, but there was no service at that spot."

The earlier color in Zander's cheeks was rapidly leaching to white. "Go on."

"Maddie was having lunch nearby that day and had offered to pick me up at the take-out point. She waited for an hour past the time when we'd agreed to meet, then called the police. About an hour after that, they found me by helicopter."

He swore under his breath.

She said nothing. Why was telling him this so brutally difficult? These words, when spoken to him, were coaxing so much shame from her that she felt choked by it.

"The helicopter transported you to the hospital?" he asked tersely.

"It did."

"And your injuries were . . . ?"

"Broken ribs. Lacerations. The worst one was an abdominal puncture. A sharp branch entered here." She indicated a spot on her outer back near where her ribs curved toward her waist. "And exited here." She pointed to the scar he'd seen on her front.

Strain crackled through the silence.

"A branch stabbed through you?" he asked.

"Through my side. Luckily for me it missed everything vital." The breezy timbre she attempted fell as flat as roadkill.

"Did you have hypothermia from the temperature of the water?" he asked.

"No. It was a hot, sunny day."

"How much blood did you lose?"

163

Almost too much. "A good bit."

"Was the surgery to repair the damage complex?"

Terribly. "Somewhat."

"Which means it was very complex. How many days were you in the hospital?"

"Only four."

Radiating restlessness, he interlaced his hands behind his skull. He peered at the water. One breath. Two, three, four. Releasing his arms, he glared at her as if she were a tangle in a book plot he was powerless to unravel. "You should have told me."

"I know."

"If a relationship is going to work, then both people have to tell each other things. They have to rely on each other."

"I . . ."

Rely. Relying on anything and anyone other than herself had never come easy for her. She found it difficult to rely on God, even. And He was all-powerful.

As far as she was concerned, reliance was way overrated. But she could tell by the set of Zander's jaw that he didn't want to hear that.

Just once—*just once!*—she'd love for someone to congratulate her on her self-sufficiency. No one ever said, *Hey, thanks for not being needy, Britt.* Or, *Props for taking care of yourself. Way to behave like an adult, Ms. Bradford. You get an A+ in girl power.* Or, in Zander's case, *Gee, thanks, Britt, for keeping quiet about your accident for the sake of my Grand Tour.*

"Why didn't you tell me?" he demanded.

"Because I didn't want to ruin your trip. And I definitely didn't want you feeling like you needed to leave whatever fabulous place you were touring last June in order to come home." She was painting herself to be more honorable than she was because she refused to admit the rest to him. Namely, that she'd been embarrassed. That she hadn't wanted his perception of her to change. "If you'd returned for that reason, at that time," she said, "it would have been terrible."

"Why?" he challenged. "Why so terrible?"

"Because the trip was important to you."

"There are things that are more important to me."

She held her breath against the waves of pleasure and fear that broke over her at his statement. This conversation was leading either to paradise . . . or disaster.

"I arrived in Merryweather almost a month ago." His words had a ragged edge. "We've had so many conversations since then that I can't count them all—"

"And I didn't mention my accident." She'd rather head him off at the pass. "I know."

"Nor did your sisters or Maddie mention it to me."

"I asked them not to."

"Why?"

"At this point, that's water under the bridge . . . or water under the fallen tree. I'm better now. Zander, I hate thinking about that day, and I hate talking about that day. Plus . . ." She struggled to pick the right words.

"You knew I'd be mad."

"Yes. And I didn't want to make you mad."

"I'm mad."

"I see that."

"You should have told me. All the other people you're close to knew this information. I'm the only one you excluded."

"You're the only one who was on a trip overseas." Her grip on her temper, and on the fact that she was at fault, began to slip.

"Did you keep it from your parents?" he asked. "They were in Africa."

"I . . . They—they're my *parents*. I had to tell them."

"And what am I to you?"

"You know what you are to me."

"I don't think I do."

"Of course you do."

"I don't. You almost died, and you didn't contact me."

She stepped close to him, scowling, her hands balled on her hips. "I didn't almost die."

"You could have died, Britt, and I'd have been on the other side of the world."

"But I didn't die!"

"But you could have. And I'd have been wrecked."

"Any of us could die any day, driving our cars or walking down the street—"

He let out a rumble of frustration, stepped forward, and cut off her argument by taking her face in his hands and kissing her.

The shock of his mouth against hers wasn't cold or dominating. The stunning contact was all glowing, sparkling warmth. Soft, firm lips. *His* lips. Against hers. Passionate and urgent to communicate something that he'd been unable to communicate with words.

I'm kissing Zander.

ZANDER is kissing me.

He smelled like expensive cologne and heat and ocean. His breath blended with hers so that she couldn't tell where his exhale ended and her inhale began. Every sensation was packed with miracles and overwhelming surprise and deep commitment. Britt's pulse thundered.

She'd had no idea, *no idea*, that kissing him could be like this, that kissing him could set her soul on fire—

Zander pulled back abruptly.

His chest hitched with his breath. He regarded her with smoky, unfocused eyes.

She stared at him, her senses reeling, her mind staggering with the ramifications of what had just happened.

Now was the time to say . . . something that would save this situation. If only she knew what that something was. Every word in her vocabulary had deserted her.

She was acquainted with physical attraction. But she was wholly unacquainted with what had just occurred. What had just occurred was physical attraction woven together with her love for Zander and their long history together—all of which had added up to make the kiss combustible.

She watched Zander's eyes clear. Watched as intensity tinged with dismay entered them.

She didn't want his dismay. She wanted to kiss him more so that she could lose herself all over in that delicious oblivion. Oblivion would provide an escape route from the talk they now must have.

"I'm sorry," he said. "I shouldn't have done that." His voice was roughened by remorse or self-condemnation—she couldn't tell which one. Did he regret kissing her because of what it might jeopardize? Or did he just plain regret kissing her?

"Let's sit," she said weakly. Her legs felt like pudding, and she couldn't take the apologetic look on his face for another second.

She sat cross-legged, her hands melded in her lap, facing the channel. He sat about a foot away, legs bent up, his forearms on his knees.

"I'm sorry," he said again.

"I'm the one who's sorry, that I didn't tell you about my accident. I should have. That I didn't is my fault."

"The kiss is my fault, though."

"I kissed you back," she reminded him.

After several seconds, she could feel his attention on her. "Britt—" he began in an anguished whisper.

"It's okay," she said.

"I don't think it is okay."

Best to go with cavalier truth. "I liked it, Zander." She risked a peek at him across her shoulder and almost laughed when his features smoothed with astonishment. Her enjoyment of the kiss had been so complete that she couldn't fathom how he could doubt it. "Did *you* like it?" she asked.

"Yes."

The sound of birdsong drifted between them. "Why did you kiss me?" she asked.

"I don't know." A pause. "I was frustrated, and I just . . . acted without thinking."

After the tumult of feeling she'd just been through, his *"I don't know"* bumped her back to earth, like a hot air balloon touching down. *"I don't know why I kissed you"* was a far cry from *"I kissed you because I've loved you wildly for years."*

At the same time, she wasn't ready to hear *"I kissed you because I've loved you wildly for years."* At this point, *"I don't know"* was on par with what she'd truthfully say if he asked her why she'd kissed him back.

The serene setting struck a stark contrast to the alarm screeching within her. She was excruciatingly aware that she needed to protect the thing that she could not lose. Their friendship.

"I don't think we should let one kiss make things weird between us," she said, then felt like a sellout because calling what had just happened between them "one kiss" betrayed the kiss's magnitude.

"I agree," Zander said.

"I'm all for living in the moment. We were living in the moment just now, and we both liked the kiss and so—good for us—no harm done." At least, she sincerely hoped that no harm had been done. "I'm sure a lot of male/female friends have kissed each other at least once during their years of friendship."

The line of his mouth took on a grim cast. "Probably so."

"And now that we've gotten a kiss out of our system, we can add it to the list of things we've done together. Which is a very long list."

"Very."

"Today we played football on the beach. There's no reason to give the kiss any more weight than the football."

A prolonged silence. When he finally spoke, he seemed to be selecting his words carefully. "I'm guessing that while you'd play football with me again, you'd rather not repeat the kiss."

"More football wouldn't be risky. But I think you and I both know that more kisses might be."

She felt more than saw him flinch.

"Ordinarily, I like the adrenaline rush of risks," she continued. "But our friendship has never been at stake in any of the risks I've taken in the past. Our friendship is much too important to me to gamble."

He gave a terse nod.

"So one kiss it is," she said, striving to project a confidence she didn't feel.

Zander sat, motionless.

"Is everything all right?" she asked.

"Yes." He rose and reached a hand down for her, then pulled her up. "Let's head back to Merryweather." They walked toward his car. "I want to try to get some pages written on my manuscript."

Relieved, she grasped the olive branch of normal conversation he'd offered. "Are you going to be able to concentrate after the football defeat you suffered?"

"I'll drown my sorrows in an iced coffee after I drop you off. Then I should be fine."

They talked in their usual way during the remainder of the drive. But talking in their usual way seemed to require twice as much effort as it had before.

The outcome they'd both agreed they didn't want had come to fruition. Things had gotten weird between them.

Her pulse tapped out a frightened Morse code to God. *Please don't let this destroy our relationship. Please, God.*

When Britt finally entered her house, emotionally wrung out, she realized that she'd forgotten all about the sea glass she'd intended to bring home as a symbol of her victory.

Card from Frank to Carolyn on their tenth anniversary:

Carolyn,
 Every day I wake up beside you and every day I can hardly believe how lucky I am. My life is golden because of you. You've brought me laughter and a home and two little girls who call me daddy. I love your heart, your gentleness, your strength. And I really love your legs.
 Don't punch me for that last comment. I'm joking.

Actually, I'm not. It's true. I love your legs.
I love every inch of you and always will. Thank you
for marrying me. For being my wife.

Love, Frank

CHAPTER
Twelve

He'd known he shouldn't kiss her.

He'd known. And he'd kissed her anyway. Now their entire relationship hung in the balance, and with it, his connection to the Bradford family.

After dropping Britt off at the Hackberry Lane Cottages, Zander made his way to Lake Shore Pine because there'd been no way he could do what he'd told Britt he intended to do—get an iced coffee and write. Writing required tremendous focus. He was only going to be able to focus on one thing today: their kiss and the conversation that followed.

For two hours straight he sat on a bench and stared at the surface of the lake. Sick to his stomach, he battled worry and blame.

Then he climbed into his car and drove country roads. He took turns at will, not caring where they might lead. Over and over again in his memory, he replayed the day's events.

Another hour slipped past.

Earlier, when he and Britt had fallen onto the sand and the length of his body had been braced above hers, he'd been like a man who'd denied himself water for far too long, then been confronted with a waterfall. By that point, he'd been dying of thirst.

Then he'd seen the scar on her stomach, and a stunned stillness had come over him.

Nothing about Britt could ever be anything less than beautiful to him, the scar included. Fierce scars suited warrior princesses. But he hadn't been able to fathom what *that* scar was doing on *her* stomach. Worse, the scar was evidence. Evidence that while he'd been gone, she'd been hurt. Badly.

For years he'd done everything in his power to protect her, to make sure that she was healthy and happy. Then, as soon as he'd let down his guard and left Washington, Britt had been involved in the kind of terrible accident he wouldn't wish on his worst enemy.

As she'd explained how she'd been injured, he'd been horrified by several things at once. The fact that he hadn't been there to help her. The fact that he'd continued his trip, oblivious. The fact that she hadn't told him something so incredibly important.

He'd tried to keep himself under control during the argument that followed, but his frustration had risen and risen until there'd been no place left to contain it.

He hadn't decided to kiss her. One heartbeat, he'd been standing there rigid and furious. The next heartbeat, he'd been kissing her. No thought had separated those two heartbeats. They'd been separated only by unstoppable instinct.

He'd imagined kissing Britt a million times. Yet the reality of kissing her . . . Britt, in his arms, their mouths intimately exploring . . . had turned him inside out.

Even now, hours later, the kiss had the power to shake him.

He pulled up at a stop sign. Was the silver BMW behind him the same one he'd seen shortly after leaving the lake?

After the police chief had questioned Nick, he'd been far more conscious of the cars surrounding him on the road. He'd seen very few black Expeditions. Those he had seen definitely hadn't appeared to be tracking him. This was the first time since that day with the chief that he'd suspected any car of following him.

He waited for the BMW to draw nearer.

It took a turn onto a private drive.

He was becoming delusional. Fabulous.

He pressed the gas.

The joy that had overtaken him when Britt said she'd liked the kiss had deserted him as soon as she'd started writing off what had happened between them as no big deal, as something they'd needed to get out of their system.

"I'm guessing that while you'd play football with me again, you'd rather not repeat the kiss," he'd said to her. He'd been able to predict how she'd respond. Even so, he'd harbored stubborn hope that she'd leave the door open a few inches to allow for the possibility of more between them.

She hadn't.

Of course she hadn't.

He shouldn't have been surprised. Which is why he couldn't explain the fresh heartbreak he'd experienced at her answer.

Or why he was still experiencing it now.

Zander hardly slept that night. The sleep he did get came to him in broken, anxious patches.

He finally gave up when daylight began to frame his room's curtains. Since he'd rather be depressed and awake than depressed and trying to sleep, he showered. He pulled on track pants, running shoes, and a T-shirt, then ran along the inn's twisting pathways.

Only when he'd exhausted himself—all he could hear was his breath, all he could think was how much his lungs hurt—did he turn back toward the inn. He needed a productive writing day today. He was falling further behind on his goals. Between now and his deadline, steady output was mandatory.

A quarter mile from his destination, he transitioned from running to walking in order to cool down.

He reached the inn's yard, lifted his gaze—

And saw Britt sitting on the inn's front steps, watching him.

His heart stuttered. He came to an immediate stop.

She wore yoga pants and a dark purple fleece sweat shirt. She'd pulled her hair into a ponytail. Gold sunshine gilded her cheekbones and mouth. Piercing brown eyes set beneath the expressive arches of her brows followed him as he crossed the remaining distance.

Has she changed her mind? Does she want more with me than friendship?

His stubborn hope wouldn't die.

Gracefully, she stood. Her hands remained in her sweat shirt's pockets. "Are you doing okay?" she asked.

"I am."

She cocked her head, and he was afraid to think what she might see in him. "Really?" she asked gently. "You looked pretty gloomy walking up to the inn just now."

"I was just deep in thought."

"About us?"

"Yeah," he admitted.

"I've been thinking about us, too. Which is why I stopped by." Britt had never shied away from hard things. She preferred to deal with difficulties head-on, then move past them. "Are we good?" she asked. "You and me?"

Are we good?

She'd posed that question to him following every disagreement that had occurred between them. He'd always tried to honor her directness with a direct answer in return. This time, though, the fully honest answer was no. They weren't good because what was between them wasn't good *for him* anymore.

He was so raw at the moment that he didn't trust himself to say that. His black state of mind could easily goad him into speaking something he might bitterly regret later.

Are we good?

"I don't know," he answered. That, too, was true. "Are we?"

"I don't know, either." She scrutinized his face. "But I'm willing to do whatever I need to do to make sure that our friendship stays strong. I can't overstate . . . how much you mean to me."

Tenderness tore free, spilling through his chest. "I can't overstate how much you mean to me," he said in a low, hoarse voice.

He could tell her that he loved her, right now, the two of them standing in the hush of a new day. Just three short words. *I love you.* The statement gathered on his tongue, waiting.

Except he knew Britt wasn't ready to hear it.

Also, he wasn't exactly handling the small rejection she'd given him yesterday well. If her decision to limit their total number of kisses to one could rock him like this, then it didn't seem possible to survive the rejection that would follow his *I love you.*

"I think we might have needed to have a longer conversation yesterday on the beach." With a gesture of her hand, she invited him to sit on the brick step she'd been sitting on when he'd arrived. "I think I rushed us, and I wish I hadn't."

He sat and used his bicep to wipe sweat from his forehead. His hair was drenched, his shirt sticking to his skin.

She took a seat beside him on the step, then bumped his shoulder with hers.

He aimed a look at her.

Coaxing mischief lit her eyes. Without words, she was daring him to lighten up. She bumped his shoulder again. He bumped her back.

"What did we not talk about yesterday that we should have?" she asked him.

"I have more questions about your accident."

That sobered her. "What would you like to know?"

He wanted to know everything. He asked her specific questions about how she'd capsized. What had gone through her mind while underwater. How much pain she'd been in. How she'd gotten free.

She answered every one in detail, and he absorbed each word, even though the scene she painted turned his chest into a cold, hollow void. Paddlers bigger and stronger than Britt had been pinned against strainers by water current until they'd drowned. If any piece of her situation had gone differently, she'd be dead.

The health flowing from her assured him that she was fine. She'd lived. But it had been a very close call. He couldn't stop thinking, *What if?* He couldn't quit visualizing the situation she'd been in and imagining all the ways it could have killed her. He couldn't stop picturing her lifeless body, pale and soaked.

He asked her about the helicopter ride that had carried her to the hospital and about her surgery. Her recovery. Her rehab. "What aftereffects do you have now?"

"Stiffness and sometimes soreness on that side of my waist. That's about it these days. It took quite a while to build up my stomach and lower back muscles, but I'm almost there now."

"Do your doctors think you should take it easy?"

"They did at first, but eventually they cleared me for strenuous exercise. The accident happened almost a year ago." A beat of quiet. "I felt like I had good reasons for not telling you, back when it happened. But after I was better, I should have told you. There's really no excuse. I should have said something about it much sooner."

"Even if you had good reasons for not telling me when it happened, you should have overruled them," he said levelly. "You should have told me right away."

"That would have been a horrible phone call to receive while you were in the middle of a trip overseas."

"Right. But I don't want you judging for me what is and what isn't too horrible for me to hear." He met her gaze. "Bad things and good things happen, and I want to know about all of them."

Her attention didn't flinch. "You're right. I screwed up, and I really am sorry. Do you forgive me?"

He nodded. "You'll tell me stuff from now on?"

"Yes. Will you tell me stuff?"

"Yes." Guilt stabbed him as he spoke the half-lie. He was angry at her for cutting him out, but he'd been cutting her out for years. He'd never told her how he felt about her. Like her, he had reasons that seemed good to him. Like her, he'd been judging what she could and couldn't hear. And even after giving her a hard time about her silence, he wasn't prepared to break his.

"What about our kiss?" she asked bluntly. "Do you want to discuss it more?"

Don't think about what kissing her felt like, he warned himself. *And whatever you do, don't look at her lips.* "No. You?"

"No. I mean, anytime you want to chat about it, I'm game. It's just that I don't really have anything else to add. Beyond what I said yesterday."

"Neither do I."

"It happened. And now I know that my friend Zander is a very good kisser." Her voice turned teasing. She hopped off the step and pulled her car keys from her pocket. "Which is useful information to know. I've been trying to set you up for years, but now I realize I was undervaluing your assets." She shot him a charming, lopsided smile.

"Were you?"

"I was. But no longer!" She sailed in the direction of the inn's small parking lot. "See you later."

"Yep." He watched her car until it disappeared from view.

The next afternoon, Nora told Willow and Britt about the series of books she'd purchased to read on her honeymoon, and Willow wondered aloud whether Nora would have time for reading on her honeymoon while Britt scanned the faces of the arriving international passengers at SeaTac airport.

Mom and Dad had spent the past two years serving as missionaries in Africa. Today they were coming home.

A family exited into the terminal after clearing customs. Not Mom and Dad.

A young couple exited. Not Mom and Dad.

"There they are!" Britt called.

Her sisters squealed, and they all moved forward en masse to give hugs. Britt, always the fastest sister, reached them first.

Her father, Garner Bradford, wrapped her in a bear hug. "Hi, sweetheart."

In response to the powerful reassurance and protection of his hug, tears pricked Britt's eyes. The degree of sturdiness in his arms hadn't changed. His bristly five o'clock shadow felt like it always had against her temple.

"Hi, Dad. Welcome home." She hadn't expected to get teary. She almost never got teary. Clearly, she'd needed a hug from her dad more than she'd realized.

Gloom had been hovering over her for the past two days since the kiss on the beach. Several times, she'd tried to pray. She wanted to trust God with the situation with Zander and experience peace as a result. But she'd had a hard time focusing her mind. She couldn't feel God's presence *at all*. So far, He'd answered her prayers with echoing silence.

Her sleep had been lousy and, at this point, her brain was exhausted from fretting over Zander. She'd done everything she could think of to set things right between them. Even so, their friendship was sputtering like a car with a glowing Check Engine light.

She didn't think he was being completely honest with her, and she wasn't being completely honest with him because yesterday, when they'd been sitting on the step and she'd looked into his eyes, she'd had to force her hands to stay down. They'd wanted to lift, tunnel into his hair, and pull his mouth to hers.

Had kissing Zander resulted in an instant addiction?

She embraced her mom, who smelled of her familiar crisp perfume. The bracelet Dad had given her during Britt's middle school years made its quiet jingling sound.

"I missed you," Mom said.

"I missed you, too." Britt took a step back to allow her sisters to complete their turns.

Garner and Kathleen Bradford were fifty-seven and fifty-five, respectively. They'd met almost thirty years ago at Bradford Shipping, shortly after her father inherited the company from his father. Her mom, who'd been working in the customer service department, had been full of plans for improving Bradford Shipping. Dad had moved her into an office near his and added her to a task force bent on saving the failing company. While pursuing their shared goals, her dad had fallen for the ambitious strawberry-blond beauty, and her mom had fallen for the green-eyed heir to the empire. The rest was history.

They'd loved each other in word and deed for decades now. The two of them were friends and allies, as well as spouses. Serving as a missionary was a dream Mom had hit upon when Britt and her sisters were little. It hadn't been Dad's dream, but because of their partnership, he'd entrusted the reins of Bradford Shipping to his managers in order to take Mom to Africa so she could live out something that had been important to her for so long.

Britt had only seen her parents twice in the past two years. They'd returned to Washington after her kayaking accident. Then they'd met up with the family a few months later in Switzerland for Willow's late summer wedding to Corbin.

Willow had decided on a destination wedding at a chalet complete with snow-crowned mountains and green pastures. Cows wearing bells around their necks had ambled through drifts of purple alpine flowers. During the entire trip, Britt had felt like a character in the children's book *Heidi*.

She'd taken stock of her parents on those other occasions, just like now.

Her mom wore her hair, which had mellowed to a pale nutmeg color, in a straight, shoulder-length cut. Couple that with her ivory complexion and passionate, persuasive personality, and most people were able to correctly deduce her Irish heritage.

Her dad's broad shoulders and square jaw proclaimed him to be the patient, steady one of the pair. The age lines marking his face and the gray streaking his thick, dark hair revealed his wisdom but did nothing to lessen his handsomeness.

They were both tanner and leaner than they'd been before they'd left for Africa. A deeper sense of calm emanated from them. When Britt had mentioned that sense of calm the last time she'd seen them, her dad had told her that serving in Africa had helped clarify what was important and what wasn't. He no longer saw the point in getting worked up over the unimportant.

"It's good to be home," Dad said, sentimental moisture gathering in his eyes. "Look at you three."

"Impressive, aren't we?" Britt asked.

"Very," Dad answered.

"I can't believe all that's happened since we left." Mom adjusted her carry-on so that it stood to her side like a short soldier. "Willow got married, and now Nora's getting married in a few weeks. Is there something in the water?"

"If so, it hasn't affected me," Britt said.

"Good," her dad joked. "That's how I like it. Stay away from boys."

"Grandma, Valentina, and Clint are all waiting at the house," Willow told them. "Valentina made borscht, so no one's going to go hungry tonight."

"Borscht," Dad said. He and Mom exchanged a laughing look. "Perfect." Valentina, their Russian nanny-turned-housekeeper, had been employed by their family since Willow was a baby. She'd been making the hearty Russian stew called borscht for so long now that it had become their unofficial family meal.

"John, Corbin, the extended family, and your friends are all champing at the bit to see you," Nora said. "We wanted to give you a little time to deal with jet lag before everyone descended on you, so we're thinking we'll cater fajitas and have a game night at John's house on Thursday."

"Sounds good," Dad said.

"Zander's still in town, right?" Mom asked Britt.

A thrill zipped through Britt at the mention of his name. "Right."

"Will he come to the game night?"

"I'm pretty sure he will, yes."

"Great," Mom said. "It's been way too long since I've seen him."

Phone call from Nora to Britt:

Nora: I've conducted some additional research into Ricardo Serra, and everything he told you about his wife checks out. They married two months ago, and as far as I can tell she's an upstanding person who is not at all involved in the underworld of antiquities theft. In fact, I'm looking at her LinkedIn profile now, and she's a commercial real-estate broker.

Britt: Huh.

Nora: I found an article about Ricardo that ran in a neighborhood magazine. According to that, he's owned and run restaurants for many years.

Britt: How many restaurants does he own?

Nora: A chain of four.

Britt: Are they successful?

Nora: As far as I can tell, they're very successful.

Britt: Interesting.

Nora: After I finished delving into his personal history, I delved into his criminal history.

Britt: And?

Nora: In addition to his two convictions, one for the crime he committed with Zander's uncle and one for the theft of the Ming figurines, he was arrested and charged one other time. In that case the charges were dropped, and he never went to trial.

Britt: What was he charged with? And when?

Nora: He and someone named Emerson Kelly were charged with stealing two Modigliani paintings from a private home on Whidbey Island in 1988. They were apprehended near the scene, but it seems that the police couldn't find any evidence to tie them to the crime.

Britt: Were the paintings recovered?

Nora: They were not. I hunted around to see if I could find out more about Emerson Kelly but couldn't. Which is strange. It's rare for me to turn up so little on a person. It seems Mr. Kelly is a bit of a ghost.

Britt: Well, if Mr. Kelly is a bit of a ghost, then my interest is officially piqued.

CHAPTER
Thirteen

Nikki says that she needs your help with Clint," Maddie told Britt the next day. "I'm sending her in with coffee."

"Copy that."

Maddie held open the swinging door that led to Sweet Art's shop.

Nikki entered, then said dramatically, "Ah, the inner sanctum of chocolate." The older woman paused, holding mugs in both hands, and surveyed the space with an appropriate air of reverence. "I've never been in here before."

"Welcome." Britt swept her arms apart grandly. "I'm always happy to lend romantic advice to earnest supplicants."

Nikki snorted. "You little pip-squeak. I don't need romantic advice from you. I'm twice your age—"

"Isn't it closer to three times?"

"—and I have more knowledge about men in my—my *eyelash* than you have in your whole body."

"I hereby kick you out of my inner sanctum for irreverence!"

"I'm not going anywhere. Maybe ever. The smell of chocolate is so thick in here that I think I might be able to get a buzz from it." Nikki set one of the mugs near Britt's elbow on the central island. "Here you are. A cappuccino."

"Thank you." While Nikki continued to look around, Britt plunged a raspberry pâtes de fruits center into tempered chocolate with a dipping fork. She tapped the fork, then scraped it along the bowl's edge so that the excess ran back down. Carefully, she placed the chocolate on parchment paper to set. "So if you have more knowledge of men in your eyelash than I do in my whole body, why do you need my help with Clint?"

"Because you know him better than I do." Nikki propped a generous hip against Britt's desk.

"Has he still not asked you out?"

"No, and I've now attended *four* Pilates classes."

"And I've called Clint once on your behalf to extol your virtues, don't forget."

"Right. And still. Nada. So now I'm in need of the most valuable commodity."

"Cacao beans?"

"Insider information. What's Clint's story?"

Britt moved another chocolate to the parchment, then picked up her mug and cradled it between her palms, smelling its fragrant steam. "I know he was raised in a farming community in central California and that he comes from a big family."

"Yes, he was the fourth of five kids. His parents remained married even though his father broke his mother's heart with repeated affairs."

"Oh. I didn't know that."

"I've already asked him all about his family and his career." Nikki waved a hand dismissively. "But I still know nothing about his romantic history, despite my attempts at prying."

"Clint is a fairly private person and he can be somewhat . . . self-conscious. He likes talking about things like karma and Native American spirituality. But he doesn't love to talk about himself."

"Listen, I adore that he's self-conscious."

"You do?" Britt certainly wasn't on the hunt for a self-conscious boyfriend.

"I do," Nikki said. "Clint's also a little naïve, which I find irresistible."

"He's sweet. Laid back."

"Both excellent qualities in a man. Especially one who's going to have to put up with me as his girlfriend."

Britt lifted one of the transfer sheets she custom ordered. Rows of stylized raspberries surrounded by tiny white polka dots created from colored cocoa butter marched across the sheet. She used her knife to cut out a raspberry design, then placed the piece of transfer paper atop a flat, hand-dipped chocolate. She depressed the top before pulling the sheet free. The raspberry and polka dot motif transferred.

"Those are gorgeous," Nikki exclaimed. "Can I have one?"

"You only like turtles."

"Gimme."

Britt handed one to Nikki and sampled another one herself. After letting the chocolate soften on her tongue, she chewed thoughtfully. The chocolate in this batch had a more nut-forward flavor than usual.

"Divine," Nikki stated.

"Is there life after turtles?"

"Maybe." Nikki chased the chocolate with a sip of her coffee. "So what's Clint's romantic story?"

"He's never been married, but beyond that I don't know much. I remember meeting a girlfriend of his at a family function once. But that was a long time ago, and I don't think he dated her long."

"Lifelong bachelors are an interesting breed." Nikki tapped a coral-painted fingernail against her mug. "What might have kept him from settling down?"

"I really don't know."

"Your next assignment is to find out," Nikki said.

"At the risk of sounding selfish, what's in it for me?"

"I'll use the Village's ad space in the *Merryweather Chronicle* to advertise Sweet Art. Instead of promoting the Village as a whole, we often try to highlight one of our fabulous vendors."

"Does Nora know that you're bribing me with advertising in exchange for a dating dossier on Clint Fletcher?"

"Nora likes to spread the love around. We give all of our vendors a turn in the sun. *When* they get their turn in the sun is completely at my discretion."

"In that case, you have a deal." Britt cut out more of the raspberries on the transfer sheet. "It occurs to me that I'm clueless about your romantic history, Nikki. Should Clint ask me, I'd like to be prepared."

"I've been married twice." Nikki reached for another chocolate, but Britt intercepted her with a shooing motion. "First," Nikki continued, "to Artie. Artie was a big, booming redneck, and I use the term *redneck* with absolute fondness. He loved Nascar, beer, and me. We married when I was twenty-three. Fifteen years later, he ran his truck into a tree after getting drunk at a friend's house watching football. No one else was injured, thank goodness."

"You knew that my friend Olivia was killed when she was hit by a drunk driver, didn't you?" Britt's group of female high school friends had been a circle of five—herself, Maddie, Olivia, Hannah, and Mia.

"I had heard that, yes. Drunk driving has taken someone from us both."

"It has."

"Such a rotten shame. When I think about how Artie died, I, very lovingly, call him a string of bad names."

A rotten shame was exactly how Britt would classify Olivia's death. Olivia had died almost three years ago, when she'd been in her mid-twenties.

Back when the accident had happened, Britt had achieved her degree at the Culinary Institute, completed her time in France, and returned to Merryweather to run Sweet Art. Construction on her cottage had just finished, and she'd moved in a few days before Mia had called early one morning to tell her the terrible news about Olivia.

She remembered sinking into one of her kitchen chairs as if

her bones had turned to water. Her heart thudded sickly, her vision resting on the moving boxes lined up against one wall of her living room, a testament to the exciting new beginning she was enjoying in her own life.

In fact, everything about her life in that season had felt like an exciting new beginning. Her career. Supporting herself. Adulthood. The world was full of trails to hike, mountains to climb, chocolates to make, and countries to visit.

The last thing she'd expected was the sudden and tragic death of a close friend. During the days before and after Olivia's funeral, she'd wrestled with God. If her perfectly healthy, young, happy friend could die one night while driving home from a restaurant dinner, then the same fate could happen to her or to anyone else she loved. And that *was not* okay with her.

Not at all.

Britt was a passionate person. The people she loved, she loved wholeheartedly. She knew that she couldn't have survived, the way Nikki had managed to, had it been her husband who'd driven a beeline into a tree. She couldn't have survived, the way her father had managed to, had it been her spouse who'd been murdered.

In the aftermath of Olivia's death, Maddie, Hannah, and Mia had all looked to her with shattered eyes. They'd needed her to have a spine of steel, and so, of course, that's exactly how she'd responded. She'd ensured that Maddie, Hannah, and Mia came through the trial as whole as possible. She'd thrown herself into her work, her romances, her activities.

She'd gone on.

When caught in the mud of difficult circumstances, she'd learned to keep trudging until her feet reached less muddy ground.

"My second husband's name was Sid," Nikki said. "He loved Roy Orbison songs, playing the trumpet, and me. He taught high school science, and he was one of those teachers that all the kids liked. Not too strict. Funny and creative. But he was a heavy smoker and had been all his life. I married him when I was forty-three. He died from lung cancer eight years later."

"I'm impressed that you continued to date after that."

"I've fallen in love with men before, between, and after my two husbands."

"And now you're ready to fall in love again."

"More than ready." Nikki drained her coffee. "I'm so much *more* than ready that even Evan at the post office is starting to look appealing to me."

Britt chuckled. "I like Evan. He has my back whenever I ship chocolate."

"He's much too young for me, and he smells like mustard, which is why I really need this thing with Clint to pan out."

"I'll do my best," Britt replied with bracing optimism.

On Thursday night, Britt arrived early to help prep John's house for the game night she and her sisters had planned in honor of their parents' homecoming.

The doorbell rang again and again as guests arrived in a steady stream. But so far, no Zander. He'd told Britt he'd come, so she kept one eye on John's foyer while mingling with familiar faces and topping off water glasses.

When Zander finally did slip quietly inside, she spotted him instantly. He stopped to talk with Willow and Corbin, which freed Britt to take his measure without his knowing.

He'd dressed up for the occasion in a white shirt with a navy-and-red striped tie and gray flat-front pants. Zander was the author of a novel that had already sold a mind-boggling number of copies. He had a photographic memory and plenty of money, especially for someone as young as he was. He'd seen far more of the world than she had. His face was sharply masculine. He held his athletic body with an alert brand of stillness, the lines of it fit and beautiful in the way that a cougar was fit and beautiful.

Even with all of that going for him, Nikki had been right when she'd commented to Britt that there was something tragic about Zander. There was. It was in the cautious, watchful impression he communicated. The solemn set of his shoulders. Also, the juxta-position between the color of his eyes—a joyous blue—and the seriousness peering out from behind them.

A yearning to bring him happiness twisted within her so sharply that it became a physical ache. From the first time she'd laid eyes on him, she'd felt compelled to lighten his load. At that time in her life, she'd been arrogant enough to imagine she could make that happen.

She was less arrogant about that now. Since his return to Merry-weather, she worried that she'd failed to bring him happiness. In fact, she feared she'd brought him unhappiness instead.

Britt's mom gave a yip of delight when she spotted Zander. Both her parents hurried toward him.

Britt approached more slowly. Stopping five yards away, she crossed her arms and observed their reunion with amusement.

Zander's gaze met Britt's as he hugged her mom. Then Mom beamed at him, placing her palms on the sides of his face. Dad hugged him, punctuating the gesture with affectionate thumps on the back. They stepped apart. Immediately, though, Dad pulled Zander in for a second hug.

When, at long last, her parents released him, Zander crossed to Britt. The two of them threaded through guests toward the fireplace at one end of the contemporary home's great room. On the way, Zander paused to shut a hallway door that stood half an inch ajar.

"When I met my parents at the airport, they didn't give *me* the palms on the cheeks or the hearty thumps on the back," Britt said.

"That's because you're just a daughter. They have more than enough of those."

"Maybe, but I'm the only daughter who's related by blood to both of them."

"A fact that you've never forgiven yourself for."

She let that statement pass like a speeding delivery truck empty of packages addressed to her. "Are you wearing a tie in order to suck up to my parents?"

"Pretty much. I knew your mom would like it."

"*I* like it. Yet you didn't wear a tie to my birthday party."

"Right. But then, you're just a daughter."

She laughed, and Zander regarded her with a deep fondness that made her mouth go dry. "I . . ." What had she intended to say? *You kissed me* was the only thing she could think of. He'd kissed her, and she'd kissed him back, and it had been amazing. That powerful knowledge hung between them so densely that it was hard to concentrate on anything other than the kiss when in his presence. "I haven't seen you in a couple of days. Did you get a lot of writing done?"

"Twenty pages."

"Very respectable. Did you spend time with your aunt?"

He dipped his head. "Carolyn and I went over paper work concerning Frank, his bank accounts, his will, and the rest of it."

Britt believed herself to be a fairly decent niece, but she wasn't in Zander's league. She was a doer, always happy to pitch in whenever her family members needed anything. Zander was good at that, too. But he was also good at *being there*, faithfully, dispensing sympathy as long as sympathy was needed. "Impressive," she said. "Catch up on sleep?"

"Yes."

"Go running?"

"Yes."

"Eat my competitor's chocolate?"

"No."

"Good. I saw the interview you did with the Seattle news station."

"Did I look like an idiot?"

"The opposite. You came across as whip-smart—"

"—and cold."

"Not cold," she corrected. "Thoughtful." And wildly handsome. She had no doubt that the station would be inundated with pink stationery addressed to him and that his book sales in the Seattle metropolitan area would spike.

Britt leaned her upper back against the shelves that framed

John's recessed TV. "Nora got back to me with the scoop on Ricardo."

"And?"

She filled Zander in on the discussion she'd had with Nora.

"She wasn't able to find out anything about Emerson Kelly?" he asked.

"Nothing. Which makes me wonder if Emerson might have gone to the trouble of removing his information from online databases. It seems a little suspicious, doesn't it? That Nora couldn't find *anything*?"

"A little. It could be that Emerson's just a private person."

"Or it could be that Emerson has something to hide." Britt mulled over the possibilities. "All we know about Emerson at the moment is that he was arrested on Whidbey Island in 1988 for stealing paintings alongside Ricardo, and that later, the charges were dropped. I say we try to dig up more information on him."

"Do you think Nora could help us locate the arrest record? For the crime on Whidbey Island in '88?"

"I don't know, but I'll definitely ask her."

She spotted Clint, Grandma, and Valentina coming their direction and beckoned them closer. This was as good a time as any to pump Clint for information on his romantic history. "Enjoying the party?"

"So far," Grandma answered. "But I've decided it would be best if I leave early."

Whenever Grandma went fishing for attention with statements like that one, Britt had learned not to bite.

"Why have you decided to leave early?" Zander asked, polite to a fault when it came to her grandmother.

"Because I know they're planning to play cards after the meal, and I don't approve of cards. Card games can quickly lead to gambling."

Valentina clucked consolingly. Her round face and plump body housed an unending supply of empathy. "Babbling not good." Despite having lived in America for decades, Valentina's grip on the English language could at best be described as loose.

191

"Gambling," Clint clarified for Valentina. "Like in Las Vegas."

"You want to go to Las Vegas, miss?" Valentina asked Grandma.

Grandma reared back, clutching her chest. "Certainly not."

"I enjoy trying my luck at the slot machines from time to time," Clint confessed.

"Oh my, *no*," Grandma replied in a scathing tone. "You should tithe that money, Clint."

"They have a lot of excellent shows in Vegas," Britt pointed out reasonably. "Sunshine. Museums."

"Shopping," Zander added. "Good hotels. Restaurants."

"I'm proud to say I'll *die* having never visited Las Vegas," Grandma announced.

Which was probably for the best. Both for Grandma's sake and the sake of the unsuspecting residents of Nevada's largest city.

"So, Clint." Britt spoke before Grandma had a chance to say more. "It struck me the other day that I don't know a lot about your personal life."

In response to her sudden shift in topic, Zander sent her an odd look.

"I've known you for quite a while now," Britt continued, "and so I feel badly that I haven't been more intentional about asking you questions, you know?"

"Sure." Clint nodded, which sent his long hair rippling. "I do. Intentionality is a really good, a really deep, practice for all of us to integrate into our daily lives."

"Scripture reading is a good practice for all of us to integrate into our daily lives," Grandma declared.

"I practice Jazzercise," Valentina stated.

"Good for you," Zander said to Valentina encouragingly.

Britt cleared her throat. "I remember meeting a girlfriend of yours a few years ago, Clint. Have there been other, ah, special women in your life?"

"Oh." Clint reddened. "Well . . ."

Britt waited, meeting his awkwardness with patience.

"No," he said. "Not very many."

"Why not?"

"I had my heart broken once," he said.

"I'm sorry to hear that."

"I'm sorry, too," Zander said. "Was it recent?"

"It was when I was eighteen." Clint gave a small shrug. "She was my first love. We'd planned to get married just as soon as I got a steady job in Hollywood. I'd barely been gone two months before she started dating someone else."

"I will make you *piroshkies*." Valentina's gaze brimmed with eager compassion. "They good for romance problems."

"And did you start dating someone else at that time?" Britt asked. "When you learned that your girlfriend had moved on?"

"No, no. I was crushed. I kept to myself for many years after that."

Britt blinked at him. His approach to dating differed in every way from her more-is-better approach. Then again, she'd never considered herself to be in love with any of the guys she'd gone out with. "And then what?"

"Finally," Clint said, "after she married for the third time and moved to New Zealand with her family, I decided that it might be time to date someone new. So I tried to. But still, to this day, I'm gun-shy." Clint shifted his weight from foot to foot. "None of my relationships have lasted very long."

"Hmm." Grandma sniffed. "Britt knows something about that."

"Maybe I need piroshkies," Britt said. If the fried buns stuffed with fillings cured issues of the heart, then Britt ought to place an order for a dozen.

"Same here," Zander murmured.

"Yes!" Valentina said. Pleasure tinted her cheeks pink in response to the sudden demand for her cooking. "They good for you."

"None for me, thank you very much." Grandma looked down her nose. "They trouble my hiatal hernia."

"At some point along the road," Clint confided in Britt, "I just figured it was too late . . . that I'd missed my chance at love."

"It's never too late for love," Britt said. "Look at Corbin. He spent years thinking that he'd blown his chance with Willow. Now they're married."

"I don't know. . . ." Uncertainty tweaked Clint's brow. "It might be better for me to work on my issues through meditation and self-actualization."

"Self-actualization," Grandma snapped. "Who cares if we know ourselves better? The point of life is to know God better."

"Love is in the air, Clint," Britt insisted. "You're interested in Nikki, right?"

His eyes softened. "I'm very interested. So much so that I'm preoccupied. I was thinking about her when I was cleaning the Marrowstone room at the inn yesterday and almost forgot to empty the trash cans."

"Excellent. Not about the trash cans," Britt clarified. "About your interest in Nikki. Good things are definitely coming your way on the romance front."

"Dance front?" Valentina asked. "I like ballet."

"Come along." Grandma led Clint and Valentina toward the kitchen, where fajitas would soon be served. "I'd like to get a spot near the front of the line."

"Love is in the air?" Zander asked Britt when the others had passed out of earshot. "What're you up to?"

"Nikki Clarkson has been hounding me about Clint. I told her I'd get the scoop on his love life."

"Do you really believe that it's never too late for love?"

"Sure. What I can't fathom is how Clint could have stayed true to his first love for the majority of his life."

"Huh," Zander said. "Imagine that."

An hour and a half later, the fajita dinner had been consumed by all, and the Bradford sisters were embroiled in a fierce game of Nertz. Each of them had a handsome man as their team member. Willow had Corbin. Nora had John. Britt had Zander. Their cousin Rachel and her boyfriend, plus one of Dad's coworkers and his wife also joined them. The remainder of the guests had chosen more sedate games in other areas of the house.

The Nertz group crouched over the breakfast table, barking out words, furiously flipping cards.

"Queen of spades!"

"Six of hearts! Who has six of hearts?"

"Jack of diamonds," Zander growled. "Anyone?"

Nora and John were losing, but what could you expect out of an academic and a man with impaired vision? John had inherited a rare genetic eye condition. Since he'd started dating Nora, his eyesight had deteriorated slightly; however, he was still able to drive and, for the most part, go about life without many accommodations.

Thanks to Britt's competitive streak, she often turned activities like yoga into contests. Even so, she and Zander were also losing.

Corbin was way too good for the rest of them. His speed and hand-eye coordination were the stuff of legends. Mere mortals could not hope to compete at Nertz against men who possessed Super Bowl rings.

"Nertz!" Willow called victoriously. Corbin spun her toward him for a kiss.

The rest of them groaned.

"Maybe we should draw names for new partners," Britt suggested.

"Hey," Zander said.

Playfulness glimmered in Corbin's brown eyes. "Can't take the humiliation of unceasing defeat?"

"I'm proud of the fact that I can't take the humiliation of unceasing defeat," Britt answered. "I'd be a doormat if I *could* take it."

"I'm keeping my wife as my partner," Corbin said. "Watching her play Nertz is the highlight of my week."

"Trivial Pursuit, anyone?" Nora suggested hopefully.

Zander's cell phone rang and he stepped away to answer. The rest of them took a break to stretch and grab drinks.

Britt had just downed a long sip of iced tea when Zander returned to her, looking shaken.

"What?" she prompted. "Who was it?"

"Carolyn. I asked her to go through Frank's things a while back. She's been working on their closet each evening, sorting and organizing."

"Okay."

"Frank kept all his shoes in their boxes, two deep, on shelves. Carolyn just opened one of the boxes, took out the shoes, and found a cell phone and charger underneath them." He gave her a eloquent look. "A cell phone Carolyn's never seen before."

Ah! Finally! A potential lead in their search for information on Frank. "What are we waiting for? Let's go."

"What about game night?"

"They won't mind if we leave. Corbin and Willow will still have several poor, unfortunate souls to beat up on." She went in search of her coat. "We're going to Carolyn's."

Actual number of pages Zander wrote since kissing Britt: None.

Time he spent helping Carolyn: Fifteen hours.

Actual quality of sleep: Tragic.

Running accomplished: Too much.

Food: Too little.

CHAPTER

Fourteen

"A re you all right?" Zander asked his aunt when she opened the door to admit them.

"I'm better now that you two are here."

When he embraced her, she held on to him for longer than usual. He stood, holding her fragile frame, allowing his stability to transfer to her until she was ready to step back.

The sound of dog paws against the hardwood floor drew Zander's attention. A chubby mutt trotted toward their position in the foyer on its short, stubby legs.

"Did you get a dog?" Zander asked.

"Yes. A dog," Carolyn answered. "I've been spending a good bit of time with friends lately. But whenever I'm here alone, I've been keeping the television on and playing music. You know, so it won't feel so solitary? None of that was helping enough." She resettled the brightly patterned scarf she wore in a loop around her neck. "I'm not usually a lonely person. In fact, I've always enjoyed time alone. But now that Frank . . . isn't coming back, whenever I'm alone here at the house it doesn't feel peaceful so much as oppressive."

"I get it," Britt said.

Though Zander suspected that Britt had never found solitude oppressive in her life.

"Sunny suggested I consider adopting a dog. I was feeling really blue earlier today, so I stopped by the animal shelter. They had a few cats but only one dog. Aurora here seemed to need someone to love her, and since the feeling was mutual, she came home with me."

Zander and Britt dropped to their haunches to greet the newcomer. "Aurora?" Zander asked.

"The people at the shelter gave her that nickname because, like Sleeping Beauty, she enjoys sleep."

Zander had never seen a dog with less in common with Sleeping Beauty. This mutt wasn't young or pretty. Her face was graying with age. Her nose was too pointy and too long for her body's proportions. Her ears drooped. Her fur grew unevenly. Aurora might have some corgi in her bloodline, though Zander suspected AKC corgis would have been disgusted by the prospect that Aurora could be their relative.

Britt scooped Aurora into her arms as they stood and asked Carolyn questions about the dog. She held Aurora confidently, rubbing beneath the dog's chin. Aurora half closed her eyes. Her rib cage expanded rhythmically.

Britt had on cargo pants, a V-neck black shirt, and gold oval earrings that sparkled against her neck. The dark mane of her hair framed her warrior princess face.

Each time he'd looked at her tonight, the sensory details of their kiss had flooded his mind. The warmth of her lips. The way she tasted. The lithe strength of her body.

She was determined and adventurous. She was a genius with chocolate. She was persistent, brave, and funny. She was loyal, and at the very core of her being, she was good.

He'd been introduced to plenty of women. Beautiful women. Impressive women. None of them had been as beautiful to him as she was. None had the mix of qualities she had that made her uniquely irresistible to him.

Could it be that no other woman had measured up to Britt

because he'd been young and shell-shocked and grasping for something to cling to when he'd fallen in love with her? Maybe the love that formed in you when you were a teenager was the most powerful love there was.

Except that no one else he knew had continued to love the girl they'd fallen for when they were fourteen.

If he hadn't met Britt until yesterday, he believed that he'd have fallen in love with her yesterday just as completely as he had all those years ago. His love for her stemmed from who she was. And who he was. And the alchemy between them.

"I took Aurora by the pet store and got all the necessary supplies," Carolyn was saying to Britt. "A bed, a leash. Bowls. Food."

Realizing that he'd been staring at Britt, Zander pulled his attention to his aunt.

"Once Aurora and I returned home," Carolyn said to him, "I decided to finish going through the closet."

"And you found a cell phone," Zander said.

Carolyn gave a subdued nod. "I couldn't believe it when I saw it." She met Britt's eyes. "I've been reorganizing Frank's side of the closet. I've found other items of his. Little notes. Spare change. A business card."

"Have you checked the cell phone yet?" Zander asked.

"No. To be honest, I'm afraid to. I'm not sure that I'm ready for another shock."

What would he do if he discovered something on Frank's hidden cell phone that would devastate Carolyn? She'd just said she wasn't ready for another shock and, frankly, he agreed. She wasn't. "Are you okay with me checking it?"

"Yes. I plugged the phone in. It's been charging in the home office."

Zander led the way into the small room at the front of the house. For a moment all three of them simply stared at the phone while Carolyn screwed her hands together into a nervous ball. The cell phone looked to be a few years old. No case. It lay there, proof of Frank's secrets.

199

"Would you like me to take Aurora?" Carolyn asked Britt.

"Actually, I'm enjoying holding her. She's lying in my arms like a warm sack of flour. It's comforting."

Zander gestured for Carolyn to take the desk chair as he powered on the cell phone. "It's passcode protected. It's asking for a four digit code."

Carolyn exhaled.

"What were Frank's usual passwords?" he asked.

"His birth year."

He tried it. Shook his head.

"Six three six three, the last four digits of his Social Security number."

He tried it, shook his head again.

"His debit card PIN number was zero two one one, his birthday and mine."

No.

After that, Carolyn had to work harder to come up with possibilities. Zander continued to enter each one, without success. "That's it for tonight," he eventually said. "The phone just froze me out."

"Will the phone allow you to try again?" Carolyn asked.

"I'll be able to try again in twenty-four hours."

"Okay, good. That'll give me time to brainstorm more passcode ideas."

Aurora snored quietly.

"Can you hack into the phone without a password?" Britt asked him.

"Not with the skills I have," he answered. "You?"

"Nope," Britt said. "I never did take up the hobby of hacking."

"I could wipe the phone, but then everything on it will be lost, which defeats the purpose." He lowered his brows as he considered Carolyn. "Uncle Frank must've been paying for this phone somehow. You never saw a charge on your family account?"

"No, and I would've noticed. Do . . . Do you think he had a bank account in his name that I don't know about?"

"Possibly."

"If so, no statements from that account ever came to the house," Carolyn said.

"He might have opted to go paperless with his banking," Zander said.

"In which case, he could have managed the account by logging in on a computer or with an app on his phone," Britt speculated.

"Which gives us even more motivation," Zander said, "to figure out this phone's code."

A week passed.

A week during which Britt continued to hope that her dangerous crush on Zander would scatter on the wind and blow away.

The two of them went hiking in Olympic National Park.

The Bradfords helped Nora transfer the bulk of her things to John's house so that she'd feel right at home when she moved in after the honeymoon.

Britt and Zander volunteered at Britt's church, providing childcare to one-year-olds. The job exhausted them both so much that they staggered to Britt's house afterward to chain-watch movies while making quips under their breath about the characters and plot in a bid to make the other one laugh.

Zander took Carolyn on a day trip to visit her daughters and help Courtney assemble her baby's nursery.

Zander brought his laptop to Britt's house one night, and they sat at her kitchen table, combing their computers for information about Emerson Kelly. They found nothing.

They visited the gym and powered through an interval workout on adjacent rowing machines that caused them both to pour sweat.

Every day, Carolyn and Zander tried—and failed—to crack the code on Frank's cell phone.

And through it all, Britt's crush on Zander remained.

It was as tenacious as a spring weed.

As strong as titanium.

"Did you ask Nora about tracking down Emerson and Ricardo's arrest record for the theft of the Modigliani paintings?" Zander asked Britt on a stormy Thursday night nine days before Nora and John's wedding.

"I did." She'd made Korean spare ribs, daikon, and chrysanthemum greens for their dinner. They'd recently finished eating, and she was handing him dishes so that he could expertly load them into her dishwasher. Zander took the pursuit of perfect dishwasher loading seriously.

"She was able to find the arrest record," she told him, "because they're public and because she understands how to request them in the right way and in the right places. The record's of no help to us, though. It only lists information we already know: Emerson and Ricardo's names, the date and place of the arrest, and the charge." Britt handed him the final two pieces of silverware and turned off the faucet.

He closed the dishwasher and straightened, a dish towel draped over one shoulder. He looked unreasonably appealing. Men who did dishes spoke her love language.

"What about the victim?" he asked. "Maybe the person who owned the stolen paintings would be willing to talk to us about the details of the case."

"You know what, Zander?" she said slowly. "That's actually sort of genius." She rushed to her computer, sliding a little in her socked feet. "I found an article the other night that talked about the theft, and I think it mentioned the owners by name." She brought up the website she'd bookmarked and skimmed the article. "There," she said triumphantly, pointing to the screen. "Grant and Callista Mayberry."

He smiled at her and, for the love of chocolate, desire zinged through her.

She called Nora while Zander scrubbed her counters and table. Within minutes, Nora produced a phone number for the Mayberrys.

"Do you want to call them or do you want me to?" Zander asked Britt.

"I'll do it. I'm less threatening and more charming."

Grant Mayberry—who sounded like a gregarious grandfather—responded to Britt's call as though she were a long-lost friend instead of a cold-calling stranger.

"My wife and I are in Europe at the moment," he told her, as casually as if he'd just said, *We're at the grocery store.* "We'll be back in five days. I'm looking at my phone calendar, and I see . . . yes . . . that I'm free a week from now. Do you and your friend want to make the trip out to Whidbey Island around four o'clock?"

"Yes! Absolutely."

"Wonderful!"

After a few more minutes of conversation, they disconnected. She extended her fist, and Zander bumped it.

"Congrats," he said.

"Congrats to you. You're the one who thought to call the victim." She padded to the living area and picked up the remote. "Movie?"

"Nah."

"More episodes of *Once Upon a Time*?"

"Actually . . ." He hooked his thumbs through his belt loops. "My flight to St. Louis is leaving pretty early tomorrow. I'm going to head back to the inn, pack, and get some sleep."

She tried not to look disappointed. It was precisely *because* she knew he was leaving for the weekend that she'd been looking forward to spending time with him tonight. "That sounds like a very responsible choice."

"I like to be responsible every now and then."

"Not me."

One dimple dug into his cheek. "I know."

Britt opened her front door for him, holding it steady as wind riffled the inky strands of Zander's hair.

Why are you leaving? You're acting weird. That's what she wanted to say and didn't. It no longer seemed advisable to say the first thing that came to mind. "I hope you have a great trip. Say hi to Daniel for me."

"I will." He looked down, frowned a little, then looked up. "Don't go kayaking alone while I'm gone."

Her lips rounded upward. "Okay."

The seconds spun out, each one elongating.

She said nothing.

He said nothing.

Finally, he gave her an extraordinarily stiff hug. The contact was as impersonal as if she were someone he'd never met who'd just handed him a congratulatory plaque at work.

He walked into the forbidding weather of a tumultuous night. Almost immediately, the darkness stole him from view.

She shut the door, groaned, then picked up a pillow and threw it irritably onto the floor. Another throw pillow. Hurl. Another. Fling.

She went to her kitchen and pulled a carton of Ben & Jerry's Salted Caramel Core from her freezer. She wasn't hungry for it, but at a time like this actual hunger for ice cream was irrelevant.

She sat on her sofa, but—*nope*—popped up within a few seconds. She carried the ice cream and spoon outside and sat on her front porch. The bad-tempered weather suited her better than the calm air indoors. Tucking her feet underneath her, she steadily spooned up bites of ice cream.

After kissing Zander on the beach, she'd been the one who'd given a speech aimed at convincing him that no harm had been done. She'd said some nonsensical thing about how they shouldn't give the kiss any more weight than playing football on the beach.

Well, harm *had* been done.

And here she was, two weeks later, still giving the kiss a tremendous amount of weight.

They'd been working hard to go through the motions of their friendship. Clearly, they were both determined to forge on and salvage what they could.

It wasn't working. Before that day on the beach, she'd feared that kissing him might wreck things.

And it had.

The time had come to face that depressing fact.

They were doing and saying the right things. But their friendship didn't *feel* right anymore. Awkwardness pervaded that which had never been awkward before. They were trapped in a painfully uncomfortable limbo and couldn't return to the way things had been.

She'd always seen Zander first and foremost as her friend. Now she saw him as a man. A man with an emotional topography buried within him that she'd yet to fully explore. A man with physical needs she hadn't acknowledged.

Maybe she should just confess her crush and tell him that she wanted to date him. He'd been the one who'd initiated their kiss, after all, which was promising. Her sisters might be right—a romance with Zander could lead them forward into something new and beautiful. Since they couldn't go backward, what did she have to lose?

Except . . . Her heart sank a little.

Her sisters were in love, and neither of them could be trusted to think like a normal, sane person.

She set the ice cream aside.

Zander hadn't said anything to her about wanting to date her either the day of their kiss or on any day since. He'd had numerous opportunities. So many! He hadn't taken any of them, which forced her to question whether he had feelings for her. And if he did, how strong those feelings truly were. Her pride would take a beating if she told him she wanted to date him and he said no thanks.

Also, her dating track record wasn't reassuring. If she'd had, say, one or two serious boyfriends in her past, then she'd have a reason to think that she could hold up her end of a long-term love. Instead, she was one of the most commitment-phobic people she knew.

Zander's heart wasn't easily given. But if he did give it to her, then she'd need to shoulder the huge responsibility that came with that. If she didn't shoulder it successfully, if she ended up trampling on his heart, then she'd lose him completely. His tendency to distance himself from people who hurt him was a hand-me-down from his childhood, a defensive tactic she couldn't blame him for.

Restlessness propelled her to her feet. She returned the remaining Ben & Jerry's to the freezer. Then she dumped her dish and spoon into the dishwasher, ruining the masterpiece of Zander's loading.

Anger throbbed in her temples, growing more insistent. She was angry with herself. And angry at Zander, too. He'd kissed her! *He'd* kissed *her*. A person shouldn't kiss someone unless they were able to tell that person they liked them. A person shouldn't kiss someone unless they were ready to deal with the issues a kiss might push to the surface. He hadn't told her he liked her! He wasn't ready to deal with the issues! If he had been, then maybe things wouldn't be so stupidly strained between them.

To add insult to injury, he was leaving and flying to Missouri, and she'd miss him. She was glad he'd carved out time for a visit with his brother. Still! This small separation was a precursor of the much longer separation that was looming when Zander returned to his Grand Tour. And all of it was making her feel like she was losing her mind.

Too agitated to sit, she began assembling ingredients from her kitchen cupboards.

She'd make chocolate.

Interested in a girl's night out? Hannah texted Britt, Maddie, and Mia two days later. *I'm in the mood to dress up, eat fancy food, then go to a club.*

Yes, please! Britt texted back. *I'm in.*

Maddie couldn't make it, she had plans with Leo. But, luckily, Mia was also game.

Hannah now lived in the town of Shelton. Mia, farther away in Kamilche. Since Shelton was the largest of the three towns and located in the middle, they decided to meet there and entrust the planning to Hannah, the most social among them.

Ordinarily, Britt's get-togethers with her high school friends were low-key. They'd cook together, then eat on the patio that jutted off the back of Mia's apartment and offered a view of the water. They'd go to a restaurant in downtown Merryweather, then walk to Maddie's place afterward for dessert.

Every once in a while, though, Hannah would get antsy and talk them all into a flashier night out. Ordinarily, Britt preferred their low-key gatherings. But this time? A flashy night out suited her perfectly.

Bring it on. Bring on the distractions of expensive food, laughter, and deafening music. She'd funnel all the edginess and dissatisfaction of the past weeks straight into her evening with Hannah and Mia.

She'd enjoy herself so much that she'd forget about her friend with the tattoos and the midnight blue eyes.

Music pounded the air inside the Dragonfly nightclub as ferociously as a boxer with a grudge. It smelled to Britt like beer, perfume, and anticipation. Looked like the inside of a kaleidoscope. And felt like a battle between the humid heat of dancing bodies and the building's industrial air-conditioning units.

After dinner, Britt, Hannah, and Mia had met up with Hannah's boyfriend, Kyle. Kyle had brought two of his friends with him. One was Reid, the guy who'd spilled his drink on Zander the night of her birthday party. Zander had hated him, a fact which made Reid more attractive this evening than he'd been before, thanks to her contrary state of mind.

Reid shouted conversation to her, and she shouted back. Britt learned that Reid played minor league baseball, was the eldest of four kids, and enjoyed skateboarding in his free time.

When her throat grew hoarse from the effort of talking, she tugged him onto the dance floor.

This was fabulous. Better than fabulous.

Reid seemed interested, which was gratifying because he was trendy, friendly, sporty, and impressively handsome.

Deliberately, she thought, *Isn't this fun? This is so much fun!* Adventure sports and chocolate making and travel weren't the only routes to pleasure.

She allowed Reid to buy her a glass of champagne. She wasn't much of a drinker, in large part because she wasn't much for relinquishing her self-control. But she and her girlfriends were enjoying a night out! She was young and healthy. She was wearing gray leather pants, a wildly colorful halter top, and earrings so long they brushed the upper tips of her shoulders. And all of this seemed to call for champagne. Just one glass.

Later, she checked her phone in the restroom and saw that Zander had sent her a second text. His first text had arrived in the midst of their Mexican cuisine meets American cuisine meets we're-fashionable-so-we're-going-to-charge-through-the-nose cuisine dinner.

He'd texted, *What are you up to tonight?*

She hadn't replied because she'd been a) a little miffed at him and yet b) hadn't wanted to upset him by telling him what she was up to.

This new text read, *Are you okay?*

He hadn't heard back from her, so he was following up. If she didn't respond, he'd worry.

Yes, she typed, *I'm at a club in Shelton with Hannah and Mia.*

Be safe, he messaged back.

Even here in the bathroom, music vibrated through the breathless female conversations. She tucked her phone into her back pocket and applied lipstick. *So much fun!* She didn't have to answer to anyone, and it felt fantastic to be so free.

Her phone buzzed.

Another text from Zander. *Who's the designated driver?*

Uber, she answered.

Will you text me when you get home to let me know you're there?

What was this? Three seconds ago she'd been thinking how wonderful it was not to have anyone to answer to. *You'll be asleep*, she typed.

Even so. Will you text me?
Sure.

She returned to her group of friends and proceeded to laugh at Reid's jokes. When he ordered her a second flute of champagne, she didn't protest. The champagne tasted amazingly delicious, and she was feeling clear-headed, so no worries on that front.

This was so much better than laughing at Zander's jokes while they watched TV. This is why she hadn't settled down. She could go out with her friends at a moment's notice. She could flirt with a cute guy she hardly knew. She could exercise her beloved independence.

The life she'd chosen was thrilling. Empowering!

Reid wore his sandy-colored hair long on top, the sides shaved into a fade. The style flattered his chiseled face.

She could predict how things would go between them. They'd text each other in the coming days and message on social media. He'd eventually invite her to join him somewhere for something, and they'd hit it off. She'd become infatuated with him and ride the giddiness of that for as long as it lasted. Then, two or four or six months from now, she'd grow bored. Her interest in Reid would deflate, and she'd ask him if they could just be friends.

She wouldn't gamble so much as one penny on the possibility that Reid might be her soul mate. No, indeed. No hope of that. Which meant that having him as a boyfriend wouldn't require her to risk her emotions or lay herself bare. All pleasure. No pain.

But not much depth, either.

She settled on a bar stool, then realized that it didn't have good mojo. "Will you switch stools with me?"

"What? Why?"

"Just switch." If she'd asked Zander to switch stools with her, he wouldn't have had to ask why.

She hooked a high heel over the rung of her new stool—better mojo—and crossed her legs.

Reid picked up one of her hands and, idly, tested the firmness of her fingertips. Then he traced circles around her knuckles with a touch so light it almost tickled. Very smoothly done. Not only did the contact between them deliver a melody of delightful sensations, it also increased the intimacy between them without a creepy factor.

She waited to feel a rush of affection for Reid. He'd earned it! Deserved it.

The rush of affection didn't come. She couldn't dredge up any feelings for him stronger than indifference.

Maybe she'd grown weary of her predictable dating cycle. Maybe her devotion to Zander had grown too big to allow room for—

She wasn't going to think about Zander tonight.

Why was having fun such hard work? She was exhausted from the exertion of it.

But she wasn't a quitter.

She gave Reid a dogged grin.

"Another glass of champagne?" he asked.

"Absolutely." Her earlier clear-headedness had dissipated. She hadn't planned to get tipsy, but now that she was . . . Wow. She remembered how fantastic it felt. Self-control was perhaps ever so slightly overrated.

Her surroundings, along with her concerns, were losing their hard edges. Everything was *fine*. Nothing to worry about. Not Zander—whom she wasn't going to think about. Not the peppermint truffle. Not Frank's mysterious past. Not the big order she needed to tackle Monday morning at Sweet Art.

She worked really hard to be the best chocolatier, friend, daughter, and sister she could be. She wasn't a burden to anyone, financially or emotionally. She took care of her business, and she helped others. She had her life together. People like her, people who had their lives together, were entitled to let their hair down every once in a while. Right?

Text messages written by Zander and deleted before sending:

Zander
Are you home yet? It's midnight.

Zander
It's 12:30 a.m. and I know you wouldn't want me to
worry and that I shouldn't worry, but I am worried. So
let me know that you're all right, please.

Zander
I'm sorry if kissing you ruined everything between us.

Zander
Your face is the face I want to see when I open my eyes
every morning. You're my sun and moon and stars. You
give my life heat and meaning and you also make me
sick with anxiety because you're not home yet and you
could be hurt or you could be drunk or you could be
making out with someone who's not me.

Zander
Home yet? It's 1:00 in the morning. There's no way I
can sleep until I know you're safe.

Zander
Did you forget to text me when you arrived home?

Zander
I love you. I've always loved you.

· · · · · · · 🎀 · · · · · · ·

Text message from Britt to Zander:

Britt
I'm home.

Zander
Cool. Thanks.

211

CHAPTER
Fifteen

The afternoon of Zander's return to Merryweather, Britt opened the door of her cottage to find him standing on the threshold. He looked tough and proficient in his lightweight hiking pants and Patagonia fleece pullover. The disordered state of his almost-black hair attested to his disdain of primping. His gaze spoke of his constancy.

At the sight of him, she curbed two urges simultaneously. The urge to punch him. And the urge to throw herself into his arms. "Hey," she said.

"Hey."

"Welcome home." She scooped up her hiking backpack and locked the front door behind her. "Did you have a good visit with Daniel?"

"I did."

"Excellent."

They talked about his trip to St. Louis on the way to the mountain to go rock-climbing.

It would be great if she could enjoy their outing by dodging this unceasing troubled tangle of reactions toward Zander. It would be great if she could transition away from the stress of today's work hours. She'd made another batch of peppermint truffles and failed at mastering the recipe yet again.

He slipped on a pair of classic brown sunglasses that would have looked right at home on Cary Grant. Desire tightened within her. The air inside the car thickened. This was *exactly* the response she'd wanted to have for Reid.

She contemplated the serious way Zander held his jaw. Noted the play of muscles running up his neck.

She'd known him very well for years upon years! How was it possible to see someone she'd known so long in a whole new light?

The familiar scents of chocolate and coffee greeted Zander when he entered Sweet Art the following afternoon.

Three female customers sat together to one side of the room, talking. Maddie was thanking another customer as she passed over a bag printed with the shop's logo.

He scanned the display case as he approached. The chocolates within gleamed. Truffles in various flavors, each topped with a unique crown—fondant, sprinkles, sea salt, sugar crystals, and more. Chocolate bark. Chocolate turtles. Hand-dipped chocolates. Molded chocolates. Fanciful chocolates. No-nonsense chocolates. Nutty chocolate. Fruity chocolate. Milk chocolate, dark chocolate, white chocolate.

When he'd been young, his taste for desserts had run toward Starbursts and Twizzlers. Later, when Britt had first developed a passion for chocolate, he'd done what he'd always done when he'd found himself in a position of ignorance in his life—he'd gone to the library, checked out every book on the subject, and committed them all to memory.

His ability to recall what he read had been the saving grace of his childhood. Books had evened his playing field for as long as he could remember. And so at first he'd studied chocolate the way he'd have studied chemistry. He'd had no personal interest in it. He'd simply been driven to learn what he could for Britt's sake.

However, during his cooking sessions with Britt, he'd comprehended more about chocolate than books had the power to teach. He'd felt the texture of it against the roof of his mouth. He'd watched Britt's whisk stirring shiny, dark brown, molten chocolate against the sides of a glass bowl. He'd heard the crunch when she'd ground down vanilla beans and sugar using a mortar and pestle.

Along the way, he'd educated his palate for chocolate the way sommeliers educated their palates for wine. He understood the chocolate-making process. He'd taught himself to differentiate the flavors of the world's three different types of cacao beans: Criollo, Forastero, Trinitario.

He'd come to love chocolate. And, since the day Britt had opened Sweet Art, he'd felt at home inside these walls. He couldn't separate Britt from chocolate or from Sweet Art. His feelings for the latter two were knotted up with his feelings for her.

"Zander," Maddie said warmly in greeting.

"Hi, Maddie."

"Britt made an emergency run to purchase forty-percent heavy cream but she said to tell you, if you arrived before her, that she'd be right back."

He and Britt were scheduled to pilot the Bradford family speedboat to Whidbey Island this afternoon to meet and talk with Grant Mayberry.

"Can a shortage of forty-percent heavy cream be considered an emergency?" he asked.

"You know Britt well enough to know the answer to that." Maddie crossed her arms. Her green eyes sized him up. "So."

"Yes?"

"What's going on with Britt lately?"

He grew instantly alert. "What do you mean?"

"She's been acting really strange for a little over two weeks now."

"How so?"

"Grumpy. Impatient."

He'd kissed Britt a little over two weeks ago.

"Do you know what might be causing this?" she asked.

"I don't."

"You don't? Or you do but you don't want to tell me?"

"I have a suspicion, but I don't want to tell you."

"Zander!"

He shrugged by way of an apology.

"Britt won't confide in me, either. I tried to get it out of her again this past Saturday, but I couldn't. And then she went out dancing with Hannah and Mia that night, and they said that Kyle's friend Reid was falling all over her."

Everything inside him turned to ice. When Britt had sent him a text Saturday night saying she was at a club, he'd known what effect she'd have on the men there. He'd worried that she'd meet someone, but it hadn't occurred to him to worry about Reid in particular. "And?" he asked tightly.

"And Hannah told me that Britt had too much champagne. Apparently, she was acting like she was determined to have a great time even if it killed her. Then Britt and Reid left the club together to go have late-night pancakes at a diner. Hannah and Mia tried to talk her into sharing an Uber home with them, like they'd planned, but Britt went to the diner instead."

He kept his face impassive. "In Reid's car?"

Maddie dipped her chin in assent.

"I'll talk to her about it."

Her look turned compassionate. "Want a chocolate?"

"No. Thank you." He was amazed that his voice sounded smooth and calm because inside him, a tornado raged.

An elderly gentleman entered the shop, and Maddie went to assist him.

Zander had gone to St. Louis to spend time with his brother because now that Frank was gone, only Daniel, Carolyn, Britt, and Britt's family knew him well and cared about him deeply. Daniel's presence grounded him and gave him a sense of belonging. He only wished he could have enjoyed his weekend with his brother more than he had.

On the flight to Missouri to see Daniel, he'd hoped that the distance from Britt might offer him perspective on their relationship. In actuality, the distance from Britt had done nothing but make him miserable. He'd spent large sections of the weekend wondering what he was doing halfway across the country from Britt.

If Britt decided to date Reid, the misery he'd endured in St. Louis would seem like a trip to Disney World in comparison.

The door to the kitchen rushed open, and Britt crossed to him. She had on a plaid shirt, jeans, boots. "Sorry I'm late."

"No problem."

They climbed into his Jeep, and he pointed them toward Bradfordwood, where'd they unmoor the family boat from the family dock, then begin their trip to Whidbey.

Less than two minutes and zero words passed before Britt said, "You're angry."

He frowned. He *was* angry. At the same time, he wasn't sure he had a right to be.

"Why're you angry?" she asked.

"I heard what happened Saturday night." He hated to experience fear or fury or possessiveness individually. The thought of her with Reid caused all three to crush down on him at once.

"Saturday night? When Hannah and Mia and I went out?"

He held his tongue.

"Who told you about that?" She paused. "Maddie?"

The best defense was a good offense. "Maddie's concerned about you. She says that you've been acting strangely lately, but that you won't talk to her about what's bothering you. Why won't you?" He cut a glance across the car.

She set her lips together and directed her attention out the side window. His question had shut her up, and he knew why.

She'd been acting strange because of their kiss or his reaction to it or her reaction to it or both. She hadn't told Maddie about the kiss because she wanted to keep it private. No doubt Britt anticipated that news of their kiss would drop like a bomb on Maddie, Hannah, Mia, and her sisters. He was willing to bet they'd all be happy. Still. They'd respond with lots of questions and opinions. Britt likely didn't have the patience to deal with that sort of fallout.

They traveled the rest of the way to Bradfordwood in silence. Britt tapped a button on her phone app to open the enormous ironwork entrance gates. Once they'd parked beside the garage, they skirted around the side of the brick mansion and began walking down the long lawn that led from the terrace to the Hood Canal far below.

"I went to dinner with Hannah and Mia on Saturday night." Britt's attention remained trained on the water as she spoke. Irritation lined her forehead. "Then we went to a club, just like I told you. Reid was there, and he and I went out for food afterward. I don't see why any of that should upset you, Zander."

"You know why I'm upset."

"Enlighten me."

"Because you got into a car with a guy you hardly know."

"I know Reid way better than some of the guys my friends have set me up with on blind dates."

"And that's supposed to put my mind at ease?"

"He's my friend's boyfriend's friend!"

"And you should always trust a friend's boyfriend's friend? How long has Kyle known Reid?"

She hesitated. "I don't know. Long enough."

"How much did Reid have to drink at the club?"

"One beer."

He gave a grunt of disbelief.

"He had one beer, Zander. He had baseball practice the next morning, so he was taking it easy."

"Reid threw back shot after shot at your birthday party."

"He didn't have any shots on Saturday night."

"Not that you saw, anyway." He *hated* that Britt was taking Reid's side against him. "You told your friends he was taking you to a diner for pancakes. Is that where he took you?"

"You're really well informed," she said dryly, voice brittle. "Yes. That's where he took me."

"And how did you get home from there?"

"Reid drove me."

"Swerving all the way?"

"No. One beer!"

"How much did you have to drink?"

"No comment."

They reached the dock, and she turned to him. When riled, she looked more like a warrior princess than at any other time. Fearfully beautiful. Spoiling for a fight.

He stared her down from his greater height, tension contracting every tendon in his frame. "Are you going to try to tell me that it's reasonable to drink too much champagne, then decide to go home with someone—"

"I didn't *go home* with him. I went to a diner with him for pancakes. Then he drove me home."

"So it's reasonable to drink too much, then let someone you don't know well drive you home?"

"Ordinarily, no. Ordinarily, it's better to stick to the plan you made with your girlfriends when you were sober. It wasn't smart of me to change my plans after I'd been drinking, I'll give you that. But this time everything worked out just fine. Reid is Kyle's friend. He had one beer. And he brought me home safely."

"And when he brought you home? Did you invite him in?" Even as the words left his mouth, Zander knew he shouldn't be speaking them.

She gave him a look of surprise, then her brows knitted thunderously.

He'd offended her with his question.

"No, Zander." She spoke with steely control. "*Of course* I didn't invite him in. Not that that's any of your business."

"It is my business because I don't want any harm to come to you," he said.

She held her chin at a mutinous angle. "I'm twenty-seven. No one's responsible for ensuring that no harm comes to me, except me."

"Fine," he gritted out.

"Good," she said in a tone that broadcasted NOT GOOD in neon letters.

She bent and began jerking free the line securing the speedboat's bow. He unwound the one at its aft.

Her carelessness with her safety made him *crazy*. He couldn't stand the risks she took—

Really? His conscience pricked him. Was that what this was about? The risks she took? Or was he angry because of a far less honorable reason?

Jealousy.

He tried to think like a rational, not-jealous person. Would a rational, not-jealous person have flown off the handle in this same situation?

To his shame, he suspected not.

She'd already admitted that it hadn't been smart to change her plans after she'd been drinking. Which was true. It hadn't been smart. But if her safety really was his motivator, then their discussion would have been far more effective at inspiring her to take more care with herself if he hadn't delivered it with so much righteous indignation. If he hadn't made her mad in the process.

The thought of her with Reid had rattled him so much that he'd lost his cool and his logic. He'd cast himself in the role of Britt's boring, holier-than-thou friend who was determined to point out her mistakes to her.

If this were a movie, she'd be the daring, fun-loving, adventurous character.

He'd be the wet blanket character nobody liked.

She jumped on board the boat, and he followed. Usually when they went out together in a car or on one of the Bradford family's boats, he drove. She preferred to ride shotgun so that she could check her phone or her trail map or her guidebook. This time, though, she lowered into the driver's seat.

Clearly, she was so irritated with him that she didn't want to give him any control.

Grinding his teeth, he took the seat beside hers. She fished the keys from their compartment and tugged on a baseball cap. Within minutes, they were speeding along the surface of the canal on their course north to Whidbey Island.

She was driving faster than necessary and people were liable to report her. He didn't say anything to her about it because he didn't want to be a wet blanket.

It would take them over an hour to reach the town of Clinton on the island's southeastern tip, which was for the best. Even though he knew he'd overreacted and might not have a right to feel animosity toward her, animosity continued to churn within him anyway. He needed time to calm down and adjust to the thought of Reid "falling all over her" at a club, Reid taking her to a diner, Reid driving her home. And Britt, letting him.

What, exactly, did she feel for Reid? She hadn't said.

Had the trip to the diner been a romantic one? Were she and Reid going to start dating now?

Betrayal burned up his esophagus like acid because, just a few days ago, she'd kissed *him* on a beach.

Then she'd said they were friends who wouldn't kiss again. And he'd let his silence become agreement.

Zander grimaced and resisted the urge to look in Britt's direction.

If he looked at her, he'd be powerless to stop himself from wanting her.

Even if she'd been swooning over Reid and even if she'd imbibed twice as much champagne, Britt would not have invited Reid into her house at one fifteen a.m.

Zander should know that. Zander *did* know that. So what was his excuse for insulting her with such a stupid question?

She didn't invite men into her home the first time she went out with them. Or even the second or the third time. Not even when she really wanted to. She hadn't wanted to invite Reid in. After he'd dropped her off, she'd spent no time daydreaming about him or hoping he'd contact her. None.

However, Murphy's Law dictated that the men you weren't interested in were always the most interested in you. This principle had held true with Reid, who'd been communicating with her steadily since Saturday night.

Reid was into her. And if only she felt the same way about him, things would be so much nicer and simpler. Instead, she was hung up on the man sitting next to her, who was staring at the shoreline as if his life depended on it.

She steered the boat, willing the wind to flush away her annoyance. The wheel beneath her hands held the warmth of the sun. Strands of her hair escaped her cap and whisked against her neck and cheeks.

She'd never been good at receiving criticism.

Once, when she'd been in the third grade, Mom had asked Nora to check Britt's math homework. When Britt had seen that Nora had marked the majority of the problems wrong, Britt had torn the math worksheet into ribbons, stormed from the house, and ridden her bike up and down Bradfordwood's drive at a blistering pace until she'd exhausted herself. To this day, when she was having a bad day, one of her family members was liable to joke, *What's the matter? Did someone make you multiply two-digit numbers?*

When Zander had told her that he knew what had happened Saturday night, the same defiance that had possessed her in response to her third-grade math homework had sparked within her. Her defenses all jumped to their feet, armor on, swords drawn. How dare he judge her? What right did he have to give her that condemning, disappointed look?

These days, when someone or something prodded the Irish temper she'd inherited from her mother, Britt typically responded well. She stayed silent and thought through the issue until she could reply civilly.

Back in third grade, she'd been wrong. Her solutions to the

math problems had literally been *wrong*, and no amount of bike riding and offended passion had changed that fact.

She strove for objectivity as she performed a mental postmortem on the argument she'd just had with Zander.

In her opinion, it really was okay to get pancakes with a friend's boyfriend's friend. She'd known Hannah's boyfriend, Kyle, for six months. She'd spent a good deal of time with Reid at her birthday party and more time with him at the club. Zander's hyper-concern about Reid's trustworthiness? Unfair. The implication that she'd gone home with Reid after pancakes? Unfair. They were just going to have to agree to disagree on those points.

Zander's concern over the decisions she'd made at the club? Fair. Maddening, but fair.

Very few people in her life had the nerve to call her out when she blew it. Zander had the nerve.

She didn't want to be the type of person who went through life insisting that her multiplication problems and her drunken choices were right, when they weren't.

It's just that . . . she *loathed* being called out. It was embarrassing. And when Zander was the one to call her out, she couldn't help but feel that she'd let him down. Which, in turn, made her fear that he'd think less of her.

No doubt, when she stopped being miffed at him, she'd be grateful to him for his forthrightness.

But she wasn't there yet. Not by a long shot.

As of right now, she was still miffed.

Once they secured the boat in Clinton's harbor, Britt sent Grant Mayberry a text to let him know they'd arrived. During her recent conversation with Grant to finalize the details of their visit, he'd insisted—*it's no trouble!*—that he'd pick them up in his car.

She tossed her ball cap into the boat, then finger-combed her hair as she and Zander walked side by side past historic buildings painted a crisp nautical white.

The Bradford family often took day trips to Orcas, Vashon, Blakely, and the rest of the nearby islands. She knew that Whidbey's one hundred and sixty-eight square miles hosted a population of more than fifty thousand spread across a smattering of towns.

Luxury homes had been tucked into the hills near Clinton to take advantage of the quieter pace of life, the separation from the mainland, and the unflagging views of Possession Sound to the west.

It made sense that Ricardo and Emerson would have tried to rob someone who lived in this sleepy place. Whidbey's police department didn't have the numbers or the ferocity of a big city force.

Britt shaded her eyes and catalogued the details of the land swelling upward from the parking lot where they waited. Clinton reminded her of a folk art painting depicting a town planted into a wooded hillside.

A royal blue convertible Mini Cooper, top down, came to an adroit stop before them. "Ms. Bradford?" the driver asked. He looked to be in his mid-seventies. His sun-reddened cheeks were set into a friendly, rectangular face topped by gray-brown hair. He'd clothed his husky body in a sweat shirt proclaiming USC across the front.

"Mr. Mayberry?"

"One and the same. Jump in!"

Zander held the door for her, and Britt slid into the back row. Before she could attempt to fasten her seatbelt, they were zooming along the road and Grant was asking cheerful questions.

She and Zander had prepared for today's meeting by researching Grant Mayberry. They'd learned that he'd founded a renewable energy company when he was young. Right from the start, his company had scaled a staircase of greater and greater success.

Grant certainly didn't appear to have been jaded by his wealth. He seemed like an extrovert who genuinely liked people.

In less than ten minutes, they reached their destination. Grant kept up a steady stream of conversation as he led them through his extremely impressive contemporary residence. The faces captured in his extensive collection of art watched them pass.

In the kitchen, he pressed glasses of lemonade into their hands. Then he ushered them to the deck. They settled onto spotless outdoor furniture positioned next to urns bursting with succulents. From this spot, Britt couldn't glimpse a single neighbor. Trees flanked them on both sides. Before them, azure water gave way to islands, which gave way to distant, snow-capped mountains.

"Thank you very much for seeing us, Mr. Mayberry," Britt said.

"Please, call me Grant."

"It was amazingly kind of you to invite us into your home, Grant," Britt said.

"Of course! It really is my pleasure." He crossed a foot over the opposing knee. "You told me a little over the phone, but why don't you start at the beginning so I know how to help you?"

"Sure," Britt answered. On the verge of pouring out all the details, she caught herself and motioned for Zander to explain. She'd come to feel very proprietary over the mystery surrounding Frank, but this mystery did not, technically, belong to her.

Zander told Grant how they'd learned of Frank's connection to Ricardo. "When we couldn't find any more information on Frank, we began collecting information on Ricardo. We found out on our own that he had been arrested here on Whidbey Island along with someone named Emerson Kelly for stealing two of your paintings by Modigliani."

"I see."

"We're hoping that researching Ricardo might lead us to a clue about Frank," Zander said.

"I'm glad to share what I know about the robbery with you." Grant flicked a few fingers in the direction of Seattle. "My wife is spending the day with our daughter and grandsons. She doesn't like to be reminded of the robbery. It's a frustrating topic for her because the paintings were never found. She'd acquired those Modigliani pieces herself, you see, at an auction. She's the art lover." A fond smile flashed across his mouth. "I've never developed an eye for it, even after all these years. As far as I'm concerned, one painting is about as good as another and none of them are irreplaceable. There's always more art in the world to purchase."

Sea gulls rode by on the breeze.

"What happened the night your paintings were stolen?" Zander asked.

"Callista and I were at a function in the city. It had been pub-licized that we'd be there because we were donating something to . . ." He ran his hand down his chin. "Someone." A good-natured chuckle tumbled from him. "Isn't that funny? I can't even remember who we were donating to now."

"No problem," Britt said. "It was a long time ago."

"I do know that it occurred to me later that the thieves almost certainly knew we were going to be away from home that night. They broke in by cutting the lines to the security system and picking the lock on the back door. They would have gotten away cleanly except that the neighbor who used to live down the road had a habit of taking his dog out for late-night walks. He saw what looked like flashlight beams inside our house and called the police."

Grant took a swig of lemonade. "By the time the police ar-rived, the robbers had left the house. One of the police officers turned on the floodlights outside and spotted two figures running in the direction of the water. The officers pursued them and were able to overtake them before they could get away in the boat they had waiting. The officers arrested them and took them to the station."

"Why were the charges eventually dropped?" Zander asked.

Grant extended one of his arms along the back of the settee. "They were dropped because the police couldn't find the paint-ings. Or Ricardo or Emerson's fingerprints inside the house, even. They figured that the robbers must have stashed the art outdoors, so they searched the boat, the land, everything. Even Callista and I hunted and hunted for those Modiglianis. We tramped around here for some time like Indiana Jones. But no luck." His wide shoulders lifted.

"What did Ricardo and Emerson tell the police they'd been doing on your property?" Zander asked.

"They said they'd been trying to find a public park, and they'd simply gotten turned around."

"I'm sorry that you lost those paintings," Britt told him honestly.

"Aw, it's all right. Like I said, they were replaceable. Callista would probably disagree with me on that, but there's no use crying over spilled milk, right? I have plenty to be thankful for." He levered himself up. "I kept everything about the robbery in a file. Earlier today, I went and found it for you. Let me grab it."

He vanished inside his house.

The silence between Britt and Zander twisted into convoluted knots in Grant's absence. Zander was sitting a foot and a half away from her on the same piece of furniture, but the distance felt like a football field.

Grief lifted within her, and she swallowed against it. She missed what they'd had.

Grant returned and set the file on the coffee table before them. "Help yourselves." He relaxed into the position he'd vacated.

Zander opened the file. Britt scooted in and leaned forward, taking care not to move so close that she'd inadvertently touch him. The page on top contained a mug shot of Ricardo and information about the arrest. The face in the photograph clearly belonged to the man they'd met, minus thirty years of wear and tear.

"Done?" Zander asked, when he'd finished reading the sheet. His brain had just recorded a mental photo of the page, and he'd still completed his reading faster.

"Done."

He flipped to the next sheet.

Britt inhaled sharply.

The mug shot revealed a young and beautiful woman with piercing, deep-set eyes. She wore her platinum hair in a short, layered pixie cut. She had flawless skin. A long and graceful neck.

Beneath the image was her name.

Emerson Kelly.

Britt glanced at Grant. "Emerson's a woman?"

"Oh yes. I'm sorry. I thought you knew."

She shook her head, her thoughts careening like bingo circles in a tumbler cage. Had any of the data on Emerson informed them that she was male?

She thought back. No.

She must have simply jumped to the conclusion that Ricardo's accomplice was male. Why? Because Emerson sounded like a man's name? Because she'd subconsciously reached the conclusion that a man was more likely to pull off a heist than a woman? Britt! Those were dumb assumptions.

"I know her," Zander said.

Britt swung her chin toward him.

He kept his focus on the page. "She's Carolyn's friend."

"She is?"

"She came into The Giftery a few weeks back when I was there. Carolyn introduced her as . . . Sunny, I think. She was wearing her hair the same way."

Britt's heartbeat thrummed. "How can we explain the fact that Emerson—the woman who was arrested here alongside Ricardo long ago—is now Carolyn's friend? What logical explanation could there be?"

"Frank had ties to Ricardo. Ricardo had ties to Emerson. And now we know that Emerson has ties to Carolyn, which means that Emerson likely had ties to Frank. Three thieves, connected."

"Three thieves pulled off the Triple Play," Britt said. The Pascal's security guard had never said he believed all three robbers to be male. He'd been too far away to see any of the three clearly, and they'd been wearing masks. "We've speculated in the past that Frank and Ricardo could have been two of the Triple Play robbers," she said. "But now it's possible that we've found all three."

"If Emerson met Frank and Ricardo in Washington in the spring or summer of 1984, then she may have been friends with Frank and

227

Carolyn ever since," Zander said. "That would explain Emerson's current presence in Carolyn's life."

Too energized to sit still, Britt edged to the front of her seat cushion. "But Carolyn said she'd never heard of or met Ricardo. Is it plausible to think that Frank would have cut Ricardo out of his family life but included Emerson in it?"

"I don't know."

"Do you ever remember meeting Emerson in the years when you lived at Frank and Carolyn's house?" she asked.

"No."

"Which seems to suggest that Sunny and Carolyn became friends recently."

"If the two women became friends recently, then their friendship can't be a coincidence."

"No," Britt said at once. "There's no way that the woman who stole Grant's paintings alongside Frank's friend Ricardo could coincidentally appear in Frank's wife's life years later."

"Which means that Sunny had a reason for befriending Carolyn. She inserted herself into Carolyn's life on purpose."

"Because of the Triple Play, I'd guess."

"And potentially," Zander said, "Frank's death."

"My!" Grant said heartily.

Britt started. She'd forgotten he was there.

"This is all very exciting," the older man said.

Was it too late to swap out Grandma for Grant? She'd love to have him for a grandparent.

"I need to call Carolyn and warn her about Sunny." Zander reached for his cell phone.

"And tomorrow we need to have a talk with Emerson."

"Go get 'em!" Grant clapped. "And be sure to let me know if you happen to cross paths with Callista's Modiglianis."

Zander's journal entry, one year ago:

I've traveled all over the world searching for things. Freedom. Experiences I can collect like shells from a beach. Culture. History. Learning. Writing inspiration.

The more I search the world, the more certain I am that the person I love the most is right where I began. Everything I truly want can be found in my own hometown.

CHAPTER

Sixteen

H e did *what*?" Maddie exclaimed the next morning.
"He kissed me," Britt answered.

"He kissed you!"

"Shh," Britt cautioned, with a glance around the interior of The Merryweather Coffee House. News traveled quickly in a small town, and Britt didn't want everyone in northwest Washington knowing by noon that Zander had kissed her. She hadn't even told her sisters yet.

A bustling morning rush filled the establishment. People dressed in professional garb ordered double shots of espresso. A group of male retirees sat at a round table, chuckling and drinking plain black coffee out of mugs. Women in work-out clothing requested non-fat lattes.

Because Britt and Zander were planning on paying Emerson a house call this morning, Britt had decided to clock in at Sweet Art after their conversation with Emerson. She'd slept in and was now indulging in the luxury of a blueberry scone paired with a cappuccino.

Earlier, she'd texted Maddie to let her know that she wouldn't be arriving at Sweet Art until later, and that Maddie was in big trouble for tattling to Zander about Britt's night out with Hannah and Mia.

Britt hadn't made it halfway through her scone before Maddie had bustled into the Coffee House.

Britt had downloaded a tracking app a few years back and added all of her close friends and family members to it. Whenever she had a hard time meeting up with one of them, she checked their location on her app. Also, should one of the people she loved run out of gas in the wilderness, she'd immediately be able to speed to their rescue. Maddie had the same app and had obviously used it this morning to pinpoint Britt.

Her erstwhile friend had ordered coffee and a thick slice of gluten-free lemon poppy seed bread. She'd situated herself across from Britt at a tiny round table adjacent to an exposed brick wall.

One might be tempted to think, looking at Maddie's kind olive green eyes and innocent face outlined by chestnut brown curls, that she had no spunk. That conclusion would be way off base.

Upon her arrival at Britt's table, Maddie had been suitably repentant about spilling the beans to Zander regarding Britt's actions Saturday night. But she'd been wholly unrepentant when she'd demanded to know what was wrong with Britt.

In a weak moment of scone bliss, Britt had opted to tell Maddie about the kiss on the beach.

"I cannot believe Zander finally kissed you," Maddie said. "That's wonderful."

"Eh." Britt pulled an unconvinced face.

"You loved the kiss, didn't you? I've always known that when you finally kissed him you'd love kissing him. I'm guessing that you've been out of sorts ever since the kiss because now you want more with him—"

"—I *might* want more with him—"

"—but you're scared of risking the relationship you have with him and maybe you're irritable because he hasn't yet made some big *I'll die unless you love me back* sort of proclamation. You're

231

not fully certain of his feelings, and you're not fully certain of your feelings, and you have no idea how to proceed from here."

Britt chewed slowly. "You're not completely wrong. Also, I'm a little ticked at him at the moment and he's a little ticked at me, so factor in that complication."

Maddie grinned. If rainbows could shoot from a person, they'd have been shooting from Maddie. She seemed not to care that her coffee was growing cold.

"I fail to see why this circumstance merits smiling," Britt said.

"It's just that I'm so happy! I've been waiting for ages for him to make a move."

"It would be easier for me to date Reid. I'm leaning toward dating Reid."

Maddie waved off Britt's gloomy declaration. "No, you're not. That's just bluster. You and I both know that, yes, it would be easier to date Reid. A lot less messy, a lot less interesting, and a lot more shallow. Reid is not the one for you. Zander is the one for you, and now it's your turn to be brave and love him back."

Britt locked her lips together.

"Before Leo and I started dating," Maddie said, "back when I was paralyzed by my own hang-ups, you confronted me about them. Remember?"

Britt took a desperate sip of cappuccino. She'd had a few straight-talking conversations with Maddie in an effort to pave the way for Maddie and Leo's romance. "That was different."

"How?"

"For one thing, I was right. You should be filled with gratitude to have me as a friend."

"*Filled.*" Maddie freed a lock of gold-highlighted hair from her hoop earring. "I'll have you know that I'm right, too. I've never been more right."

"For another thing," Britt said, "those times that I lectured you really did help you along with Leo."

"Yes, and I'm about to return the favor."

Britt tipped her head toward Maddie's drink. "Your coffee's getting cold."

Maddie ignored Britt's comment. "Remember when you didn't make the soccer team our junior year?"

"What does that have to do with anything?"

"Hear me out. We found out about that from Gretchen King, whom we hardly knew, because you didn't tell us. And when we asked you about not making the team, you shrugged it off. You wouldn't talk about it or cry or shake your fist at God or . . . anything."

"Good."

"Not good, because you loved soccer. It had to have crushed you when you didn't make the team."

"You're finding fault with me because I didn't cry over it?" Britt asked.

"I'm finding fault with you because you wouldn't open up and let us help you with your hurt."

Britt gaped at her. She was strong. So what?

"Remember how much you wanted that apprenticeship in France that you applied for first? You told me all about the master chocolatier you'd be working under and his chocolate empire and his awards and even where you'd live. And then you weren't chosen for the apprenticeship."

"I'm not really enjoying these particular memories—"

"You swept that rejection under the rug like it didn't matter."

"I got another apprenticeship. It worked out fine."

"And then," Maddie continued, "when Olivia died, you were the one patting our backs and handing us tissues."

"Somebody needed to."

"Nobody needed to. We could have all been heartbroken together."

"I beg to differ—"

"Don't even get me started on how you acted after your kayaking accident. You could hardly sit! You could hardly walk. Yet trying to force you to accept help from Hannah and Mia and me—"

"And all the other people you recruited."

"You have a lot of friends!" Maddie set her palms on either side of her plate. "Trying to force you to accept help was like trying to turn back the tide of the ocean."

Scowling, Britt brushed crumbs from the table.

"I could go on and on, listing example after example," Maddie said.

"Of what, exactly? My independence?"

"Take any positive attribute to its extreme, and you'll find something negative."

"How can independence be a bad thing?"

"It's a bad thing when it costs you the love of a man who would do anything in the world for you."

Britt opened her lips. Closed her lips. Opened them again. "You don't know that Zander would do anything in the world for me."

"I *do* know that he'd do anything in the world for you. We all do. Me. Hannah. Mia. Your sisters. Your parents. Zander's brother. Zander's aunt. And you know it, too. Here." Maddie leaned across the table and lightly tapped the area of Britt's heart. "But you're scared."

"*Scared?*"

"You're the most courageous person I know. Except about this one aspect of your life."

"That's not reassuring."

"To love Zander is to lean on him, to a degree," Maddie said. "It will require you to forfeit some of your freedom, Britt. You'll have to let him in and trust him more than you've ever trusted anyone . . . with all of it. Your joy and your pain. Your successes and your failures."

The idea of blubbering about her pain and her failures to Zander sounded awful to her. He appreciated her self-sufficiency! He'd told her so.

"I'm simply trying to say," Maddie said in a calm, reasonable tone, "that a romance with Zander will demand vulnerability."

"You've been dating Leo for five months and now—"

"And now I'm an expert. Yeah, yeah." Maddie squeezed Britt's hand. "I'm not an expert on dating. But we've been friends for a long time. I am an expert on you."

He and Britt hadn't patched things up.

Usually Britt insisted that they resolve their disagreements. But, so far, she was letting the disagreement they'd had yesterday drift past like an inner tube down a river.

He glanced at her as they made their way up the walk to the development where Emerson lived. He was having a hard time reading her. Ever since he'd picked her up ten minutes ago, she'd seemed almost carefully neutral. Was she no longer mad at him? Was she still mad but choosing to avoid the topic? Why?

Britt wore a loose white top with a wide opening at the neck that stretched from shoulder to shoulder. Gray jeans. Black sandals that fastened around her ankles. She'd painted her toenails dark purple. Her long hair was down today and a few of the lighter, more amber-colored strands glinted in the morning sunlight.

What would happen if he took hold of her shoulders, settled her against the wall next to Emerson's front door, and kissed her? Hard.

The rebel in him wanted to try. She disrupted him with her presence, her scent, her eyes, her words. He wanted to disrupt her even half as much.

Zander pushed Emerson's doorbell, thrust his hands into the pockets of his jeans, and held himself immobile.

Carolyn had informed them that Sunny had moved to town two and a half months ago and that she'd met Sunny shortly after, when she'd come to The Giftery to shop. The two women had struck up a friendship. They'd taken to sharing lunch a few times a week and talking on the phone in between.

Carolyn had supplied Zander with Emerson's address, which had led them to this unremarkable zero-lot-line complex.

Emerson answered the door, her face registering mild surprise at finding her friend's nephew on her doorstep. "Good morning. Zander, isn't it?"

"It is." If Emerson had inserted herself into Carolyn's life on purpose, then he'd bet that she knew his name far better than she was letting on. He introduced Britt and the two shook hands.

Emerson had clothed her slim frame in exercise pants and a long-sleeved turquoise work-out top. Her blond hair gave her a youthful look, though he guessed her to be at or near Frank's age—in her mid-sixties.

She balanced her weight on one bare foot and casually draped her other foot across it. "What can I do for you?"

"Carolyn said that she told you about the research we've been doing into Frank's death," Zander said, getting straight to the point.

"She did."

For weeks now, he and Britt had been trying to find the combination of clues that would unlock the secrets of Frank's past. He'd used up most of his patience and, at this point, needed the truth from Emerson. If there was an unseen threat at play, the truth would give him a shot at protecting the people he loved.

"Back when Frank was known as James Ross, he and a friend named Ricardo Serra robbed a gas station," Zander said. "Yesterday, Britt and I traveled to Whidbey Island because Ricardo was arrested there in 1988. We looked at mug shots of both Ricardo and his accomplice, which is how we discovered that Ricardo's accomplice . . . was you." Zander pulled out his phone and showed her the picture of her mug shot that he'd taken yesterday at Grant's house.

Emerson did not flinch. She raised the inmost points of her eyebrows so slightly it almost wasn't perceptible. The response communicated interest far more than shock or fear. "I'd love to know how you gained access to those mug shots," she said calmly.

"We met with the victim," Britt answered. "He kept a file of all the information he received about the case."

Emerson took a step back from the door. "Care to come inside?"

Zander followed Britt into a condo that smelled of baking pumpkin pie and reminded him of a Rooms to Go showroom. The living room furniture seemed staged to appeal to the widest possible percentage of people, which made him suspect that Emerson was renting the place furnished.

Emerson gestured for him and Britt to take the armchairs. She lowered herself onto the patterned sofa next to the fireplace and crossed her legs with catlike grace. A novel, pen, day planner, and fuzzy throw blanket rested on the cushion beside her.

"We don't believe that you and Ricardo were in search of a public park on Whidbey Island the night that Grant and Callista Mayberry's paintings were stolen," Zander said.

Emerson matched his steady gaze with her own.

"We also don't believe," he continued, "that it's a coincidence that you showed up in Merryweather a month before Frank died. And we don't believe it's a coincidence that you and Carolyn became friends."

Emerson remained quiet for a long period of time.

"I'm not sure if any part of your friendship with Carolyn is genuine." Zander's palms tightened on the chair's armrests. "But if you care about her at all, then telling us what you know might enable us to keep her safe."

"Or telling you what I know might end up endangering you all," Emerson offered mildly.

Foreboding pricked the skin at the back of his neck. "Be that as it may, we'd still like to hear what you know."

Emerson appeared to weigh her options, and he had the sense that no amount of argument would rush her.

"I'm going to need to borrow your phones and frisk you to make sure you're not wearing electronic recording devices." Emerson spoke in a no-nonsense way, as if she'd just mentioned that the forecast called for rain.

"Agreed," Britt said at the exact moment that Zander said, "Deal."

It seemed that Emerson had decided to talk to them. He understood why she'd first want to be sure they weren't recording her.

They gave her their phones, which she carried toward the back of the condo.

He frowned at Emerson's day planner, across from him on the sofa. Did he have time to check it? Should he risk checking it now, right before she might come clean? If she caught him, she might change her mind—

She returned. He and Britt rose so that Emerson could give them both a thorough pat down, then she went to stand near the electric fireplace. Nonchalantly, she leaned a shoulder against the mantle and crossed her arms. "What would you like to know?"

"Were you, Ricardo, and Frank the ones who pulled off the Triple Play?" Zander asked.

"Yes."

Her admission thumped the breath from him. Frank, Ricardo, Emerson. The Triple Play thieves.

"A contact of mine in Chicago let me know that Frank and Ricardo were moving to Seattle," Emerson said.

"They didn't come to Seattle specifically for the heist?" Britt asked.

"No, they came because Ricardo had family there. I'd had my eye on the Pascal for some time, and I had a good bit of the job planned. In order to pull it off, I knew I needed partners. I got to know Ricardo and Frank over the course of several weeks. I came to trust them and, eventually, we started making plans."

The only difference between Emerson and Zander's father? Emerson was a successful thief. His father, unsuccessful. Because of his experience with his dad, Zander comprehended much about Emerson. He could expect her to have only one code and only one motivation. Self-interest. "Did Frank actually work construction in the city, or was that just a cover story?" Zander asked.

"He worked construction. We all had day jobs."

Thieves with day jobs. They'd contributed to the community they'd stolen from.

"We decided that Frank would case the Pascal," Emerson said. "In order to visit the museum frequently without arousing suspicion, I felt that he should become a museum member. But we couldn't have him in the museum's system under his real name.

So he remained James Ross in the other spheres of his life, including at work. Whenever he visited the Pascal, he visited as Frank Pierce."

"Did he choose the Frank Pierce identity?" Britt asked.

"No, I did. I drove out of town and walked around a cemetery until I found a grave for a male born around the same time as Frank."

"We visited that cemetery," Zander said. "In Enumclaw."

"Enumclaw. Yes."

"Your heist was a success," Britt prompted.

Emerson didn't fidget or shift. She held herself with uncommon stillness. "Except for the fact that Frank was shot."

The data they'd found so far pointed to the believability of what Emerson was saying. Even so, the conversation had a surreal quality to it. They were talking about *Frank* . . . having committed one of the most famous unsolved crimes in the county. His Uncle Frank was the man who'd insisted he make his bed every day before school, who'd taken him to his first professional basketball game, who'd ribbed him about spending too much time playing video games, who'd loved him.

"Where did you take Frank to get the bullet wound treated?" Britt asked.

"My brother had graduated from med school and was doing his internship at that time. We took Frank to his house, and he did the best he could to stitch Frank up. It wasn't ideal, and it wasn't according to my plans." A twitch of consternation crossed her mouth, and he could tell that it still bothered her that something about the heist had gone wrong.

Ricardo had lied to them when he'd said he knew nothing about Frank's bullet wound, when he'd said he and Frank had lost touch after moving to Seattle.

"Had you planned for Frank to continue to visit the Pascal after the heist?" Britt asked.

"I had, because I felt attention would be drawn to him if he suddenly severed his visits after a crime had been committed. We had to wait longer than I would've liked for his leg to recover. But as soon as he was well enough, he resumed his visits to the museum. I intended for him to show himself at the Pascal for a couple of months, then gradually taper off his attendance in a way that wouldn't raise anyone's eyebrows." She released a disapproving sigh. "Instead, he fell in love with Carolyn and neither Ricardo nor I could talk him into giving her up. By then, it wasn't as if Frank could tell Carolyn what he'd done or confess that he'd been pretending to be someone he wasn't for months. So he did something I didn't endorse. He cut ties with his previous life and he became, permanently, the man he'd told Carolyn he was."

"Did you keep in contact with him after that?" Britt asked.

"Not regularly. If the police had found one of us, then communication between us could have brought down the others."

Zander paced. Stopped. Faced Emerson. "Why did you reenter Frank's life this year?"

"Because Frank is the one who took *Young Woman at Rest* by Renoir."

He glanced at Britt just as she glanced at him. Her brown eyes had gone bright with the satisfaction of discovery.

Britt turned her profile toward Emerson. "That painting hasn't been seen since the day it was stolen."

"You believe that Frank still has it," Zander guessed. "And you want it for yourself."

A wry dimple marked Emerson's cheek. "Well? Yes. Frank didn't seem to have any use for it."

How dare she find humor in any corner of this? His uncle was dead. "You tracked Frank down. Then what? Threatened him? Blackmailed him?"

She rested one foot over the other again. "I've never had the need for brute force. I simply had a few conversations with Frank during which I tried to talk him into letting me sell the painting. I proposed that we'd split the profits fifty-fifty."

"And he said?"

"No."

"So you befriended Carolyn, hoping she might lead you to the painting," Zander said.

Emerson nodded.

"Have you been following me?" he asked.

"No."

"Do you know someone named Nick Dunlap?"

"No."

He couldn't decide whether or not she was telling the truth. "The fact that you've remained in Merryweather for a month and a half after Frank's death tells me that the painting is still missing."

"It's still missing," she confirmed.

"I assume that you've been searching for it," Britt said.

"Yes. But so far, I haven't been able to find it."

"How can you be sure that Frank didn't sell it long ago?" Britt asked.

"I've spent my entire professional life doing business with a certain group of people. If Frank had sold it, I'd have known."

A timer let out a beeping sound, and Emerson disappeared into the kitchen, he supposed to take her pie from the oven. He heard the whoosh of a drawer.

He jumped up and flicked open her day planner to the week she had bookmarked, this week. The hinge on the oven door rasped. He memorized the notations on the pages as quickly and accurately as he could. The oven door rasped again.

He landed back in his chair. Britt gave him a look that communicated her approval the second before Emerson strode in.

"How did Frank die?" he asked when Emerson returned to her position at the fireplace. The smell of pumpkin, which he'd always liked in the past, became suffocating.

"I don't know."

"We're aware that Frank received an upsetting phone call his final day at work," Britt said.

"He got in his car and drove off," Zander said. "And that was the last anyone saw of him before he was found dead in his car the next day. Are you the person who called him at work?"

241

"No."

"Do you know who did?"

"No. Listen, here's what's pertinent at this point." She tucked a short piece of hair behind her ear. "We need to acknowledge that I might not be the only person who's aware that Frank was in possession of *Young Woman at Rest*. Certainly Ricardo's aware, and there's no telling who he's told. It's in your best interest to figure out where Frank has been storing that painting. The sooner you get it out of your possession, the better—for the two of you and for Carolyn. Do you have any idea where it might be?"

He'd never tell her if he did. "Not yet."

"When you do come up with ideas, contact me. I'll check them out. If I find the painting, I'll take care of the entire situation. None of you will have to risk anything or get your hands dirty in any way."

"You'll sell it on the black market." His voice was flat.

"*I'll take care of it*," Emerson reiterated. "You'll receive fifty percent of the profits, which will amount to a tremendous sum. Enough to ensure that Carolyn never has another financial worry in her lifetime. Enough to set you both up very comfortably."

Britt came to stand next to him, aligning herself with him wordlessly.

Earlier, he hadn't been able to read her. But he knew exactly what she was thinking now. She was thinking, *no way*. Britt wouldn't allow Emerson to have the painting. Not for any price.

"If you let me handle it, you won't have to worry about anyone else knocking on your door in search of the Renoir," Emerson said.

"Who else might knock on my door?" he asked. "I'd like names."

"I can't give you names. But, like I said, several people may be aware that Frank had the painting. If I take possession of the painting, that becomes a non-issue for you. It's a win-win outcome."

"Except for the Pascal," Britt observed.

"The Pascal is doing just fine," Emerson replied. "It owns approximately seven hundred masterworks at last count."

Taut quiet encircled them.

"Will you consider my offer?" Emerson asked.

"Yes."

"And contact me with ideas regarding the painting's where-abouts?"

"Yes." He wanted Emerson to hope that they might come through for her with a tip that would lead her to the Renoir. She was too smart to injure potential allies.

"I'll retrieve your phones." She did so, then held her front door open as they passed through.

"Do you happen to know where Grant Mayberry's Modiglianis ended up?" Zander paused on her front step.

"I've no idea."

"Because I get the impression that his wife might like them back."

"I've no idea." Emerson spoke firmly, despite that she no doubt had every idea of the paintings' whereabouts. She'd shared all that she was going to share. The Modiglianis were lost.

Once inside his Jeep, Zander turned over his phone and discovered a yellow Post-it note stuck to the back. On it, Emerson had written her phone number.

They'd driven a good two miles before Britt spoke. "Your uncle stole a masterpiece and kept it hidden for more than thirty years." She set her sandals on his dashboard and bent her knees up toward her chest. He could remember her sitting that exact way in the passenger seat of every car he'd ever driven.

"It's hard to believe."

"Incredibly."

And now Britt was tangled up in an art heist worth millions because of her friendship with him.

Until the day at the Central Library, he hadn't suspected that Frank had a connection to the Triple Play. By then, Britt was already deeply involved. It would have been difficult to talk her out of helping him with Frank's case at that point. Still. He should have tried. Instead, he'd continued to include her for his own selfish reasons.

"What did Emerson have written in her day planner?" Britt asked.

"Not much. She had arrows over certain hours of each day with a Z beside them."

"Your first initial. What could that mean? That she's following you during those hours? Researching you?"

"I don't know. She also had 'Cindy's birthday' written on Monday. She had 'Claire' written next to 12:15 p.m. on Wednesday. 'Mom' was written next to seven p.m. on Thursday. And 'Video call with Tom' was written next to eight a.m. on Friday."

"Tom?" She grew instantly alert. "Could that be Tom R? As in Nick Dunlap's Tom R?"

"She didn't have Tom R written down. It just said 'Video call with Tom.' Tom's a very common name."

"Maddeningly common. Still, it's possible that Emerson's connected to the same Tom that Nick's connected to. Emerson. Tom. Nick. Could all three of them be working together?"

"I don't know." He was sick of not knowing.

Britt absent-mindedly tapped a finger against her lip. "I don't think, by the way, that Emerson told us all that she did back there because she cares about Carolyn's safety," she said.

"No."

"She told us for reasons of her own. She hasn't had any luck finding the painting, and she wants it badly enough to try a new tactic. The new tactic is us."

"I'm certain that she didn't tell us everything she knows. I'll call Detective Shaw as soon as I drop you off."

"Good, though I'm not sure what the detective can do since we have no idea where the painting is."

"Plus, the statute of limitations on the Triple Play would keep anyone from charging Emerson with robbery at this point."

"Even if the detective were to confront Emerson with the information she just gave us, she'd almost certainly deny the whole conversation."

At an intersection, Zander looked over at Britt.

He wanted to lock her in a tower to protect her.

He wanted her to put her feet on the dashboard of every car he'd ever own for as long as he lived.

Most of all, he wanted to break the uncomfortable tension that had existed between them since their kiss.

"*Young Woman at Rest* was first stolen from the Pascal family by the Nazis." Britt toyed absent-mindedly with a lock of her hair. "It was the favorite painting of Annette Pascal's grandmother, so the family mounted a huge search for it. After years of effort, they finally brought it home."

"Right."

"We're the ones who have the ability to bring it home to the Pascals a second time, Zander. We have to find that painting."

"*I* have to find that painting."

"With my assistance."

He said nothing, though he had no intention of allowing Britt to get any more mixed up in this situation than she already was.

"Emerson Kelly is not going to get anywhere near *Young Woman at Rest*," Britt continued. "When we find the painting, we're going to return it to Annette Pascal."

Without a doubt, Carolyn would settle on the same goal.

Which meant that he had to find a way to unearth the painting. Return it to the Pascal Museum. And do so without risking any of their necks.

"But why?" Carolyn's oval face communicated her shock.

Zander had dropped Britt at her house, then driven to Carolyn's. He'd just finished relaying their conversation with Emerson to his aunt.

"Why in the world would Frank have held on to a priceless work of art all this time?" Her gray eyes beseeched him.

"I don't know." He scratched the back of his neck. "Can you think of why he might have kept it?"

"No. I have no clue why. None." She pressed two shuddering

fingers against her forehead and rubbed. "Zander. *Young Woman at Rest* is precious to Annette Pascal. I can't bear to think that Frank's had it . . . that he's kept it from Annette all this time."

They were sitting at Carolyn's kitchen table. Aurora slept on the floor, her chin resting on Carolyn's foot.

Zander extended a hand to his aunt, just as he'd done many times since Frank's death. She wrapped her slim fingers around his.

"I know that you've already been searching through the contents of the house," Zander said.

"Yes. I'm almost finished."

"What about the attic? Could he have stored a painting in your attic?"

"I mean . . . I suppose it's possible."

"I'll take a look around up there. This house doesn't have a basement, does it?"

"No."

"Do you rent storage space anywhere?"

"No."

"Do you own any other properties?"

"We don't."

"Could he have stored the painting in the garage?"

She chewed the inside of her lip. "The garage holds gardening tools and car equipment. *My goodness.* Surely Frank wouldn't have stored a painting by Renoir in our attic or in our garage."

"It's unlikely. I'm just trying to think through all the possibilities."

Releasing his hand, she stood. Aurora startled awake and scrambled to her feet. Carolyn moved to the window and stopped, her attention fastened beyond the pane of glass. "How could Frank have stolen a piece of art? Any piece of art, but especially a piece of art that belongs to the Pascal? I consider Annette to be a friend! Every time I had lunch with Annette or received a card from her, I told Frank about it. He had numerous opportunities to confide in me. Why didn't he confide in me?"

Zander had no answer.

"It's too late now to give Frank a piece of my mind about that painting. Just like it's too late now to tell him I love him." Her voice broke, and tears piled onto her bottom eyelashes.

"But perhaps it's not too late to make it right," Zander said. "With any luck, we can still return *Young Woman at Rest* to Annette Pascal."

Phone call from Detective Kurt Shaw to Zander:

Kurt: After we got off the phone earlier, I contacted the FBI's Art Crime Team. They'd like to talk to you about Frank, the Triple Play, and the missing Renoir.

Zander: Excellent.

Kurt: I gave them your number, so expect a phone call.

Zander: Is there any chance that they'll send an agent out?

Kurt: A good chance. In fact, I'm hopeful that they will. They told me, though, that they won't be able to get anyone here for at least a week.

CHAPTER
Seventeen

Zander ran along a dirt path that led him deeper into the dense green of the Washington forest. He drew cold early morning air into his chest. His running shoes hit the earth in a measured cadence. Sweat stung one of his eyes.

He kept going. He'd told himself he'd run to the waterfall, and he was determined to do what he'd set his mind to do.

After the meeting with Emerson yesterday, he'd stayed with Carolyn for several hours. They'd gone through every square inch of the attic. Every hall and bedroom closet in the house. Every cupboard big enough for a painting. He'd even gone underneath the house to search the crawl space around the pier and beam foundation. They hadn't found the painting. Nor had they succeeded at unlocking Frank's cell phone, despite several more passcode attempts.

Later, he'd spoken to Jennifer Delacruz, an agent with the FBI's Art Crime Team. He'd explained everything he knew about Frank and the Triple Play. She'd said she'd be in touch.

Then he'd attempted to write. He'd fallen behind his progress goals on his current manuscript, and the stress of that was beginning to press on him like a boulder. He'd had plenty of time to write while in Merryweather. The only legitimate reason for his lack of productivity was lame but true: He hadn't been able to concentrate.

Between his preoccupation with Britt and his pursuit of Frank's secrets, Zander couldn't seem to recover his focus. His grief over Frank's death had turned creativity into a luxury he was suddenly too poor to afford . . . in a way that had nothing to do with his bank balance.

The hiking trail tilted upward, then curled to the left, shadowing a stream flowing in the opposite direction.

He was tired of grief. Of the helpless feeling that Frank's case had plunged him into. Of his frustration concerning Britt.

He rounded a corner, and the waterfall appeared before him. The flow cascaded from a crevice high above, falling past gleaming black rocks before crashing into a dusky blue pool.

With a huff of relief, he stopped running and leaned over, hands braced on his knees. He stayed there for several minutes, sucking air. Then he walked back and forth beside the pool to cool his body.

He'd seen one other person, a man walking his dog, back near the base of the wilderness area. That had been forty minutes ago.

Loneliness squeezed in on him as surely as the trees and plants.

Moss crept over every surface. Vines, like sleeping snakes, decorated branches. White-gray sky watched over him as if it disapproved.

Loneliness had found him during the years when he and Daniel had fended for themselves in St. Louis. It had followed him to every faraway place he'd visited the past year and a half. Now it had chased him into the heart of the forest.

Everyone Zander knew appeared to deal with loneliness better than he did. Was his loneliness a character flaw? Or was he simply someone who had a need for connection buried deep inside him, like a time capsule beneath concrete?

He sat on a rock embedded in the hill and studied the clearing. Gradually, as the sun broke free and poured honey-colored light over the pool, he understood that he wasn't fully alone.

No humans were near. But he could sense God's presence in this remote place.

He'd sensed God's presence this very same way the day of the fire. His first night in his new bedroom at Frank and Carolyn's house. After one of his early cooking sessions with Britt, when they'd sat on Bradfordwood's terrace eating cupcakes and watching the sun set. The day he'd learned he'd been offered a college scholarship. When he'd felt led to try his hand at writing a book. Standing on a towering cliff overlooking the English Channel.

God had made a way for Zander to accomplish everything he'd accomplished so far. He'd been beside him all along. Was beside him even now. Yet somewhere along the way Zander had grown unsure of God, and so he'd stopped depending on Him.

If God wanted to condemn him, he understood.

If God was angry with him, he understood.

Here's the thing, though. *He* was also angry with God.

Zander's childhood had made him defensive, quick to protect himself by pulling away from people he suspected he couldn't trust. He knew that wasn't the right reaction to his unanswered prayers, but he didn't know how to fix his response. He'd tried to cure himself of his disillusionment by attending church on Sunday, no matter where he traveled.

It hadn't worked.

Turning his hands so that his palms faced up, Zander made himself bend his head to pray. He asked God to forgive him, but even as he did, his soul felt cold and distant. He asked God to protect Britt, Carolyn, Courtney, and Sarah. He prayed for wisdom concerning Britt.

His mind wandered.

He continued praying.

His mind wandered.

He groaned with frustration and, pressing to his feet, gave up. It seemed sacrilegious to pray such a lousy prayer when he should be experiencing genuine gratitude. In light of the crucifixion, what right did he have to complain?

None. He was lonely *and* selfish.

He ran back in the direction of his car without peace or resolution, his thoughts gravitating to Britt.

He had loved her for so, so long.

He was hers. There was no changing his course, no getting over her, no moving on.

He'd ruined their friendship by kissing her. Trying to recapture what they'd had before was useless. So he should tell her how he felt.

His pace cut off. He stumbled to a stop.

For years, he'd been asking God for Britt's love. But not once had he taken action to obtain her love. The timing hadn't been right. He'd had far too much to lose.

He didn't have as much to lose now.

Surprised conviction coursed from the top of his head to his feet and back again. It was time to tell her.

If she didn't want to date him, then she didn't.

But if she did—

She wouldn't.

But if she did . . .

She wouldn't.

It felt foolish, stupidly reckless, to let himself hope.

He'd tell her. And then he'd deal with what came.

After six months of planning, Nora's wedding weekend had finally arrived.

Britt completed her responsibilities at Sweet Art at two on Friday, then ran by the grocery store. She stocked her fridge and performed a final inspection to make sure her home was ready for the two female cousins who were slated to stay with her tonight and tomorrow night.

She drove from her place to Nora's Bookish Cottage to drop off a celebratory box of chocolate she'd made special for the occasion. For half an hour, they sat on Nora's back deck, drinking Nora's homemade tea blend, talking, and eating chocolate.

Then Britt continued to Bradfordwood to help Mom, Dad, Valentina, and Clint with preparations. Her parents were hosting several family members, both at the main house and at the inn. Willow and Corbin were housing the rest.

She returned home in time to welcome her cousins, shower, and dress for the rehearsal.

Nora had opted to marry John at the Hartnett Chapel, the quaint white clapboard structure that reigned over Merryweather Historical Village. Since the chapel wasn't large enough to accommodate all the guests, rows of white chairs would be arranged on the village's central green and the ceremony would take place on the chapel's elevated front porch.

Happily, tomorrow's forecast promised a rainless, partly sunny, seventy-degree day. Nora wasn't going to have to activate her back-up rain plan, which meant the wedding party didn't need to practice in two venues. Only one.

During the rehearsal, the wedding coordinator put the couple, the four bridesmaids, the four groomsmen, the two flower girls, the ring bearer, the attendants, the ushers, and the parents and grandparents of the bride and groom through their paces.

That done, the group gathered with visiting family for a rehearsal dinner hosted by John's parents. The evening overflowed with conversation, affection, and tiramisu.

Every time Britt turned around, she was approached by a distant relative of hers or John's. The evening was completely and totally full. . . . Or it would have been, if Zander's absence hadn't shot a hole straight through the center of it.

The emotions that warred within her whenever she was with him lately exhausted her. She wanted to feel relieved over the opportunity to take a night off. Instead, she simply felt hollow.

When she fell into bed that night, she willed sleep to come. Defiantly, her brain raced. Nora—*her* Nora—was getting married tomorrow. And then both of her sisters would be married.

She could probably look forward to nieces and nephews soon,

which rocked, because she intended to be the coolest aunt in the history of aunts.

She didn't pine for marriage and, truthfully, it would have rubbed her the wrong way if her sisters hadn't married before her. Even so, a trace of sorrow swirled within her because, after Nora's wedding, she wouldn't be able to relate to either of her sisters about this new and enormous aspect of their lives.

They'd both have husbands. They'd both be *wives*. Wives! Willow and Nora were building homes in Marriage Land, a place Britt had no access to.

Consciously, she relaxed her muscles, then tested some yoga breathing.

A picture of Zander materialized in her mind. He was walking toward her the day he'd returned to Merryweather from his Grand Tour. His body language communicated isolation. Yet the attention he fixed on her revealed how much he valued their relationship. A smile stole over his mouth almost as if it didn't have permission. His eyes were world-weary. His soul, loyal.

Her heart reached out with stark longing.

She wasn't ready for marriage. But a renegade portion of her did want a great love.

"You look beautiful," Dad said to Nora the next day.

"You do," Britt, Willow, and Mom all immediately agreed.

Nora loved vintage-inspired clothing, and that preference carried over to her wedding dress. She wore an off-the-shoulder white gown. The snug bodice and three-quarter-length sleeves had been overlaid with delicate lace. A satin belt encircled her waist, highlighted at the front by a pin glittering with gems. Her taffeta skirt jetted out into a wide circle. In lieu of a veil, a small tiara graced her head. She'd parted her hair on the side, then let it glide smoothly down to her shoulders.

The elegant effect harkened back, in a subtle way, to the 1950s.

Today, on her wedding day, she looked like the most stunning version of herself.

The ceremony was scheduled to start in ten minutes, at five p.m., and all of Nora's one thousand plans had come together seamlessly. The wedding party, wedding coordinators, hair and makeup people, florist, and photographer had been using the MacKenzie Timber Barn, which stood next to the Hartnett Chapel, as a staging area. When Dad had asked if he could speak with them just now, they'd gathered in one of the barn's private back rooms, decked out in their finery.

Dad, in a tux. Mom, in a beaded sheath the hue of champagne. Willow and Britt, in their blush-colored bridesmaid dresses. Britt, who'd never been a fan of constricting garments, approved. Her chiffon skirt flowed to the floor in easy, dreamy, elegant lines.

Each bridesmaid had been free to choose a hairstyle that the stylist then accented with pale pink rosebuds. Willow had gone for an elaborate low bun. Britt had opted to let the stylist weave the roses into a loose braid.

They held one another's hands, forming a circle.

The Bradford family.

"John's a lucky man," Dad said.

"And a wonderful one," Mom added.

"Grandma would say he's too handsome." Britt winked at Nora.

"Which proves that John's exactly as handsome as he should be," Willow said.

John was far more than a pretty face. He was a Medal of Honor–winning former Navy SEAL. He'd encountered hard things, and so had Nora. The challenges only served to make this day all the sweeter.

"Ever since you were small . . ." Mom's attention landed on Willow, Nora, then Britt. Drop earrings swung from her ears. "Your dad and I have prayed over you, asking God to bless and guide you. It's amazing to see the ways He's doing just that."

"It really is amazing," Dad said. "When you were little, and you were supposed to be sleeping because it was past your bedtime, I remember hearing you talk about your future weddings."

"Nora wanted a dragon-themed wedding on top of a volcano," Britt said.

"That's very true," Nora concurred. "And I fully intended to marry Harry Potter. Willow wanted to get married in Sleeping Beauty's castle at Disneyland."

"Right." Willow's smile dazzled. "I had my heart set on marrying Dawson from *Dawson's Creek*." She eyed Britt with amusement. "You wanted to hold your wedding on a yacht in Alaska."

"And I planned to marry the cute guitar-playing guy from *The Princess Diaries*."

They all laughed.

"Our plans didn't exactly come to fruition," Willow said.

"Thank goodness," Nora said, "seeing as how my future husband, Harry Potter, is a fictional character."

"Your real-life marriage," Dad said to her, "is going to be terrific. We wish you and John all the best, honey. We're really proud of you. If Robin could have been here, I know she'd have been every bit as proud as we are." Their family always acknowledged Nora's mom, Robin, at pivotal moments in Nora's life.

Tenderness softened Nora's face. "Thank you, Dad."

"No crying," Britt warned. "Those of us wearing makeup are absolutely *not* allowed to cry right now."

"An excellent point," Mom said. "We'll finish up by simply saying that we love you."

"I love you all," Nora replied. "Thank you for . . . well, you know what. Everything. All these years." Her voice began to wobble.

"No crying!" Britt said. "Quick, Dad. Say a prayer."

Dad thanked God for his wife and for his girls, then earnestly prayed for God's grace to flow through the marriage of his middle daughter, Nora.

The second of the two flower girls kept hunching over to pick up the petals that the first flower girl had dropped. Britt spotted the little girl's antics as she made her way up the central aisle between the white folding chairs positioned on the lawn. Nora's OCD flower girl added the ideal note of spontaneous charm to the wedding ceremony.

Britt ascended the chapel's steps clasping a bouquet bursting with shades of pale pink, vermilion, and white. When she took her position and turned to face the guests, she pinpointed Zander without having to scan the crowd. She just . . . knew . . . he was sitting in the middle on the bride's side. His dark gray suit looked stunning against his white shirt and pale gray tie.

Nora and John exchanged their vows in front of the chapel's peaked blue door, which was crowned by a garland of the same flowers that comprised the bridesmaids' bouquets.

Across from Britt, the guys' white tuxedo jackets reflected the sunshine. Above, spring leaves murmured happily. Birds wheeled into the sky with soft song.

When John and Nora were pronounced husband and wife, they shared an excellent kiss. Then the string quartet launched into the triumphant strains of "Ode to Joy" as the audience applauded.

Britt's attention flicked to Zander. All the normal people were watching the bride and groom. Not him.

He was looking steadily back at her.

Zander seemed to have disappeared. She'd lost sight of him fifteen minutes ago.

The dancing portion of the wedding reception had begun thirty minutes before, and Britt was currently partnered with the OCD flower girl on the dance floor. So far the band had been playing slow love songs that everyone knew and all the guests felt comfortable dancing to.

Britt held one of the girl's hands high. Her skirt flared out as she executed a spin. "Again?" the girl asked.

"I'd be happy to spin you as many times as you'd like."

Britt's mom and dad swept past. She could tell that her mom had just said something witty because her dad gave a low, appreciative chuckle. Corbin whispered into Willow's ear, and her oldest sister blushed in response. Nora rested her head against John's chest as the two moved to the beat of the song. Nikki and Clint ambled by, Nikki's fingertips pressing five dents into the shoulder of his suit jacket.

Despite Britt's efforts to shore up Clint's confidence, he still hadn't gathered enough nerve to take Nikki out on a date. The pep talk she'd given him about asking Nikki to dance had achieved greater success, however, which made her feel as self-satisfied as a cotillion parent.

When Britt had told Nikki that Clint was gun-shy about romance because of his first love's unfaithfulness, Nikki had grown even more determined to win the battle for Clint's heart. Clint and Nikki had attended more Pilates classes, and Nikki had stopped by the inn a few times to deliver kombucha, his favorite drink, to him while he worked.

Britt fully expected to have them well on their way to lovebird status within the next two weeks.

She gave the flower girl another spin.

Nora's reception venue had been designed by a protégé of Frank Lloyd Wright. This enormous space—with its three walls of windows and honey-toned wood floors—had once housed its owner's collection of antique cars.

For dinner, Britt had been seated at a table with Zander, Grandma, Valentina, Valentina's husband, Clint, Nikki, and Grandma's sister. Zander had been perfectly polite to her and everyone else at the table. Conversation had bubbled easily. He had not, however, been *normal*. He was trying too hard. The ongoing weirdness persisted between them.

Until recently, their friendship had seemed sturdy to her, broad and reliable, like a boardwalk. Only now did she realize that their friendship may have been more like a two-inch-wide balance beam all along. Or perhaps it *had* been a boardwalk before. And had become a narrow beam when they'd kissed.

While eating hors d'oeuvres, she'd struggled to pay attention to anything other than Zander's hand, maneuvering his fork. While eating salad, she'd tried not to notice the spicy scent of his cologne. While eating steak, she'd caught herself peering at his profile.

The song ended and the flower girl scampered to her mom. Britt still couldn't spot Zander, and his absence was beginning to make her edgy. He hadn't left yet, surely? Parties drained him. Most likely, he'd retreated outside for a breather.

Britt returned to her table to scoop up her coat, then slipped outdoors.

A stone pathway lit by magical lanterns took her past a pond dotted with lily pads in bloom. Rivers of dianthus, forget-me-nots, and poppies surged against jade lawns. Night wind gusted against her, and she thrust her arms into the sleeves of her dressy black wool coat.

Like at the ceremony earlier, she searched for Zander more by feel than by sight. The quality of the atmosphere altered slightly, and she left the path—

There. He was sitting on a bench at the far side of a small circle of grass rimmed by trees.

Thanks to the landscape lighting that provided gold-toned illumination from above and below, she could discern the details of his features as she neared. What she saw there caused her breath to jam up.

He was watching her with a look of raw honesty. It was a look that spoke of resolution and vulnerability.

And in that moment, before a word had been spoken, she comprehended that they'd fallen off their balance beam for good. And that nothing would ever be exactly as it had been again.

Wedding toast from John to Nora:

Nora, your courage humbles me. Your intelligence challenges me to be the man you deserve. Your faith makes mine stronger. Your laugh is my favorite sound. Your optimism brings light to dark places. Your dreams convince me to hope. Your love takes my breath away.

I feel incredibly fortunate to be your husband.

I love you.

CHAPTER
Eighteen

D id the introvert in you need a vacation from the party?"
Britt sometimes preferred to ease into difficult conversations the way she eased into too-hot bath water. Slowly.

"I don't have the stamina for that many hours of socializing in a row."

"I know." She sat next to Zander on the bench. They gazed at the garden while the things they weren't saying gathered shape and mass.

"I'm overly protective of you," he said. "I shouldn't have come down on you the way I did for changing your plans that night at the club and leaving with Reid."

"I shouldn't have changed my plans after I'd been drinking."

"I should have resisted the urge to lecture you."

"I should have taken your lecturing on the chin."

"Forgive me?" he asked.

"Yes. Forgive me?"

"Yes."

The pressure surrounding them did not lessen. On the contrary. It intensified.

Zander had more to say. Zander had worse to say.

Fear ran ghostly fingertips down Britt's spine.

The music from the reception was much softer here, but still audible thanks to the French doors that had been left open. A new song began and Britt recognized its opening bars. "Alone," by Heart.

Zander held out a hand. "May I have this dance?"

"You may." She placed her hand in his and kicked off her shoes. The cool grass felt like heaven against the soles of feet that weren't used to wearing a new pair of heels for five hours straight. They swayed together. Her, in a romantic dress that gleamed from beneath her unbuttoned coat. Him, in his suit.

Whenever she'd been between boyfriends at a time when a formal high school dance had rolled around, the two of them had gone together. In fact, they'd been each other's dates to prom their senior year of high school. She'd worn a jade green gown that, in retrospect, had been seriously ill-advised. He'd been such a good sport that he'd worn a jade green cummerbund and bow tie to match.

They'd danced just the way they were now too many times to count. Normally, they talked or laughed or sang along. Tonight, the lack of conversation or laughter or singing created a tense void.

The band reached the song's chorus: "*Till now, I always got by on my own.*"

Zander's hair was slightly shiny and perfectly in place, which meant he'd used gel for the occasion. He'd shaved his hard cheeks smooth. His eyes reminded her of midnight lagoons.

"I'm worried about what I need to tell you." Lines grooved Zander's forehead. "I haven't said anything yet. And already, I'm worried."

"Just go ahead and say whatever you need to." Honestly! She couldn't take much more of this.

He ducked his head in a nod, broke contact with her, and took a few steps back. His jacket separated as his hands pushed defensively into the pockets of his pants. They studied each other, two old friends whose relationship had grown complicated.

"I love you," he said. His vision did not waver from hers.

Astonishment and elation and concern slammed into her simultaneously, rendering her mute.

"I have always loved you," he said. "I don't think that fact comes as a surprise to you. Does it?"

She blinked at him, trying to acclimate.

"I have always loved you," he'd said.

"I . . ." She didn't know how to frame her response because his declarations were both shocking and—after her conversations with her sisters and Maddie—not shocking. They were *both*.

"It's not that I feel deserving of your love," he continued. "I don't. I accept that you don't love me back, and I even regret my feelings for you because if they didn't exist, then we could go on being friends for a long time. But they do exist, so I'm struggling to continue doing . . ." He motioned between them. "This."

"What do you mean by 'this'?" she asked with false calm. Fiasco! She knew the answer to her question.

"Our friendship. Before I went away I was better able to deal with my emotions. We were friends, and friends was better than nothing because I had you in my life and because our friendship was great. But since I returned, my emotions have been making me miserable."

He'd said that he loved her. Then followed that up by informing her that she was making him miserable. "What are you suggesting?"

"I don't know what I'm suggesting."

"That we end our friendship?" The two of them did *not* give up on each other. They did *not* let go of each other. Indignation muscled its way to the front of her thoughts. She stepped forward and used the flat of her palms to push him in the chest.

Startled, he fell back a step.

She set her hands on her hips. "Did it ever occur to you to ask me how I feel about you?"

"I think I know how you feel about me."

"You have no idea how I feel about you."

He looked at her as if she'd just announced that the koi in the pond were performing a play.

"You should have had a conversation with me about this," she said.

"We are having a conversation about it."

"We should have had a conversation about this sooner."

He scrubbed his hands into his hair, ruining the neat alignment she'd noticed earlier. Then, with a sound of frustration, he dropped his arms. "How do you feel about me?" He appeared to brace for bad news.

"I'm not sure. Which is why there's no way that you can know, Zander. My feelings for you have been changing."

A pause. "Changing?"

"When we kissed, the dynamic between us shifted. I haven't been able to find my equilibrium since."

"Why? You got everything you wanted the way you wanted it after we kissed. You said you thought it would be best if we didn't repeat the kiss. And I said okay."

"My brain was so scrambled after we kissed that I hardly knew what I was saying. My knee-jerk reaction was to safeguard our friendship."

He drew an uneven breath. "Have you changed your mind? You're going to have to spell it out for me so that I can understand. What is it you want?"

"I want to kiss you," she told him bluntly.

He looked like he'd been poleaxed.

Collecting her bravery, she drew herself upright. "That's what I wanted five seconds after our kiss. And that's what I've continued to want every day since. It's just that I'm wary about getting your hopes up or my hopes up about the future. I don't want to cause you or myself pain. I can't guarantee . . . anything."

The band began to play "Keep on Loving You" by REO Speedwagon.

"Maybe we should do what other people do when they like each other," she suggested. "Maybe we should try dating and see where it leads."

He still hadn't moved. "You want to date me?"

For the first time since she'd found him in the garden, she smiled. Despite his photographic memory and an extraordinarily high IQ, he seemed to be having difficulty comprehending English. She understood why.

When something had been the same for an eon, it was mind-bending to realize that it was suddenly different. A micro-evolution had occurred in their relationship. "Yes. I want to give dating you a try."

"And . . . you want to kiss me? Is that what you said?"

A tendril of hair drifted in front of her face. She tucked it behind her ear. "When I told you on the beach that I liked our kiss, that was an understatement. In fact, it was such a big understatement that it might be considered either a sin of omission or a lie."

His gaze homed in on her.

"That kiss was earth-shattering," she stated. "In the best possible way."

He walked slowly toward her, closing the distance between them until they stood less than a foot apart.

Desire began to singe the edges of the clear-headedness she was trying to maintain. "Was it earth-shattering for you, too?" Her voice emerged faintly hoarse.

"Yes. Earth-shattering."

"Do you want to give dating me a try?" she asked.

He released a rasp of amusement. "Britt. I've been wanting to give dating you a try since I was fourteen."

"You're not worried?"

"About what?"

"That our dating relationship will crash and burn, which will end up ruining everything between us?"

He thought about it for a drawn-out space of time. His attention traveled down to her lips, held there, then returned to her eyes. "I'm terrified." He moved in even closer.

She positioned her bare feet between his dress shoes and lifted her chin. She could feel his breath on her lips, and her heart was racing at what felt like double its usual speed. Until now, Zander's love for her had been hypothetical. She hadn't known how she'd feel if and when she came face-to-face with the reality of it.

Now she knew. She wasn't scared. She definitely didn't want to run. The opposite, in fact. Despite her track record with men, regardless of the epic disaster that might be looming—she wanted this. She was willing to accept a level of danger in exchange for the opportunity of more with him.

He inclined his face toward hers with exquisite deliberation, seeming to test every nuance of her response.

She caught her bottom lip in her teeth. Let it go. Patience wasn't usually her thing, but she made herself wait. If he could draw out the anticipation of pleasure, then so could she.

His eyelids sunk closed. His lips met hers. In less than a second, the kiss turned passionate. His hands framed her face. Her hands wound behind his neck and insistently pulled him closer.

The rest of the universe ceased to exist. No sounds penetrated but those they were making. No heat but that which they were building. No sensations but these. No people in the world but him. She'd been waiting for this kiss for days that felt like years.

Zander communicated his devotion to her clearly. She expressed that she adored him and depended on him and understood him. She could stand on this spot and kiss him all night. . . .

Except for the fact that she was MIA from Nora's wedding.

Oh, who cared? She could kiss him for just a little while longer.

After a few more minutes passed, she forced herself to lean back. He regarded her through hazy eyes.

"I should probably get back to the reception, seeing as how it's my sister's reception, and I'm a bridesmaid." She promptly ruined the effect of her words by kissing the edge of his jaw.

"I agree." He kissed her forehead.

"Someone might begin to wonder where I am." She hugged him tighter.

"You're right." He trailed kisses toward her collarbone.

Gasping, she angled her head to the side to grant him better access.

"You're right," he said again, this time with more clarity and force. He lifted his head. "I'll go back in with you."

"Okay." *It would be good, Britt, if you could make yourself move now.*

He gave her a wolfish smile. It was rare to see him smile like that, which made it all the more powerful.

She slipped on her shoes, and they walked toward the reception. When they'd almost reached their destination, she pulled him to a halt. "It might not be the best idea to steal Nora's thunder in any way tonight."

"No hand-holding at the reception? No kissing? No one the wiser?" He'd read her mind.

"Exactly. You and I are the wiser, though. Which feels like enough for now."

"More than enough."

Their eyes met and the knowing look in his caused her senses to leap with delight.

"What are your plans after this?" she asked.

"I don't have any. You?"

"My cousins are staying with me, so I have to get them settled for the night. After that, I'm free."

"Want to meet me somewhere?"

"Yes, but where? There's no privacy at my place."

"There's none at the inn, either."

Her face brightened. "Sweet Art is private. Meet me there forty-five minutes after we leave here?"

"I'll be there."

She proceeded Zander—her new boyfriend and oldest friend—into Nora and John's boisterous celebration.

———

Zander reclaimed his seat at their now-empty table, feeling nothing like the man who'd eaten dinner here. Then it had felt like he'd been in the Upside Down, made famous by the TV show *Stranger Things*. Now he found himself in the Right Side Up.

He watched Britt check in with her family members, then dance with her dad. He couldn't fully believe what had just happened between them. It was too good to be true. Too sudden to trust. Too unexpected to have actually happened.

But it had.

He chuckled as he studied the palms of his hands to verify the reality of them. People were going to think he was crazy, sitting here smiling to himself and staring at his hands.

The girl he loved liked him back. She wanted to kiss him. She wanted to date him.

Thank God. He was finally going to get the chance with Britt that he'd been waiting for, and not just since the ninth grade. He'd been born for this chance. If this chance resulted in anything less than marriage and him loving her and her loving him until death, then he'd be finished. There'd be no recovering from a breakup—

He wasn't going to let himself think about that tonight. He was self-aware enough to know that he could be pessimistic and that he worried too much. He refused to let those weaknesses spoil anything about this night.

"You're back," Britt's grandmother Margaret said to Zander. She approached, Valentina and Clint in her wake. Zander rose and pulled out her chair for her. All four of them settled into their seats. "Was Britt with you just now?" Margaret asked. "I noticed she was gone, too."

"Yes. We stepped outside to get some air." A visceral memory of kissing her flashed through his mind. "Compared to the temperature outside, it feels hot in here." He slid out of his jacket and rolled up his sleeves.

Margaret's chin tightened. "You know I've never approved of those tattoos. It says in Leviticus that God's people shouldn't put tattoo marks on themselves."

"Yes, ma'am." He knew better than to point out that it also said in Leviticus that God's people shouldn't wear clothing woven of two kinds of material . . . like the dress she was wearing.

"In the ancient world," Clint said, "tattoos played a very cool role in rituals and traditions."

"Not in *Christian* rituals and traditions," Margaret snapped. "Imagine the Apostle Peter with tattoos."

Valentina inclined her friendly face toward Margaret. "Heater?"

"Peter," Zander said.

"You cold, miss?" Valentina asked. "Should I get your coat?"

"No, I'm quite comfortable," Margaret said. "Thank you."

"Are you referring to the mechanic named Peter who lives in Shelton?" Clint asked. "He's got a tattoo on his neck, and he's a legitimate genius with transmissions."

Zander laughed.

"I'm referring to the Peter who was Jesus Christ's disciple," Margaret clarified sharply.

"Icicle?" Valentina asked.

"*Disciple.*"

Clint responded with a look of contrition. Valentina, with one of confusion.

Margaret's attention sliced to Zander. His amusement caused her to narrow her eyes.

He couldn't help it. Britt wanted to date him. He'd be smiling for days.

"When will you be returning to your trip?" she asked.

So long as he and Britt were dating, he wasn't going anywhere. "I'm not sure."

"I hope you plan to avoid Amsterdam," Margaret said.

"Yes, ma'am."

Margaret sniffed. "Britt tells me that your book has done very well."

"Far better than I expected."

"Have you ever considered writing about the stoning of Stephen?" Margaret asked.

"Moaning?" Valentina asked.

"Stoning," Margaret repeated in a louder tone. "I've always thought that would make an excellent topic for a novel."

"I'll keep that in mind."

"I have this book idea," Clint said. "About this actor who goes to Hollywood and actually *meets* his muse. You know? The two of them could do all these really cool things together, like paddle-boarding and ceramics. Or they could create some of those really big bubbles, you know? Those bubbles that are as tall as a man?"

"Sure. Interesting thought, Clint."

"I think romance would be for you to write," Valentina proposed. "You could tell story about Russian woman coming to America as mail-order bride."

"Fascinating idea."

"Yes." Valentina patted his forearm. "Romance be good thing for you to write about, sir. Very good."

Zander hadn't planned on staying all the way until the end of Nora and John's wedding reception, but now a crane wouldn't be able to drag him away.

He put in an admirable amount of time chatting with Margaret, Valentina, and Clint, even though their conversation reminded him of a trip through a fun house at a fair.

He mingled with reception guests.

Eventually, he and Britt stood across from each other holding lit sparklers as Nora and John ran through the row of guests and climbed into a waiting limo.

Zander had a great deal of affection for Nora. He liked John. He was happy for them. Everyone had had a wonderful time at their ceremony and reception. Neither had been boring or drawn-out.

Even so, he couldn't have been more glad to see them leave.

Britt squared away her cousins in record time. Record time! Thus, she beat Zander to Sweet Art.

She waited for him in the kitchen, almost unbearably impatient for him to arrive. She'd changed into yoga pants and a long-sleeved work-out top, and passed the time by sitting cross-legged on her desk chair and posting pictures from Nora and John's wedding to social media. While she waited, Zander's words *"I have always loved you"* replayed again and again in her memory.

He'd loved her this whole time. The ramifications of that: enormous.

For one thing, it must have been hard, incredibly hard, on him to have been such a good friend to her all these years while wanting to be more than her friend.

For another thing, she'd taken on a big responsibility tonight when she'd kissed him.

The love he'd extended to her was a sacred trust. She needed to handle it with extreme care. His parents' love hadn't proven trustworthy. He'd just lost his uncle. She absolutely had to prove herself dependable in this situation.

In fact, she wanted to prove herself to be better than dependable. She wanted to make up for the pain she'd caused him in the past.

When she heard footsteps on the walkway outside, she raised her head to see him push through Sweet Art's back door. He'd changed, too. Into jeans and a hoodie.

"Hey," she said.

He crossed to her and threaded his strong hands into her hair until they supported the base of her neck. Just like that, no preamble. He traced his thumbs along her jaw. "Hey."

This wondrous new thing between them was *way* too big and powerful to contain. She'd considered herself to be a romance guru because she'd mowed through an impressive number of boyfriends. She'd been Zander's girlfriend for all of two and a half hours, and already, she could see that her self-acclaimed knowledge about matters of the heart had been pitifully lacking. Embarrassingly incomplete. Her other relationships had been pleasant and diverting, but they hadn't been anything like this.

She remembered elementary school worksheets that had asked her to circle the item that wasn't like the other. If she could line up all her previous boyfriends and Zander, she'd put an enormous circle around Zander.

He kissed her then, tugging her away from coherent thought on an ebb tide of pure, sweet, aching bliss.

Zander's journal entry, six years ago:

Britt's been living in France for a year now. In two days, I'll be taking my second trip to see her there.

I can't afford international travel. But I can afford the separation between us even less, so I've been tutoring students to earn money and eating ramen for dinner.

It's worth it.

Since she's been gone, I've felt as though there's a river separating me from everyone and everything else. That river is Britt. That river is France.

My plane leaves in forty-eight hours. Which means I'll see her again in sixty-three hours and twenty-eight minutes.

Finally.

CHAPTER
Nineteen

Britt and Zander stayed awake all night.

They laughed and kissed and talked. They made peanut butter cookies together at three a.m. They marveled over the two of them, together as more than friends. Friends, still. But it was the "more than" part that neither of them could get over. It was that part that held the astonishing power of a hurricane. It might take them weeks to accustom themselves to it.

Britt hoped that it took her years, because exploring this horizon was like unwrapping a golden box, hiding inside another golden box, hiding inside another golden box.

They parted reluctantly at six, and Britt returned to her cottage. She slipped on pajamas and whipped up waffle batter. Energy blazed along her nerve endings. By the time her cousins made their way downstairs, sliced fruit, fresh-squeezed orange juice, bacon, and waffle fixings awaited them. She felt invincible!

If only invincibility lasted longer. Exhaustion felled her around the time her cousins left, at eleven.

She texted Zander to let him know that the coast was clear. He appeared less than ten minutes later. While he went around the downstairs living area shutting drawers, doors, and cupboards, she brought pillows down from her bedroom. They collapsed onto her sofa. He reclined, pillows behind his lower back, legs stretched out. She lay on her side on the sofa, a pillow beneath her head.

"What movie is guaranteed to put us right to sleep?" Zander asked.

"Without giving us nightmares." She scrunched her face, racking her brain.

"*A River Runs Through It*?"

"*Babe*?"

"*Babe* is perfect."

A pink pig trotted around a farm onscreen while relaxation sank over Britt like a warm blanket.

Zander was here. They were holding hands. It was Sunday, and she had nowhere to be for the rest of the day. No responsibilities.

When she woke, she could tell by the quality of the light that late afternoon had arrived. Slowly, she squinted and turned toward Zander. He was already awake. He was still reclining, but he'd twisted his torso to face her. One of his arms rested along the sofa's top and his chin rested on his bicep. He was watching her.

This was the best way to wake up. Ever.

"Hungry?" he asked.

"Mmm-hmm."

"How about I take you out to dinner?"

Butterscotch schnapps!

The revelation came to Britt near noon the next day while she was washing her hands at Sweet Art's kitchen sink. That's what her peppermint truffle needed in order to achieve greatness. She'd add butterscotch schnapps to the cream, then infuse the cream with a cinnamon stick.

Of course! She could already taste the balance of it.

She'd been about to take a break for lunch. Instead, she launched into a fresh flurry of activity in order to test her inspiration.

When Zander arrived at two to take her mountain biking, she

greeted him at Sweet Art's back door carrying a tiny plate bearing a peppermint truffle.

His attention raised from the truffle to her. "You did it, didn't you?"

"Yes. Finally!"

He gently lifted the chocolate.

She watched him eat it.

"It's excellent," he pronounced.

"Thank you." His praise regarding chocolate meant more to her than the praise of anyone else, because his praise was educated.

"What did you do to it since the last time I tasted it?" he asked. "I can't put my finger on what you changed."

"Good. I don't like to be obvious."

"Well?"

"I added butterscotch schnapps to the cream, then infused it with cinnamon."

"Do you feel like Edison when he invented the lightbulb?"

"Very much so. It seems that having you as a boyfriend has taken me to a higher plane of chocolate creativity."

"Is that so?" He set the plate aside and drew so close he had to incline his chin to keep eye contact with her.

Her breath shallowed. She placed her palms on his chest.

"Imagine what you'll be capable of," he said, "after having me as a boyfriend for another week. The Nobel Prize for chocolate?"

"Undoubtedly," she whispered. "Don't forget the Medal of Freedom."

His fingers interlaced behind her waist. "I'm happy to do whatever I need to do on behalf of chocolate."

"Anything for a good cause?"

"Whatever it takes."

"Maybe having me for a girlfriend will take you to a higher plane of writing creativity."

"It already has. I wrote eighteen pages today."

She went up on her tiptoes and set her lips against his in a kiss as diaphanous as sunshine. The magnetism between them built with a glorious rush of intensity—

"Ready?" came Willow's voice, followed at once by the creak of the door that led to the shop. "I'm here to pick you up—"

Britt only had time to jerk a few inches away from Zander. His arms remained behind her. One of her hands bunched the fabric of his shirt.

Willow's face slackened comically. Quickly though, a grin burgeoned on her lips. "Well, well, well."

Maddie rushed to a stop at Willow's shoulder. She gaped at them with excitement.

Britt and Zander stepped sheepishly apart.

Britt wouldn't have minded keeping the change in her relationship with Zander to herself for a little while longer. At the same time, she was sensible enough to know that hiding the truth from people who were as close to her as Maddie and Willow would quickly cost her more effort than it was worth. She was too busy being blissful right now to bother with secrecy.

"We had plans to help Mom and Dad put Bradfordwood back to rights this afternoon." Willow pointed a thumb behind her shoulder. "Now that all the wedding guests have gone. Remember?"

"Oh. That's right." Her focus on Zander had obliterated everything else from her head. Shoot. She'd been looking forward to mountain biking with him. "I'd forgotten. Sorry that I made plans with you, too, Zander."

"No problem." He pulled his car keys from his pocket. "We'll go mountain biking another time."

"You're not going to stay and face this firing squad with me?" Britt joked.

"I have faith in your ability to face firing squads without my help." He winked and closed the door behind him.

"*You and Zander are together?*" Willow asked.

"We are."

Maddie released a squeak of delight.

"Since when?" Willow wanted to know.

"The wedding reception."

"It's about time," Maddie said.

"Oh my goodness." Willow hugged Britt. "This is the *best* news."

"Are you happy?" Maddie asked.

"Very happy," Britt said.

Willow clapped.

"I just don't want you to get too worked up," Britt said. "This is all very new. We're just enjoying ourselves."

"Except you know you can't just enjoy yourself with Zander, right?" A trace of seriousness seeped into Willow's demeanor.

"I know."

"He loves you."

"So he's told me."

"He has?" Maddie asked.

"Yes, once. However, we've been a couple for less than two days, so I'm hoping you'll understand why I'm not quite ready to print wedding invitations."

Willow extracted her phone.

"Who are you texting?" Britt asked. As far as she was concerned, her relationship status update could spread via Merryweather's usual communication channel: avid gossip.

"I'm telling Nora," Willow answered. "In Fiji. If I don't immediately pass this news along to her, she might never forgive me. And if she never forgives me, then who's going to loan me books?"

Near dinnertime that night, Zander waited for Britt.

They'd decided to meet at the bench situated a five-minute walk into the forest behind the Inn at Bradfordwood. Here, the stream stretched into a wide bend. The air smelled of sun-warmed pine needles. Blue lupine colored the opposite bank.

He'd spent a good portion of his life waiting for Britt. However, now that they were together, waiting no longer depressed him. He could easily wait for her here for hours.

He felt like a man who'd been praying for relief from migraines for years. And had now, suddenly, been cured. He was without pain. Healthy. Content.

Zander hadn't been peaceful or trusting in the face of his unanswered prayers about Britt. God had seen fit to answer his prayers anyway. The truth of his faithlessness in comparison to God's generosity left him both grateful and guilty.

His guilt and the knowledge that God could take Britt away at any moment were the only two things keeping Zander from a sense of complete satisfaction.

He rested the back of his head on the bench, his face slanting to the cloudy sky.

Since Nora's wedding, he hadn't told Britt again that he loved her because he knew better than to rush her or pressure her. Dating Britt Bradford was like trying to tame a bobcat. If he gave her any reason to think he wanted to take away her freedom, he'd lose her.

Thus, he was holding a part of himself back verbally. And trying his best to hold a part of his heart back, too. He wasn't succeeding fully. However, the need to try to protect himself had been ingrained in him. Life had taught him that he needed an insurance policy of some kind, always.

When he heard a twig snap, he straightened.

Britt came into view. The confidence in her stride told him just how at home she was on these acres. A warrior princess in her own territory.

The majority of his life, he'd not lived in a place that he could classify as "home." But whenever and wherever he was with her, he was understood and accepted.

Her presence was home to him.

She lowered onto the bench and interlaced her hand with his. "I'm bummed that I stood you up for mountain biking. Can I get a rain check on that?"

He pulled their joined hands to him and kissed the back of her hand. "Sure."

"What did you spend the afternoon doing?"

"Searching Carolyn's house a second time."

"Find any paintings by Renoir?"

"None. So then I searched their land. I wondered if maybe Frank could have put the painting in a protective box of some kind and buried it."

"And?"

"Nothing I saw on the property made me think that's what happened."

"Where could he have hidden it?"

"I wish I knew. I can't imagine where he hid it and neither can Carolyn."

"We really need to get inside Frank's cell phone." She reached out and idly traced his bottom lip with her fingertip.

Playfully, he caught her finger in his teeth.

She shrieked, laughing. Then grew more serious as she watched the pad of her finger graze his jaw, skim down the side of his throat, trace the neckline of his shirt. "I'm lucky to have you."

"I'm luckier." He held himself immobile, his heart striking his ribs.

Zander was certain that of the two of them, he was the luckiest. He was also the one who loved the most, which left him exposed.

A warning bell sounded deep inside him. He'd gambled all on this relationship. If things didn't work out, he'd lose his best friend and one of the only families he'd ever had.

Already, he was acting with as much caution as possible. What more could he do? He and Britt were together. He didn't want his dread of losing her to ruin the joy of having her.

One perfect week slid by.

When Britt was making chocolate, Zander was writing. When Britt was off work, the two of them were together.

They hiked and kayaked and sailed and watched movies. They hung out with Carolyn and with Britt's family. They hunted for the painting in Frank's office building and at Frank and Carolyn's church. They cooked side by side and shared their plates at restaurants.

Britt's parents had long called Britt and Zander inseparable. But now, except for work hours and sleep hours, they really were.

Britt sat in her living room, reading her most recent book purchase, *Chocolate-Making Through the Centuries*.

When Zander had finished his pages for the day, she'd encouraged him to spend the afternoon attending to the marketing responsibilities his publisher had added to his plate. The two of them had made plans to drive to Shelton to hear a band this evening.

Unfortunately, the Monday evening weather seemed to have other ideas. A spring storm had stalled overhead and instead of decreasing, the drenching rain only seemed to be strengthening.

She kept expecting him to text her to say he'd arrive to pick her up after the rain. So far, he hadn't. And so far, she'd learned that archaeologists had unearthed a ceramic vessel on the Gulf Coast of Mexico that contained the chemical footprint of cacao. They'd dated the vessel to approximately 1750 BC.

1750 BC! Maybe Zander would be willing to travel with her to Mexico later this year to check out the site and try the chocolate from that region—

Her doorbell rang. She startled, then hurried to her door. Surely, he hadn't braved the downpour—

He had. He stood on her front step, soaked. His dark hair gleamed black with moisture. His eyelashes formed spiky points. His white shirt clung to his chest in translucent swaths. His jeans looked like they'd been dipped in a lake. Behind him, gray streaked vertically to the earth with a droning white noise.

Self-deprecation tipped up his lips. "I didn't want to be late."

He was soaked and probably cold, and she wanted to nurture him almost as much as she wanted to launch herself into his arms. "I was thinking you'd arrive after this let up."

"I told you I'd be here at six, so I'm here at six."

Trustworthy Zander, who always did what he said he'd do. Now that she thought about it, that quality was unusual. It wasn't even something she expected from most of her friends and acquaintances. It was commonplace for people to agree to do a thing, then rationalize it or excuse it away when that thing became too challenging or too boring.

"Come inside," she said.

"And drip all over your floors? I don't have anything to change into, so there's no point in coming in."

"But you must be chilly."

"Nah. It feels kind of good actually." He slowly walked backward down her steps, still facing her, until he'd left her porch.

He was standing unprotected beneath a storm and enjoying it.

Her own sense of adventure kicked in. She raced into the downpour after him. He caught her just the way he had the day he'd returned from his Grand Tour.

The pelting rain snatched Britt's breath, even though Zander had been right . . . this late May rain wasn't cold. It held summer's promise far more than winter's memory.

"I didn't want you to get wet." Laughter stitched through his statement.

"I wasn't about to let you have all the fun."

"But you'd done your hair and put on makeup. . . ."

"I couldn't care less."

"One of these days your spontaneity is going to bite you." He grinned.

"Says the water-logged man. You were spontaneous first."

"I was punctual. *You* were spontaneous."

"If I get hit by a lightning bolt, we'll both agree that my spontaneity bit me." Her clothing became heavy, its dampness pressing against her skin. Droplets rolled down her forehead and cheeks.

Zander looped an arm under her knees, then carried her along one of the decorative pathways that bisected the large flower garden at the heart of the Hackberry Lane Cottages.

He came to a stop in the center of the green space, and she slid to standing. He didn't release her from his hold.

The water formed a drumming veil around them. All the cottages had vanished from view as surely as the two of them had vanished from view of the cottages. Probably a good thing. Poor Mrs. Witherspoon would call the police if she spotted Britt kissing a man in the middle of a monsoon.

"You're not allowed to get hit by a lightning bolt," Zander told her, his hard-planed face uncompromising. "If you did, then I'd have to jump in front of the next one and Aunt Carolyn would be mad."

"You wouldn't have to jump in front of the next lightning bolt."

"Yes, I would." He spoke soberly. "Because you're everything to me."

Heat blossomed in her chest.

"I'd stand in a thousand storms for you," he said.

He didn't see her as the pampered youngest sister, the Bradford daughter with too many advantages and too little common sense. She wasn't as sensitive as she should be. She was overly focused on her work, and in fact, had been known to forget things—even important things she ought to have remembered—for hours and days at a time. She had commitment issues. She could be too reckless and even harmfully self-sufficient.

Zander knew all that. Yet, he'd always chosen to focus on her best qualities, not her worst.

To be valued the way he valued her filled the crevices Britt's insecurities had chiseled.

Her hands tunneled into his wet hair, and she drew his mouth to hers. Pounding rain without. Pounding emotions within.

———

Dimly, Zander realized that the rain was lessening.

He regretted that it was, because that meant their privacy was lessening, too.

"Do you think Mrs. Witherspoon can see us?" Britt asked against his lips.

"Not yet, but soon."

"Bummer."

He stared down into her flushed face, overwhelmed by how beautiful she was. . . .

And an idea slipped into his brain.

He swept saturated tendrils of Britt's hair away from her eyes. He'd thought of a passcode. A passcode to try on Frank's cell phone.

He'd thought of it because he now comprehended why Frank had been willing to leave his past life behind, to never again see his family members or be known by the name he'd been given at birth. Frank had been willing to do all of that and far more because of love.

LOVE.

Zander visualized the cell phone's screen. Five six eight three would spell out the word love.

"Let's dry off. And go hear a band." He took her hand, and they retraced their route in the direction of her house.

He'd try his new passcode idea on Frank's phone when he was by himself. On the off-chance he was right and unlocked the phone, he wanted time to search its contents, think, then settle on the safest course of action alone.

Note passed between Zander and Britt in eleventh grade:

ZANDER: Do you need help studying for your trig test this weekend?

BRITT: I'm in big trouble in that class, but I don't want you to spend your weekend explaining trigonometry to me.

ZANDER: Who else do you know who can explain trigonometry to you?

BRITT: Good point.

ZANDER: I'll come over to your house tonight, and we'll get started.

BRITT: I'll make you apple pie as payment.

Note passed from Hannah to Britt in eleventh grade:

HANNAH: Did you notice how Olivia followed Zander around at the party Friday? I think she might be into him. They'd look amazing together with their black hair and blue eyes.

BRITT: Totally! I really love Olivia. But I don't think her personality is quite right for Zander. They're not a fit.

Letter slipped under Mr. Finch's door by Britt in eleventh grade:

Mr. Finch,

I'm so glad you coach the boys' soccer team. You're really good at it! Great job!

I only have one piece of constructive criticism. You don't play Zander Ford enough. He's super talented, and I sincerely believe that he could score a lot of goals and help your team to a winning record if he didn't spend so much of the game on the bench.

Thanks for your consideration. Go Panthers!

—A concerned fan

283

CHAPTER
Twenty

The next morning Zander drove past the employee lot behind The Giftery, confirmed that Carolyn's car was parked there, then continued to Frank and Carolyn's house. He let himself inside with the key that Frank had given him the day he'd moved in.

He found Frank's phone charging on the desk in the home office.

Aurora padded into the room, her tail wagging and her homely dog face smiling.

"Hey, sweetheart." He scratched her chin and then, when she rolled onto her back, obliged her by scratching her belly.

Sitting on the desk chair, he picked up the cell phone. Aurora pawed his pant leg. He ignored her. More insistent pawing.

"Come on up, then." Since Aurora had the vertical jump of an elephant, he lifted her dead weight onto his lap.

Immediately, she rested her chin on the crook of his elbow and closed her eyes.

He brought Frank's phone to life, then slowly tested his newest passcode theory.

Five. Six. Eight. Three.

With swift obedience, the phone unlocked.

Zander stared at it in astonishment.

No way.

LOVE had been Frank's passcode.

His tiredness vanished. All other distractions fell away like a deck of cards from a child's hands.

One of the app icons displayed on the phone belonged to Pacific Trust Bank. The rest of the apps looked like ones that had come preloaded onto the phone.

Zander tapped the Pacific Trust Bank icon. The app requested another password. This roadblock, he'd anticipated. He reached for the notepad on which Carolyn had jotted down all the passwords that she and Frank had ever used. The bank would no doubt demand a long password that contained a mix of numbers, uppercase and lowercase letters.

He scanned the list of known passwords, looking for one that matched those characteristics. The third one he tried, Frank&Caro1986, worked.

Account information filled the phone's screen, and Zander released an amazed exhale. He scrolled through the list of withdrawals and deposits.

On the fifteenth day of every month, Frank's employer deposited money into the account. On the first day of every month, a company called The Residences withdrew money from the account. The deposit from his employer and the withdrawals to The Residences were set to trigger automatically. Scattered between those two static transactions, Frank paid utility bills. Because Frank had steadily deposited more than he'd paid out, he'd built up a five-thousand-dollar balance.

Zander tapped on the hyperlink for The Residences. The app provided a phone number and an address in Olympia, Washington.

He memorized both.

Carefully, he placed Frank's phone on the desk, as if rattling it might cause the clue to disappear. He picked up his own phone and ran a search for The Residences.

The seven-story apartment building gave the impression of modern solidity. According to The Residences home page, it had opened its doors eight years before.

He returned his attention to Frank's phone and checked the date of the first rent payment Frank had made to The Residences. Eight years ago. In fact, that was the first payment he'd ever made via mobile banking using this bank account.

Assuming Frank had moved *Young Woman at Rest* to The Residences eight years ago, Zander had no way of knowing where he'd kept it prior to that time. Wherever it had been, Frank hadn't paid for storage or rent fees via mobile banking.

How could he pinpoint Frank's apartment number?

Frank must've been receiving rent and utility bills either via his mailbox at The Residences or via his email inbox. Or both.

Zander launched the email app. Sure enough, he found a row of bills inside the inbox. He opened the most recent statement from the electric company and—*there*.

Right at the top of the bill, it listed Frank's address. *4030 Oak Fern Way, #618, Olympia, Washington*.

Zander stared at the address until it blurred.

The top desk drawer released an accusing creak as Zander opened it. Since Frank's death, Carolyn had kept many of his personal items here. His wallet. His business cards. His keys. His other phone, the non-secret one. The spare change he'd left on the kitchen counter the last time he'd been at the house.

Zander scooped up Frank's keys. Nothing about the ordinary split ring holding several plain keys would arouse anyone's interest. Yet, Zander would bet that this ring held the key to Frank's apartment at The Residences. If anyone questioned Frank about that particular key, it would have been easy for Frank to shrug and say the key had been there so long that he'd forgotten what it opened.

Zander went to the back door, let Aurora out, then stood on the stoop. Should he take the keys without saying anything to Carolyn? Or should he ask to borrow them?

He had no idea how often she went through Frank's things. If he took the keys without telling her and she realized they were missing, she'd go into a panic, and he'd have to backpedal. Better to tell her. He'd say he planned to take the keys to a friend to see if the friend could give him information about them.

He hated lying to her. But since lying might protect her, he'd lie.

Aurora returned. She sat and peered up at him with a combination of kindness and disapproval, as if she could read his mind.

He'd take Frank's cell phone, too. LOVE was not an extremely tricky four-letter word. It had evaded him for days, but now that he'd hit on it, it seemed almost elementary. Carolyn could come home from work tonight and figure it out. It was only a matter of time before Britt did.

At this point, he didn't want either of them to know about The Residences. The meeting with Emerson had confirmed that there might be others—maybe several others and maybe dangerous others—who were aware that Frank possessed *Young Woman at Rest*. Until the FBI arrived, knowledge about Frank's apartment in Olympia could do nothing for Carolyn or Britt except endanger them.

He stuffed Frank's phone and keys into his sweat shirt pocket, filled Aurora's water dish, then locked the door behind him on his way to his car.

He sat behind the wheel in silence, searching the view for Emerson or any other suspicious person or vehicle. He saw nothing unusual. Even so, he could very well be under surveillance, and the information he'd just learned felt like it was flashing from him like the lights on top of a police car.

He drove a few miles, then parked in a lot adjacent to a busy restaurant.

He texted Carolyn, asking to borrow Frank's phone and keys and giving his reasons why.

In under a minute, Carolyn replied that he was welcome to borrow Frank's phone and keys.

Zander dialed Jennifer Delacruz, the FBI agent he'd spoken with on the phone after meeting with Emerson. He explained that he may have discovered the location of the painting. She informed him that she was currently on assignment in Georgia. However, she and her partner would shoot to arrive in Washington in four days' time to follow up on his lead.

After they disconnected, Zander eyed Frank's keys, resting in the Jeep's cupholder.

He had an address. And he had keys.

For more than eight weeks, he'd been searching for information. Now that he'd finally obtained it, he was almost desperate to act on it.

He wouldn't act on it, though.

It was smartest to wait until Agent Delacruz arrived and let her take over the case.

He returned to the Inn at Bradfordwood and sat at the desk in his room. However, he didn't even open his laptop. After staring out the window for countless minutes, he scoured through Frank's phone. He checked its browsing history—none. He checked its phone contacts—none. No recent calls to or from the phone.

The drive to Olympia would only take forty minutes. He needed to be free by two, when Britt got off work, because they were going out on the Bradford family sailboat with her mom and dad this afternoon.

He had plenty of time to drive to Olympia, try Frank's keys on #618 at The Residences, and return to Merryweather without tipping off Britt.

No.

He'd wait for the FBI.

That afternoon, he did his level best to behave as if his mind was fully present. Britt's parents bought it, but Britt did not.

"What's wrong?" she asked in the car on the way back to the Hackberry Lane Cottages. "Something's bothering you. You're distracted."

"Sorry. It's just that I can't stop thinking about the painting."

The next day, his nerves stretched tighter and tighter. Questions about the mysterious interior of #618 consumed his thoughts.

Again that night, Britt asked him what was wrong. Again, he blamed his preoccupation on the painting.

He tried to eat breakfast at the inn the next morning and couldn't manage it.

What if the apartment in Olympia stood empty? Even if Frank had been storing the painting at The Residences, it's possible that Emerson's reappearance in his life had changed everything. Maybe Frank had moved the painting. Or maybe he'd sold it? Or perhaps, in the days since Zander and Britt had met with Emerson, Emerson had located the painting and removed it from #618.

What if the FBI agents flew to Washington based on the strength of his tip and found nothing? No painting? No evidence?

The prospect of wasting their time and money settled over him like a dark fog. If he drove to Olympia and checked the apartment, he'd be far better informed. He'd know whether his information merited a visit by the FBI.

Through the inn's front windows, Zander caught sight of Clint's truck approaching. No doubt, Clint would let Zander swap cars with him for the day.

If someone was tailing Zander, they'd be waiting and watching for his Jeep. If they were following his movements remotely through a tracking device, that device would be connected to the Jeep. He could drive Clint's truck to Olympia undetected—

No. He shouldn't go.

He was going to have to go. He couldn't stand to sit on the address of Frank's apartment at The Residences for another minute.

He rose from the dining room table, his face settling into resolute lines, and went in search of Clint.

Britt entered The Giftery carrying a large cardboard box containing the shop's most recent chocolate order.

"Britt!" Carolyn hurried to hold open the door leading to the shop's storage space.

Britt passed by her, set the box on the work table within, and hugged Carolyn. "Good to see you."

"Good to see you, too."

They returned to the retail area, where a husband and wife were studying the folk art display and a twenty-something woman was perusing bath products.

"How's everything going with Zander?" Bashful interest shone in the older woman's eyes. Britt knew she was really asking—*"Is your romance with my nephew blissful? Yes? I hope?"*

Without exception, Britt's friends and relatives had been thrilled to learn that she was dating Zander. They'd said things like, "Finally!" and "It's about time!" and "You two are meant to be together."

Carolyn had been among the happiest when greeted with the news. Britt supposed this was because she understood better than most the solitary state of Zander's heart.

"Everything's going great," Britt answered honestly. If there was one thing that was less than ideal about dating Zander, it was the fact that she couldn't be with him twenty-four hours a day. "How are you?" she asked Carolyn.

"I'm hanging in there."

Sorrow shrouded Carolyn. However, she no longer had the drawn, pale look of a person who had a knife pressing against her ribs.

"Has Zander's friend been able to find out anything about Frank's keys or phone?" Carolyn asked.

Britt wrinkled her brow. "I'm afraid I don't know anything about that."

"No?"

"No."

Carolyn's hands made a fluttery movement just anxious enough to reveal that she believed she'd told Britt something she shouldn't have. "Oh well. It's no big deal. I'm sure he just forgot to mention it."

"Zander delivered Frank's keys and phone to a friend of his?"

"Yes, two days ago. I guess his friend is knowledgeable about phones . . . and keys. I've been hoping something good might come out of it."

"Wonderful," Britt said brightly. "I'm hopeful, too. Fingers crossed!" She headed to the door, explaining as she went that she had to get back to Sweet Art, but that she'd see Carolyn again soon.

Once out of sight of The Giftery's windows, she came to a halt. Placing her hands on her hips, she frowned at the sidewalk.

Two days ago Zander had taken Frank's keys and cell phone. He'd said nothing about it to her. Unfortunately, she didn't believe he'd said nothing because he'd forgotten to mention it, as Carolyn had suggested.

He'd deliberately remained silent on the subject.

For the past two days, he'd been distracted. Every time she'd asked him why, he'd said he was worried about the painting. She'd accepted that answer because he was her boyfriend and because concern wasn't out of character for him. Also because she trusted him.

Her thoughts ticked like a clock.

Zander definitely did *not* have a friend with supernatural knowledge about keys and phones. If he had, he would have told her so. He would have taken Frank's keys and phone to his friend weeks ago.

Had Zander figured out the passcode to Frank's cell phone?

Surely, *surely*, he would have told her if he had.

But if he still didn't know the passcode, why did he have a sudden need of Frank's keys? He'd only need the keys if he'd learned of a house or a storage locker or an apartment that needed opening.

The most likely possibility . . . *Let this not be true.* The most likely possibility was that he'd figured out the passcode, searched the information on Frank's phone, and learned of a potential location for the painting.

Her stomach give a sickening lurch. She didn't want to believe that Zander would cut her out of something that had been their joint project.

Except he himself had admitted to her that he was overly protective of her. It wasn't much of a stretch to imagine that he'd cut her out in an attempt to keep her safe.

He'd also admitted to her that he loved her. But now he was

treating her as if she wasn't worthy of so much as a *discussion* about the painting's location. As if he couldn't rely on her to protect sensitive information. As if she were a child he had to make decisions for.

She pulled her phone from her pocket and speed-dialed his number.

.... ❦ ....

Phone call from Britt to Zander:

Zander: Hello?

Britt: Hey, I just saw your aunt Carolyn when I was dropping off chocolate at her store, and she told me that you took Frank's cell phone and keys to a friend of yours a few days ago.

Zander: Yeah, I did.

Britt: You didn't tell me about this development.

Zander: I didn't? I meant to. It's hard for me to think straight when I'm around you. You look at me, and my brain goes blank.

Britt: Who is this friend?

Zander: A guy named Ryan who I used to work with.

Britt: You've never mentioned him before.

Zander: He wasn't a close friend. I know him well enough to know that he's a genius with phones, though. I thought maybe he could figure out a way to hack into Frank's phone without compromising any of the contents.

Britt: And he's also a genius with keys?

Zander: More so than I am. Since we're stuck, it seemed like it might be helpful to let someone with fresh eyes take a look.

Britt: Are you at the inn, writing?

Zander: Yep.

Britt: Okay, got to go. I'll see you later.

CHAPTER
Twenty-One

Zander was lying.

Britt's heart reverberated slowly like a bass drum. *Boom. Boom. Boom.*

He was lying.

She activated the tracking app on her phone because back when she'd set it up, she'd added him to it. It took the app a few seconds to pinpoint Zander's location, a small space of time that stretched wretchedly long with the premonition that he was not at the inn, writing, like he'd told her.

The circle representing Zander appeared on the app's screen, traveling south on Highway 101. Nauseating proof. She'd just caught him in a lie.

He was fifteen minutes outside of town. Not a tremendous head start. If she drove fast, and she liked to drive fast, she could probably shave off a few minutes of his lead.

Boom. Boom. Boom.

A quaking had begun deep inside her torso. It was fear, she realized. She was afraid that their whole relationship was abruptly, horribly at risk.

She'd been so careful of him. She hadn't imagined that he might not be as careful of her. It hadn't occurred to her to doubt him.

Not once. Now, however, as she stared at her tracking app, she saw that she shouldn't have been so blindly naïve.

Zander. *Zander* had lied to her. He'd lied.

Big, bottomless misery hovered above her, waiting to swallow her whole. The only thing that could generate that level of misery was equally big and bottomless attachment.

She cared about Zander even more than she'd realized.

When she got to wherever he was going, he had a lot of explaining to do.

The fourth key Zander tried on the door of apartment #618 slid easily into place, then turned the deadbolt with a solid *click*.

He entered, then locked the door behind him. Cool, moist air enveloped him.

One of the keys had actually *worked*.

He was inside his uncle's secret apartment.

A contemporary kitchen that looked like it had never been used gave way to a living area. The space held the minimum amount of furniture. A simple table with four chairs. Beyond that, two sofas and a coffee table. Cream curtains partially covered the windows at the rear of the space. An open door led to a bedroom containing a bed with a beige comforter.

If the painting had once been here, was it now gone?

He flipped the light switches and illumination flooded down. As he progressed through the kitchen, the living room's right-hand wall became visible first. Three easily recognizable oil paintings had been suspended there. All were knock-offs of famous works. Monet's *Water Lilies*. Van Gogh's *Starry Night*. Degas' ballerinas.

He walked farther and was finally able to glimpse the left-hand wall.

In the center of it hung a painting.

It was a painting he'd seen many times before in articles about the Triple Play, on microfiche, on computer screens, in the books he'd checked out about Renoir. Very few people had seen this particular masterwork face-to-face in the past thirty years. Now all at once, he was in that number.

Young Woman at Rest.

Oil on canvas. Painted in the year 1876 in the impressionist style by the famously brilliant Frenchman Pierre-Auguste Renoir. Owned by the Pascal family since 1931. Taken by the Nazis in 1941. Found and returned after a painstaking search by Annette Pascal's grandparents and father in the year 1968. Stolen again in 1985 by James Richard Ross, who later became Frank Joseph Pierce.

A simple wooden frame bordered the painting. Brightness shone against the textured brushstrokes, each one melting into the next with awe-inspiring skill.

Zander's memory supplied the subject's name. Nina Lopez. Nina had lived more than a century before, yet to this day, her skin glowed with youth. Golden brown hair flowed over one shoulder onto her floral dress. Her liquid eyes looked out from the picture thoughtfully, almost as if she had been waiting with long-suffering patience to be found.

A hush fell over Zander, quieting his body and mind.

This piece of art was far more timeless than he was.

Every detail of it proclaimed *masterpiece*.

He glanced again at his surroundings. It seemed that Frank had done what he could to ensure the painting's security. He'd furnished the apartment, likely so that nothing about this interior would arouse suspicion should staff from The Residences need to enter. He'd even added other impressionist works to the room. Anyone who observed them would think that this apartment's renter liked European art from the late 1800s. They'd have no reason to imagine that one of these pieces might be an original.

Frank had positioned the curtains so that the sunlight couldn't quite reach *Young Woman at Rest*. The thermostat read *70*, which ensured an environment neither too hot nor too cold. A whir sounded from the direction of the ceiling vent above, which didn't match the others. Had it been fitted with a humidifying device? The moisture in the air seemed to attest to that.

Up until now, there'd still been a chance Frank hadn't been involved in the Triple Play. Emerson could have been lying. The clues they'd followed might have led them down the wrong path. But now he was looking directly into the face of the Renoir and the certainty that his uncle had stolen it.

The uncle he'd loved.

No person was perfect. He wasn't. His parents hadn't been. But back when he'd come to live with Frank and Carolyn, they'd both seemed as close to perfect as people could be.

Maybe it had made him feel safer to think that, and in those days, he'd needed a sense of safety in order to function. Maybe thinking that had just been simpler for him.

This painting testified to the fact that Frank had made a colossal mistake. Around the time of his wedding to Carolyn, Frank had placed his trust in a God who forgave even the most colossal mistakes. But if Frank's faith had been genuine, why hadn't he taken steps to make amends for his mistake? Why hadn't he returned *Young Woman at Rest* to Annette Pascal long ago? Without too much difficulty, Frank could have done so without incriminating himself.

Zander took a few steps back, to get a more distant perspective on the painting, and spotted an envelope on the coffee table. Written across it in Frank's familiar handwriting was one word.

Carolyn.

Carefully, he picked it up. The business-sized envelope held a stiffness, the kind of stiffness that worked its way into paper as it aged.

He knew what to do about the painting. He'd leave it here until the FBI came to retrieve it.

But this letter? Frank had intended this for Carolyn and only Carolyn. If he left it here, the FBI would very likely take it. As the letter's rightful owner, Carolyn deserved to open it herself and read it first.

He carefully folded it and slid it into the back pocket of his jeans. After the FBI had custody of the painting, he'd explain everything to Carolyn and give this letter to her—

Someone knocked on the apartment's door, the sound unnaturally loud in the silence. Zander jerked. His chin whipped around.

"Zander?" Britt called from the hallway.

Terror contracted his heart.

Had Emerson learned of his trip here? Had she somehow gotten hold of Britt?

He ran to the door. Splaying a hand on its wooden surface, he looked through the peephole. As far as he could tell, Britt was alone on the other side. As he watched, she turned and moved in the direction of the next door.

His thoughts shot in a thousand different directions. He opened the door. "Britt."

She whirled. He looped a hand around her arm and tugged her into the apartment. She'd probably only been in the hallway for a short time, but he felt frighteningly exposed.

All of his careful plans, his precautions on her behalf, were racing through his fingers like water.

They faced off. Him, shocked and rattled. Her, with a tight, accusatory expression on her face.

"How did you know I was here?" he asked.

"The tracking app on my phone. Remember? I connected your phone to it years ago. Before your trip."

He'd forgotten. Pressure banded around his chest. He might be having a heart attack. *Think, Zander.*

"When Carolyn told me you'd taken Frank's phone and keys, I knew that, at the very least, you'd deliberately kept that information from me. Then when I called you, I could tell you were lying. So I checked the app."

"And followed me here."

"I couldn't find your car—"

"I swapped cars with Clint."

"—but the tracking app showed me which corner of the building you were in. I started at floor one. I've been knocking on all the doors in this corner on every floor."

Think. If he was going to protect her, he first needed to think through the dangers she may have brought with her. Then decide how to counter them.

"You've found the painting. Right?" She spoke without inflection, proceeding into the apartment. When she spotted the Renoir, she simply stood, observing it.

She wore white jeans, a loose turquoise shirt. She'd woven her hair into a messy braid that snaked over one shoulder. She looked just like she always did, except for the waves of betrayal pouring from her. She was furious with him.

He was terrified for her. "Did you drive here in your car?" he asked.

She gave a rigid nod.

"No one followed you?"

"No."

"That doesn't mean they don't know where you are."

"How? I've been keeping an eye on my rearview mirror ever since the day you told me you thought Nick was tailing you. I've never once suspected that anyone was following me."

"Emerson knows you've been hunting for the painting with me. She may have placed a GPS device on your car." In that case, Emerson could be right on their heels. They might only have minutes to evacuate.

Britt looked at him sharply. "A GPS device?"

He jerked his chin.

"If you suspected that they might have put a GPS device on my car, why didn't you say so?" she asked.

Why *hadn't* he warned her? In retrospect, keeping her in the dark struck him as unforgivably stupid. "Because I didn't plan for you to come anywhere near this painting. Look, we need to get out of here." Urgency marked each word. "This piece of art is worth a fortune. There are plenty of people in the world who wouldn't hesitate to kill us both to get their hands on it."

"If I've inadvertently led those people here, then I've also led them to the painting." She gestured to the Renoir. "We can't let them have this."

"Yes, we can." If his choices were risking Britt or letting the painting fall into the wrong hands—no contest. He'd let the painting go. "Let's leave—"

"We're taking the painting. We need to cover it in something." She rushed to the curtains. "Give me a leg up."

"Britt."

"Give me a leg up."

He cupped his palms and lifted her. She raised the edge of the curtain rod from its support, tipped the rod down, and let one of the curtain panels pool on the floor.

Zander set *Young Woman at Rest* on the curtain, and they hurried to wrap it in folds of cloth. He lifted the painting, and they dashed into the hallway. He didn't bother locking the door behind them.

Elevator or stairs? "Let's take the stairs," he decided. Fewer cameras.

They'd leave Britt's car here and drive Clint's anonymous truck straight to . . . to Detective Shaw. They only had to make it to the police station in Merryweather. Yet under these circumstances, Merryweather felt much too far away.

Maybe it would be better to take the painting to the closest police station. Here, in Olympia. That's what he'd do. He'd take it to the nearest station and entrust it to the police, who were much better equipped to protect it than he was. Then he'd get Britt far away from it.

Their breathing accelerated as they sprinted down the final flight of stairs. They reached the first floor and pushed through the exit doors that emptied to the parking lot. He led the way as they ran toward Clint's truck.

The mild, cloudy day appeared harmless. Peaceful. Light wind rustled the bank of trees at the perimeter of the lot. Clint's truck waited for them, just forty yards or so away.

They sped toward it.

Twenty yards.

All four doors of a black G-Class Mercedes SUV parked nearby opened simultaneously. Four men climbed from it. Immediately, their focus centered on Zander and Britt.

His gut pitched. They ran faster.

"I'd slow down if I were you, Zander," one of the men called.

Zander cut a look over his shoulder. The one who'd spoken was Nick Dunlap. And he'd drawn a gun.

Instantly, Zander stopped. Britt ran a few more paces before pausing to assess the situation. Her eyes met his and a wordless conversation passed between them.

Go, he pled. She wasn't carrying the painting. He was. So they were unlikely to shoot her. If she continued forward, she might be able to get away. *Go!*

She gave a minuscule shake of her head. *I'm not leaving you.*

God, Zander prayed. *God.*

These men knew his name. If they knew that, then they knew what he held.

They'd come for the Renoir.

They hadn't come to hurt Britt. She was unarmed. If he cooperated with them and handed over the painting, then they'd have what they wanted and they'd let Britt go.

Nick holstered the weapon as he and the other three men neared. Zander placed himself between them and Britt. They were all wearing slim, custom-made suits. All looked like Nick did, with weathered faces and muscular frames.

One appeared to be in his mid-fifties. The others were younger. Nick. Then one with recessed eyes. One with thick, black hair.

"Out for a stroll on this pleasant day?" the oldest one asked Zander and Britt in an amused Scottish accent. Wrinkles fanned out from his eyes. He wore his graying hair short and a gold signet ring on one of his fingers.

Neither Zander nor Britt answered.

Tension had overtaken Zander's entire body.

"Tom," Nick said to the older man, nodding as a sedan pulled around the corner of the building in their direction.

Tom. This was the Tom connected to Nick and Emerson.

"It's all right," Tom said to Nick. "Zander and Britt here are too intelligent to try to signal the driver. They know they'd just end up putting him or her in jeopardy and that really wouldn't be fair, seeing as how the driver isn't involved in this at all."

The sedan drew even with them. The old woman behind the wheel gave them a benign scan and continued on.

Tom flicked his fingers toward the covered painting. "That looks heavy. We'd be glad to carry it for you—"

"Who are you?" Zander asked.

"We're the ones who've gone to a lot of time and expense to locate that painting," Tom answered.

Zander held eye contact with Tom. "Both the Pascal Museum and the FBI are offering a reward for this painting. If you'll let us return it, we'll let you pocket the reward money."

In response to Zander's offer, Tom's attention roved to Britt. He aimed a smile at her—both tender and cold—that turned Zander's blood to ice. "Interesting proposition. Except that the reward money is just a drop in the bucket compared to what I can get for the painting."

"Turning it in is fast and easy," Britt said. "No risk."

"There's always risk, love."

"But not the kind of risk that could land you in jail," she said.

Tom chuckled. "I've dealt with the risk of jail for close to forty years now. I've even been an inmate a time or two."

"We'll hand the painting over to you," Zander said. "And you'll let us go."

"You'll hand the painting over," Tom agreed. "I'm not so sure about that last part."

"You'll have what you want, and you'll let us go," Zander stated.

"But you see, I want two things." Casually, Tom resettled and smoothed his suit jacket. "I want the painting, and I want to get out of the country with it safely. If I let you go, you'll run inside that building," he inclined his head toward The Residences, "call the police, and make it more difficult for me to get out of the country."

301

"No, we won't," Zander said flatly. "You have my word."

"I never accept a stranger's word," Tom said kindly. "In fact, I never accept the word of a friend. Or even a brother, for that matter."

Panic twisted every second into an endurance test. "In that case, tie us up inside Frank's apartment."

"Not a bad idea. Just to show you how reasonable I am, I'll compromise. I've got one seat available in the car, so I'll leave one of you here inside the apartment. I'll take the other as collateral, to ensure the silence of the one we leave behind."

"I'll go," Zander said, grabbing on to the thread of hope Tom had offered. They'd restrain Britt at The Residences, and they'd take him. That, he could live with. He couldn't live with the prospect of them loading her into their SUV.

"Zander," Britt hissed.

"What?" Tom asked Britt in the same understated, entertained tone he'd been using since the conversation began. "You don't like that plan?"

"I don't want you to take him," she said. "He's told you that we won't interfere with your plans, and we won't. Tie us both up in Frank's apartment."

Tom regarded them with approval. "Look at the two of you. Both trying to protect the other. Charming." He caught Nick's eye. "Put Britt in the car and leave Zander in the apartment."

The thread of hope Zander held snapped.

Nick and the one with the recessed eyes immediately came forward.

"It's not personal, Zander," Tom was saying in his Scottish brogue. "It's just business."

The one with recessed eyes attempted to thrust Zander to the side. Zander stayed on his feet and shoved the painting into his arms. Nick came at him. Zander swung, his punch connecting with Nick's jaw.

Out of the corner of his eye, Zander saw Britt racing toward the nearest entrance to The Residences.

The dark-haired one bolted after her.

Pain exploded against the side of Zander's face. In the split second when his attention had been diverted, Nick had landed a blow. Zander came up swinging. He and Nick exchanged punches—a haze of fists and force and hurt—until the other one rushed Zander from the side, tackling him to the ground.

Zander tried to twist—

Both men thrust him onto his stomach. A knee pressed into the small of Zander's back. Zander rotated his head toward Britt, praying she'd made it inside the building.

Instead, the dark-haired man had pinned her arms in front of her and was hauling her back toward them. She was kicking, struggling. "Zander!"

"Britt," he rasped. He heaved against the weight immobilizing him.

"I'm sorry," she cried. "Zander! I'm sorry."

A prick stung the side of his neck, and his vision began to gray.

Britt writhed, doing her best to land blows against her attacker's legs as the man continued to cart her to the SUV.

No.

His worst nightmare was playing out before him. Britt, in danger because of a situation with his uncle that he'd involved her in.

Britt!

Unconsciousness submerged him.

Text message from Carolyn to Zander:

Carolyn

Britt came by the store earlier, and I told her how you'd taken Frank's keys and cell phone to your friend. She seemed surprised, so I simply wanted to let you know that I'd talked with her. I love you.

CHAPTER
Twenty-Two

Zander was in high school again.

He and Britt stood side by side at Bradfordwood's kitchen counter, making cinnamon rolls at ten o'clock at night. She'd pulled her hair up into a high ponytail and wore a navy and gold sweat shirt that said *Merryweather Panthers* across the front.

She explained to him how to roll the dough so that it was thick but not too thick.

He watched her. Slim arms. Graceful hands. Serious concentration in the familiar angles of her profile. When she had the dough how she wanted it, she scooped up handfuls of the cinnamon-sugar mixture to sprinkle on top.

She gave him a nudge and peered up at him laughingly. "C'mon, Zander Ford. You have to pull your weight." She scooted the bowl of cinnamon sugar in his direction, and he went to work.

"No One" by Alicia Keys played quietly and the scent of bread dough filled the air. But it was Britt—it had always been Britt—who commanded his senses most.

She rolled and sliced the dough, then slid a pan full of rolls into the oven. "They'll be gorgeous when they've baked and we've drizzled them with frosting."

You're gorgeous.

She wrapped her arms around his neck. "Zander?"

His breath fled. "Yes?" Mighty emotions, too big to control and almost too big to bear, expanded inside him.

"I love you."

Elation came swift and deep in response.

Except . . . something seemed off. Not quite right. He kicked his misgivings to the side.

Her hands bracketed his face, and she arched onto her toes to bring their eyes closer to level. She gave him a winsome smile. Then her lips met his.

Only, she hadn't kissed him in high school. She'd never told him she loved him. Reality began to intrude. At first he fought to thrust it away because he longed to cling to the dream. But then a nagging sense—that there was something he needed to focus on in the real world—slithered around him.

Whatever it was, this dream was better. He tried to wrap his arms around Britt, to keep her with him, but she dissolved, and he was left with nothing but darkness.

He woke filled with regret because the dream had ended.

Why was he . . . Cobwebs blanketed his brain. Why was he stretched out . . . on such a hard surface—

My God. Terrible realization split into his mind. In a single pulse, everything that had happened rushed into his memory. The four men. Him, stomach-down on the parking lot's asphalt. Britt flailing as one of the men wrestled her toward their SUV. He'd felt a sting in his neck, and then . . . nothing. Until now.

Tom had said to tie him up and leave him in Frank's apartment. That's exactly where he was, in the living room, hardwood floor below him. The lights were on. The humidifier whirred. A nail poked from the wall where the painting had hung.

A piece of what he guessed to be duct tape covered his mouth. He tried to move and discovered that his feet were cinched together with a plastic restraint. His hands were likewise bound in front of him at the wrists.

He looked for Britt, though he knew, in the place where his worst fears seethed, that she was gone.

Gone.

The men had taken both the painting and Britt.

Dread made a grab for his throat. His nose strained to push air into his lungs. He'd told Tom he'd go with them. He'd wanted it to be him. But Tom must have been able to tell how Zander felt about Britt. Tom had decided to leave behind the one who loved the other because the one who loved would be less likely to gamble with the life of the one who'd been taken by going to the authorities.

Britt's well-being was one of the most important things in Zander's life. His desire to protect her had motivated his choices for years. But if Tom thought that he'd pursue Britt's safety in this situation through silence, then Tom had misjudged him.

Zander would move mountains and oceans to get her back.

He levered himself into a sitting position and checked his watch. He'd been out for approximately twenty minutes. With effort, he inched toward the wall shared by the apartment next door. He banged it with his feet. Then he banged the floor. Then the wall.

He needed someone to hear him. He needed someone to come.

When his legs began to shake with exhaustion, he used his hands. His knuckles grew bloody. As much as his body protested, he found he could master it far better than his mind.

His mind turned on him like poison. He worried that no one would answer his pounding. He worried about the things Tom and his men might do to a young and beautiful captive. He worried that he wouldn't be able to find her. That he'd go to the police and they'd search and search and . . . nothing. He worried that Britt wouldn't make it through this alive.

He ceased his movement long enough to catch his breath, to pray.

Right here and right now, when it mattered, Zander knew who to turn to. The fire of his predicament brightly illuminated what was, and wasn't, important.

His head bent beneath the weight of his remorse. For years,

he'd nurtured his complaints, content to bind himself to God with duty. His behavior shamed him now, so much his chest ached with the force of it.

The God he'd failed was the same one—the only one—who could shield Britt now.

Zander had been unfaithful, and if God operated on human rules of fairness, then he would have no right to ask God anything. God would have every right to turn away and shut His ears to Zander's pleas.

But against all odds and all comprehension, God didn't operate on human rules. He'd trampled fairness when He'd sanctioned the most unfair act of history—the crucifixion. Because of that, Zander had been made right with God. He was God's son. A son full of mistakes. But a son, nonetheless.

Zander's unfaithfulness couldn't negate God's faithfulness. Faithfulness was inseparable from God's character. And so Zander could be sure that here, where no one else might be able to hear him, there was One who *would* hear. One who could be counted upon to listen.

Zander prayed, empty-handed and undeserving. He begged God to forgive him. He begged God to keep Britt safe. He begged God to send someone to free him.

Renewed energy flowed in his limbs by the time he ended the prayer. He hit his feet against the wall over and over. He prayed. Hit his feet against the wall. Prayed.

At last, a knock finally sounded at the door. "It's management," a female voice called. "Everything all right in there?"

He thumped furiously with his feet until he heard a key turn in the lock. Relief blurred Zander's vision when a middle-aged woman wearing a navy business suit entered. Her face blanched at the sight of him. She reassured him that she'd get help, used her phone to alert a coworker, then knelt beside him. Her name tag read *Crystal*.

Gingerly, she peeled the duct tape from his mouth.

"Scissors," he said.

She placed a quick follow-up call requesting scissors. "Are you all right?" Fear and concern stamped her face.

No. He was not all right. "I'm fine."

"Who did this to you?"

"I'd rather not say. Do you see my cell phone or my keys?"

"Wait a sec." She hurried around the space. "No. I'm sorry, I don't."

They'd taken his method of communication and his method of transportation.

Crystal returned to his side. "What happened?"

"Some men stole something from me." He wasn't referring to the painting. "And left me here."

"I'm so glad that Mrs. Jenks, in the apartment below yours, called to tell us about the noise you were making."

Another woman ran in with scissors. Her name tag identified her as *Pam*.

"If you'll cut the tie around my wrists, I'll cut the one around my ankles," Zander said.

It took some muscle to sever the plastic tie, but after a few moments, Pam managed it.

Zander took the scissors, cut the tie around his ankles, and ascended to his feet. "I'm going to need access to a phone and a car."

"We'll call the police," Crystal, clearly the more senior of the two, replied. "Our security protocol—"

"*I'll* call the police," Zander informed them in a tone that didn't invite discussion. "A woman's in danger, and I need to do this my way, or she could get hurt. Do you understand me?"

Crystal reached for a necklace that wasn't there, as if seeking reassurance from it. "Yes, but . . ."

"You might need to see a doctor," Pam said. "Your face." She motioned. "And your hands."

"I'm fine," he repeated, irate at the time they were costing him. "I need a phone and a car. Immediately."

"Who *are* you?" Crystal asked.

"My name is Zander Ford."

Pam gave a squeak. "I read your book."

"Mr. Ford," Crystal said. "You can't expect us to hand over our phone or car. Come to the office and you can use the landline. We'll call a taxi—"

"He can borrow my phone and car," Pam offered.

"Pam!"

Ignoring her boss's exclamation, Pam walked as quickly as her short legs allowed toward the elevator bank. Zander followed.

"Pam," Crystal repeated.

"Like I said," Pam told Crystal, "I read his book. I know he's an upstanding person—"

"You know nothing of the kind."

The three of them stepped into the elevator. "It seems like he's in a desperate situation, and that a woman's life is on the line," Pam said to Crystal. Her attention jumped to Zander. "So, yes. I'll let you borrow my phone and car."

"Thank you."

Within minutes, Zander was sitting behind the wheel of Pam's ten-year-old Mazda. Before starting the car, he ran a search in her smart phone's app store for the tracking app Britt had used earlier today to track him. He'd gotten the same app back when she'd told him about it, then deleted it before leaving on his trip. He might be able to use it now in reverse, to track Britt.

He downloaded the app, then signed in with his username and password. The app remembered him and showed him the locations of the few people he'd connected. However, it couldn't pinpoint Britt. Instead, next to her name on his list of contacts, it read *Customer Offline*.

The men who'd taken her must have disabled her phone.

He took a jagged breath as he struggled to get ahold of himself. Then he dialed Detective Kurt Shaw as he pulled onto the road in the direction of Merryweather.

Kurt came on the line, and Zander provided a terse explanation of events. He gave a description of the men, their Mercedes, and the license plate, which he pulled up from memory.

"Do you have any idea where they might be taking her?" Kurt asked.

"None. They mentioned that they want to get the painting out of the country. That's all I know."

"They could be heading to the Canadian border. Or to an airport."

"Or to a boat. I think her phone's out of commission. Even so, can you try to locate its position?"

"I can try. I'll notify Chief Warner and the sheriff's department immediately."

"Don't forget the FBI. Grab a pen. I'll give you Agent Delacruz's number." He rattled off the digits.

"I'd like for you to meet with us at the station," Kurt said. "How long will it take you to get here?"

"Thirty minutes."

They disconnected, and Zander purposely recalled the day he and Britt had visited Emerson. He visualized, in detail, the sticky note Emerson had stuck to the back of his phone. Black numbers on yellow paper.

He punched the digits into Pam's phone. No one answered. When asked to leave a message, he said, "This is Zander Ford. Call me back." He dialed her number again. No answer. He swerved to the side of the road and came to a stop so that he could text her. *Pick up the phone. This is Zander Ford. It's an emergency.* He sent the text and pulled back onto the road.

He called her again. "Pick up," he growled.

She picked up. "Hello?"

"It's Zander." For the second time since he'd climbed into the Mazda, he recounted Britt's kidnapping.

Emerson Kelly had not told them everything she knew the day they'd spoken with her. If anyone had information on the four men who'd taken Britt, it was her.

Emerson responded to Zander with silence.

"Emerson?" he said sharply.

"I'm very sorry this happened." She spoke in a tone so tightly controlled it made him suspect that he'd shaken her. "I wish you would have contacted me as soon as you hit on a suspected location for the painting. I could have prevented this."

She was blaming him, and her arrow struck home because he deserved blame. Britt had led Tom and his men to The Residences. But she never would have gone to the Residences if he hadn't gone there first or if he'd told her that they might be monitoring her car. He'd had no business making the trip to Olympia today. He should have stayed in Merryweather and waited for Agent Delacruz. If he had, none of this would have happened.

An image of Britt's family—her parents, her sisters, her grandmother—rose before him. His gut roiled at the thought of having to tell them that Britt had been taken.

He cleared his throat, scattering the image. "The only thing that matters now is rescuing Britt. I have to know what you know about Tom and Nick and the others."

Again, no reply.

He reached a stoplight and squeezed shut his eyes against a tide of desperation. "I believe that you're honorable." It was a lie. He strongly suspected that Emerson had no honor. He'd pegged her as a person who, like his father, acted solely in her own best interests. "You cannot allow an innocent woman to die because she got herself involved with a painting stolen in a heist you planned. I trust that you *won't* allow that."

Silence.

"Emerson!" he shouted. He had tears in his eyes as he sent the car hurtling through the intersection when the light turned green. His hands, bloodied at the knuckles, strangled the steering wheel.

"I'm here," she said.

"I need you to help me. *Now.*"

"What are you planning?"

He hesitated. Tom was holding Britt as collateral in order to keep Zander from going to the police. At this moment, Zander was driving as fast as he could in the direction of the police. If Emerson

311

was working with Tom and she informed Tom that Zander hadn't kept his end of the bargain, Britt could pay the price.

However, Emerson had sounded genuinely surprised just now, when Zander had told her what had occurred. If she was in league with Tom, why hadn't she driven to Olympia today to retrieve the painting with the others?

His instincts were telling him that they'd need Emerson's knowledge if they were going to have a hope of finding Britt. In exchange for that knowledge, he was going to have to depend on a woman he didn't trust.

"I'm planning to work with the Merryweather police, the sheriff's department, and the FBI to bring Britt home. If you help us, I'll make sure you're compensated."

"I'm not interested in your money. However, your friends might be able to offer me something I am interested in."

"I'm on my way to the Merryweather police station. Will you meet me there?"

"Yes. Bring the highest-ranking people you can. I'll bring my attorney."

They'd chained Britt to a pipe.

She couldn't see what they'd done, exactly, because the pipe ran up the wall at her spine, and they'd fastened her wrists together behind her back on the far side of the pipe. They'd used a rigid binding—plastic, maybe—to restrain her wrists. It had no give. She'd been pulling and twisting and tugging without success ever since they'd left her in this room. Maybe thirty minutes ago? All she'd managed to do was chafe the skin on her wrists and cause a few of her fingers to turn numb.

She eyed her industrial surroundings. Stained concrete floor. Dirty cream-colored paint. Exposed ductwork.

In Olympia, they'd handcuffed her before stuffing her into the middle seat in the Mercedes' second row. She'd expended so much energy fighting them that her sawing inhales and exhales had been the only sound inside the SUV when it had pulled away from The Residences. As soon as she'd recovered her breath, Nick had pulled a hood over her head, and Tom had turned on Guns N' Roses.

Agonizing fear and guilt had stretched her time in the Mercedes, making every minute grueling. Her thoughts churned the entire drive. *What have I done? Is this really happening to me? It can't be. It is. What have I done?*

It wasn't until they'd deposited her here, released her handcuffs, secured her arms behind the pipe—her fighting them every inch of the way—that they'd finally whipped off the hood. Then they'd shut the door behind them, leaving her here alone.

She'd been sitting on the floor, her mind rioting, ever since. She'd kept it together by asking for God's strength and by focusing on how to escape and by ignoring the full-blown panic attack hovering over her.

Just a few hours ago, she'd been in her clean, orderly, familiar kitchen at Sweet Art, boxing chocolate in preparation to make deliveries.

Now she was here.

When she'd discovered that Zander had lied to her, she'd let anger submerge caution.

"This piece of art is worth a fortune," Zander had said to her earlier. *"There are plenty of people in the world who wouldn't hesitate to kill us both to get their hands on it."* Until she'd seen Tom and the others with her own eyes, the people Zander had been afraid of had seemed as imaginary to her as storybook pirates. It certainly hadn't occurred to her that the pirates might use GPS on her car to guide them to Renoir's masterpiece.

She hated that her carelessness had led Tom to *Young Woman at Rest*. And she really hated that she'd put Zander in danger. What if they'd taken *him* instead of her? And it had been all her fault?

She could—she *would*—bear the stress of the situation she found herself in now. She couldn't have borne it if Zander had been the one taken.

The last time she'd seen him, he'd been unconscious on the

surface of the parking lot. What if they'd hurt him? What if they hadn't simply tied him up inside Frank's apartment—

Stop it. She couldn't let her train of thought go there.

They'd tied him up inside the apartment at The Residences, and he'd be fine.

She chewed the edge of her lip.

She wished she'd stopped by to see Nora last night after she and John had returned from Fiji. She wished she and Willow had taken the day trip to Bellingham's galleries they'd been planning. She wished she'd done a better job of telling her parents that she'd had the best childhood possible because of them. And she desperately wished her last minutes with Zander hadn't been blistered by her temper.

Text message from the co-pilot of Tom's private plane to Tom:

> We've made up time in the air and will be arriving earlier than expected, in one and a half hours.

CHAPTER
Twenty-Three

The first time Zander entered the Merryweather police station's conference room, Detective Shaw had informed him and Carolyn that Frank's autopsy revealed a bullet wound.

Same oval wood table. Same framed print of the American flag. This time, however, there were more players.

Kurt Shaw had taken the seat next to Zander. Across from them sat Police Chief Warner and a captain from the sheriff's department. Kurt had contacted Agent Delacruz, who'd been patched in via video conferencing on an iPad. Two FBI agents were en route from the nearest satellite office.

While they waited for Emerson and her attorney to arrive, Zander had been answering questions. At Kurt's urging, he was holding an ice pack against the swelling on the side of his face.

The sensation of the ice pack irritated Zander all out of proportion. Not because of the sting of cold. But because every second he held it there marked another second of time wasted.

They needed, they *all* needed, to *take action.*

The other men appeared somber and intense, but none revealed outwardly the roiling anxiety he felt inwardly.

"How about I get you something to eat or drink?" Kurt asked. "You look pale."

"Thank you, but no." He couldn't even think about food—

The door opened. Emerson and her attorney, a serious man wearing glasses and a gray suit, entered. The attorney shut the door behind them, and they took the two seats at the head of the table.

"Good afternoon," Emerson said.

"Afternoon," the others responded.

Zander set the ice pack on the table.

Emerson wore a black shirt and black jacket. She broadcasted a regal brand of calm as she introduced herself and her attorney. Kurt introduced everyone else to her.

"Shall we begin?" she asked.

"Please," Chief Warner answered.

Emerson stacked one palm on top the other on the table's surface. "I'm willing to provide you with all the information I have on Tom Randolph, the man who kidnapped Britt Bradford. Are you familiar with Tom Randolph?" she asked Agent Delacruz.

"I am."

"Then you know that his operation is huge and has been, up until now, impenetrable to law enforcement. In exchange for my testimony against him, I want immunity and I want witness protection."

"That will take time," Delacruz said.

"We'll have to work with the DA's office in order to make that happen," the chief said.

"Yes," Emerson responded. "I'm aware."

Zander had been right about Emerson. She was here because she'd decided it was in her own best interests to turn on Tom and align herself with the police and FBI. He didn't care why she helped them. Or what she got out of it. Or whether the FBI would be able to bring Tom Randolph down. He only cared about Britt. "We don't have time to spare," Zander said unequivocally. "We can't wait for the DA."

"Which is why," Emerson said, "in an act of good faith, I'm willing to tell you at this time the things I know that might help you find her."

"Good." The chief gave a businesslike nod. "Go ahead."

Emerson straightened her posture. "Tom and I run in the same circles and have for many years. The difference between us is that I'm an independent contractor, and Tom has put together a kind of syndicate. He deals in art, diamonds, and jewelry. Almost a year ago, I contacted him because I needed financial backing in order to pull off a very large job. He gave me the money. Unfortunately, the job went bust. Tom wanted his money back with interest. I had funds but not enough to cover what I owed Tom, so I flew to Washington to talk with Frank. I knew he had a painting worth the kind of money that would clear my debt."

"*Young Woman at Rest*," Agent Delacruz said.

"*Young Woman at Rest*," Emerson concurred. "In order to assure Tom that I was good for the money, I told him about Frank and the painting. Then I came to Merryweather to see if I could convince Frank to let me sell it."

Kurt's pen scratched against his pad of paper as he took notes.

"For the first few months after I arrived here," Emerson continued, "Tom allowed me to work on Frank my own way and at my own pace. At the end of March, Tom's patience ran out. He sent some of his men here." Her gaze sought Zander's. "One of them was Nick Dunlap. Was he there today?"

Zander nodded.

"Nick and the others picked me up, and then Nick called Frank at his jobsite. He told Frank he wanted to speak with him and that if he declined they'd be forced to grab Carolyn or one of his daughters to compel him to talk. Then they recited the address of Carolyn's workplace and of his daughters' homes."

"So Frank agreed to speak with them," Zander said.

"Yes. Nick gave him the address of a remote spot north of town. As soon as Frank got there, they handcuffed us both. They put hoods over our heads and pushed us into the back seat of the van they were driving. They took us to a holding room and chained us to a pipe."

Zander swallowed back the image of Britt, hooded. Britt, chained to a pipe.

"Nick called Tom to ask him what he wanted him to do next. Tom was relatively close at that time, in California. He told Nick to wait, that he'd fly up the following morning, and speak to Frank and me personally. Nick left."

"And?" Zander asked.

"And Frank was extremely upset. He was fearful for Carolyn and his girls. As the hours went by, he began to complain of chest pain. He was panting, struggling to breathe. Dizzy. I yelled for help but no one came." Emerson frowned. "I could twist my arm just enough to see my watch, which is how I know that Frank died at 5:11 a.m."

His uncle had died tied to a pipe, robbed of medical intervention, as well as the ability to contact the people he loved.

"By the time Tom arrived, Frank had been dead for more than two hours," Emerson said. "Tom was furious. He had Nick and the others take Frank's body back to Frank's car and park it on a road where Frank would be found."

"Did they set you free at that point?" Chief Warner asked.

"They did, yes. They put a hood over my head and returned me to my car. Tom decided to leave Nick in Merryweather with me. The two of us were given the task of finding the painting."

"And you hoped Carolyn would lead you to it," Zander said.

"At first, I thought that Frank might have mentioned the Renoir in his will and, if so, that Carolyn would confide in me."

"But he didn't mention it in his will," Zander stated.

"That's correct."

"So you and Nick started following me."

"Initially, we followed Carolyn, her daughters, and you. But when you and Britt visited the cemetery in Enumclaw, we realized that the two of you were actively investigating Frank's history. From then on, we concentrated most of our attention on you and Britt, which proved the right play in the end. You were the ones who paved the way to the painting."

"Why help us now?" the chief asked. "Tom has the painting. Doesn't that mean your debt is paid?"

"Had I found the painting shortly after arriving in Merryweather, Tom would have taken it as payment. But now he's invested time and money and men in this pursuit. I'm betting that they've come to view the painting as payment for the work they've put in here in Washington. Which means they'll view my busted job as a separate event and still want to collect on that." Her manicured eyebrow arched. "Neither Tom nor Nick contacted me today when they set off for Olympia, which assures me that they don't consider me to be their partner."

Kurt opened his laptop. "It's likely that they've taken Britt to the same place they took Emerson and Frank."

"I agree," Chief Warner said.

"Where did you and Nick meet Frank after Nick called Frank at the jobsite?" Kurt asked Emerson.

Emerson provided an address.

"How long would you estimate you drove after leaving that location?"

"Thirty minutes or so."

"At approximately what rate of speed?"

"The top speed that the roads around here allow."

Kurt went to work on the computer.

The chief adjusted his chair to face Emerson more fully. "What else can you tell us about the room where you and Frank were held? Any detail, no matter how small, could be helpful."

"I heard the sound of airplanes taking off and landing," Emerson said, then went on to describe the room's details.

Kurt turned the computer screen toward the occupants of the table. It showed a detailed map, a portion of which was circled. Shaw pointed to the circle's epicenter. "This is where Frank met Nick after leaving the construction site. I determined the search area based on the amount of time they traveled and the speed at which they traveled. Within the search area, there's only one airstrip. Jefferson Airport." He pointed to its location. "It services private jets."

He zoomed in on the airstrip and indicated its nearby structures.

"There are a network of hangars and commercial buildings adjacent to the airport that were built in the 1950s. Old enough to line up with Emerson's account of the room where she was held."

"I'll get a search warrant for those buildings," the chief said.

Agent Delacruz spoke from the iPad. "I'll pull up the information I have on those warehouses and forward it to you immediately. I'll also contact The Residences to see if they have surveillance footage of their parking lot."

"I'll be meeting with my SWAT team in fifteen minutes," the captain said.

"Thank you." The chief looked to Kurt. "Take Zander and Emerson and have them ID all the suspects involved in the kidnapping."

"Yes, sir."

Zander sat next to Emerson in Kurt's office as she supplied names for Tom and his men. After each name, Kurt pulled up a photo for him and Emerson to positively identify. The faces of the men who'd taken Britt would be burned into his psyche forever. So far, they'd ID'd three. Only one left.

Kurt's screen revealed a picture of Nick's blunt features and thick neck.

"Yes," Emerson said. "That's him."

Kurt looked to Zander.

"Yes. Nick's the one who was following me several weeks back."

"Got it."

Emerson's hands, intertwined on her lap, had never clenched as she'd turned on one former accomplice after another. Her attorney hovered at her shoulder.

"I'll send this information to the SWAT team now," Kurt said.

From what Zander could tell, Kurt had access to a substantial amount of information on each of the men they'd named. Now at least SWAT would know whom they were up against.

The clock drew Zander's attention. Tom had told him he wanted to leave the country. How much more time did they have until he did just that? Would he take Britt when he went? If so, how would Zander find her? What if Tom had already loaded her into a plane and departed?

"Is there anything else you can tell us about Tom?" Kurt asked Emerson. "How he usually operates? What his objectives might be currently and how he might try to execute them?"

"Certainly."

Zander continued to watch the clock while Emerson spoke, impatience causing his knee to bounce and his fingers to scratch painfully at his opposite elbow. A scream was building in his windpipe. He wanted to scratch and scratch until he tore off skin.

Six and a half minutes later, Emerson finished.

"Anything else?" Kurt asked.

"I have a great deal more to share with the FBI. About the jobs Tom has executed. His syndicate, and all the other players involved in that. But I've shared everything that can be of use in the operation you're about to undertake. And now I'd like a cup of tea. Do you have a break room?"

"We do."

"You'll be able to find me there."

Zander stood when she stood. Emerson observed him for a drawn-out moment. Then she inclined her head slightly. He inclined his. She preceded her attorney from the office.

Zander faced Kurt. "How much longer?"

"Not long. SWAT is fast."

"Not fast enough."

"They're fast. Any faster, and they'd make a mistake. You don't want that."

"No."

Kurt came around his desk and set his palms on Zander's shoulders. "It's our job to locate Britt and get her home safely. Not your job. *Ours.* We're good at our job."

"I'm going to the warehouses with you."

Kurt's grip tightened. "In situations such as these, when some-one's been abducted, we'll occasionally bring a loved one along to comfort the victim when we recover them. I will bring you along, I promise you. But only if you'll agree to remain in my squad car during the operation. I can't allow you to jeopardize this mission."

"Understood," Zander said. "And agreed."

Britt's captors offered to escort her to the bathroom.

She declined.

They brought a bottle of water to her, unscrewed it, and held it to her mouth. She tried one sip, but when the water hit her knotted stomach, it immediately wanted to revolt. She kept the sip down, but barely. "Please," she said. "No more water."

"We wouldn't want you to get thirsty," the one called Nick told her.

"I'm not thirsty." Through the open door behind him, she could see two of the men nailing a rectangular wooden crate shut. It looked as though they'd almost finished packing the Renoir in preparation to transport it. She didn't read celebration in their body language. Not yet—they hadn't gotten the Renoir off American soil. But she did read something close. Assurance. They knew they were almost to the finish line.

"Anything else you need?" Nick smiled. His regard slid down her body and up again.

Her skin crawled. "No."

"Sure?"

"Very. Where are you taking the painting?"

"That's none of your concern."

"Will you leave me here when you go?"

"That's up to Tom, and he hasn't decided yet. Personally, I'd be happy to have you come along."

"I'd rather stay." She far preferred her chances here, tied to a pipe, than on an airplane with them.

322

"In case you hadn't noticed, you're our hostage." He rose and left, closing her back inside her solitary box.

Moisture pressed hard against her eyes. Fiasco.

Do not cry, Britt. Do not.

She prided herself on the fact that she never cried. Right now, tears seemed less useful and more destructive than ever.

Closing her lids, she concentrated on sliding air deeply in and out of her lungs while she carefully constructed a meticulous picture of Zander in her mind.

Zander's decision to cut her out when he'd unlocked Frank's phone and his subsequent lie to her about his location had hurt her. Those actions still hurt. But a crisis had a way of stripping away shallow hurts to reveal the much larger emotion beneath. At the moment, her hurt was made almost insignificant by the magnitude of the primary thing she felt for Zander.

Love.

Her throat constricted. Why hadn't she told him she loved him? He'd been brave enough to tell her how he felt. Why hadn't she had the guts to do the same?

Maybe because she hadn't known for sure that she loved him until now. Maybe because she'd been more than content with how things had been, just as they were, since Nora's wedding. Maybe because commitment had never come easy for her. Maybe because she'd been smug in the belief that she had time . . . that she could always sort through her feelings and articulate them at some future point.

The sound of a distant airplane engine punctuated the indistinguishable murmur of the men's voices on the far side of the wall. The metal pipe bled cold against the back of her skull.

She loved Zander.

Of course she did.

They could read each other's minds. They could communicate with a look. She knew the minutiae of his personality. He was honorable and loyal. Complex and brilliant. Wary and wry.

She'd harbored a piercing compassion for the despondent, betrayed kid who'd needed a home. Now she loved the man he'd become, even though her love for him was not a revelation that comforted her.

For one thing, it had come at a ridiculous time. *Too little, too late* had never been more accurate.

For another, the idea of loving him brought a cape full of fears billowing behind it. This circumstance was scary enough. Love for Zander couldn't fortify her at this point. It could only weaken her.

And so . . . no.

Love? Just no.

This was not the time for love. Considering her predicament, there might never be a time for it.

The truth of that wrenched through her, causing physical pain.

If she was going to survive this, then she needed to place a partition between herself and thoughts of Zander.

And so she did.

The barrier put distance between them in a way that allowed her heart to continue pumping and her bravery to stabilize.

"Will SWAT be able to pinpoint Britt's location within the warehouses based on the Mercedes?"

"They'll try. If they aren't able to get a visual on the Mercedes, they'll begin searching the warehouses systematically." Kurt steered his GMC along the winding road leading to remote Jefferson Airport. They followed a squad car that held Chief Warner and one of his deputies.

The SWAT team would arrive before they did. Kurt, the chief, county officers, emergency vehicles, and more would hang back or advance depending on the communication they received from SWAT.

"And when they find Britt?" Zander asked.

"They'll likely deploy a flash bang."

"Which is harmless, yes?"

"Yes, but when it detonates, it puts off so much light, sound, and smoke that it's disorienting."

"What if one of the guys is holding her hostage?"

"SWAT is trained to handle it. They'll likely negotiate first. If that breaks down, they may take the attacker out."

God. It was a prayer. A plea. *Come through for Britt. Stand between her and danger. I believe that you can. I believe that you will.*

Please, I beg of you.

A small plane descended toward earth against the bruised gray of the cloudy sky.

They were close.

Note passed from Zander to Colton in twelfth grade:

> I heard that you tried to pressure Britt into leaving Maddie's party with you. When she said no, you yelled at her.
>
> Treat Britt like that again, and I'll beat you up.

Note passed between Mia and Britt in twelfth grade:

MIA: That girl you set Zander up with was so pretty! Did they hit it off?

BRITT: At first. They went out three times, and then he told me he didn't think it was going to work.

MIA: Why?

BRITT: Because she got way too serious about him way too quick. I tried to give her a Zander 101 course before they went out, and I warned her not to do that, but she clearly didn't listen.

MIA: She's crazy! You have super high standards for Zander's girlfriends. She was lucky that you offered to set her up with him in the first place.

BRITT: Exactly!

MIA: Zander doesn't date much. Doesn't he get lonely?

BRITT: No. He has me.

MIA: I thought you'd picked a winner for him this time.

BRITT: I thought so, too, for a few days. But now I see that I was wrong. I don't think her personality is quite right for Zander. They're not a fit.

Note written by Britt when she was in twelfth grade:

Dad, can you please call the admissions director at University of Washington–Tacoma to confirm our appointment with him and Zander on Saturday? Everything has to go perfectly because we NEED that man to offer Zander a full ride. Should we casually mention that USC is desperate for Zander? You're going to say no, since that would be a lie. But you're good at negotiation, so I'm counting on you to come up with something (not a lie) that will still work.

CHAPTER
Twenty-Four

An explosion from the adjoining room caused Britt to jerk upright.

Immediately, she heard shouting. Scuffling. Then gunfire.

Her heart rate bolted into a sprint. What had happened?

She levered her feet underneath her and pushed herself to standing.

Urgent male voices. More thudding.

Tom slid inside the room where she was being held and closed the door. He strode toward her, face grim.

Whatever was going down in the next room—it couldn't be good for Tom. He might even have decided to free her to use her as a shield.

She had no intention of serving as his shield.

The second he released her, he'd doubtless try to grab her. Then what? Force her cooperation by pointing a gun at her?

The clamor in the next room continued as Tom lifted a pair of cutters to the restraint binding her wrists.

The instant her wrists sprang apart, Britt lunged away from him. She'd been assessing the rusty metal bar lying on the room's floor since they'd caged her here. She lifted it now.

He came at her fast. She swung the bar with all her might. He jerked out of its path and continued to advance. She swung again. Again. Without success. The heaviness of the metal sucked the strength from her arms. She gathered her energy and sliced the bar through the air—

He caught it in midair and attempted to yank it from her.

Her fingers clenched the bar, fighting to hold on.

Tom gave a mighty pull. Metal scraped her palms as Tom wrenched it from her and tossed it aside. It landed with a terrible clatter.

He made a swipe for her. She dodged just beyond his reach. Angrily, he thrust a hand inside his suit jacket—

The door banged open, and a SWAT officer filled the opening. His vision and his gun's sight swerved past Britt before stopping on Tom. "Freeze."

Time seemed to spin as Britt and the officer waited for Tom's response.

"Hands where I can see them," the officer said, approaching. A second officer followed him in. Then a third.

Gradually, Tom lifted his palms.

Two of the officers descended on him. The third made his way to Britt. "Ms. Bradford? Are you all right?"

He wore so much gear—helmet, loaded vest, arm guards—that he almost looked like RoboCop. However, his eyes were kind.

"I'm fine." Her voice sounded sturdier than she felt. The visual evidence was telling her that she might be safe. But her adrenaline wasn't buying it. Streams of it coursed through her, making her feel faint and like she could swim the English Channel and shaky and hyper alert all at the same time.

Through the door, she saw the debris of the exchange between Tom's men and the officers. Overturned chairs. Strewn papers. A man's arm, lying motionless against the floor at an unnatural angle—

Her attention skittered from that sight, rising to observe more SWAT team members entering the space.

"Right this way, Ms. Bradford," the one with the kind eyes said.

He took a gentle hold of her elbow and steered her forward.

"Have you found the painting?" she asked.

The officer tapped the rectangular crate as they passed. "I believe this is it, right here."

"You'll . . . make sure it's in there?"

"We'll make sure."

They progressed down a hallway, a foyer.

She'd been saved. Freed.

People were talking. Sounds were swirling around her. Yet it felt strangely as though she had cotton in her ears . . . as if she were floating through a loud movie of a crime scene inside a bubble of drastically subdued sound.

"Britt?"

The spell altered just enough to allow her to distinguish her name.

"I'm Detective Kurt Shaw."

He was tall and bald. "Nice to meet you," she replied automatically.

"Are you okay?"

"Yes."

"Are you sure?"

"Yes. I'm fine."

"Good." His astute gaze ran over her. "Looks like your wrists are injured."

Surprised, she noticed that he was right. In addition to the scratches on her palms from the pipe, the tie had chafed her skin in places until it bled. "It's—" She found she needed to swallow. "It's just scrapes. I was trying to tug my wrists free."

"All right. We'll get that taken care of outside." He made a mannerly gesture for her to go through the doors ahead of him. They emptied into a crowded parking lot.

"Zander helped us find you," Kurt said.

Her chest throbbed at the mention of Zander's name.

"He's here," Kurt continued. "Would you like to see him before we have someone look at those wrists?"

"Yes. I'd like to see him."

Squad cars jammed the lot. A van. An ambulance.

Numerous people were going about their professional duties, yet she had the sense that they were all also cataloguing her appearance. She was their . . . kidnap victim.

She was exactly who she'd always been, just more than a little shaken up. The idea that these people saw her as something different—*kidnap victim*—was an odd revelation to absorb. So odd, she felt the bubble rising around her again.

To these people, she was like the daughter in the movie *Taken*. Which tempted her to grab a megaphone and make an announcement. *I'm perfectly fine, everyone! No harm done.*

"He's just there." Kurt pointed. "I'll come get you in a minute."

Britt glanced in the direction he'd indicated and saw Zander, standing as still as a tree in the middle of a swarming army. He was watching her, red and blue lights revolving behind him. Slowly, she walked forward.

His feet were braced apart. His arms hung by his sides, his knuckles angry red. He wore the black T-shirt and worn jeans he'd had on earlier. Furrows marked his inky hair. His fair skin was whiter than usual, which caused the bruise that ran beneath one eye and across his cheekbone to stand out starkly in contrast.

He had the look of a vase that had been fractured but hadn't yet broken apart.

It had been a very bad day for them both.

When she reached him, he enveloped her in his arms. Her head notched into its place just beneath his chin, her ear pressed to his heart. He rested his jaw against the top of her head.

They were circled by benevolent, heroic strangers who'd successfully rescued her and reclaimed *Young Woman at Rest*. However, he was the only person here who knew her. And he was wondrously familiar.

The luxurious scent of his cologne soothed her. His body heat warmed her. His arms communicated physical power and emotional commitment.

Neither of them spoke. And neither let go.

She remained exactly where she was, holding him tightly. Bit by bit, the volume of their environment rose back to its proper level.

Her emotions billowed, pressing outward against the inside of her skin, making her feel as if she were on the verge of sobbing . . . which she didn't understand. She and Zander were both fine. She should be nothing but happy in this moment. She was happy. It's just that she wasn't *only* happy.

She was also angry at Tom and his men. Horrified that she hadn't been able to do more to defend herself or to escape. Ashamed and relieved and anxious simultaneously. Most of all, she felt helpless. Today's events had stripped her sense of security from her. So much so, that she wanted to dissolve against Zander.

Except that if she lost control of herself now, she worried that it might be very ugly and very public. She *could not* weep in front of all these spectators. Or Zander, even.

She cherished him. Her heart was steely toward many things, but the section of it that belonged to him had gone alarmingly tender.

Back when she'd been ten years old and had burned her inner wrist, accepting her mom's comfort had seemed to Britt like a liability. In this situation, loving Zander seemed like a liability, too. Best to keep the partition between them a little while longer. Until she had her feet back underneath her, she needed a sliver of distance.

She adjusted her position so that she could study his battered face. "You're going to have a black eye."

He regarded her gravely. "Your hands are bloody."

"You have a bruise on your cheek."

"The hem of your shirt is ripped."

"Your knuckles are a mess."

"Your hair is one big tangle."

At that, her lips quirked into a curve.

"I was worried," he said.

A simple sentence. Yet she comprehended its weight. He didn't want to burden her by saying more, because he probably felt that

331

he'd gotten off lighter than she had today. *I was worried* was an understatement the way *pail of water* was an understatement for *ocean.*

"I was worried about you, too."

"I wish I'd told you as soon as I unlocked Frank's phone."

"What was the passcode?"

Dark lashes accentuated his slightly bloodshot midnight blue eyes. "Love."

"Ah."

"I also wish I'd never gone to Olympia," he continued. "The FBI told me they were coming. I should have waited."

She might be jumbled at the moment, but she was too fair to let him think this was his fault. "I wish I hadn't chased you to Olympia without thinking through all the possibilities. I ended up bringing Tom down on us. I'm really sorry."

"I'm sorry that I mixed you up in this. Britt, I would never want to hurt you—"

"I know."

Tension lined his brow as he took in the contours of her face. "What did they do to you?"

"They put a hood over my head and drove me here. Then they secured my wrists behind a pipe and left me alone in a grimy room." *And I thought they might kill me, and I thought they might have killed you.* "That's all."

He waited for her to elaborate, but she didn't want to talk about it more.

"That's all," she repeated.

"Are you all right?"

"I am."

Again, he waited. "Britt."

"I'm all right, and I need for you to believe that I'm all right so that I can go on being all right." Her voice betrayed her by trembling a bit.

Understanding tinged his face. "You can tell me whatever you need to."

"I know. But I don't need to tell you anything more at this particular moment."

"Okay." He lifted first one of her wrists, then the other. His jaw turned brutally grim—

"Excuse me," Kurt called. "If you're ready, Ms. Bradford, the paramedics can check you out."

She and Zander walked to the ambulance. Britt sat on the vehicle's open bumper while the paramedics checked her vitals and tended to her wrists. She asked Zander question after question about the things that had happened to him after she'd left The Residences, until she understood how the SWAT team had found her.

Minutes later, they sat in the back seat of Kurt's SUV on their way to the Merryweather Police Station to give their statements.

"Do you want to call your parents or do you want me to do it?" Zander asked.

She didn't want to do anything. She only wanted to sit, allowing this car to carry her along, watching the scenery blur by. Her limbs had become as heavy as lead.

However, if Zander called her parents on her behalf, then her family would be even more upset than they were already going to be. "I'll call. Do you have your phone?"

"No, they took it from me."

"They took mine, too."

"You can use mine." Kurt passed his cell phone back.

She dialed her dad, the more even-keeled of her parents. Using a this-is-no-big-deal tone, she recounted everything that had happened.

Her dad informed her that he and Mom would meet her at the station and that she'd spend the night with them. She attempted to protest, but he quickly overruled her, and she didn't have the energy to argue.

She returned the phone to Kurt.

Zander interlaced his fingers with hers and placed their joined hands on his thigh. The back of his head rested against the seat. His attention slid to her, and he squeezed her fingers.

Once again, her thin defenses began to splinter—

Stop it, Britt. Keep it together.

Tipping her temple against the cool window, she returned her gaze to the world beyond.

Britt glanced at the clock positioned on the bedside table of her room at Bradfordwood. 5:14 a.m. Dawn.

She flicked her focus to the night-light plugged into her bathroom counter's backsplash. When she'd been small, a night-light that depicted a cow jumping over the moon had occupied that spot. After that, a dog night-light. After that, a chocolate cake night-light. After that, this simple and classy adult model.

She'd outgrown the need of a night-light long ago. She didn't sleep with one at home. Yet during all the awake hours sandwiched in between the lousy three and half hours of sleep she'd managed during the night, she'd focused on the night-light while her mind rampaged.

The illumination it gave *should* have been reassuring. It was steady and warm and it saved her from coal black darkness. She kept waiting to experience its reassurance. But so far, she hadn't.

After her parents had brought her here from the police station last night, they'd offered to make her a big dinner. She hadn't been up for it. Instead, she'd parked herself in front of the TV. Eventually, her dad had delivered a dinner of her childhood comfort foods on a TV tray—peanut butter and jelly sandwich, carrots, Cheetos.

After that, her sisters had stopped by and everyone had clucked over her and given her fretful looks, which she'd loathed. Claiming tiredness, she'd excused herself as early as possible and retreated here, to her old bedroom, to hide. She'd talked on the phone with Zander, who hadn't pressured her to spill her guts, which she'd appreciated. Even so, the sound of his voice had caused tears to rush to her eyes, so she'd kept it brief.

Sleep had seemed like the antidote for the exhaustion weighting her body, so she'd showered, changed into the pair of pajamas her mom had loaned her, and crawled beneath the covers. The more she'd strained for relaxation, however, the less her muscles had wanted to loosen. The more she'd tried to fill her mind with peaceful thoughts, the more it had fixated on the moments when Tom's men had wrestled her into their car.

A quiet sound drew Britt's attention to the hallway door. It slid open a few feet, revealing a feminine silhouette. Her mom, checking on her.

"I'm awake," Britt said.

"Rough night's sleep?"

"Sadly, yes. You too?"

"Sadly, yes. It's early. You should try to get more sleep."

"Nah." Britt scooted up so that she was sitting against the pillows propped against the antique metal headboard. "I'd rather start the day now than lie here trying to sleep."

Mom neared and clicked on the lamp next to the clock.

"First the kayaking accident and now this." Britt squinted as her eyes adjusted. "I've decided to avoid death-defying situations for a while."

"That's a resolution I can fully support." Mom, wearing a white fleece robe, lowered herself to the edge of the mattress near Britt's legs. "How long do you think your decision to avoid death-defying situations will last? I'd like to pace myself." Her quick smile transformed her face.

"I think I might be able to make it a whole month," Britt teased.

"A whole month?" Mom asked wryly. "As long as that?"

"As long as that."

Mom liked to pull her strawberry blond hair into a topknot for sleep. The style was very similar to the style Britt favored when making chocolate. Mom's hair was shorter, though, so several strands had come undone to glide around her ears and neck. "I can't stop thinking about what happened to you yesterday."

"Me neither. I want to feel like myself again." The prospect of feeling this unsettled for days? Intolerable.

"Yesterday was really, really scary, Britt. I'm afraid it might take some time for you to feel like yourself again."

"I hope not."

Mom's brown eyes seemed to see right down into the hidden valleys of Britt's personality. "You've never been a complainer."

"No."

"I mean, when you were a teenager, you'd complain about what was being served for dinner or Dad's driving or the temperature inside the house."

"Don't forget that terrible radio station you used to play. I complained about that."

"But you never complained about the really hard things."

"It's just . . . not my way."

"I get that. We both love our independence, you and I. And yet, there were times . . . there *are* times . . . when I worry that you don't feel you have the right to saddle us with the difficult stuff because of our family dynamics or our history or both."

"You want me to saddle you with the difficult stuff?"

"Of course I do." Compassion infused every word. "If it would help."

"You've all endured more than I have."

"No one in our family is keeping score to determine who's endured the most or least. You know that, right? We're not in competition with one another."

"I know that in theory. But I'd feel like an idiot if I melted into a puddle in front of you guys simply because I was placed in a room by myself for a few hours and got some scrapes on my hands."

"Every person in this family is going to need support occasionally. Even you."

Skepticism pushed upward within her, but her mom leveled an adamant I'm-right-about-this face at Britt, so there was no point in disagreeing.

"Even you," Mom insisted.

Britt considered the beloved angles of her mom's cheekbones, chin, and forehead. Kathleen Bradford hadn't sailed through life on calm seas only. She'd faced her share of storms and lived to tell the tale. "How did you survive your dad's death?" Britt asked. She genuinely wanted to know. Her mom had only been seven when the small plane her dad had been piloting crashed.

"I survived because I let God carry me through it." She smoothed the long ends of her robe's belt. "Here's what I know for sure: You can rely on Him in the hard as well as in the easy. If He leads you into something hard, then He'll provide the grace you need to bear up under it."

That sounded wildly oversimplified. And at the same time, beyond reach, because Britt had no idea how to actually apply that advice to herself. How could she let God carry her?

Dad strode into the bedroom, the handles of two mugs clasped in one hand, the handle of a third in his other hand. "Morning, sweetheart."

"Not you, too," Britt said to him. "Couldn't sleep?"

"Nope. You're a grown-up, even though I want you to know that I—"

"Never gave your permission for that to happen."

"Exactly. Like it or not, you'll always be my little girl." He extended one of the mugs.

She accepted it from him. Coffee, hot and fragrant. "Thank you."

He passed the next mug to her mom, then went to the window and parted the curtains. Beyond, black trees formed a lacework pattern against a brightening lavender sky.

"We'll make you breakfast," Mom said.

"Yes! Buttermilk pancakes." Dad looked so excited at the chance to make her favorite that she didn't have the heart to tell them she wasn't hungry. In truth, she was anti-hungry. The thought of food made her nauseous.

"I'll stay home, and you and I can take the boat out," Dad said. "Or watch movies. Or read. We'll spend the day relaxing."

"Thanks, but I'm going to go to work today."

Mom frowned. "It might be smart to take a day or two to recover."

"Except that I hardly got any work done yesterday, and the chocolate isn't going to make itself."

"You always make sure you have enough inventory," Dad said. "You can afford to take a few personal days."

"I can, but I want to go in." Work would keep her hands—and hopefully her brain—occupied. She *craved* that. "My kitchen is more tranquil than a spa."

They regarded her doubtfully. She could read their tiredness and concern. Yet overlaying those things was clear evidence of their serenity. They were worried about her, yes. But they felt normal. They felt like themselves. They weren't about to jump out of their skins, like she was. Thus, they couldn't fully understand.

"Well . . . if you're sure," Dad said.

"I'm sure." Britt spoke with a certainty she did not feel.

Letter Frank left for Carolyn in the apartment at The Residences:

Carolyn,

If you're reading this, it probably means that I'm dead. It definitely means that you've found the painting.

I want to explain.

Even as I write these words, I'm aware that my secrets are unexplainable and unpardonable. Still, I want to make sure that you know a few important things.

1) I was one of the three thieves involved in the Triple Play. <u>Young Woman at Rest</u> by Renoir is my share of the heist.

2) My real name is James Richard Ross. I decided to use an alias back when I was casing the Pascal Museum. Which is why, when I met you, I introduced myself as Frank Pierce.

3) I didn't intend to fall in love the summer we met. But after just a few conversations with you, I was sunk.

When I began to fall in love with you, I considered calling off my involvement in the heist. I wish I had. Back then, I didn't know whether you'd ever come to feel for me what I felt for you. Also, at that point, I was deeply involved in the planning of the heist, and the others were counting on me. I told myself I couldn't let them down.

4) I was shot in the leg by a security guard as I ran from the Pascal. For two weeks I waited to return to you while I recuperated. That entire time, you were the only thing on my mind. I was motivated to get better for one reason and one reason only. You.

5) Leading up to the heist, I was prepared to sell the Renoir. But afterward . . . after you . . . everything I thought I wanted and thought I'd do shifted. I no longer wanted to do the dishonorable thing and sell the painting for my own profit. So I kept it.

6) Many times over the years I decided to return <u>Young Woman at Rest</u> to the Pascal. I laid the groundwork to do just that. But each time, just as I was about to take action, stress would eat away at me, and I'd second-guess myself. I was terrified that I'd get caught. I've always been terrified of that. If the police had found a way to trace the painting back to me, then the truth would've come out. I'd have been hauled away, which I deserved. You, Courtney, and Sarah would have been devastated, which you didn't deserve.

7) After a time, I came to view the painting as an insurance policy. It's by far the most expensive thing I've ever had. After our girls were born and the weight of responsibility became heavier, I couldn't force myself to let go of the security the painting represented. What if you or our girls got sick and I had to pay medical bills? What if our house burned down? What if something happened to me that made it impossible for me to support you?

If there'd come a time when I needed to sell the painting to rescue you, or our girls, I would have sold it in a minute. I'd have had to lie to you about the origin of the money. But I'd have done it.

There are many important things in this life, but none as important to me as our family.

Now that you understand these things about me, I'm scared as I sit here . . . thinking about how you might feel. I know you'll feel betrayed by my lies. I need you to understand that I kept this secret because I wasn't brave enough to risk losing your love.

I'm afraid you'll wonder how much of our life together was true. The answer: All of it was true. I kept a painting and my past life hidden. But every day of our marriage has been real. Every time I told you I loved you, I was telling the honest truth.

My early years were fighting and struggle. My years with you have been peace and joy. If I had a whole book to fill, I could never tell you all the ways you gave hope to a hopeless, good-for-nothing man.

I love you. I love our girls.

Please forgive me for my mistakes. Please forgive me for stealing what did not belong to me and for remaining silent about things I should have spoken.

You gave me a life, Carolyn. A real, full life, complete with everything I could have asked for. We didn't have the money the painting could have brought us, which was fine with me because I knew that, between us, we had something far more valuable.

If I'm gone, please know that I'm grateful for every hour I had with you. I received beyond what I ever should have received, and I know how lucky I am.

<u>I love you very much.</u>

Frank

CHAPTER
Twenty-Five

That night, Valentina made borscht for the Bradford family.

Britt decrypted the message Valentina was seeking to send her through borscht-code: *You encountered a dreadful patch of turbulence yesterday, Britt, but you're back on smooth air now, and you're perfectly safe.*

Unfortunately, the *you're perfectly safe* part of the message wasn't computing.

Britt was setting Bradfordwood's dining room table because her sisters, their husbands, and Zander were due to arrive any minute. She could hear her parents talking with Grandma, Clint, and Valentina in the kitchen. Her dad had turned on all the downstairs lights inside the rambling brick mansion to counteract the drizzly weather outside. The smells of beef, tomato, and potato permeated the home's interior.

Last night she'd understood that her night-light should be comforting. Now that same surreal certainty had returned—her surroundings *should* be comforting. Yet her anxiety persisted. The things that ought to combat it weren't having any effect, including the hours she'd spent at Sweet Art today. She'd been unable to concentrate and had thrown out one of the batches of dark chocolate pistachio bark she'd attempted.

The sound of the front door opening reached her. She set down the final piece of silverware and turned. Through the opening between the dining room and foyer, she watched Zander enter. He wore his gray Atari T-shirt and carried two loaves of French bread. His concentration homed in on her as she approached. An affectionate smile softened the planes of his face.

They'd spoken on the phone twice today and texted often, but this was the first time she'd seen him since they'd parted at the police station yesterday. She knew he was cataloguing her condition down to the tiniest detail, and she had the sinking sense that he was perceiving more than she wanted him to.

"Hey." She flashed a grin that she hoped would quash his qualms about her or distract him or both.

"How are you?"

She could tell that he wanted an honest answer. She responded with a pat answer. "I'm doing pretty well." Carefully, she set her hand on his injured cheek. "Your bruises have gotten worse. Do they hurt?"

"Only when I'm awake."

Even this simple touch, her palm to his face, contained both physical power and mighty love. It frightened her, just how much power and love it contained.

Zander was beautiful to her, and the bruises only served to make his outer and inner beauty more obvious. She yearned to pull him into the coat closet, feel his lips on hers, and allow the delicious sensations of kissing him to drown out the noise in her head. What she needed, though, was to take a step back so that she could keep the partition between them, because that was the only option that would give her a shot at maintaining her equilibrium.

She removed her hand and took a step back.

His mouth flattened with concern.

Concern. She couldn't continue to bear everyone's concern much longer. Least of all, his.

"Thanks for bringing bread." She adjusted her one-shoulder

royal blue top. "You can take it back and hand it to one of my parents."

"Britt—"

"How about we talk later, when everybody else goes? I think I heard a car outside." She checked the front drive. "Yep. John and Nora are here."

Zander hesitated.

"I'll be there in a minute," she told him.

He made his way toward the kitchen just as Nora and John bustled indoors. Britt had seen Nora last night but not John, so she gave him a hug, which he returned using the arm that wasn't holding a dish of peach cobbler.

"It was considerate of you to wait until we were back from our honeymoon before getting yourself kidnapped," he said.

"I'm nothing if not considerate."

John smiled, his face ruggedly handsome. "I wish I could have been there to help yesterday, even though my vision's not what it once was."

"Shortly after Nora met you, she told me that you could fell dragons. Right, Nora?"

"That's correct." Nora hung her rain jacket on the coatrack. "I stand behind my assertion."

"For what it's worth, I don't think you need 20/20 vision to fell dragons, John," Britt said.

"First of all, I've only felled two dragons in my time," John told Britt. "And they were both kind of small." He carried the cobbler out of sight.

"There goes my husband." Nora flourished her hands in the direction he'd gone. "I can't believe I get to use the term *my hus-band* now. It makes me giddy every single time."

"Great. Then use it like crazy."

"My husband sent me flowers at work today."

"Did he?"

"Yes, because he's an excellent husband. Also, my husband helped me make tonight's peach cobbler."

"Fascinating."

"And tomorrow, my husband's planning to take me to the movies—"

"You know what, Mrs. Lawson?" Britt interrupted.

"That's the other thing I can't get enough of! Mrs. Lawson—"

"I amend my earlier statement. Don't use the term *my husband* like crazy."

The door swung open again, this time admitting Willow and Corbin.

"Since I saw you last, I hear that you managed to mix yourself up with a gang of art thieves," Corbin said to Britt. He held a tray of appetizers and far more than his portion of charisma.

"Yep."

"Impressive, even for you." His auburn hair was shaved short, and scruff darkened his cheeks. His professional football player's stature always made her feel like the shortest girl in the class.

"Think how tediously peaceful things would be around here if it wasn't for me." Britt wasn't really joking. If left to mature Willow and studious Nora, the Bradford family would be a dead bore.

"I wouldn't mind a little tedious peace," Willow commented.

"Same," Corbin agreed.

"You can count on me to provide you with plenty of tedious peace, as always," Nora assured them.

"Much appreciated, Nora," Corbin said. "Where's John?"

"My husband's in the kitchen."

"Heading that way myself." He left the three Bradford sisters together in Bradfordwood's grand entrance hall.

"*Your husband's* in the kitchen?" Willow repeated to Nora. Humor danced in her jade green eyes.

"Yes. My husband—"

"Don't get her started," Britt said to Willow.

"Fine." Willow crossed her arms over her simple ivory sundress. No one could make simple look chic more effortlessly than Willow. "Let's talk about you instead."

Britt's mood twisted south. "Not necessary—"

"You went through something terrible yesterday," Willow stated.

"Not *that* terrible," Britt said.

"Pretty terrible," Nora said.

Willow held Britt's eyes. "I'm worried about you."

"What can we do to help?" Nora asked.

"Nothing. I'm fine—"

"No, really," Willow said, unruffled. "What can we do to help?"

They weren't going to let her brush them off. Persistent sisters. Which meant she'd have to think of something that would appease them. "You can bring Ben & Jerry's to my place on Sunday after church. We can eat it for lunch."

"Done," Nora said.

"And you'll talk to us then? About everything that happened and how you're dealing with it?" Willow asked.

Britt winced. "Not if I can help it. I'm grateful to you for wanting to comfort me and all. But honestly, I don't want to talk about it yet. Or even think about it. All I really want to do is hang out with you and laugh and eat ice cream."

"Understood," Willow said. "But are you communicating about this with someone? Zander?"

Again, not if she could help it.

"He can relate because he went through it, too," Nora pointed out.

"And he's a great listener," Willow said.

"And he's as reliable as the Rock of Gibraltar," Nora said.

"And he loves you," Willow said.

"So do we," Nora added. "But if you'd rather talk to him about it, we get it."

For the first time, a blip of quiet inserted itself into the conversation. "Are you done now?" Britt asked.

"I am," Willow said. "Are you done, Nora?"

"Yes. I'm ready to join *my husband* in the kitchen."

Britt rolled her eyes. Her sisters linked arms with her on either side as they made their way toward the others.

Mom, Dad, Willow, Corbin, Nora, John, Zander, Grandma, Clint, and Valentina talked and snacked on appetizers while the stew simmered. Britt flitted from one person to the next, trying to prove to them all that she was just fine. Her inner attention was split, however. One third of her focus stayed where she wanted it—on the conversation. One third tried to suppress a roiling sense of fear. One third was preoccupied with Zander.

He was quieter than usual. Several times, she caught him surveying her with an inscrutable expression.

When Valentina declared the borscht ready, they moved into the dining room. Britt had forced herself to eat a pancake this morning and half the sandwich Maddie had brought to her for lunch. She still wasn't hungry. She watched the pat of butter she'd spread on her crusty slice of French bread soften. She chewed a bite, waiting for her brain to register its deliciousness. But it didn't. Perhaps because her stomach had contracted with nerves.

Her passion for food, the thing that had motivated her entire career, had deserted her.

Though Zander was sitting next to her, he felt as far away as Guam. That uncomfortable truth wasn't helped by the swoony happiness shooting from Nora and John and Willow and Corbin in rosy bursts.

If you were one of three sisters and the other two had recently married, you deserved a medal.

"You look shaken by the ordeal you went through yesterday," Grandma said to Britt, taking a stab at sympathy.

"No, I'm not shaken. I'm right as rain!"

"The beef in this dish might not be the best thing for your state of mind," Grandma continued. "Or your waistline. It's very rich."

Britt fantasized about picking Grandma up, carrying her to the canal, and throwing her in. "I'll go easy on the beef."

Grandma cupped a hand around her mouth, as if telling Britt a secret, despite the fact that she was sitting across the table. "Be sure to take some Milk of Magnesia later. I always do after eating Valentina's borscht. Keeps me regular."

"Yes!" Valentina piped up. "Warm milk before bed help you sleep, miss."

"Meditative music helps me fall asleep," Clint told Britt.

Grandma gave Clint a suspicious look. "What's meditative music?"

"Therapeutic sounds and melodies. You know? Played on instruments like the dulcimer, the pan flute, and wind chimes."

"Wind chimes are not an instrument," Grandma stated. "They're a porch decoration for those who aren't at home with the natural sounds of God's world."

Britt had to wonder whether God considered Grandma's cantankerous voice to be one of the natural sounds of His world.

"I just pop a Tylenol PM when I'm having trouble sleeping," Corbin said.

"No, no, no." Willow shook her head. "The most natural thing, Britt, is melatonin."

"I exercise to improve sleep," John told her.

"I read," Nora said.

She needed to mount a counteroffensive in order to end this sleep intervention. "Thanks, everyone, for the helpful suggestions, but how about we move right along to the topic of Clint dating Nikki? All in favor, raise your hands." Poor Clint. It was cowardly of her to turn the spotlight from herself to him. But there you had it.

Everyone raised their hands.

"I don't want to pressure you or anything," Nora said to Clint, "but Nikki really is great. She's worked with me for several years now, and she's someone who says what she thinks. She's confident and sassy, but she's also genuinely good-hearted."

Clint blushed. He'd removed his cowboy hat politely when he'd come inside. His long, thin hair shone beneath the chandelier. Women all over America would pay to get their hair that shiny.

"What do you think?" the never-shy Corbin asked him. "Are you interested in dating Nikki?"

"I . . ." Clint stammered. "I'm very interested. Yes."

"It says in Scripture that it is not good for man to be alone,"

Grandma said, though she herself had been single for most of her life.

"What's preventing you from dating Nikki?" Mom asked.

"I'm not real convinced that . . . she likes me."

"*She does!*" all three Bradford sisters said in unison.

"Jinx!" they said in unison again.

How could Clint possibly doubt Nikki's interest? The woman was as subtle as a bulldozer.

"Ask her out." Corbin smiled his megawatt smile.

"Do you really think so?" Clint asked the table at large, earnestly curious. Britt had never met a man who required as much confirmation as Clint Fletcher.

"Yes, I very think so," Valentina said with her heavy Russian accent.

"*Yes,*" the rest of them said.

"Though we really shouldn't force dear, sweet Clint," Nora pointed out.

"Aw, a little force wouldn't hurt him." Britt grasped her water goblet and thumped it in time to the syllables. "Clint and Nikki. Clint and Nikki."

Almost everyone joined in with Britt's chant, thumping their glasses. Two abstained. Nora regarded Clint with laughing apology. Grandma's face, framed by the fur of Old Musty, had reverted to its default setting of disapproval.

"*Clint and Nikki. Clint and Nikki.*"

"Okay, okay." Clint threw up his hands good-naturedly. "I'll ask her out."

A resounding cheer arose.

"Your grandmother was right," Zander said to Britt later that night.

"If so, that would be the first time since 1971."

"When she said earlier that you were shaken," he continued. "She was right about that."

Her body stiffened.

Everyone had stayed to help clean up after dinner, then left for their respective homes thirty minutes ago. The night sky had cleared. The light rain of earlier had whisked away, leaving behind a bright moon, stars, and an endless supply of clean, cool air. Thus, Britt and Zander had decided to move their party for two outside to the fire pit at the back of the house.

She'd dried off one of the Adirondack love seats while he'd gotten a fire going. Now they were sitting close, hands intertwined, feet propped on the lip of the fire pit, a blanket draped over them. It was private here, with a wall of brick at their back. Outdoor lanterns mounted to the exterior of the house flickered.

Britt had been feeling claustrophobic inside and had imagined that this was just what the doctor ordered. Space. Nature.

What she didn't need? Zander pointing out that her grandmother had been right. That she was shaken.

Great Scott. He was well-meaning. They were all so well-meaning. But their well-meaningness was suffocating her.

"When I arrived you said we'd talk later," Zander reminded her.

"I know." She released a strained sigh. "But for now can we just rest and look at the stars? It would be nice if I didn't have to fill the next few minutes with words."

He remained silent, and so did Britt. However, the silence didn't coast with peacefulness, the way she'd hoped it might. It snapped with tension.

"I'm off my game," she finally admitted.

"I know. I could tell as soon as you walked out of the warehouse yesterday. The dinner we just had drove the point home."

"I expected to feel . . . nervous . . . when I was trapped in that room. And even for a few hours afterward. Sure. Fine. But it's been more than a day, and I'm nowhere close to getting my groove back."

"Yesterday was traumatic, Britt."

"Yet you seem to have bounced back."

"I haven't. Yesterday was my worst day." He spoke upward, to the night sky. "Worse than the day of the fire in St. Louis. It was

349

so bad, I'm still dazed by it. I can't stop replaying the things that happened. I can't stop thinking about all the things that could have happened to you . . . and almost did. At the same time, I'm incredibly relieved that none of those things did happen."

"I wish I were relieved. Instead, I mostly feel scared and help-less, which are two things I can't *stand* to feel." She adjusted her position to face him. Likewise, he faced her. She ran a fingertip down his cheek and along the edge of his jaw.

"Why do you think—" he began.

She kissed him. Because she was desperate to. Because kissing him would blot out everything else, including his probing questions.

Need rose between them like a flash flood. His hands slid into her hair and she gloried in the lithe power of his body.

She'd wanted this kiss to drown out everything else. Perversely, it was forcing her to confront too many things simultaneously. Her love for Zander. Her vulnerability. Her fears and weaknesses and shortcomings. She could feel herself beginning to crumble beneath the enormity of it all. Tears burned her throat.

She could either trust Zander more than she'd ever trusted anyone, crumble, then deal with the embarrassing rubble. Or she could do what she'd always done—hold herself together and resist the temptation to crumble. Her ability to hold herself together was one of her greatest sources of pride. The bedrock of her personality.

She broke away and scrambled to her feet. The blanket puddled on the ground.

He regarded her with glowing eyes for a long moment, then straightened to standing.

"I can't do this right now." She couldn't deal with her emotions for him while struggling to acclimate to the fact that she'd been stuck in a car, hooded, then chained to a pipe while a man lost his life in the adjoining room.

Tread cautiously, Britt. He's trying to support you the best way he knows how. Don't hurt him.

She didn't want to hurt him. No part of her wanted to hurt

him, but she wasn't stable enough right now to handle the zigzags of joy and defenselessness that loving him brought.

———

Zander fought to keep his face neutral.

Britt's words didn't have to mean disaster. *They don't have to*, he told himself fiercely. Yet he was already panicking inside.

His chest was still rising and falling rapidly from the intensity of their kiss. In his peripheral vision he could see a scattering of lights at the base of the shoreline across the Hood Canal. The shifting and swelling mass of black water between him and that shoreline mimicked the unsettled tide of his soul.

"I'm ridiculously attracted to you," she said. "Ridiculously. Over-the-top attracted to you."

"Then kiss me some more."

"I want to." Her turbulent eyes, set into the warrior princess face he knew so well, communicated conflict. "At the same time, kissing you . . . talking to you, being with you . . . makes me feel like I'm going to fall apart."

"Why?"

"I think because . . . when I'm with you, I'm aware that I'm with someone I can count on."

"Good. Because you are."

"Not good, because yesterday and today I've felt all wobbly and weepy in your presence."

"Be wobbly and weepy, then. It's fine with me if you are."

"It's not fine with me, though." Her chin firmed. "I don't want to depend on anyone's strength but my own."

He knew her complexities better than just about anyone on the planet. He wanted to help her. He wanted her to trust him. He wanted to shatter the detachment she was using to keep herself separate from him. But this time he didn't know how.

"I think I need to be alone for a couple of days," she said. "It's not your fault. And I don't want you to get worked up over it because it's no big deal. It's just . . . I think some solitude might help me get my head straight."

Pain stole the oxygen from his lungs. No big deal? She was pushing him away.

He'd known since they started dating that he was opening himself up to ruin if she ever pulled back. It was a chance he'd been willing to take because their relationship these past weeks was the best thing that had ever happened to him. "You think staying away from me is going to allow you to get your head straight?"

Winds of regret gusted in the brown depths of her irises. "Yes."

"I don't see how taking a break from me is going to make anything better."

"That's because you're not inside my head, experiencing what I'm experiencing."

"Then let me in."

"That sounds good on paper. Except that being near you is only confusing me more."

"Don't shut me out."

"I'm not trying to shut you out! I'm crazy about you. I'm simply trying to find my way back to my right mind. In order to do that, I need a few days apart from you, Zander. Just a few days."

She was in shock. She was scared. He'd say yes to any request she made. It's just that he *hated* this particular request. More, he doubted whether saying yes to a separation between them would benefit her.

"Why can't you see what I see?" he asked. Like black veins in white granite, anger began to thread its way through him. "The whole earth can rise and fall around us and, of all things, this relationship of ours is the one thing we need to hold on to. When hardships come, when the dust settles, when I'm on my deathbed, I will still be holding on to you, Britt."

She stood very still, ferocity and fragility evident in the lines of her posture.

Britt didn't feel the same way that he felt.

She never had, which had always been his torture. Years of pent-up frustration coalesced within him. *Why?* Why couldn't she value what he valued?

He crossed to her, took her face in his hands, and kissed her hard. "Hold on to me," he rasped.

She didn't answer.

"Please," he said.

"I'm not letting go of you, Zander." Each word emerged quiet but decisive. "I just. . . . need a few days."

He gazed at her, willing her to change her mind. *Change your mind. Hold on to me.*

She didn't back down.

With a growl, he stalked from her in the direction of his car.

She didn't come after him or call out.

He didn't look back.

Zander's journal entry:

The day CPS took me from my mom, I was numb, reeling, and angry. That's how I feel tonight, even knowing that, unlike in the case of my mom, Britt is fine.

We've gone off-course, and I'm sick to my stomach because I know that over time, even a small change in course can take you to an entirely different place.

I don't want to go any place where Britt isn't.

However, I don't know how to get us back on course. I want to fix it.

I'm powerless to fix it because she wants time away . . . from me.

From me.

CHAPTER
Twenty-Six

Nikki stuck her head into Britt's kitchen at Sweet Art near midday on Monday. "Maddie tells me there's a ripple in the force field of your romance with Zander Ford."

Perhaps if she ignored Nikki, the older woman would go away.

"And that you're really crabby because of it," Nikki added.

"Maddie!" Britt called. "Please escort your ambassador out of my kitchen!"

"Maddie's not going to rescue you, honey."

Britt continued cleaning the inside of her refrigerator. The sound of scrubbing joined the sound of conversation from the shop floor and the wheeze of the espresso machine.

"Come outside with me," Nikki said.

"No."

"It's a beautiful day, and I want to talk to you about the ripple in the force field."

"No."

"If I have to announce to all your customers that you're glum because you had a fight with your boyfriend and then publicly invent juicy stories about each and every one of Zander's tattoos, I will."

"That's not nice."

"Don't mess with me, little Bradford." Nikki gave her a challenging glare, which was, frankly, impressive. Nikki had on a long tangerine shirt and leggings. That, along with her sprayed bangs and heavy makeup, made her look like a 1980s' roller derby champion who wouldn't hesitate to elbow competitors to the rink floor.

"Fine." Britt slipped off her chef's coat and followed Nikki outdoors to one of the benches facing the large, smooth stretch of lawn at the heart of Merryweather Historical Village.

The early June weather was acting like an unloved child putting on its best behavior in a last-ditch attempt to win the love of a parent. Sunlight fell over them. Children played on the grass. Britt acknowledged these things with all the emotion of a scientist jotting down lab results.

Ordinarily, she relished fabulous weather. Ordinarily, she exercised every day. Ordinarily, she was pleasantly obsessed with chocolate. Ordinarily, she cooked at home. Ordinarily, she liked her life.

But not since Friday night and her exchange with Zander at the fire pit. Since then, she'd been despondent.

After he'd left, she'd returned to her cottage. She'd slept horribly. Spent most of Saturday on her sofa in her pajamas watching episodes of *Once Upon a Time*. Slept horribly. On Sunday she'd attended church, then spent time with her sisters. Paced her cottage. Slept horribly.

She'd believed she'd improve if left to her own devices. On the contrary, she'd continued to deteriorate mentally, physically, and emotionally. Her well-being was tumbling away from her, beyond her reach. Making matters worse—her conviction that she'd wounded Zander, which was exactly what she'd set out *not* to do.

"I'm meeting Clint here for our first official date in just a minute," Nikki announced. "Which is why I stopped by Sweet Art. He's taking me to lunch, so I thought I'd buy some chocolate so I can treat him to dessert. Of course, as far as I'm concerned, he *is* the dessert." She guffawed. Intimidating roller derby Nikki had seemingly departed in search of the nearest happy hour.

355

"I'm not convinced that your romantic bliss over Clint is the medicine I need at this particular moment."

"Thank you for bringing Clint around, by the way. I knew you could convince him to date me. My faith in you was not misplaced."

Both women watched a toddler run by, shrieking with laughter.

"Zander is a gorgeous man," Nikki declared. "If I could eat him up like a topping on a sundae, I would."

"You think all men are gorgeous."

"I think gorgeous men are gorgeous," she corrected. "You'd be a world-class fool to let that man slip though your fingers. Now tell me what went wrong so Auntie Nikki can repair it."

"Did Nora tell you what happened on Thursday? The painting and the abduction and all of that?"

"Yes."

"Afterward, I started feeling . . . overwhelmed by Zander. Every time I was around him it was like I was weaker instead of stronger."

"Mmm-hmm."

A long moment slipped past. "What does *mmm-hmm* mean?" So far, this therapy session stunk.

"You're scared. Naturally, what happened on Thursday reminded you that you can die and that Zander can die, too. Mortality is terrifying. And loving someone from the bottom of your heart is terrifying, too. So you ran into your rabbit hole to hide from the kind of transparency that could crush you to smithereens."

Britt gathered words to refute Nikki's diagnosis. At the last second, though, she held them back. Nikki might not be completely wrong.

"I've had my eye on you, and I've seen one boyfriend after another pass through your life," Nikki said. "It seems to me that you've kept them all at arm's length." Nikki pulled a small Sweet Art box from her purse and opened the lid to reveal four truffles. "I'm going to speak to you in the language of chocolate because it's what you understand. Here." She nudged the box in Britt's direction. "Take one."

"No, thank you."

"*Take one.*" Roller derby Nikki returned and aimed a fiery expression at Britt.

"I thought these were for you and Clint."

Nikki scoffed. "I bought a bigger box for Clint and me. This is the box I was planning to eat in the bathtub tonight."

Britt selected one of her newly debuted peppermint truffles.

"Take a bite," Nikki ordered.

Britt did so. She tasted the flavors and textures. Swallowed. Lifted the truffle to her mouth to pop in the remaining bite—

Nikki slapped what was left of the truffle from her hand. Britt squawked as it went flying into the air, tumbling end over end, then landing in the grass.

"What did you do that for?" Britt asked.

"To teach you an object lesson." She pointed a freshly painted coral nail at the chocolate remnant. "Your experience with the chocolate didn't end very well. Did it?"

"No."

"Are you sorry that you took a bite of it when you did?"

"I . . . No. I'm glad I got to eat some of it before you committed chocolate-icide."

"Precisely. You and I, we need to embrace the love that comes our way for as long as it lasts. If we let fear interfere, we'll miss the sweetness. And the sweetness is too, too good to miss."

Here was someone who'd dared love—and all the frailties that came with that—and experienced heartbreak twice. Even so, Nikki was willing to dive in again. Her dad, her sisters, Leo, Clint. They'd all been willing to dive in again. Meanwhile, Britt quaked at the idea of diving in even once. "I'm sort of awed by your ability to enter into something that leaves you so defenseless."

"I'm never defenseless. I have God."

Britt glanced toward the chapel where Nora and John had married. Her taste buds still registered dark chocolate and peppermint. This therapy session hadn't stunk as much as she'd first feared. Yet an obstinate part of her still refused to reverse her stance, to break down, reach out, and call Zander.

She'd sent him a text this morning, saying that she'd see him at the ceremony at the Pascal Museum on Thursday, when *Young Woman at Rest* would be formally returned. He'd responded with one word: *Fine*. Nothing more. Which is how she intended to leave things between them until Thursday.

Nikki rose and adjusted her shirt. "Clint!"

He ambled across the lawn toward them.

"Hi, handsome." Nikki welcomed him with a kiss on both cheeks.

"Hey," Clint said bashfully. "Hi, Britt."

She unfolded herself from the bench. "Hi, Clint."

Nikki looped a hand around his forearm. "Have I mentioned lately how much I appreciate a man who's not afraid to show his bare arms? If not, I want you to know I do appreciate it. You've got great arms."

"And you," Clint appeared to think himself duty-bound to give Nikki a compliment in return, "are wearing really nice perfume."

Nikki raised her eyebrows suggestively. "It's called Poison."

"But it's not really poison," Clint said with an edge of doubt.

"You'll have to sip some from my wrist to find out."

Clint turned pink and laughter rumbled from Nikki. "Ready for lunch?"

"Ready. You?"

"So, *so* ready." Nikki winked at Britt as she turned Clint toward the parking lot.

Britt watched them go, then scooped the discarded chocolate from the ground and lobbed it into the nearest trash can.

Across town, Zander sat at his desk inside his room at the inn, staring through the window before him.

Going through his days without Britt, without hope of seeing her or talking with her, had drained the color from his life like water from a bathtub. He'd caught up with his writing goals. The story was coming together, and he was on pace now to finish his manuscript ahead of schedule. But he couldn't make himself care.

He missed her.

She'd told him she was on the edge of falling apart, and now it was his turn to stand on that same cliff. So far he'd kept himself from coming undone by forcing himself to eat, sleep, write, and exercise. He'd been praying long and often. And he'd been telling himself that this situation was going to lead him and Britt to better things.

It had to. He couldn't accept or even think about the alternative.

As happy as his relationship with Britt had made him since Nora's wedding, it hadn't been without flaws. She'd never told him she loved him, and he hadn't been able to tell her that he loved her without fearing that he'd scare her. And—as the aftermath of her abduction proved—she wasn't willing to confide in him.

He wanted their love to go far deeper than that. With every molecule of him, he was certain that their love could go deeper. Would go deeper.

He'd made himself plain to her on Friday night. She'd said she needed time. He'd given her time. Now he had to have faith that the God who'd heard and answered the prayers he'd prayed when he'd been trapped inside Frank's apartment would use this no-man's-land of pain to take him and Britt where they needed to go. Together.

Standing, Zander stretched his arms overhead. Then he hooked his thumbs through his belt loops, his attention still latched on the scene outdoors.

He'd waited thirteen years for Britt.

Winning her heart wasn't a short game. It had proven itself to be a very, very long game.

He was a shell of himself without her. His hands itched to touch her and his eyes longed to see her.

But for her, he would force himself to be patient.

For the remainder of Monday, all of Tuesday, and most of Wednesday, Britt tried to wrestle her mental health into submission. She wrestled with it while looking over business accounts and making chocolate. At home in front of the television. In bed when sleep evaded her.

Almost a week had passed since Tom's men had kidnapped her. In that time she'd survived on little but gumption and prepackaged food.

By dinnertime on Wednesday, she'd exhausted her supply of both.

Dizzy with tiredness, she peered blankly at the kitchen cupboard in her cottage for five minutes. Despite her body's weariness, her brain churned with fears. *You're helpless. You're out of control. You're not safe. Not even here. You're not safe anywhere.* She couldn't bear the agitated hamster wheel of her thoughts. She'd felt better after she'd been impaled by a tree branch than she did now.

Hands trembling, she assembled ingredients for a salad on her cutting board. As she chopped a carrot, the tip of her knife nicked her index finger. The spot stung. Then blood welled.

Britt cursed and examined the cut. It wasn't serious. It didn't require stitches. It was just the kind of ordinary, garden variety incision that happened to people who cooked.

Even so, overwhelming despair and frustration built inside her as she watched blood drip from it. The pressure of her emotions increased and increased.

She squirted a drop of soap on the cut, ran it under water, flicked the water off angrily, and pressed a paper towel against her finger.

The pressure increased even more. Her heart began to race. Her breath grew shallow. Her skin turned clammy—too hot and too cold at the same time. Faintness gusted through her, and she struggled not to vomit.

Her mind broke free of its leash. *You're going to have a heart attack like Frank. You can't get enough air into your lungs.*

Terrified, she grabbed for her phone. Leaning on the counter

360

for support, she exited the kitchen and shuffled toward the living area in her socks. She'd rest on the sofa—

She didn't get that far. Halfway there, she braced her palm on the wall and fought a losing battle to master her body. She crumpled to the floor. Hunching forward, she planted her arms on her upraised knees.

Her pulse beat out a rhythm of alarm as she dialed Zander on her cell.

"Hello?" he said.

"Zander . . ."

"I'll be right there. Are you at home?"

"Yes."

He'd understood everything she needed him to understand from the state of her voice alone.

It would take him fifteen minutes to get here from the inn, a length of time that seemed impossible. She couldn't stand this for fifteen more seconds, let alone fifteen more minutes.

She pulled her mom's words from her memory as urgently as if they were a lifeline. *"You can rely on Him in the hard as well as in the easy. If He leads you into something hard, then He'll provide the grace you need to bear up under it."*

Britt desperately longed for that to be true.

Her eyes squeezed shut. *God*, she prayed. *Save me.*

She'd been submerged by a situation she couldn't power through. Couldn't talk herself out of. Couldn't evade. The self-sufficiency she'd used to treat every other difficulty of her life was worthless to her now. She'd failed to deal with or even acknowledge numerous injuries and sorrows.

She wasn't fine.

She'd hadn't been fine many, many other times.

She wasn't fine.

I'm relying on you, she told God shakily. *Not me this time. Only you.*

She hung on to Him for one minute. Then, eventually, two minutes. Three.

He didn't make everything better by quieting her body the way that she wanted Him to. Her body and mind continued to rage. But His presence turned her brutal predicament from something she could not endure into something she could endure, through His power.

She sensed His nearness, His mighty Spirit. Resolutely, He funneled courage into her. As she gave her weight over to Him, He began to carry her, the way her mom had said He would.

Another minute passed. Another. The tighter she gripped Him, the more dependable she found Him to be.

What an idiot she'd been. So full of willful confidence in her own capability. Her sisters and parents and Maddie and Zander had all been right about her. She'd trusted in herself and ended up on her butt in her living room, incapacitated. A week ago she'd been going about her life as if she had it all under control. Now that illusion of control had been shattered.

The truth: she was small and frail. Horrifically human. The Bible was right when it said her life was like a mist that would soon vanish. On the day of her kayaking accident and the day of her abduction, she'd seen just how susceptible she was to death. Her time on earth? Incredibly temporary.

God Most High couldn't be more different. He was creator of heaven and earth. The Ancient of Days. Her intuition could only grasp at a fraction of His size and even that fraction was *vast*.

How could such an all-powerful God love her enough to meet her here?

She didn't know how. She only knew that, incomprehensibly, He did love her that much.

Because He *was* here.

When she heard Zander's footsteps on her front porch, gratitude unfurled within her. He knew where she hid her spare key and, sure enough, she heard it twist in the door lock. She lifted her face in time to see him enter. He wore track pants and a black athletic shirt, and he looked healthy and normal and strong.

Zander. Her best friend. She wanted to fist her fingers into his shirt in order to keep him next to her. Always.

He knelt before her, his features tense.

"My heart's . . . been pounding," she told him. "And I'm . . . short of breath."

"Are you dehydrated?" he asked.

"No."

"Panic attack?"

"Maybe. I . . . think so."

"Is it getting worse? Or better?"

"It might be getting . . . a little better."

"What's this?" He indicated the paper towel still wrapped around her cut.

"I sliced my finger. It's not bad . . . though."

He sat, pulled her onto his lap, and braced his back against the wall. She lay against the incline of his chest, his arms wrapped around her. "Let's work on breathing," he said. "We'll start with three counts in, three counts out." They breathed in unison. Gradually in, gradually out. "Can you slow it down even more?" he asked her after a time.

She nodded.

Mercifully, her mind began to release its terror. Her heart quieted. The aftermath left her weak, shaky, and holding on to her composure by a strand as thin as a spider web.

"Better?" Zander asked.

"Slightly."

"I'm going to get you some water." He set her gently down.

"I can get it."

"I know you can. But let me get it for you." He returned with a glass of ice water.

She accepted it and took an experimental sip.

He must have remembered where her medicine drawer was located, because he lowered himself before her, holding a tube of antibacterial ointment and a bandage.

With the sort of concentration she'd guess brain surgeons used when operating, he removed the paper towel and studied the small incision on the pad of her finger. He dabbed ointment onto it, then applied the bandage.

The crumbling sensation his nearness had evoked since her abduction overtook her. This time, she wasn't equal to it. Watching him doctor her finger *slayed her*. A panoramic view opened in her memory of all the things he'd done for her, all the things he'd sacrificed for her. Tears started streaming down her cheeks.

He stared directly at her. She knew she looked a wreck, but she gazed levelly back at him, tears and all.

"Water," he suggested.

She drank more water. She cried and drank. Drank and cried. Eventually, she drained the glass.

He lifted her in his arms and carried her upstairs to her bedroom. After he'd deposited her on her bed, he created a backrest out of her array of throw pillows.

She cried.

He climbed onto the queen bed with its white duvet and propped his upper body on the pillow ramp. Then he looped an arm underneath her, and curved her in beside him. She rested her head on his shoulder. He took hold of her hand, then tucked their joined hands between them.

"This isn't so bad, is it?" he whispered, referring to their cozy position.

"This is mortifying," she whispered back, tears flowing.

"Not for me. I get to be here, with you, and there's nowhere I'd rather be."

"I'm a mess."

"No. It's just that you're not bulletproof. That's all."

"I want to be bulletproof."

"None of us are."

"You're pretty much perfect, Zander. It's nauseating."

"I beg your pardon. I have lots of weaknesses."

"Which are?"

He must have grabbed a box of tissues from the bathroom after depositing her on her bed, because he offered the box to her now. She took two.

"I can be reclusive," he said.

"You like to spend time alone."

"I'm gloomy."

"You're realistic."

"I'm terrible with strangers."

That, she agreed with. She shrugged and blotted her eyes.

"I can't walk past an open drawer or cupboard without closing it. I need matching hangers and all my clothes have to face the same way. I can't stand by and watch people load a dishwasher the wrong way."

She attempted a shuddering breath. "Your ability to expertly load a dishwasher isn't an imperfection."

"Yes, it is, because I have to load a dishwasher the right way even if the people who own the dishwasher haven't invited me to."

It seemed that her tears were bottomless.

"I hate ketchup," he said. "I used to spend too much time playing video games. And I can't set a timer for an odd number."

"Scandalous."

"But my biggest weakness by far . . ."

"Yes?"

"Is you."

Her heart was coming apart at the seams.

"I'd give up anything," he said. "For you."

"I don't deserve that."

"You do deserve it. That, and more." He brought the tissues to her again.

She tossed the used ones over the side of the bed and took two more. "You admired my independence. I know you did."

"I still do. You're the most independent woman I know. Today won't change that."

"I'm soaking your shirt with my tears."

"You're being honest. You're giving me the first chance I've ever had since I met you to be here for you."

"It's mortifying," she repeated.

"I love you," he told her, undaunted.

Her crying shook her shoulders.

"I've been all over the world," he said, "but you are the most beautiful thing I've ever seen. You're my treasure and my compass. If you'd died last Thursday, then my life would have been over, too."

Britt hadn't known her body could contain this much splendor and grief simultaneously. Since the moment she'd met Zander, she'd wanted to use her strength to rescue him. But now he was leveraging his strength to rescue her.

"Have I made myself clear?" he asked.

She nodded against his chest.

Then she sobbed for an hour straight.

He massaged her scalp. He smoothed the long fall of her hair. He rubbed her back.

She cried for the things her family members had suffered, things that had left their marks upon her childhood.

She mourned the death of her close friend Olivia.

She sobbed because she'd been wrong to go kayaking after a flood and wrong to not tell Zander about her injuries and wrong to not accept comfort or help from the people who loved her. She cried because her kayaking injury had hurt and because it still hurt sometimes.

She mourned because she'd felt so wretchedly powerless last week in the parking lot at The Residences and later in that room at the warehouse. Her sense of security had been yanked away and she was sorry, very sorry, that it had.

She cried because Zander loved her and she loved him back, and she wasn't worthy of his devotion or this astonishingly wonderful bond that existed between them.

She sobbed because her ridiculous pride had kept her from relying on God, the one—the only one—she should have been relying on all this time.

When she finally spent all her tears, her eyes were puffy but the sin, the anxieties, and the lies she'd told herself had been expunged from her soul. Her body could relax. At last, her mind could settle.

She'd been driven low, and it had humbled her. But when she'd been driven low, she'd found God there. The God she'd known since childhood had gently lifted her chin. He was on her side. She could afford to let go of her own tattered competency.

She drifted to sleep in Zander's arms.

A few times during the night, she became aware of him shifting. Closing the curtains. Turning out the lights. But he always returned immediately, and thank goodness for that. Because as soon as he came back and she felt his arm beneath her head or his fingers enclosing hers or his heartbeat beneath her ear, she tumbled back into deep, restful sleep.

Letter from Zander to his mom two weeks after he started high school:

Dear Mom,

I know you were worried about me making friends. I don't want you to be worried. I have a friend. A girl named Britt Bradford. She sits beside me in English and walks with me from English to art. She saves me a place at her lunch table, and we talk after school when we're waiting for our rides outside.

She grew up in Merryweather, so she knows everyone and introduces me to everyone—which is more people than I even want to meet.

She lives in this big mansion, and I went there yesterday to eat dinner with her parents. Then Britt and I made brownies, but not out of a box. They turned out really good.

I'm okay, Mom. You don't have to worry about me.

CHAPTER

Twenty-Seven

She hadn't told Zander she loved him.

That was Britt's first conscious thought upon waking the next morning and realizing that he was gone.

He'd been here—all night. But now he'd left. And she hadn't had the chance to tell him she loved him.

She'd meant to! Wanted to, badly. She'd been waiting until her nose wasn't running and her eyes weren't puddled with tears—

Oh no. The ceremony at the Pascal was today.

She could tell by the light creeping around the edges of her curtains that it was full morning. What if she'd overslept and missed it?

She lunged toward her nightstand and angled her clock so that she could see its face. 7:54.

Relieved, she flopped onto her back. She'd told her parents she'd be ready when they swung by to pick her up at nine o'clock. They were allowing an hour and forty-five minutes for the drive to Seattle, and another fifteen minutes to park and find their seats in time for the eleven o'clock ceremony. That left her a good hour to eat, shower, and get herself ready.

A paper crinkled beneath her elbow. She lifted it and squinted at the writing.

*If you wake in time for the ceremony, I'll see you
there. If not, no problem. I'll call you right after. Sleep is
more important.*

Zander was a fantastic man. Pure platinum! But he was also
completely wrong. Sleep was not more important than today's
ceremony at the Pascal marking *Young Woman at Rest*'s return to
the family and the museum where the painting belonged.

She'd fallen asleep when? Around seven thirty last night? She'd
gotten more than enough sleep.

She levered upward to sit on the edge of the mattress. Her white
duvet was still tucked beneath her throw pillows because she had
slept in yesterday's clothes on top of her made bed. Tentatively,
she walked to her bathroom, then downstairs.

She felt unsteady inside still. Physically weak. But the scratching
nervousness that had been trapped within her had finally quieted,
thank God.

For the first time in days, she was hungry. Gloriously hungry.
Sunlight slanted over her as she prepared coffee, bacon, a veg-
etable hash, eggs. Two butterflies lit on the flowers in the flowerbox
mounted outside her kitchen window. One of them took to the
air, wings flashing.

Yesterday's panic attack/sobbing fit hadn't fixed her in one fell
swoop. She didn't feel fully safe, even standing in her locked house
inside her close-knit community. Nor did she feel one hundred
percent like herself. But she felt more like herself than she had
since the day she'd driven to Olympia to confront Zander at The
Residences, and that was enough.

Yesterday had hollowed her out somehow. God had used the
situation to perform spring cleaning. It had been painful. Very.
But it had also swept away the debris that had been separating
her from God.

Her breakfast gave her the energy she needed to shower, blow-
dry her hair, do her makeup, and pick out clothing.

She sighed as she regarded her reflection in her bathroom mirror.

She'd chosen her favorite lavender maxi dress and accessorized it with a long necklace. If anyone looked closely, they'd notice that her eyes were swollen. She slid her feet into a pair of gladiator sandals and made her way to the parking lot.

Right on schedule, her family pulled up in Mom's white Suburban, Dad at the wheel. Britt climbed aboard. Mom, Dad, Willow, and Nora had all been adamant about attending the intimate, invitation-only ceremony at the Pascal, and her dad had been adamant about driving them there. Britt suspected that he'd insisted on driving because he wanted to make life easier for her in the wake of her abduction. Ordinarily, that would have grated on her. But accepting Zander's help last night hadn't been awful. So why not accept her dad's help, too? There were worse things than relaxing in the back seat, flanked by her sisters on either side, just like in the old days.

When they arrived at the Pascal, they were shown to a ballroom at the back of the museum. The mahogany floors smelled of lemon-scented polish. The windows and chandeliers cast illumination over towering cream walls and the rows of guests. At the front, a podium equipped with a microphone waited next to an easel that supported the painting, currently covered with fabric. A security guard stood a few feet from it, hands clasped before him.

Among those present, Britt recognized some of Carolyn's friends and co-workers. She pegged several guests as reporters and photographers. The rest must be connected to the Pascal family or to the museum.

At the stroke of eleven o'clock, an elegant woman dressed in a black pique suit jacket, tailored pants, and low-rise patent leather heels made her way to the microphone. She'd dyed her hair such a dark red that the shade reminded Britt of cherry cola. Each strand had been coiffed into a short and flattering style. Her very fair skin shone beneath modest makeup.

Annette Pascal. Eighty-seven years old and the epitome of girl power.

"Thank you for coming." She didn't fidget or stoop toward the microphone. "This is a grand day, a day I've been anticipating for thirty-four years."

Where was Zander? As she'd been doing since she took her seat, Britt scanned the space like a child scanning the sky for Santa Claus. She didn't see him.

Annette detailed her family's colorful history with *Young Woman at Rest*.

Still no sign of Zander.

"I took over as museum director," Annette was saying, "just a few months before the Triple Play robbery occurred. My father and grandparents had already brought the painting back to us once, after it was taken by the Nazis. In the aftermath of the Triple Play, it fell to me to do the work they'd done before me, to recover the painting yet again. My fervor to return Pierre-Auguste Renoir's *Young Woman at Rest* to this place has never wavered, not for a moment. Even so, the painting remained elusive. Until this day." She permitted herself a self-satisfied smile. "I can't help but think that my father and grandparents are very, very proud this morning."

The audience applauded enthusiastically.

"A family from Merryweather, Washington, located the painting. I'm sure that you may have additional questions about the painting's discovery, but no details beyond those will be divulged. The family has declined the reward that our museum and the FBI offered. They've also asked that their identity not be made public and that their photo not be taken. I don't mind admitting that I had to twist their arm a little to convince them to come today. But in the end, they honored my heartfelt request. Please welcome them."

More applause. Britt twisted, clapping, to watch Carolyn enter. Then came Zander's cousins, Courtney and Sarah. Then Zander. He wore a navy suit. White shirt. Pale blue tie.

Annette made more remarks, thanking the police and the FBI for their excellent efforts.

Britt could no longer concentrate. Indeed, she couldn't move her attention from Zander. He stood farthest from the microphone and a little removed from his cousins—on the fringes, exactly where he'd so often existed in life. His hair was gleaming, his expression serious as his focus centered on her.

The tenderness in his eyes was for her. For her. The certainty of that caused goose bumps to tingle on her skin and her heart to lift.

He gave her a look that asked, *How are you?*

She inclined her head and smiled a little, assuring him that she'd improved from "basket case" to "a few notches above basket case."

She didn't want Zander to exist on the fringes anymore. She wanted to break his isolation over her knee like a brittle stick. She wanted to throw the pieces of that stick into a roaring fire until they'd turned to ash.

He was a diamond. And he was hers.

Annette persuaded Carolyn to speak. Carolyn expressed regret at the length of time that had passed since the painting was stolen. She informed the guests that she and her family didn't desire thanks or recognition of any kind. She insisted that all the credit was due to Annette, law enforcement, and the research of her nephew Zander and his friend Britt.

Willow poked Britt with her elbow.

Carolyn told Annette how very grateful she was to see the painting reunited with its rightful owner.

Together, Annette and Carolyn gripped the hem of the fabric covering the painting, then lifted it up and over. The woman depicted on canvas was revealed with a dramatic *whoosh*. She peered at the assembled guests with her knowing smile.

The artwork gleamed even more here than it had inside the apartment in Olympia.

Carolyn stepped out of the way so that Annette could pose for pictures with the painting. Several important-looking people joined her for more pictures. Cameras snapped.

The ceremony ended, and the audience rose and began to mingle.

Britt looked down the row at her family. Willow. Nora. Dad. Mom.

"It was so inspiring to hear about the painting's story," Mom said. "What a remarkable—"

"Super remarkable!" Britt jolted to her feet. "If you'll excuse me, I've got to go . . . talk to Zander about something. I'm sure he can give me a ride home. Thanks for coming with me. Really, thanks."

They regarded her with startled bemusement.

"Uh . . . sure, honey," her dad said. "You're welcome."

"I'll see you in Merryweather," she said. "Later. Not today. Another day. Soon."

Britt hurried to the front of the room. Zander's cousins and aunt were ensconced in discussions, so she was free to grab Zander's hand. She towed him from the room like a teacher marching a misbehaving student to the principal's office. Except faster.

"Hello," he said dryly, when they were in the hallway.

She took a set of stairs. Dragged him down more corridors. Finally, she found an exit door. It emptied into a private walled garden.

Zander had told her that Frank and Carolyn had once eaten lunches together in this very same courtyard. Ivy climbed brick. Lilac trees dripped clusters of white flowers. A border of moss gave way to planting beds bursting with pink hydrangeas.

They were blessedly alone.

Their hands remained joined as he faced her. "You okay?" he asked.

"I'm wobbly. But better than I was yesterday."

"You look gorgeous."

"*You* look gorgeous. Thank you for . . . everything, Zander. For staying with me so that I could sleep last night and bandaging my finger. And all the rest of it, too. Years' and years' worth."

He gave her a crooked smile. "You're welcome."

He looked like what he was. Honorable. Dedicated. Smart. The lines across his forehead gave faint witness to his years and his hardships.

Wind riffled the trees. Her mouth went dry. "Renoir's painting came home today," she said.

"Yes."

"Thanks to you."

"Thanks to us," he corrected.

"*Young Woman at Rest* belongs here."

"I couldn't agree more."

"In exactly the same way, you belong with me," she said. "And I belong with you."

Hard-fought hope fractured his expression.

Some things simply *were*. Like the seasons. The sun and the moon. The tide. She and Zander were like that. They were.

"I love you," she said.

He stared at her in amazement.

"I love you," she said again.

He took a step closer, looking determined and more than a little possessive. They were just inches apart.

"You belong with me," he vowed. "And I belong with you."

"Yes."

He set his forehead on hers. They both closed their eyes.

Britt's chest clutched with rightness and joy.

His fingers lightly cupped the back of her neck. She latched her hands around his wrists, feeling the warmth of his skin.

He pulled away just enough to meet her eyes. "Did you say that you loved me?"

She laughed. "I did."

"You love me?"

"Yes."

"You do?" he asked again, as if he needed to make positively certain.

"Yes. I love you, Zander."

"And you're never going to tell me you need a break from me again?"

"No. In fact, if you ever decide to finish your Grand Tour, you're going to have to take me with you."

"If you love me—"

"—which I do—"

"—then my Grand Tour is finished," he said. "And I'm glad because my time overseas brought me to the conclusion that you're the only thing worth traveling for. I've loved you since I was four-teen, and I'll love you for longer than eternity lasts. All I want is the chance to show you that and tell you that every single day."

She blinked at him, speechless.

He bent and gave her a kiss so sweetly passionate that a lilac blossom felt its vibration and shook loose to *ping* off Britt's arm.

Zander walked her backward until her shoulder blades settled against ivy. He planted one hand on the garden wall and continued to kiss her.

Their kisses flowed from hurried kisses filled with impatience, to soft kisses filled with exploration, to deep kisses filled with promises too profound for words.

She wrapped her arms around him and drew him closer. She wanted to weep and laugh and dance. But mostly she wanted to kiss him and kiss him some more—

A drumming noise and muted shouts interrupted them.

They both looked in the direction of the ruckus.

Her family stood at a window a floor above them, hooting and pointing at them and grinning.

This walled garden wasn't quite as private as previously sup-posed.

"Never mind them," Britt whispered, her lips hitching up at the corners. "Give me the longer-than-eternity-lasts speech again."

"I'll love you for longer than eternity lasts."

"And all you want . . ." she prompted.

"Is the chance to show you that and tell you that every single day."

She released a blissful sigh. "That's a very, very good speech. I love you, Zander."

"I love you, Britt." Then he spoke the word that would become their shared pledge for the rest of their lives. "Always."

"Always," she murmured, in the instant before his mouth low-ered to hers.

Epilogue

Written in Britt's bridal scrapbook on the page titled Wedding Day Highlights:

Just five days have passed since our wedding. We left the Costa Rican beach where we were married the morning after the ceremony and drove here, to a resort built into a mountainside in the thick of the rain forest.

At the moment, Zander is off finalizing the details of the surprise he's planning for me tomorrow—a chocolate-tasting tour. Since I'm here on our balcony, pretending not to know what he's up to, and since someone more organized than I am (Nora) stuck this scrapbook in my suitcase, and since my memory isn't as good as Zander's, I figure it's best to go ahead and record our wedding highlights now.

The perfect highlights:
- The tears in my dad's eyes when he arrived to walk me down the aisle.
- The cool sand beneath my toes and the blues and buttery yellows of the sunset over the ocean.
- Our vows.
- The moment when I glanced to the side during the ceremony and saw Willow and Nora smiling back at me.

- The prayer my mom spoke over us before we ate dinner under the stars.
- The dance Zander and I shared with Willow's baby girl and Nora's baby boy clasped between us.

The imperfect highlights:
- The moment when my wedding band slid off the pastor's Bible. Zander made a grab for it and missed. So it was sand-speckled when he slid it on my finger.
- The flower-covered *Z* that hung from the back of Zander's chair at dinner kept sliding to the side to form the letter *N*. We kept tilting it back. It kept sliding to the side. Eventually, we decided Nander had a nice ring to it.

The biggest highlight of all:
Zander.

More specifically, Zander, in his suit, with those Dickensian orphan eyes gazing at me with steadfast joy.

When I look back at our story, I can't believe I didn't force him to become my boyfriend when I was fourteen. If I'd known then what I know now, I would have. Only, I didn't know it then. Nor for a long time afterward. I think that's because God couldn't trust me with Zander until recently. Had I fallen in love with him at fourteen, I'd have screwed it up, because I wouldn't have understood how rare and valuable this love between us is.

It amazes me that Zander waited for me as long as he did, that he didn't give up, get over me, and fall for someone else. I've told him this more than once, and he always says that he tried to get over me, but couldn't.

It's as if God kept my heart distant and Zander's heart loyal until we were both ready for God's plan to unfold.

I'm grateful. The God I've come to lean on understands me better than I understand myself. Ultimately, His timing was perfect.

Because sitting here, on my honeymoon, with hummingbirds sipping from the flowering tree beside me, I do understand . . . down to the bottom of my soul . . . how rare and valuable this love between us is.

When I first began to fall for him, I remember worrying that loving Zander might be a liability. As it turns out, loving someone who's trustworthy and sacrificial is not a liability. Quite the opposite. The chance to love Zander and be loved by Zander is the greatest gift of my life.

I'll fight for him. I'll protect him. I'll make sure he has a place to belong and a family to belong to. I'll put his best above my own.

Five days ago, I vowed to love and cherish him for the rest of my life, and that's exactly what I intend to do.

Zander was the highlight of my wedding day.

Zander. My best friend, my husband.

Always.

"Trust in the Lord with all your heart and lean not on your own understanding; in all your ways submit to him, and he will make your paths straight."

PROVERBS 3:5–6

Questions for Conversation

1. Becky really enjoyed casting two good friends as the hero and heroine of *Sweet on You*. Were you friends with your husband or boyfriend before you started dating? What do you think friendship adds to a romance depicted in a novel?

2. How did the setting of Britt's chocolate shop, Sweet Art, affect the experience of reading this story? How did the troublesome peppermint truffle serve as a metaphor?

3. The theme of *Sweet on You* is reliance. Name a few ways in which that theme played out over the course of the story.

4. Which part of *Sweet on You* struck you as the most romantic?

5. Why do you think Becky chose to add a secondary romance between Nikki and Clint to this story?

6. Some of you may have tried to research *Young Woman at Rest* by Renoir. That particular piece of art is fictional. However, Becky used a real piece by Renoir entitled *Young Woman Seated*, which features model Nina Lopez, as inspiration for

the painting described in *Sweet on You*. What do you like or dislike about book and movie storylines that revolve around a heist?

7. How did the plot line impact the romance in *Sweet on You*?

8. In the novel, Kathleen says the following words to Britt about God: "If He leads you into something hard, then He'll provide the grace you need in order to bear up under it." Do any scriptures come to mind that support that statement?

9. How did the epistolary elements at the end of each chapter enhance the novel? Do any of them stick out in your memory as especially charming or impactful?

10. What facets of the Bradford family did you find unique, appealing, or enjoyable?

Becky Wade is the 2018 Christy Award Book of the Year winner for *True to You*. She is a native of California who attended Baylor University, met and married a Texan, and moved to Dallas. She published historical romances for the general market, then put her career on hold for several years to care for her children. When God called her back to writing, Becky knew He meant for her to turn her attention to Christian fiction. Her humorous, heart-pounding contemporary romance novels have won three Christy Awards, the Carol Award, the INSPY Award, and the Inspirational Reader's Choice Award for Romance. Becky lives in Dallas, Texas with her husband and three children. To find out more about Becky and her books, visit www.beckywade.com.

Sign Up for Becky's Newsletter!

Keep up to date with Becky's news on book releases and events by signing up for her email list at beckywade.com.

More from Becky Wade

Willow Bradford is content taking a break from modeling to run her family's inn until she comes face-to-face with NFL quarterback Corbin Stewart, the man who broke her heart—and wants to win her back. When a decades-old family mystery brings them together, they're forced to decide whether they can risk falling for one another all over again.

Falling for You
A Bradford Sisters Romance

You May Also Like . . .

After a broken engagement, genealogist Nora Bradford decides focusing on her work and her novels is safer than romance. But when John, a former Navy SEAL, hires her to help find his birth mother, the spark between them is undeniable. However, he's dating someone, and Nora is hesitant. Is she ready to abandon her fictional heroes and risk her heart for real?

True to You
A BRADFORD SISTERS ROMANCE

NFL star Gray Fowler is receiving death threats. Out of concern, his team hires a protection detail, but Gray is indignant when he meets his bodyguard. How can an attractive woman half his size protect him? Former Marine Dru Porter is, in fact, more than capable. But as danger rises, can Dru and Gray entrust their lives to one another?

Her One and Only

Scarred from his time in the military, horse trainer Jake Porter is content living a solitary existence. At least he was until his childhood friend Lyndie James comes back into his life and starts tearing down the walls he's built around his heart.

A Love Like Ours

BETHANYHOUSE